THE GRAND
ADVENTURE

•

PHILIP JOSÉ FARMER

THE GRAND ADVENTURE

MASTERWORKS OF SCIENCE FICTION
AND FANTASY

•

A BYRON PREISS
VISUAL PUBLICATIONS, INC. BOOK

BOOK DESIGN BY
ROBERT GOULD AND ALEX JAY

BERKLEY BOOKS, NEW YORK

For Phil

THE GRAND ADVENTURE
Masterworks of Science Fiction and Fantasy

A Berkley Book/published by arrangement with
Byron Preiss Visual Publications, Inc.

PRINTING HISTORY
Berkley trade paperback edition/November 1984

Special thanks to John Silbersack for his help in making the selections for this
collection. Additional thanks to the author's agent, Ted Chichak; Ann Weil;
Roger Cooper, Susan Allison and Ony Ryzuk of Berkley Books; and Joan Brandt.

Book design by Robert Gould and Alex Jay/Studio J.
Cover design by Robert Gould and Alex Jay.

·C·O·N·T·E·N·T·S·

THE PEORIA-COLORED WRITER

As Hector pursued Patroclus around and around the walls of Troy, the great god Zeus weighed their fates in the scales of destiny, and Patroclus was found wanting. So, Patroclus died.

In any fight, unless there's a draw, someone has to lose.

The above event from Homer's *The Iliad* occurred to me when Byron Preiss asked me to write a general introduction to this collection. I was to evaluate in it my writing career. I was also to describe the times and places where I wrote my stories, how I felt then, what kind of a situation I was in then, what effect that had on my writing then, and so on.

What he requested was very difficult and perhaps near-impossible. To do it, I must split myself so that one of my half-personae could look objectively at the other. Or perhaps I should say that I was required to cut myself into three parts. One would be the god Zeus; one, the victorious Hector; one, the loser Patroclus.

The difficulty with this task is that it involves my self-image. Self-images are what we like to think we are. But, usually, the self-image corresponds very little to reality. If a person tries to look objectively at himself or herself, that person often fails to be critical or perceptive enough. A very few, like Jean-Jacques Rousseau in his *Confessions*, go to the other extreme and make themselves out to be worse than they are.

Humankind, among other things, is *Homo self-fooling us*.

This introduction is not supposed to be a confessional or psychological self-analysis. It's to be an evaluation, a weighing of my career as a writer. If it is, then it has to have standards of comparison. Against what or whom? Dostoyevsky, Twain, Fielding, Balzac? Janet Dailey or Albert Payson Terhune? Or those in my field: Heinlein, Clarke, Ellison, Lem, Le Guin, Lin Carter, E. C. Tubbs? Or against the goals I set for myself, goals which had little to do with other writers? Well, that's not quite true. In my very early days, I was ambitious to be the American Dostoyevsky or twentieth-century Melville.

No. "Ambitious" is not the correct word. I had dreams, but I never worked to realize my dreams.

When I first told myself that I would be a writer someday, I meant that I'd be a mainstream writer. Though I'd been an ardent reader of science-fiction since the age of eight, I did not intend to be a science-fiction writer. I did think that I might write an occasional science-fiction work between mainstream short stories and novels. But being known as a science-fiction writer was not in my dreams.

Here I am, sixty-six years old, and my career as a mainstream writer seems to be a near-failure. I am not, however, grieving over it, nor have I given up. I regard this career as something that has just been long delayed in starting. Only now am I beginning it.

Until I've given birth to at least ten mainstream novels, I will not be able to say whether I've been a success, a failure, or an also-ran as a mainstreamer. I hope that I'll find out long before the tenth is completed. I'll be eighty then.

What I lacked in the early part of my writing career was the high-burning, all-consuming, and ever-driving flame. The flame that makes a writer write and write and to hell with the consequences or the circumstances. When this flame envelops you, it makes everything and everybody—family, friends, jobs—subordinate to the desire to write. If they have to suffer, too bad. The ambition comes first; all else is secondary.

This species of writer takes a job only when it's necessary to keep himself and his family from starving, and sometimes not then.

(There may be female counterparts of this type of writer, but I don't know any.)

The species of writer to which I belonged accepts his responsibilities as a writer and does his best—well, his near-best—to fulfill them.

I worked at mundane, boring, and physically exhausting jobs for many years. When I was on the second or third shift, I wrote in the mornings. When I was on days, I wrote in the evenings. And I tried to write as much as I could on the weekends when I was not working at the steel mill.

I also read a lot, and we had a social life that was not busy but still occupied a certain amount of time.

My wife complained because I did not spend enough time with her and the kids. She was justified in this, but, on the other hand, she knew when she married me that I wanted to be a writer. She just had no idea of what it was going to be like. Neither did I.

I tried to make a compromise on the time allotted for family demands and for my writing. Like many compromises, it satisfied no one. But, like most, it worked, though with a sixty percent efficiency.

That was not a bad rate when you consider that most human beings only operate at sixty percent or less of their potentiality. And that our cultures only develop about fifty percent of their citizens' potentialities. Or that our economic systems only work at about sixty percent of their potentiality.

If our automobiles operated at that low an efficiency, we would junk them.

I was not as hard-working as a writer or as a father and a husband as I should have been. I drifted. Instead of altering the course of events by a fierce determination to succeed and a willingness to sacrifice others, I let events carry me along. The years passed, and I had written a few mainstream short stories, all of which had been rejected, and a few science-fiction short stories, also rejected. I had written the first quarter of what was intended to be a mammoth mainstream novel. I had written the first fourth of a mystery novel. There were a few sonnets and triolets in the drawer, none of which had been sent out.

On January 26, 1952, I was thirty-four years old, had worked about ten years at Keystone Steel & Wire, and had sold one story, a 12,000-word novella, to a pulp-magazine, *Adventure*. "O'Brien and Obrenov" had gone first to the *Saturday Evening Post*, and the editor had said that he would buy it if I would cut out a drunk scene. I was tempted. The *Post* was a very prestigious publication, and it paid well. But I finally said no; I sent the story to *Argosy*. Its editor liked it very much but said that it was too long for *Argosy*. However, he did send it on to Ken White, the editor of *Adventure*. And he purchased it.

In 1952, I looked at the story, published in 1946, and wondered if this was not only my first but my last printed work. Should I quit the steel mill and try for a master's degree in English? In 1949, I had gone back to college. I had a year and a half of courses to complete, having picked up a freshman year at the University of Missouri in 1936–1937 and a sophomore year and one semester of a junior year at Bradley College, Peoria. My wife, the driving force in our family, had said that she was tired of my drifting and was fed up with my wasting my brain and body at the steel mill. So I made arrangements to work a straight night shift, forty-eight hours a week, at Keystone, and I took seventeen semester hours at Bradley. My wife began to take classes designed to get her a medical technologist's degree.

Some of our expenses were paid for by the G.I. Bill, but there was not enough to cover the monthly house payments, food and clothing, etc. I had to work the night shift and study when I had the time and cut my sleep to five or six hours a day. In addition, we had a rousing social life, having met a group of G.I. Bill students who had formed a sort of pre-Beatnik community. In 1950, they were still called "bohemians."

I got my B.A. in English and Creative Writing in 1950 and then collapsed from physical exhaustion. Nevertheless, I took several courses on the master's level when the winter semester started. But I was no longer able to work a straight night shift; some of my fellow workers at Keystone wanted the night shift—I don't know why. I arranged for the two special tutoring courses available and took them. But from then on I'd have to take day courses at Bradley. To do that, I'd have to become a full-time student, and we just did not have the money. I had to work.

By then, I had decided that I really did not want to be a teacher. I'd talked to some teachers about their work, about faculty politics, about the low pay, and I said, "No. I don't want to be a teacher. I don't have the temperament. I'm a writer, and that's that."

There was, however, a vast gulf between being a writer—there are many of those—and being a successful writer, of whom there are few.

I looked at the career of Bob Bloch, author of hundreds of short stories and several novels. He had sold his first story to *Weird Tales* magazine when he was seventeen and had continued to sell steadily since. Yet he had not become a full-time writer; he had worked at several jobs and had written an abundance of stories in his spare time. Why had I not done this?

"Many are called but few are chosen."

Was I one of the multitude of called-but-rejected?

Or was it that I just had not tried hard enough?

The ancient Greek philosopher, Heraclitus, said, "Character determines destiny."

Was my character that of a self-defeatist?

A psychologist, a student counselor at the University of Missouri, had told me that I was a self-defeater.

Well, I thought, what if that was true? That did not mean that I could not change my character. I have always believed in free will, even though I was heavily influenced by Mark Twain's determinism when I was young. I don't think that we're robots. What we *are* are semi-automatons who have free will. We can, in the psychical sense, lift ourselves by our bootstraps.

I do believe in genetic determinism, and the discoveries made in recent years have confirmed this belief. I also believe that environmental effects determine, to a certain extent, the direction the genetic drives will take. But there's a third factor, free will, that can override, to a certain extent, the integrated effects of genes and environment.

We are not robots.

Still, sometimes, when I'm depressed, I think that perhaps Twain and Vonnegut are right: We are automatons moved by events and the bad chemicals in our body. But I get over this and regain my unscientific near-religious belief that we do have free will. If many use their free will to choose not to use their free will, that's their problem.

If people choose to believe that they are incapable of salvation, that they must rely on the coming of

Christ or Mohammed or the Great Pumpkin to save them, then they have abandoned the free will that God or Nature or Whomever gave them.

It's up to the species *Homo sapiens* to save itself.

So far, we've done a bad job of that.

But science-fiction writers, the best of them, anyway, are concerned about the future and the welfare of humankind. They're idealists, the best of them, and they know what's gone wrong in the past and what's wrong now, and they hope that they can show how we can develop our potentiality to be human beings. The trouble in the past and now is that most of us have been people but not human beings. Here and there, now and then, a genuine human being comes along as an example to the rest of us. We can see what we could be, should be, if we realize the potentiality in us. Unfortunately, the real human beings are usually killed by the people. Or, if the examples and the teachings of the real human beings are taken up, then the people distort the teachings, corrupt them, and use them for their own purposes.

The semi-robots kill the human beings one way or another.

Good science-fiction writers try to show how we could become human beings. Or, if they don't do that, they show what has kept us from achieving the goal of evolution.

By that I mean that the main purpose of evolution is to get us to the stage where we, *Homo sapiens*, can see that this universe is not senseless. And, having seen, we can then use that perceived order and purpose for good ends.

So far, no one, not even the founders of the great religions or the great philosophers, has been able to prove that the universe is not senseless.

Science-fiction writers know that we must work the

future as if it were dough. We must bake bread from that dough and cast the bread upon the waters of infinity-eternity. What comes back on the tide is usually ruined bread. But *Homo sapiens* is also *Homo optimus*, and we keep trying.

At the same time that we're optimists, we're also realists. We know that humankind is an imperfect animal and will never achieve Utopia. We don't think that Utopia would be desirable because we then would have no goals to work for. But a near-Utopia would be a society in which every person would have open to him or her everything which could enable the realization of full potentiality.

Homo sapiens is also the only animal that's not perfect. All the others fit one hundred percent into their environments and flourish as long as the environment does not change. *Homo sapiens* operates more from rationality than from instinct—despite the fact that it's also irrational—and if the environment does not suit it, it changes the environment. But it, unlike other animals, makes mistakes because it is imperfect. At the same time, *Homo sapiens* can create civilizations and art and music and literature and new social institutions because it is an imperfect animal. Though it keeps screwing up, it has the potentiality to achieve near-perfection.

Homo sapiens is also the only irrational animal. But it has two types of irrationality. One is what I call the Bad Well of Irrationality, and the other the Good Well of Irrationality.

It's the waters from the Bad Well that make for such irrational things as tribalism, clanism, nationalism, sexism, racism, unrealistic ideologies, and self-righteous religionism.

At one time, these things had survival value. They kept the tribe or the nation from perishing because each tribe or nation was surrounded by other tribes or nations that wanted to destroy them.

But that time has long been gone. The only tribe or nation that should exist now is the tribe of Earth or the nation of Earth.

As you know, that state does not exist now, and the chances for its coming into existence are few.

The Bad Well spreads its waters everywhere.

The Good Well is that which makes for compassion, sympathy, and empathy. It also leads to religious impulses, to a high code of ethics, to a desire to make a society which will enable each person to develop his or her full potentiality as a human being. Some have more potentiality than others, but every one should have the chance to realize his or hers to the full.

I pause now. I consider and contemplate.

What I've been doing is retyping a 9500-word introduction.

But I've been veering away from the rough draft before me. I've been going off on tracks I had not considered traveling when I first wrote this.

So, I'm writing a new and much shorter introduction. I'm cutting this considerably. Eliminating thousands of words about what situation I was in when I wrote this or that story and how I felt then. I've already done that in the introductions to the stories herein. It's neither necessary nor desirable to describe how I felt when I wrote other stories or how I slowly gained experience in living and found out more and more about people, and then began selling my fiction and became, finally, a full-time writer in 1969 at the age of fifty-one. Nor is it necessary to describe how I became more or less successful and began to reap the rewards of my writing only when I had reached the age of sixty, a time when most people are seriously thinking of retiring.

That's all right. Better late than never. Anyway, I've

always been a slow starter and a slow developer. I'm not a dasher; I'm a marathon racer. More of a tortoise than a hare.

Well, that's not quite true. It was the hare who took naps now and then, and I sure did that. So call me a tortoise-hare.

In my first draft of this introduction, I had written a lot of stuff that might be interesting. Such as revealing that Betty Friedan, the feminist pioneer, an organizer of NOW and the author of *The Feminine Mystique* and other influential books, was a sophomore at Peoria Central High school when I was a senior. I also described how, though I've been mainly concerned with the issues of future societies, infinity, eternity, and the purpose of the cosmos, my writings have reflected a certain provincialism. They've been streaked with my origins. Though I do write of things beyond the solar system, I am a Peoria-colored writer. No person escapes his origins.

But all this is not really important, and it should be reserved for a book-length autobiography. This introduction is too limited in space for all that I wanted to put in it.

I'll just list the things I've learned while writing and what the themes of my writing have been and have become. I think that I knew all this unconsciously when I started writing, but it took years of living to make these things known consciously to me.

1. Things are seldom what they seem.
2. Everybody has a self-image, and that usually does not correspond with reality.
3. For every advantage, there's a disadvantage and vice-versa.
4. Without personal immortality, this universe is meaningless.
5. If we were not given immortal souls, then we

must create our own. (That is one of the basic premises of my Riverworld series.)

6. We are not robots, nor are we, as Woody Allen says, "Monads with windows." We do have free will, but we don't use it very often.

7. *Homo sapiens* is both rational and irrational, and the Bad Well of Irrationality is what we usually drink from. But the Good Well is there to be used.

8. Some people think that there are many realities. There is, however, only one. We just do not know yet what that is.

9. Despite all I've said, it might be best if science-fiction writers forget they're prophets and philosophers and just stick to telling stories. They're as irrational as the other members of *Homo sapiens*.

AN OVERVIEW OF THE FAIR

•

The paramagnetic airliners fly from all over the world to this city on the Atlantic Ocean. Here, where once was only sullen lifeless water and the top of the Atlantic Ridge is eleven thousand feet down, is an island. It exists because the nations of Earth long ago agreed to transport their garbage, trash, and junk to this spot and dump it. In a short time, the accumulation made a body of land one hundred and twenty miles square rising from the Atlantic Ridge. Who would have thought that there was so much to be rid of in this world?

Now, New Atlantis is a small country, a separate nation that, in twenty years, will be the area of the state of Indiana. In forty, it will rival Texas in area. After that, the garbage, trash, and junk will be dumped into the Pacific.

There are mountains, rivers, and forests on this pleasant land, the lower and major part of which is trash. I'd like to ignore what some have inevitably and not always vindictively made of this, claiming that the present Fair is trash piled on trash. But I can't. I must point out to the critics and scoffers that all good and original and worthwhile things and beings—and the worthless, too—are reconstituted trash. Living plants and animals and humans are made up of the molecules which once formed the dinosaur and the moa, Og the Caveman and Cleopatra. We're all reconstituted recycled trash. So, critics, you who are also reassembled molecules of the dead and decayed, let's have no more cruel—and invalid—jests.

Bacon, the capital city of New Atlantis, is at the mouth of a wide river which empties into the best and one of the largest harbors of the world. Just outside

Bacon, I got off the liner and was driven ten miles through rich farmlands and a forest to the World Farmer Fair. I wish that I could report that there were thousands of cheering and tickertape-throwing people lining the entrance avenue to the Fair. However, I had come incognito and so had avoided the ceremonies, the gift of the key to the city, the luncheons, the speeches, and the tour of the waterworks. Truth was that I was afraid that I would not be offered these even if I came under my own name. New Atlanteans are used to World Fairs; this year's had followed many and many more would succeed this. Last year, Doctor Isaac Asimov came to view the Fair dedicated to him, and the only notice the locals took was a small item in the newspaper about the presence of the American author and scientist, Dr. Azimuth.

The taxi stopped after what seemed a long journey. I got out, paid the driver, paid the ticket taker, and passed through the Fair gates. I stood for a long while in the huge tourist crowd looking at the shining and towering pavilions. I will describe these in the special pavilion introductions. For the moment, the reader may refer to the Fair illustration. The front exteriors of these buildings are shown in it.

My reaction to the vista was one of awe and, I must admit, gratification.

Before I go on, however, I must tell you that I know that some of the tourists in the crowd and some of you readers are secret agents of Arcturus IV. You multiple-personality beings are here to view these architectural wonders and to ponder among yourselves just why Earthpeople would erect them in honor of anyone so humble and impoverished. After all, I am a single persona and so would be in the lowest class if I were an Arcturan. It should, however, occur to you that anyone who writes about so many subjects and so many different worlds may not be a one-person.

I might even be worthy of being made an honorary Arcturan. After the full-scale invasion and conquest, of course.

And so, wondering among these wonders, these lofty and wide-spread glitters, the pavilions five, I decided to enter one. I would not take a guided tour. Why should I need anyone to explain anything in the buildings? Did not I, in a sense, create these buildings? Are there any mysteries about them that a guide could illuminate for me?

In fact, there is one mystery here which neither the guides nor the tourists will ever know. I only may enlighten the curious about the tiny door leading to a small room in the rear of each pavilion. I alone have the key to these rooms. No one else has ever entered these rooms. I wish it were otherwise. I wish that I could take you with me into the mystery these rooms hold. But I cannot.

Don't feel bad about this. You, too, have such a room, though it is in your soul, not in a building.

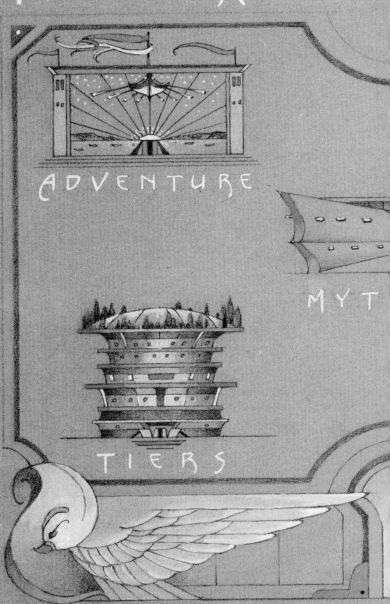

THE GRAND

ADVENTURE

MYT

TIERS

ADVENTURE

PSYCHOLOGY

OLOGY

SPACE

THE WORLD OF TIERS PAVILION

•

Some of you may not be familiar with my World of Tiers series. For your benefit, I'll explain why this many-leveled Tower-of-Babylon structure is at the Fair. It represents one of my more popular series, which consists of seven books. The final one, if I remember correctly, was published in A.D. 1999. This was the year that one of my great-grandchildren, Kickaha José Farmer, was born, named after both the protagonist of the series and myself. If he had been born in the early 1980's, I would have objected because I would not have wanted to inflict the kid with such a bizarre name. Life is hard enough. But nowadays so many have such "weird" given names that his is just one of a multitude.

The World of Tiers Pavilion should perhaps have been set inside the Adventure Pavilion. Most people regard it as a basically *adventure* science-fiction or fantasy series. It is, however, really more than *just* that and could have been placed inside the Mythology Pavilion, too. In fact, the Fair designers were thinking of that in the beginning, but they decided that the series was popular enough to warrant its own pavilion. I pointed out that that sort of logic demanded that the Riverworld series also have its own building. They did not agree. Anyway, putting the Adventure Pavilion inside the Mythology Pavilion would have required an enormously larger structure, not to mention one brobdingnagially more expensive.

I love the word *brobdingnagian*, have ever since I read Swift's *Gulliver's Travels* at a very young age. I like to think that I sometimes write brobdingnagially.

The World of Tiers series is about, among other things, a richness of artificial pocket universes occupying the same space as that of our own *natural* universe. The pocket universe which gave this series its name (a name I did not choose) has only one planet, one moon, and one sun. The moon and sun revolve around the planet, a concept which would have pleased pre-Copernicans. The planet is shaped somewhat like the pavilion, each level having its own rivers, mountains, plains, forests, and type of human beings. The water supply of the planet rises from the top level, Atlantis, and many rivers flow over the edge of the tier, dropping for ten thousand feet or so to the next level. Eventually, the cataracts fall into the sea, which rings the lowest level.

The tourist sees herein (the pavilion) my beasts, birds, reptiles, humans, and some rather strange non-Terrestrial creatures as they are in my series. One, looking exactly like my hero, Paul Janus Finnegan, a.k.a. Kickaha the Trickster, goes through various adventures described in the series. The therioids and androids are, of course, doll-size.

I love this pavilion. My only complaint about it is that it was not built on a one-to-one scale. I can't have everything, however. Sometimes, though, I wonder: Why not?

THE PAVILION OF PSYCHOLOGY

•

This severe and austere building has the least impressive exterior of the five. Perhaps that is because the artist was influenced by the theme and was thinking of Skinner's Box when he designed it.

And what is this monolith in front of the building? What is it supposed to represent? To me, it looks like a long rigid finger pointing upward in the universal gesture of defiance. Is it possible that the artists misread the editor's instructions? Did he think that this pavilion was dedicated to Proctology?

I wish that it had been. I could have had a lot of fun with that.

The interior of the pavilion, however, is as rich, varied, and striking as the human psyche. The walls are ridged, folded, and fissured to resemble the cortex of the human brain. Through them run arteries of a startling joyous-scarlet and veins of a deep melancholy-blue. Near the entrance are the statues of some of the world's greatest psychologists. They are not images of, as you might expect, Freud, Jung, Adler, Sullivan, Horney, *et al.* Here stand towering painted marble figures of those who are, to me, the really great psychologists: Mark Twain, Fyodor Dostoyevsky, Charles Dickens, Honoré Balzac, François Rabelais, Michel Montaigne, William Shakespeare, Henry Miller, Woody Allen, and Jane Austen.

This building, like the others, is multilevel and has at least a hundred tableaux depicting not only scenes but moods from my works. My favorite is the concluding scene from my novel, *UFO Versus IRS*. This portrays that moment when the Internal Revenue Service, after a long and harsh and even bloody persecution of two Vegans disguised as human beings, is forced to refund the Vegans one hundred and thirty trillion dollars.

THE SPACE PAVILION

•

This monument-museum looks vaguely like a rocket. The resemblance is heightened by the two bright beams shooting from vast holes beneath the overhang. At night, they are an eye-hurting white and really look like the exhausts from a rocket. The artist for the illustration, however, forgot to put in the smoke rising from the ground where the beams strike; that is, the steam from ground vents which simulates the smoke. The steam increases the illusion of fierce ravening raw energy smiting the concrete.

During the day, the two pseudoblasts are colored a bright orange so that they may be seen in the daylight.

You enter the building through a door that looks small in the illustration but is in reality eighty feet wide. You gasp because you seem to be suddenly floating at the edge of black and abysmal space. Space with a big S. Space. In fact, you are much lighter because of the antigravity field permeating this vast enclosure. Constellations, exploding nebulae, and single stars circle slowly, themselves whirling, above and below you. You are standing on a transparent floor, the solidity of which is your only assurance that you are not indeed in true Space, the universe around you on all sides.

Sometimes, you do not have even that assurance. Now and then your movements will propel you a few inches into the air.

Because of the scale of the heavenly bodies, you cannot see at first the model of the starship described in "Shadow of Space." But the ship does indeed swell as it supposedly surpasses the speed of light, and, presently, its walls coincide with the walls of the universe and then pass out of your sight. Or seem to. After a minute, the ship reappears, being in its decelerating and hence shrinking state. Its crew also shrinks. In three minutes, the starship has dwindled to a speck of light and then nothing.

The ship and its crew are holographic deceptions, of course, but very realistic ones.

This simulation of Space is awesome, staggering, and

achingly beautiful. Man has imitated Nature here, but the feeling, if any, that this is a fake passes quickly. You are face to face with that which, perhaps, you would rather not face. This is the most beautiful of all things that God has to offer. The most beautiful of all nonliving things, that is (what can surpass the beauty of a human baby?). This is the most beautiful of God's spectacles: the naked stars in Space.

I went back to this pavilion seven times before leaving the Fair.

THE ADVENTURE PAVILION

•

Mostly, I'm supposed to say in these pavilion-introductions what I like and don't like about them — what I think is superb and thrilling or absurd and ludicrous or discrepant and lacking. The trouble with this approach is that my reactions may not, more probably won't be, yours. On the other hand, most of you will have to take my word for the quality or nonquality of these pavilions. Very few of you, so I've been told, will ever travel to New Atlantis.

The design for the front of the Adventure Pavilion is both striking and symbolic. The rays from the semihemispherical roof of the tiny pavilion seem to buoy up an ancient galley or a Viking longship. The rays could be some sort of antigravity rays, which scientists tell us is impossible. (But how do they know what will be possible in the distant future?) The fusion in the design is consonant with my works, which range from future technology to the ancient and historical. The long ago *was* fuses with the far distant *to-be*.

However, with my sense of perversion or perverse sense that has both delighted and disgusted readers, I also see the front design of the pavilion as something other than just described.

The little structure in the foreground could be a doorless outhouse, a way-station for the relief of the adventurers who pass this way. (No pun intended.) The Vikings in the airborne longship are descending on the gravity-softening rays and intend to get rid of what Nature demands they not carry around too long.

High adventure is fine, but even it has to obey natural dictates. Realism—a touch of it here and there, anyway—makes the fantasy more believable. Surely, King Arthur had a dropseat in his suit of armor.

I cannot fault, try though I did, the interior of the Adventure Pavilion. It has moving tableaux depicting almost all of my stories, short or long. The designers perceived, quite rightly, that all of the stories are, in more than one sense, adventure stories. Even my short story, "Buddha Contemplates His Novel," is an adventure. And my "Immanuel Kant Falls On His Categorical Imperative," though it does not have much action, is an adventure story. Thus, any story here is also in the other pavilions, but the representative tableau has different scenes in each building.

One of my favorites in this pavilion is from my short story, "Cheap Street Hell," an afterlife tale in which some publishers (eighty-seven percent of those having existed or now existing) are in a hell run by authors. The latter dispense the food, water, cigarettes, drugs and booze which they receive from *above*. The authors are required by contract with *above* to pass on fifty percent of the Heavenly CARE packages to the publishers. But, by the time the food and goodies trickle down through various departments to the publishers, the publishers are lucky to get ten percent.

I add that honest publishers have a special place in Heaven, where they sit on the right hand of God, though not very near.

THE PAVILION OF MYTHOLOGY

•

There is a good reason why the building dedicated to my mythology is in the center of the Fair and between those erected to the World of Tiers, Adventure, Psychology, and Space. Mythology is a glue, perhaps the most widely used but no doubt the strongest, that holds society together and keeps the individual from falling apart. We are born into myth, live by and through myth, and die swaddled in myth. In fact, many myths say that death is not the end of our story but the beginning of another, a sequel. This is an irrational idea based upon no scientifically valid evidence whatsoever. To which rational statement most people say, "So what?"

Cats and dogs, despite their long association with human beings, have no mythology. Apes, despite their close resemblance to *Homo sapiens*, have no mythology. Only a sentient species has mythology. Only those species capable of rationality are capable of being irrational.

Your narrator, who is both rational and irrational, has tried in his fiction to demonstrate that all of humanity is just like him. He admits, however, that some are more rational than others. But there are also different systems of rationality and of logic.

Enough of that. The pavilion before us is dedicated to the ancient, present, and possibly future mythology of *Homo sapiens* and other species as seen or experienced through your narrator. It is this which we will briefly tour.

Let's pause before this magnificent structure which is so huge and heavy, yet looks as if it's about to lift and wing away at any moment. It is named Mythology, but is it rightly named? *Mythology* comes from the Greek *mythologia*, a telling of tales or legends, legendary lore;

from *mythos*, word, speech, legend, story, and *-logia*, from *legein*, to speak. Mythology is the science or study of myths and legends. Or a book of or about myths. Or myths collectively; especially, all the myths about a specific being, or those myths, fables, or traditions interwoven with the history, origin, deities, etc. of a specified people.

Myths are also used in the sense of consciously made-up lies.

So saith Webster's.

Homer took the myths and legends handed down to him by many others and put them together and improved them. If you grant that *The Iliad* and *The Odyssey* are not only poetry but, in a sense, the first two novels, then you have also granted that the first two novels are still the best ever written. Nobody has beaten Homer in the novel-writing field. And nobody has beaten him at creating his personal mythology. Though he inherited various epos, legends, fairy tales, folk tales, and fragments of lays, he not only added to them, he did considerable editing. The results were works which reflect not only racial and national myths, but these as strained through Homer. Hence, his mythology is also personal.

Lesser Homers followed—for instance, Edgar Rice Burroughs, Lester Dent, and Walter Gibson. These created modern myths, those of more recent vintage. Tarzan, Doc Savage, and The Shadow were created in the 1930's, but they are still alive today. They fascinated me when I was young, still do, and I have extended their biographies in my mythology.

For instance, you step into the gargantuan dome which forms the first half of this pavilion. You see on your right a jungle tableau. Traveling through its upper regions is a rather new hero, as newness goes, Tarzan, John Clayton, Viscount Greystoke, Lord of the Jungle,

Chief of the Waziri tribe. As I've tried to show in my *Tarzan Alive* and some pastiches, Tarzan is also the ancient Sun Hero, Oedipus, Hercules, Odysseus, and the native American Trickster or African Anansi, the trickster Spider. Though his setting is modern, as modernity goes, he is an archetype which appeals to, makes resonant, the primal archetypes existing in us. He is also a highly individualized man, the archetype as seen by Burroughs. And as seen through my extensions.

But my main function is to tell you my reactions to the contents of the pavilions, not to describe them all. I walk past the Tarzan tableau to a copy of "The Adventure of the Peerless Peer." This copy needs a structure this size to house it. It's a truly massive volume, a leather-bound book forty feet high. It leans against a pillar and is open, revealing words big enough for even the almost blind to read. Every "i" is as tall as the "I" that stands admiringly before it. The capital letters are as tall as basketball players.

Beyond the book is a vista which seems to be seen from afar. There is the mighty King Kong on top of the Empire State Building, one paw holding the archetypal blonde heroine-victim, the other clutching an Army biplane he's plucked out of the air. And there is Doc Savage, the golden-eyed and bronze-skinned giant, hurling around enemies about whose evilness there is no doubt. And there is Glinda the Good, the ravishing red-haired witch-ruler of the Quadlings of the Land of Oz. And there in a murky alley deep in the canyons of Manhattan, sidling along, a big .45 automatic in each fist, his eyes blazing in the darkness, laughing maniacally, is The Shadow.

In other vistas are Sherlock Holmes and Dr. Watson, Rip van Winkle and Jesus on Mars.

This half of the building houses those heroes and heroines of mythology, ancient and modern, whom I loved so much when young that I could not endure that no more stories would be written about them. So I wrote more stories.

The prolonging of the life of the heroes of others is, however, only a small part of my writings. Most of my heroes and heroines are of my own creation. Thus, these figure in the big majority of the tableaux and the colossal one-book limited editions leaning against pillars carved with the faces of gargoyles and ghosts, goddesses and ghouls, giants and jinns. Here is the future Roman Catholic priest, Father John Carmody, hanging in midspace with an egg growing from his chest. There is Ralph von Wau Wau, the giant German police dog with a genius I.Q., the admirer and emulator of Sherlock Holmes, author of the best seller, *Some Humans Don't Stink*. And there is one of my favorite characters, Fobo, the Wogglebug of Ozagen, running desperately down the street to save the human hero of *The Lovers* from his own stupidity.

Here, as in the other buildings, are tableaux of almost all of my stories. What are they doing in the Mythology Pavilion?

Answer: Though many of the stories are threaded with or based upon the racial mythology of *Homo sapiens*, the collective unconscious of the hybrid ape-angel known as Human Being, all also figure forth my private, my personal, mythology. Hindbrain, forebrain, and the peculiar psyche of PJF go hand in hand here. Trimurti. The trinity. Everything is in threes. Yet one.

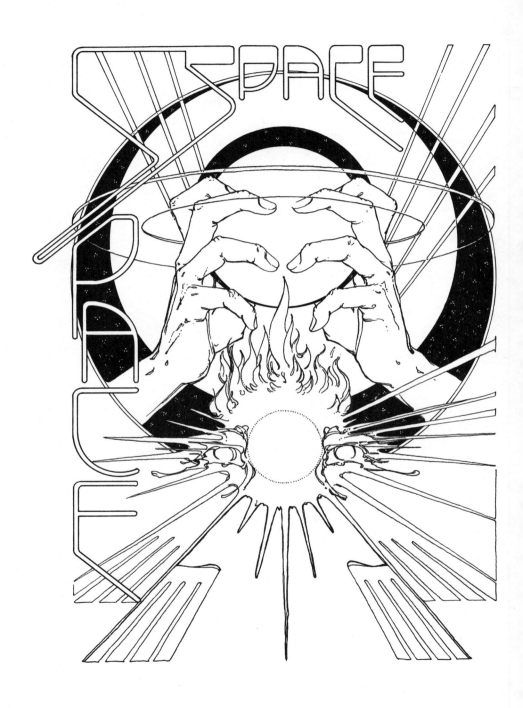

THE SHADOW
OF SPACE

"My little old maiden aunt in Iowa won't understand this," Gene Roddenberry said. "It'd be too far out for her. Besides, do you have any idea how much money it would cost to do the special effects and make all the models we'd need?"

Roddenberry, the producer of the soon-to-be-launched Star Trek series, and I were in his office. He had just read my treatment for a script. (A treatment is a prose description of the basis for a TV or movie script.) The maiden aunt in Iowa he referred to may or may not have existed. But he used her as a standard for what the TV audience would understand and how they would react. If she could not comprehend what was going on, then the treatment would be rejected. Apparently, his aunt just would not grasp a show based on my treatment; she'd be bewildered.

While he was telling me this, I was looking at a lavalite on his desk. It was the first time I'd ever seen one. In fact, I had never even heard the word "lavalite" before. The red thermoplastic globs in the heated transparent liquid in the bottle rose, split, curled, twisted, expanded, shed parts of themselves, formed dragon and cloud shapes, cooled near the top of the bottle, sank, met other globs, merged, and settled near the bottom. There, reheated, they rose again, splitting off and writhing like sick amoebae.

The lavalite was a visible reflection, a solid analogy, to my thoughts and sensations. They, like the heated plastic globs, were twisting and turning, rising and falling, forming strange shapes. So were my guts. But I was cool. I maintained my composure.

And, at that very moment, gazing at the lavalite, I got an idea for a story. Roddenberry would never accept it for his show, and, anyway, I wanted to make a novel from the idea. Some years later, I did, and it was issued as The Lavalite World, a volume in my World of Tiers series.

"It's out, definitely out. Not for me," Roddenberry said. He spoke in a kindly but determined tone. I could not change his mind. I was not going to try. What did I know about the demands and restrictions of (so-called) science-fiction TV shows?

Now, looking back, I can see that he was right. The idea of a faster-than-light spaceship expanding until it burst out of our

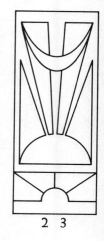

2 3

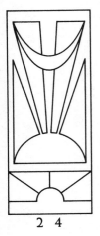

universe would be too far out for most TV viewers. At that time, anyway. Now we have a somewhat more sophisticated audience, one conditioned by Star Trek, Star Wars, The Empire Strikes Back, Close Encounters of the Third Kind, Alien, Scanners, and The Lathe of Heaven.

Or would the majority still be unable to grasp this concept? Many would, but many more might not.

I thanked Roddenberry and left with the rejected treatment. I then wrote another treatment for another possible script for Roddenberry. That, too, was rejected as being even more far out.

"Too confusing," Roddenberry said. "You have to remember that some viewers will tune in on the show in the middle of it. They'd never understand what was going on, and I doubt that those who watch it from the beginning would. Besides, the viewer will have interruptions to distract him. Commercials, going to the toilet, phone calls, the kids and the dog raising cain. And so on."

So I said to hell with TV treatments and went back to writing fiction for magazines and books.

I should not have given up. I should have written more treatments and made sure that they were on a less abstract level, less difficult to translate into the visual-audial medium: film. I could then have written scripts based on my treatments and made a pile of money. Other science-fiction writers I knew in Los Angeles did so, and so did many writers who knew little of science-fiction. Their scripts showed it. But I must have felt, deep down, that Star Trek did not want the kind of stuff that I wanted to write.

However, I am, among other things, economical. At least, I am when it comes to ideas. Both the ideas I'd proposed in my treatments were too good to let die. So I used one of the treatments as a springboard for the story you are about to read. It was changed considerably. Captain Kirk and Mister Spock et al. were replaced by other characters, the story now took place far beyond any frontiers of space that the Enterprise would ever cross, and I did not worry about special effects, models, and vast sums of money to produce it. Nor about whether my readers would understand it. I knew that they would.

Just as I was finishing "The Shadow of Space," I heard that a man named Joe Elder was in the market for stories for an anthology titled Eros in Orbit. It would be sexual science-fiction, no tabus, no holds barred. I sent my offering to Elder, and he rejected it with the comment that it was too raunchy for him and that I was not in good taste. Words to that effect. He even sounded indignant that I would dare send the manuscript to him.

This was not the first time that I had received such a rejection letter. But I had not expected it. Had he not said that there would be no tabus?

What was the scene that aroused his puritanical ire and made him forget his promises that there would be no holds barred? It was something that seemed to me to be rather mild and also to be integral and appropriate to the psychological aspects of the tale. It was not something thrown in for sensationalism.

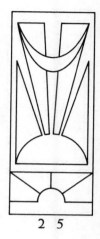

I don't want to preshow too much of this story, so I'll just say that the spaceship Sleipnir went into the womb of the colossal dead woman floating in outer space. Really outer space. I had the Sleipnir do that so that crew would be psychologically comforted. It needed such badly. It would literally be back in the womb. But, apparently, my vivid description of the Brobding-nagian vagina and pubic hair was too much for Joe.

I had the choice of putting the ms. in the trunk—as we say in the business—or making some changes. So I had the spaceship enter the woman's mouth—after all, that should satisfy those with an oral fixation—and I sent it to a magazine. It was printed there, and it has since appeared in a number of anthologies, some of them edited by academics.

Some of the editors who purchased "The Shadow of Space" would have accepted the original version. But, though I considered using that, I did not.

Why?

I have this strange thing about my stories. I believe that they are true. They did happen or will happen. I'd be tampering with reality if I altered a story to any significant extent once it's been printed.

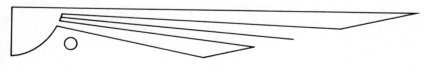

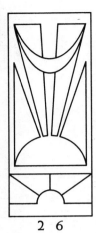

This story is standing as printed.

But, as you shall see later, I did change my mind about altering significantly one story. Circumstances forced me to do that. But I rationalized that it was right to do so. After all, there are many parallel universes. In some, the South did win the battle of Gettysburg, Napoleon did successfully invade England, and various Philip José Farmers wrote different stories from those written in this universe or wrote differing versions.

Do I contradict myself?

Walt Whitman and I say, "Very well. I contain many contradictions."

Thesis, antithesis, and synthesis.

The PJF of one universe writes a story. The PJF of another writes a different version. The PJF of a third universe writes a story which combines both.

Perhaps all three PJF's are linked at night when they dream. They share their dreams.

The klaxon cleared its plastic throat and began to whoop. Alternate yellows and reds pulsed on the consoles wrapped like bracelets around the wrists of the captain and the navigator. The huge auxiliary screens spaced on the bulkheads of the bridge also flashed red and yellow.

Captain Grettir, catapulted from his reverie and from his chair, stood up. The letters and numerals 20-G-DZ-R hung burning on a sector of each screen and spurted up from the wrist-console, spread out before his eyes, then disappeared, only to rise from the wrist-console again and magnify themselves and thin into nothing. Over and over again. 20-G-DZ-R. The code letters indicating that the alarm originated from the corridor leading to the engine room.

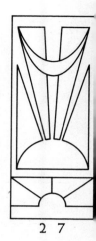

2 7

He turned his wrist and raised his arm to place the lower half of the console at the correct viewing and speaking distance.

"Twenty-G-DZ-R, report!"

The flaming, expanding, levitating letters died out, and the long high-cheekboned face of MacCool, chief engineer, appeared as a tiny image on the sector of the console. It was duplicated on the bridge bulkhead screens. It rose and grew larger, shooting towards Grettir, then winking out to be followed by a second ballooning face.

Also on the wrist-console's screen, behind MacCool, were Comas, a petty officer, and Grinker, a machinist's mate. Their faces did not float up because they were not in the central part of the screen. Behind them was a group of marines and an 88-K cannon on a floating sled.

"It's the Wellington woman," MacCool said. "She

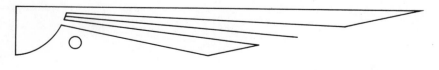

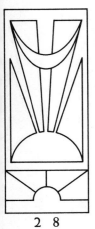

used a photer, low-power setting, to knock out the two guards stationed at the engine-room port. Then she herded us—me, Comas, Grinker—out. She said she'd shoot us if we resisted. And she welded the grille to the bulkhead so it can't be opened unless it's burned off.

"I don't know why she's doing this. But she's reconnected the drive wires to a zander bridge so she can control the acceleration herself. We can't do a thing to stop her unless we go in after her."

He paused, swallowed and said, "I could send men outside and have them try to get through the engine room airlock or else cut through the hull to get her. While she's distracted by this, we could make a frontal attack down the corridor. But she says she'll shoot anybody that gets too close. We could lose some men. She means what she says."

"If you cut a hole in the hull, she'd be out of air, dead in a minute," Grettir said.

"She's in a spacesuit," MacCool replied. "That's why I didn't have this area sealed off and gas flooded in."

Grettir hoped his face was not betraying his shock. Hearing an exclamation from Wang, seated near him, Grettir turned his head. He said, "How in hell did she get out of sick bay?"

He realized at the same time that Wang could not answer that question.

MacCool said, "I don't know, sir. Ask Doctor Wills."

"Never mind that now!"

Grettir stared at the sequence of values appearing on the navigator's auxiliary bulkhead-screen. The oh-point-five of lightspeed had already climbed to point-nine-six. It changed every four seconds. The point-nine-six became point-nine-seven, then point-nine-eight, point-nine-nine and then one-point-oh.

And then one-point-one and one-point-two.

Grettir forced himself to sit back down. If anything was going to happen, it would have done so by now; the cruiser *Sleipnir*, two hundred-eighty million tons, would have been converted to pure energy.

A nova, bright but very brief, would have gouted in the heavens. And the orbiting telescopes of Earth would see the flare in twenty-point-eight light-years.

"What's the state of the *emc* clamp and acceleration-dissipaters?" Grettir said.

"No strain—yet," Wang said. "But the power drain . . . if it continues . . . five megakilowatts per two seconds, and we're just beginning."

"I think," Grettir said slowly, "that we're going to find out what we intended to find out. But it isn't going to be under the carefully controlled conditions we had planned."

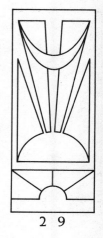

The Terran Space Navy experimental cruiser *Sleipnir* had left its base on Asgard, eighth planet of Altair (alpha Aquilae), twenty-eight shipdays ago. It was under orders to make the first attempt of a manned ship to exceed the velocity of light. If its mission was successful, men could travel between Earth and the colonial planets in weeks instead of years. The entire galaxy might be opened to Earth.

Within the past two weeks, the *Sleipnir* had made several tests at oh-point-eight times the velocity of light, the tests lasting up to two hours at a time.

The *Sleipnir* was equipped with enormous motors and massive clamps, dissipaters and space-time structure expanders ("hole-openers") required for near-light-speeds and beyond. No ship in Terrestrial history had ever had such power or the means to handle such power.

The drive itself—the cubed amplification of energy

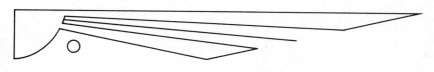

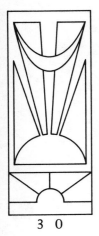

produced by the controlled mixture of matter, anti-matter and half-matter—gave an energy that could eat its way through the iron core of a planet. But part of that energy had to be diverted to power the energy-mass conversion "clamp" that kept the ship from being transformed into energy itself. The "hole-opener" also required vast power. This device—officially the Space-Time Structure Expander or Neutralizer—"unbent" the local curvature of the universe and so furnished a "hole" through which the *Sleipnir* traveled. This hole nullified ninety-nine-point-three per cent of the resistance the *Sleipnir* would normally have encountered.

Thus the effects of speeds approaching and even exceeding light-speed, would be modified, even if not entirely avoided. The *Sleipnir* should not contract along its length to zero nor attain infinite mass when it reached the speed of light. It contracted, and it swelled, yes, by only 1/777,777th what it should have. The ship would assume the shape of a disk—but much more slowly than it would without its openers, clamps and dissipaters.

Beyond the speed of light, who knew what would happen? It was the business of the *Sleipnir* to find out. But, Grettir thought, not under these conditions.

"Sir!" MacCool said, "Wellington threatens to shoot anybody who comes near the engine room."

He hesitated, then said, "Except you. She wants to speak to you. But she doesn't want to do it over the intercom. She insists that you come down and talk to her face to face." Grettir bit his lower lip and made a sucking sound.

"Why me?" he said, but he knew why, and MacCool's expression showed that he also knew.

"I'll be down in a minute. Now, isn't there any way we can connect a bypass, route a circuit around her

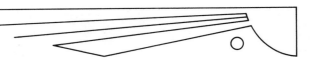

or beyond her and get control of the drive again?"

"No, sir!"

"Then she's cut through the engine-room deck and gotten to the backup circuits also?"

MacCool said, "She's crazy, but she's clear-headed enough to take all precautions. She hasn't overlooked a thing."

Grettir said, "Wang! What's the velocity now?"

"Two-point-three sl/pm, sir!"

Grettir looked at the huge starscreen on the "forward" bulkhead of the bridge. Black except for a few glitters of white, blue, red, green, and the galaxy called XD-2 that lay dead ahead. The galaxy had been the size of an orange, and it still was. He stared at the screen for perhaps a minute, then said, "Wang, am I seeing right? The red light from XD-2 is shifting towards the blue, right?"

3   1

"Right, sir!"

"Then . . . why isn't XD-2 getting bigger? We're overhauling it like a fox after a rabbit."

Wang said, "I think it's getting closer, sir. But *we're* getting bigger."

II

Grettir rose from the chair. "Take over while I'm gone. Turn off the alarm; tell the crew to continue their normal duties. If anything comes up while I'm in the engine area, notify me at once."

The exec saluted. "Yes, sir!" she said huskily.

Grettir strode off the bridge. He was aware that the officers and crewmen seated in the ring of chairs in the bridge were looking covertly at him. He stopped for a minute to light up a cigar. He was glad that his

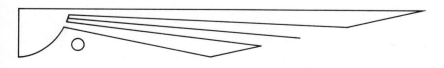

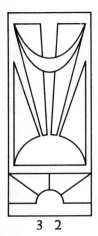

hands were not shaking, and he hoped that his expression was confident. Slowly, repressing the impulse to run, he continued across the bridge and into the jumpshaft. He stepped off backward into the shaft and nonchalantly blew out smoke while he sank out of sight of the men in the bridge. He braced himself against the quick drop and then the thrusting deceleration. He had set the controls for Dock 14; the doors slid open; he walked into a corridor where a g-car and operator waited for him. Grettir climbed in, sat down and told the crewman where to drive to.

Two minutes later, he was with MacCool. The chief engineer pointed down the corridor. Near its end on the floor were two still unconscious Marines. The door to the engine room was open. The secondary door, the grille, was shut. The lights within the engine room had been turned off. Something white on the other side of the grille moved. It was Donna Wellington's face, visible through the helmet.

"We can't keep this acceleration up," Grettir said. "We're already going far faster than even unmanned experimental ships have been allowed to go. There are all sorts of theories about what might happen to a ship at these speeds, all bad."

"We've disproved several by now," MacCool said. He spoke evenly, but his forehead was sweaty and shadows hung under his eyes.

MacCool continued, "I'm glad you got here, sir. She just threatened to cut the *emc* clamp wires if you didn't show up within the next two minutes."

He gestured with both hands to indicate a huge and expanding ball of light.

"I'll talk to her," Grettir said. "Although I can't imagine what she wants."

MacCool looked dubious. Grettir wanted to ask him what the hell he was thinking but thought better of

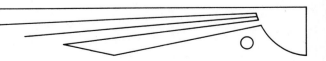

it. He said, "Keep your men at this post. Don't even look as if you're coming after me."

"And what do we do, sir, if she shoots you?"

Grettir winced. "Use the cannon. And never mind hesitating if I happen to be in the way. Blast her! But make sure you use a beam short enough to get her but not long enough to touch the engines."

"May I ask why we don't do that before you put your life in danger?" MacCool said.

Grettir hesitated, then said, "My main responsibility is to the ship and its crew. But this woman is very sick; she doesn't realize the implications of her actions. Not fully, anyway. I want to talk her out of this, if I can."

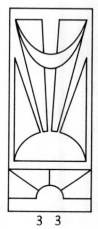

He unhooked the communicator from his belt and walked down the corridor toward the grille and the darkness behind it and the whiteness that moved. His back prickled. The men were watching him intently. God knew what they were saying, or at least thinking, about him. The whole crew had been amused for some time by Donna Wellington's passion for him and his inability to cope with her. They had said she was mad about him, not realizing that she really was mad. They had laughed. But they were not laughing now.

Even so, knowing that she was truly insane, some of them must be blaming him for this danger. Undoubtedly, they were thinking that if he had handled her differently, they would not now be so close to death.

He stopped just one step short of the grille. Now he could see Wellington's face, a checkerboard of blacks and whites. He waited for her to speak first. A full minute passed, then she said, "Robert!"

The voice, normally low-pitched and pleasant, was now thin and strained.

"Not Robert Eric," he said into the communicator.

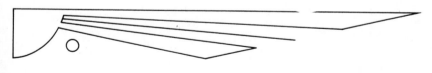

"Captain Eric Grettir, Mrs. Wellington."

There was a silence. She moved closer to the grille. Light struck one eye, which gleamed bluely.

"Why do you hate me so, Robert?" she said plaintively. "You used to love me. What did I do to make you turn against me?"

"I am *not* your husband," Grettir said. "Look at me. Can't you see that I am not Robert Wellington? I am Captain Grettir of the *Sleipnir*. You *must* see who I *really* am, Mrs. Wellington. It is very important."

"You don't love me!" she screamed. "You are trying to get rid of me by pretending you're another man! But it won't work! I'd know you anywhere, you beast! You beast! I hate you, Robert!"

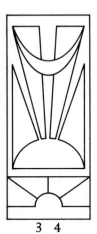

3   4

Involuntarily, Grettir stepped back under the intensity of her anger. He saw her hand come up from the shadows and the flash of light on a handgun. It was too late then; she fired; a beam of whiteness dazzled him.

Light was followed by darkness.

Ahead, or above, there was a disk of grayness in the black. Grettir traveled slowly and spasmodically towards it, as if he had been swallowed by a whale but was being ejected towards the open mouth, the muscles of the Leviathan's throat working him outwards.

Far behind him, deep in the bowels of the whale, Donna Wellington spoke.

"Robert?"

"Eric!" he shouted. "I'm *Eric!*"

The *Sleipnir*, barely on its way out from Asgard, dawdling at 6200 kilometers per second, had picked up the Mayday call. It came from a spaceship midway between the twelfth and thirteenth planet of Altair. Although Grettir could have ignored the call without reprimand from his superiors, he had altered course,

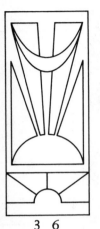

and he had found a ship wrecked by a meteorite. Inside the hull was half the body of a man. And a woman in deep shock.

Robert and Donna Wellington were second-generation Asgardians, Ph.D.s in biotatalogy, holding master's papers in astrogation. They had been searching for specimens of "space plankton" and "space hydras," forms of life born in the regions between Altair's outer planets.

The crash, the death of her husband, and the shattering sense of isolation, dissociation, and hopelessness during the eighty-four hours before rescue had twisted Mrs. Wellington. Perhaps twisted was the wrong word. Fragmented was a better description.

From the beginning of what at first seemed recovery, she had taken a superficial resemblance of Grettir to her husband for an identity. Grettir had been gentle and kind with her at the beginning and had made frequent visits to sick bay. Later, advised by Doctor Wills, he had been severe with her.

And so the unforeseen result.

Donna Wellington screamed behind him. Suddenly, the twilight circle ahead became bright, and he was free. He opened his eyes to see faces over him. Doctor Wills and MacCool. He was in sick bay.

MacCool smiled and said, "For a moment, we thought . . ."

"What happened?" Grettir said. Then, "I know what she did. I mean—"

"She fired full power at you," MacCool said. "But the bars of the grille absorbed most of the energy. You got just enough to crisp the skin off your face and to knock you out. Good thing you closed your eyes in time."

Grettir sat up. He felt his face; it was covered with

a greasy ointment, pain-deadening and skin-growing *resec.*

"I got a hell of a headache."

Doctor Wills said, "It'll be gone in a minute."

"What's the situation?" Grettir said. "How'd you get me away from her?"

MacCool said, "I had to do it, Captain. Otherwise, she'd have taken another shot at you. The cannon blasted what was left of the grille. Mrs. Wellington—"

"She's dead?"

"Yes. But the cannon didn't get her. Strange. She took her suit off, stripped to the skin. Then she went out through the airlock in the engine room. Naked, as if she meant to be the bride of Death. We almost got caught in the outrush of air, since she fixed the controls so that the inner port remained open. It was close, but we got the port shut in time."

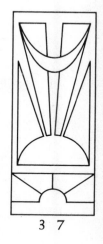

Grettir said, "I . . . never mind. Any damage to the engine room?"

"No. And the wires are reconnected for normal operation. Only—"

"Only what?"

MacCool's face was so long he looked like a frightened bloodhound.

"Just before I reconnected the wires, a funny . . . peculiar . . . thing happened. The whole ship, and everything inside the ship, went through a sort of distortion. Wavy, as if we'd all become wax and were dripping. Or flags flapping in a wind. The bridge reports that the fore of the ship seemed to expand like a balloon, then became ripply, and the entire effect passed through the ship. We all got nauseated while the waviness lasted."

There was silence, but their expressions indicated that there was more to be said.

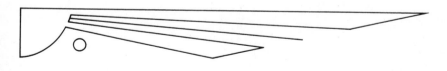

"Well?"

MacCool and Wills looked at each other. MacCool swallowed and said, "Captain, we don't know where in hell we are!"

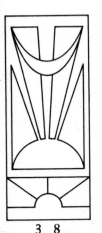

III

On the bridge, Grettir examined the forward EXT. screen. There were no stars. Space everywhere was filled with a light as gray and as dull as that of a false dawn on Earth. In the gray glow, at a distance as yet undetermined, were a number of spheres. They looked small, but if they were as large as the one immediately aft of the *Sleipnir*, they were huge.

The sphere behind them, estimated to be at a distance of fifty kilometers, was about the size of Earth's moon, relative to the ship. Its surface was as smooth and as gray as a ball of lead.

Darl spoke a code into her wrist-console, and the sphere on the starscreen seemed to shoot towards them. It filled the screen until Darl changed the line-of-sight. They were looking at about twenty degrees of arc of the limb of the sphere.

"There it is!" Darl said. A small object floated around the edge of the sphere and seemed to shoot towards them. She magnified it, and it became a small gray sphere.

"It orbits round the big one," she said.

Darl paused, then said, "We—the ship—came *out* of that small sphere. *Out* of it. *Through* its skin."

"You mean we had been inside it?" Grettir said. "And now we're outside it?"

"Yes, sir! Exactly!"

She gasped and said, "Oh, oh—sir!"

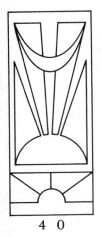

Around the large sphere, slightly above the plane of the orbit of the small sphere but within its sweep in an inner orbit, sped another object. At least fifty times as large as the small globe, it caught up with the globe, and the two disappeared together around the curve of the primary.

"Wellington's body!" Grettir said.

He turned away from the screen, took one step, and turned around again. "It's not right! She should be trailing along behind us or at least parallel with us, maybe shooting off at an angle but still moving in our direction.

"But she's been grabbed by the big sphere! She's in orbit! And her size! Gargantuan! It doesn't make sense! It shouldn't be!"

"Nothing should," Wang said.

"Take us back," Grettir said. "Establish an orbit around the primary, on the same plane as the secondary but further out, approximately a kilometer and a half from it."

Darl's expression said, "Then what?"

Grettir wondered if she had the same thought as he. The faces of the others on the bridge were doubtful. The fear was covered but leaking out. He could smell the rotten bubbles. Had they guessed, too?

"What attraction does the primary have on the ship?" he said to Wang.

"No detectable influence whatsoever, sir. The *Sleipnir* seems to have a neutral charge, neither positive nor negative in relation to any of the spheres. Or to Wellington's . . . body."

Grettir was slightly relieved. His thoughts had been so wild that he had not been able to consider them as anything but hysterical fantasies. But Wang's answer showed that Grettir's idea was also his. Instead of replying in terms of gravitational force, he had talked as

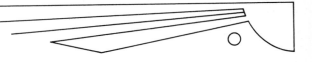

if the ship were a subatomic particle.

But if the ship was not affected by the primary, why had Wellington's corpse been attracted by the primary?

"Our velocity in relation to the primary?" Grettir said.

"We cut off the acceleration as soon as the wires were reconnected," Wang said.

"This was immediately after we came out into this . . . this space. We didn't apply any retrodrive. Our velocity, as indicated by power consumption, is ten megaparsecs per minute. That is," he added after a pause, "what the instruments show. But our detector, which should be totally ineffective at this velocity, indicates fifty kilometers per minute, relative to the big sphere."

Wang leaned back in his chair as if he expected Grettir to explode into incredulity. Grettir lit up another cigar. This time, his hands shook. He blew out a big puff of smoke and said, "Obviously, we're operating under different quote laws unquote *out here.*"

Wang sighed softly. "So you think so, too, Captain? Yes, different *laws.* Which means that every time we make a move through this space, we can't know what the result will be. May I ask what you plan to do, sir?"

By this question, which Wang would never have dared to voice before, though he had doubtless often thought it, Grettir knew that the navigator shared his anxiety. Beneath that apparently easy manner and soft voice was a pain just beneath the navel. The umbilical had been ripped out; Wang was hurting and bleeding inside. Was he, too, beginning to float away in a gray void? Bereft as no man had ever been bereft?

It took a special type of man or woman to lose himself from Earth or his native planet, to go out among the stars so far that the natal sun was not even a faint

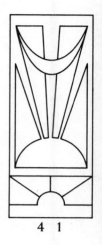

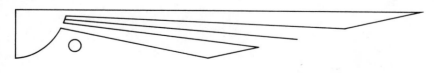

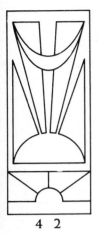

glimmer. It also took special conditioning for the special type of man. He had to believe, in the deepest part of his unconscious, that his ship was a piece of Mother Earth. He had to believe; otherwise, he went to pieces.

It could be done. Hundreds did it. But nothing had prepared even these farfarers for absolute divorce from the universe itself.

Grettir ached with the dread of the void. The void was coiling up inside him, a gray serpent, a slither of nothingness. Coiling. And what would happen when it uncoiled?

And what would happen to the crew when they were informed—as they must be—of the utter dissociation?

There was only one way to keep their minds from slipping their moorings. They must believe that they could get back into the world. Just as he must believe it.

"I'll play it by ear," Grettir said.

"What? Sir?"

"Play it by ear!" Grettir said more harshly than he had intended. "I was merely answering your question. Have you forgotten you asked me what I meant to do?"

"Oh, no, sir," Wang said. "I was just thinking. . . ."

"Keep your mind on the job," Grettir said. He told Darl he would take over. He spoke the code to activate the ALL-STATIONS; a low rising-falling sound went into every room of the *Sleipnir*, and all screens flashed a black-and-green checked pattern. Then the warnings, visual and audible, died out, and the captain spoke.

He talked for two minutes. The bridgemen looked as if the lights had been turned off in their brains. It was almost impossible to grasp the concept of their being outside their universe. As difficult was thinking

of their unimaginably vast native cosmos as only an "electron" orbiting around the nucleus of an "atom." If what the captain said was true (how could it be?), the ship was in the space between the superatoms of a supermolecule of a superuniverse.

Even though they knew that the *Sleipnir* had ballooned under the effect of nearly three hundred thousand times the speed of light, they could not wrap the fingers of their minds around the concept. It turned to smoke and drifted away.

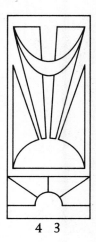

It took ten minutes, ship's time, to turn and to complete the maneuvers which placed the *Sleipnir* in an orbit parallel to but outside the secondary, or, as Grettir thought of it, "our universe." He gave his chair back to Darl and paced back and forth across the bridge while he watched the starscreen.

If they were experiencing the sundering, the cutting-off, they were keeping it under control. They had been told by their captain that they *were* going back in, not that they would make a *try* at re-entry. They had been through much with him, and he had never failed them. With this trust, they could endure the agony of dissolution.

As the *Sleipnir* established itself parallel to the secondary, Wellington's body curved around the primary again and began to pass the small sphere and ship. The arms of the mountainous body were extended stiffly to both sides, and her legs spread out. In the gray light, her skin was bluish-black from the ruptured veins and arteries below the skin. Her red hair, coiled in a Psyche knot, looked black. Her eyes, each of which was larger than the bridge of the *Sleipnir*, were open, bulging clots of black blood. Her lips were pulled back in a grimace, the teeth like a soot-streaked portcullis.

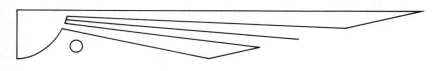

Cartwheeling, she passed the sphere and the ship.

Wang reported that there were three "shadows" on the surface of the primary. Those were keeping pace with the secondary, the corpse, and the ship. Magnified on the bridge-bulkhead screen, each "shadow" was the silhouette of one of the three orbiting bodies. The shadows were only about one shade darker than the surface and were caused by a shifting pucker in the primary skin. The surface protruded along the edges of the shadows and formed a shallow depression within the edges.

If the shadow of the *Sleipnir* was a true indication of the shape of the vessel, the *Sleipnir* had lost its needle shape and was a spindle, fat at both ends and narrow-waisted.

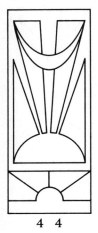

When Wellington's corpse passed by the small sphere and the ship, her shadow or "print" reversed itself in shape. Where the head of the shadow should have been, the feet now were and vice versa.

She disappeared around the curve of the primary and, on returning on the other side, her shadow had again become a "true" reflection. It remained so until she passed the secondary, after which the shadow once more reversed itself.

Grettir had been informed that there seemed to be absolutely no matter in the space outside the spheres. There was not one detectable atom or particle. Moreover, despite the lack of any radiation, the temperature of the hull, and ten meters beyond the hull, was a fluctuating 52.22° plus-or-minus 2.22° C.

IV

Three orbits later, Grettir knew that the ship had diminished greatly in size. Or else the small sphere

had expanded. Or both changes had occurred. More-over, on the visual screen, the secondary had lost its spherical shape and become a fat disk during the first circling of the ship to establish its orbit.

Grettir was puzzling over this and thinking of calling Van Voorden, the physicist chief, when Wellington's corpse came around the primary again. The body caught up with the other satellites, and for a moment the primary, the secondary, and the *Sleipnir* were in a line, strung on an invisible cord.

Suddenly, the secondary and the corpse jumped to-ward each other. They ceased their motion when within a quarter kilometer of each other. The secondary re-gained its globular form as soon as it had attained its new orbit. Wellington's arms and legs, during this change in position, moved in as if she had come to life. Her arms folded themselves across her breasts, and her legs drew up so that her thighs were against her belly.

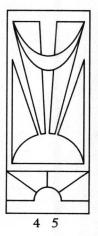

4 5

Grettir called Van Voorden. The physicist said, "Out here, the cabin boy—if we had one—knows as much as I do about what's going on or what to expect. The data, such as they are, are too inadequate, too con-fusing. I can only suggest that there was an interchange of energy between Wellington and the secondary."

"A quantum jump?" Grettir said. "If that's so, why didn't the ship experience a loss or gain?"

Darl said, "Pardon, sir. But it did. There was a loss of fifty megakilowatts in oh-point-eight second."

Van Voorden said, "The *Sleipnir* may have decreased in relative size because of decrease in velocity. Or maybe velocity had nothing to do with it or only partially, anyway. Maybe the change in spatial inter-relationships among bodies causes other changes. In shape, size, energy transfer and so forth. I don't know. Tell me, how big is the woman—corpse—relative to the ship now?"

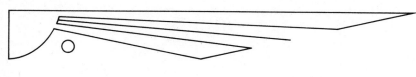

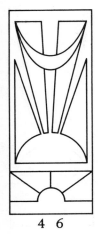

"The detectors say she's eighty-three times as large. She increased. Or we've decreased."

Van Voorden's eyes grew even larger. Grettir thanked him and cut him off. He ordered the *Sleipnir* to be put in exactly the same orbit as the secondary but ten dekameters ahead of it.

Van Voorden called back. "The jump happened when we were in line with the other three bodies. Maybe the *Sleipnir* is some sort of *geometrical catalyst* under certain conditions. That's only an analogy, of course."

Wang verbally fed the order into the computer-interface, part of his wrist-console. The *Sleipnir* was soon racing ahead of the sphere. The ship and secondary were now approximately equal in size. The corpse, coming around the primary again, was still the same relative size as before.

Grettir ordered the vessel turned around so that the nose would be facing the sphere. This accomplished, he had the velocity reduced. The retrodrive braked them while the lateral thrusts readjusted forces to keep the ship in the same orbit. Since the primary had no attraction for the *Sleipnir*, the ship had to remain in orbit with a constant rebalancing of thrusts. The sphere, now ballooning, inched towards the ship.

"Radar indicates we're doing twenty-six-point-six dekameters per second relative to the primary," Wang said. "Power drain indicates we're making twenty-five thousand times the speed of light. That, by the way, is not proportionate to what we were making when we left our world."

"More braking," Grettir said. "Cut it down to fifteen dm."

The sphere swelled, filled the screen, and Grettir involuntarily braced himself for the impact, even though he was so far from expecting one that he had not strapped himself into a chair. There had been none

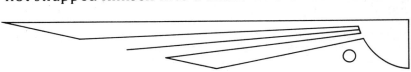

when the ship had broken through the "skin" of the universe.

Grettir had been told of the distortion in the ship when it had left the universe and so was not entirely surprised. Nevertheless, he could not help being both frightened and bewildered when the front part of the bridge abruptly swelled and then rippled. Screen, bulkheads, deck and crew waved as if they were cloth in a strong wind. Grettir felt as if he were being folded into a thousand different angles at the same time.

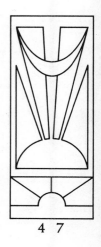

Then Wang cried out, and the others repeated his cry. Wang rose from his seat and put his hands out before him. Grettir, standing behind and to one side of him, was frozen as he saw dozens of little objects, firefly-size, burning brightly, slip *through* the starscreen and bulkhead, and drift towards him. He came out of his paralysis in time to dodge one tiny whitely glowing ball. But another struck his forehead, causing him to yelp.

A score of the bodies passed by him. Some were white; some blue; some green; one was topaz. They were at all levels, above his head, even with his waist, one almost touching the deck. He crouched down to let two pass over him, and as he did so, he saw Nagy, the communications officer, bent over and vomiting. The stuff sprayed out of his mouth and caught a little glow in it and snuffed it out in a burst of smoke.

Then the forepart of the bridge had reasserted its solidity and constancy of shape. There were no more burning objects coming through.

Grettir turned to see the aft bulkheads of the bridge quivering in the wake of the wave. And they, too, became normal. Grettir shouted the "override" code so that he could take control from Wang, who was screaming with pain. He directed the ship to change

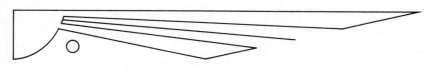

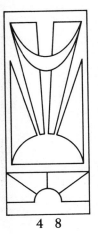

its course to an "upward vertical" direction. There was no "upward" sensation, because the artificial g-field within the ship readjusted. Suddenly, the forward part of the bridge became distorted again, and the waves reached through the fabric of the ship and the crew.

The starscreen, which had been showing nothing but the blackness of space, speckled by a few stars, now displayed the great gray sphere in one corner and the crepuscular light. Grettir, fighting the pain in his forehead and the nausea, gave another command. There was a delay of possibly thirty seconds, and then the *Sleipnir* began the turn that would take it back into a parallel orbit with the secondary.

Grettir, realizing what was happening shortly after being burned, had taken the *Sleipnir* back out of the universe. He put in a call for corpsmen and Doctor Wills and then helped Wang from his chair. There was an odor of burned flesh and hair in the bridge which the air-conditioning system had not as yet removed. Wang's face and hands were burned in five or six places, and part of the long coarse black hair on the right side of his head was burned.

Three corpsmen and Wills ran into the bridge. Wills started to apply a pseudoprotein jelly on Grettir's forehead, but Grettir told him to take care of Wang first. Wills worked swiftly and then, after spreading the jelly over Wang's burns and placing a false-skin bandage over the burns, treated the captain. As soon as the jelly was placed on his forehead, Grettir felt the pain dissolve.

"Third degree," Wills said. "It's lucky those things—whatever they are—weren't larger."

Grettir picked up his cigar, which he had dropped on the deck when he had first seen the objects racing towards him. The cigar was still burning. Near it lay a coal, swiftly blackening. He picked it up gingerly.

It felt warm but could be held without too much discomfort.

Grettir extended his hand, palm up, so that the doctor could see the speck of black matter in it. It was even smaller than when it had floated into the bridge through the momentarily "opened" interstices of the molecules composing the hull and bulkheads.

"This is a galaxy," he whispered.

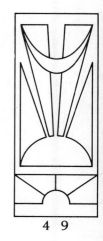

Doc Wills did not understand. "A galaxy of our universe," Grettir added.

Doc Wills paled, and he gulped loudly.

"You mean . . . ?"

Grettir nodded.

Wills said, "I hope . . . not our . . . Earth's . . . galaxy!"

"I doubt it," Grettir said. "We were on the edge of the star fields farthest out, that is, the closest to the— skin?—of our universe. But if we had kept on going . . ."

Wills shook his head. Billions of stars, possibly millions of inhabitable, hence inhabited, planets, were in that little ball of fire, now cool and collapsed. Trillions of sentient beings and an unimaginable number of animals had died when their world collided with Grettir's forehead.

Wang, informed of the true cause of his burns, became ill again. Grettir ordered him to sick bay and replaced him with Gomez. Van Voorden entered the bridge. He said, "I suppose our main objective has to be our re-entry. But why couldn't we make an attempt to penetrate the primary, the nucleus? Do you realize what an astounding . . . ?"

Grettir interrupted. "I realize. But our fuel supply is low, very low. If—I mean, *when* we get back through the 'skin,' we'll have a long way to go before we can return to Base. Maybe too long. I don't dare exceed a

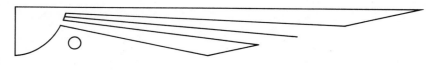

certain speed during re-entry because of our size. It would be too dangerous... I don't want to wipe out any more galaxies. God knows the psychological problems we are going to have when the guilt really hits. Right now, we're numbed. *No!* We're not going to do any exploring!"

"But there may be no future investigations permitted!" Van Voorden said. "There's too much danger to the universe itself to allow any more research by ships like ours!"

"Exactly," Grettir said. "I sympathize with your desire to do scientific research. But the safety of the ship and crew comes first. Besides, I think that if I were to order an exploration, I'd have mutiny on my hands. And I couldn't blame my men. Tell me, Van Voorden, don't you feel a sense of... dissociation?"

Van Voorden nodded and said, "But I'm willing to fight it. There is so much..."

"So much to find out," Grettir said. "Agreed. But the authorities will have to determine if that is to be done."

Grettir dismissed him. Van Voorden marched off with a straight back and an angry set to his shoulders and neck. But he did not give the impression of a powerful anger. He was, Grettir thought, secretly relieved at the captain's decision. Van Voorden had made his protest for Science's sake. But as a human being, Van Voorden must want very much to get "home."

V

At the end of the ordered maneuver, the *Sleipnir* was in the same orbit as the universe but twenty kilometers ahead and again pointed toward it. Since there was no attraction between ship and primary, the *Sleipnir* had

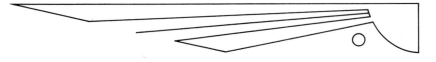

to use power to maintain the orbit; a delicate read-justment of lateral thrust was constantly required.

Grettir ordered braking applied. The sphere expanded on the starscreen, and then there was only a gray surface displayed. To the viewers the surface did not seem to spin, but the globe completed a revolution on its polar axis once every thirty-three seconds.

Grettir did not like to think of the implications of this. Van Voorden undoubtedly had received the report, but he had made no move to notify the captain. Perhaps, like Grettir, he believed that the fewer who thought about it, the better.

The mockup screen showed, in silhouette form, the relative sizes of the approaching spheres and the ship. The basketball was the universe; the toothpick, the *Sleipnir*. Grettir hoped that this reduction would be enough to avoid running into any more galaxies. Immediately after the vessel penetrated the "skin," the *Sleipnir* would again be braked, thus further diminishing it. There should be plenty of distance between the skin and the edge of the closest star fields.

"Here we go," Grettir said, watching the screen which indicated in meters the gap between ship and sphere. Again he involuntarily braced himself.

There was a rumble, a groan. The deck slanted upwards, then rolled to port. Grettir was hurled to the deck, spun over and over and brought up with stunning impact against a bulkhead. He was in a daze for a moment, and by the time he had recovered, the ship had reasserted its proper attitude. Gomez had placed the ship into "level" again. He had a habit of strapping himself into the navigator's chair although regulations did not require it unless the captain ordered it.

Grettir asked for a report on any damage and, while waiting for it, called Van Voorden. The physicist was bleeding from a cut on his forehead.

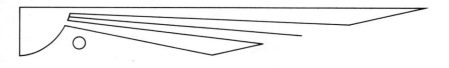

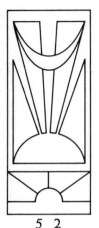

"Obviously," he said, "it requires a certain force to penetrate the outer covering or energy shield or whatever it is that encloses the universe. We didn't have it. So—"

"Presents quite a problem," Grettir said. "If we go fast enough to rip through, we're too large and may destroy entire galaxies. If we go too slow, we can't get through."

He paused, then said, "I can think of only one method. But I'm ignorant of the consequences, which might be disastrous. Not for us but for the universe. I'm not sure I should even take such a chance."

He was silent so long that Van Voorden could not restrain himself. "Well?"

"Do you think that if we could make a hole in the skin, the rupture might result in some sort of collapse or cosmic disturbance?"

"You want to beam a hole in the skin?" Van Voorden said slowly. His skin was pale, but it had been that color before Grettir asked him the question. Grettir wondered if Van Voorden was beginning to crumble under the "dissociation."

"Never mind," Grettir said. "I shouldn't have asked you. You can't know what effects would be any more than anyone else. I apologize. I must have been trying to make you share some of the blame if anything went wrong. Forget it."

Van Voorden stared, and he was still looking blank when Grettir cut off his image. He paced back and forth, once stepping over a tiny black object on the deck and then grimacing when he realized that it was too late to care. Millions of stars, billions of planets, trillions of creatures. All cold and dead. And if he experimented further in trying to get back into the native cosmos, then what? A collapsing universe.

But the *Sleipnir* had passed through the "skin" twice, and the rupture had not seemed to cause harm. The surface of the sphere was smooth and unbroken. It must be self-regulating and self-repairing.

Grettir stopped pacing and said aloud, "We came through the skin without harm to it. So we're going to try the beam!"

Nobody answered him, but the look on their faces was evidence of their relief. Fifteen minutes later, the *Sleipnir* was just ahead of the sphere and facing it. After an unvarying speed and distance from the sphere had been maintained for several minutes, laser beams measured the exact length between the tip of the cannon and the surface of the globe.

The chief gunnery officer, Abdul White Eagle, set one of the fore cannons. Grettir delayed only a few seconds in giving the next order. He clenched his teeth so hard he almost bit the cigar in two, groaned slightly, then said, "Fire!"

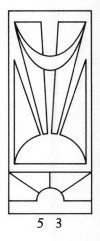

Darl transmitted the command. The beam shot out, touched the skin, and vanished.

The starscreen showed a black hole in the gray surface at the equator of the sphere. The hole moved away and then was gone around the curve of the sphere. Exactly 33 seconds later, the hole was in its original position. It was shrinking. By the time four rotations were completed, the hole had closed in on itself.

Grettir sighed and wiped the sweat off his forehead. Darl reported that the hole would be big enough for the ship to get through by the second time it came around. After that, it would be too small.

"We'll go through during the second rotation," Grettir said. "Set up the compigator for an automatic entry; tie the cannon in with the compigator. There shouldn't be any problem. If the hole shrinks too fast, we'll enlarge it with the cannon."

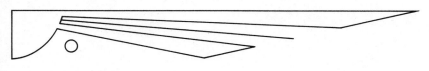

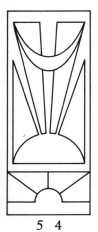

He heard Darl say, "Operation begun, sir!" as Gomez spoke into his console. The white beam spurted out in a cone, flicked against the "shell" or "skin" and disappeared. A circle of blackness three times the diameter of the ship came into being and then moved to one side of the screen. Immediately, under the control of the compigator, the retrodrive of the *Sleipnir* went into action. The sphere loomed; a gray wall filled the starscreen. Then the edge of the hole came into view, and a blackness spread over the screen.

"We're going to make it," Grettir thought. "The compigator can't make a mistake."

He looked around him. The bridgemen were strapped to their chairs now. Most of the faces were set, they were well disciplined and brave. But if they felt as he did—they must—they were shoving back a scream far down in them. They could not endure this "homesickness" much longer. And after they got through, were back in the womb, he would have to permit them a most unmilitary behavior. They would laugh, weep, shout, whoop. And so would he.

The nose of the *Sleipnir* passed through the hole. Now, if anything went wrong, the fore cannon could not be used. But it was impossible that . . .

The klaxon whooped. Darl screamed, "Oh, my God! Something's wrong! The hole's shrinking too fast!"

Grettir roared, "Double the speed! No! Halve it!"

Increasing the forward speed meant a swelling in size of the *Sleipnir* but a contraction of the longitudinal axis and a lengthening of the lateral. The *Sleipnir* would get through the hole faster, but it would also narrow the gap between its hull and the edges of the hole.

Halving the speed, on the other hand, though it would make the ship smaller in relation to the hole, would also make the distance to be traversed greater.

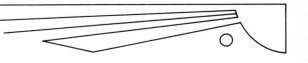

This might mean that the edges would still hit the ship.

Actually, Grettir did not know what order should be given or if any order would have an effect upon their chance to escape. He could only do what seemed best.

The grayness spread out from the perimeter of the starscreen. There was a screech of severed plastic running through the ship, quivering the bulkheads and decks, a sudden push forward of the crew as they felt the inertia, then a release as the almost instantaneous readjustment of the internal g-field canceled the external effects.

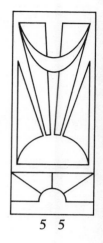

Everybody in the bridge yelled. Grettir forced himself to cut off his shout. He watched the starscreen. They were out in the gray again. The huge sphere shot across the screen. In the corner was the secondary and then a glimpse of a giant blue-black foot. More grayness. A whirl of other great spheres in the distance. The primary again. The secondary. Wellington's hand, like a malformed squid of the void.

When Grettir saw the corpse again, he knew that the ship had been deflected away from the sphere and was heading towards the corpse. He did not, however, expect a collision. The orbital velocity of the dead woman was greater than that of the secondary or of the *Sleipnir*.

Grettir, calling for a damage report, heard what he had expected. The nose of the ship had been sheared off. Bearing forty-five crewmen with it, it was now inside the "universe," heading toward a home it would never reach. The passageways leading to the cut-off part had been automatically sealed, of course, so that there was no danger of losing air.

But the retrodrives had also been sliced off. The *Sleipnir* could drive forward but could not brake itself

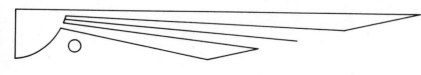

unless it was first turned around to present its aft to the direction of motion.

VI

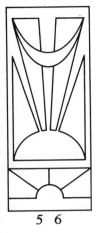

Grettir gave the command to stabilize the ship first, then to reverse it. MacCool replied from the engine room that neither maneuver was, at the moment, possible. The collision and the shearing had caused malfunctions in the control circuits. He did not know what the trouble was, but the electronic trouble-scanner was searching through the circuits. A moment later, he called back to say that the device was itself not operating properly and that the troubleshooting would have to be done by his men until the device had been repaired.

MacCool was disturbed. He could not account for the breakdown because, theoretically, there should have been none. Even the impact and loss of the fore part should not have resulted in loss of circuit operation.

Grettir told him to do what he could. Meanwhile, the ship was tumbling and was obviously catching up with the vast corpse. There had been another inexplainable interchange of energy, position, and momentum, and the *Sleipnir* and Mrs. Wellington were going to collide.

Grettir unstrapped himself and began walking back and forth across the bridge. Even though the ship was cartwheeling, the internal g-field neutralized the effect for the crew. The vessel seemed level and stable unless the starscreen was looked at. When Grettir watched the screen, he felt slightly queasy because he was, at times, standing upside down in relation to the corpse.

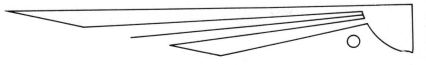

Grettir asked for a computation of when the collision would take place and of what part of the body the *Sleipnir* would strike. It might make a difference whether it struck a soft or hard part. The difference would not result in damage to the ship, but it would affect the angle and velocity of the rebound path. If the circuits were repaired before the convergence, or just after, Grettir would have to know what action to take.

Wang replied that he had already asked the compigator for an estimate of the area of collision if conditions remained as they were. Even as he spoke, the compigator screen displayed the answer.

Grettir said, "At any other time, I'd laugh. So we will return—literally—to the womb."

The card had also indicated that, the nearer the ship got to Wellington, the slower was its velocity. Moreover, the relative size of the ship, as reported by radar, was decreasing in direct proportion to its proximity to the body.

Gomez said, "I think we've come under the influence of that . . . woman, as if she'd become a planet and had captured a satellite. Us. She doesn't have any gravitational attraction or any charge in relation to us. But—"

"But there are other factors," Grettir said to him. "Maybe they are spatial relations, which, in this 'space,' may be the equivalent of gravity."

The *Sleipnir* was now so close that the body entirely filled the starscreen when the ship was pointed towards it. First, the enormous head came into view. The blood-clotted and bulging eyes stared at them. The nose slid by like a Brobdingnagian guillotine. The mouth grinned at them as if it would enjoy gulping them down. Then the neck, a diorite column left exposed by the erosion of softer rock; the cleavage of the blackened Hima-

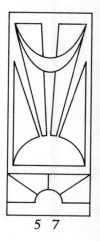

57

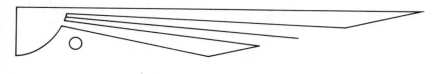

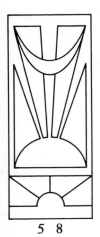

layan breasts; the navel, the eye of a hurricane.

Then she went out of sight, and the secondary and primary and the gray-shrouded giants far off whirled across the screen.

Grettir used the All-Stations to tell the nonbridge personnel what was happening. "As soon as MacCool locates the trouble, we will be on our way out. We have plenty of power left, enough to blast our way out of a hundred corpses. Sit tight. Don't worry. It's just a matter of time."

He spoke with a cheerfulness he did not feel, although he had not lied to them. Nor did he expect any reaction, positive or negative. They must be as numb as he. Their minds, their entire nervous systems, were boggling.

The compigator showed a corrected impact prediction. Because of the continuing decrease in size of the vessel, it would strike the corpse almost dead-center in the navel. A minute later, the screen predicted impact near the coccyx. A third display revised that to collision with the top of the head. A fourth changed that to a strike on the lower part on the front of the right leg.

Grettir called Van Voorden again. The physicist's face shot up from the surface of Grettir's wrist-console but was stationary on the auxiliary bulkhead-screen. This gave a larger view and showed Van Voorden looking over his wrist-console at a screen on his cabin-bulkhead. It offered the latest impact report in large burning letters.

"Like the handwriting on the wall in the days of King Belshazzar," Van Voorden said. "And I am a Daniel come to judgment. So we're going to hit her leg, heh. *Many, many tickle up her shin.* Hee, hee!"

Grettir stared uncomprehendingly at him, then cut him off. A few seconds later, he understood Van Voor-

den's pun. He did not wonder at the man's levity at a moment so grave. It was a means of relieving his deep anxiety and bewilderment. It might also mean that he was already cracking up, since it was out of character with him. But Grettir could do nothing for him at that moment.

As the *Sleipnir* neared the corpse, the ship continued to shrink. However, the dwindling was not at a steady rate nor could the times of shrinkage be predicted. It operated in spurts of from two to thirty seconds duration at irregular intervals. And then it became evident that, unless some new factor entered, the *Sleipnir* would spin into the gaping mouth. While the head rotated "downward," the ship would pass through the great space between the lips.

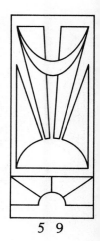

And so it was. On the starscreen, the lower lip, a massive ridge, wrinkled with mountains and pitted with valleys, appeared. Flecks of lipstick floated by, black-red Hawaiis. A tooth like a jagged skyscraper dropped out of sight.

The *Sleipnir* settled slowly into the darkness. The walls shot away and upwards. The blackness outside knotted. Only a part of the gray "sky" was visible during that point of the cartwheel when the fore part of the starscreen was directed upwards. Then the opening became a thread of gray, a strand, and was gone.

Strangely—or was it so odd?—the officers and crew lost their feeling of dissociation. Grettir's stomach expanded with relief; the dreadful fragmenting was gone. He now felt as if something had been attached, or reattached, to his navel. Rubb, the psychology officer, reported that he had taken a survey of one out of fifty of the crew, and each described similar sensations.

Despite this, the personnel were free of only one anxiety and were far from being out of danger. The

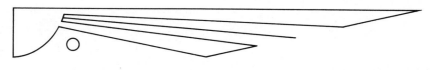

temperature had been slowly mounting ever since the ship had been spun off the secondary and had headed towards the corpse. The power system and air-conditioning had stabilized at 62.22° C for a while. But the temperature of the hull had gone upwards at a geometric progression, and the outer hull was now 2500° K. There was no danger of it melting as yet; it could resist up to 56,000° K. The air-conditioning demanded more and more power, and after thirty minutes ship's time, Grettir had had to let the internal temperature rise to 66.5° C to ease the load.

Grettir ordered everybody into spacesuits, which could keep the wearers at a comfortable temperature. Just as the order was carried out, MacCool reported that he had located the source of malfunction.

"The Wellington woman did it!" he shouted. "She sure took care of us! She inserted a monolith subparticle switch in the circuits; the switch had a timer which operated the switch after a certain time had elapsed. It was only coincidence that the circuits went blank right after we failed to get back into our world!"

VII

"So she wanted to be certain that we'd be wrecked if she was frustrated in her attempts in the engine room," Grettir said. "You'd better continue the search for other microswitches or sabotage devices."

MacCool's face was long.

"We're ready to operate now but... hell! We can't spare any power now because we need all we can get to keep the temperature down. I can spare enough to cancel the tumble. But that's all."

"Forget it for now," Grettir said. He had contacted

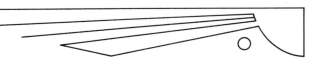

Van Voorden, who seemed to have recovered. He confirmed the captain's theory about the rise in temperature. It was the rapid contraction of the ship that was causing the emission of heat.

"How is this contraction possible?" Grettir said. "Are the atoms of the ship, and of our bodies, coming closer together? If so, what happens when they come into contact with each other?"

"We've already passed that point of diminishment," Van Voorden said. "I'd say that our own atoms are shrinking also."

"But that's not possible," Grettir replied. Then, "Forget about that remark. What is possible? Whatever happens is possible."

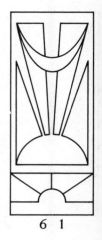

Grettir cut him off and strode back and forth and wished that he could smoke a cigar. He had intended to talk about what the *Sleipnir* would find if it had managed to break back into its native universe. It seemed to Grettir that the universe would have changed so much that no one aboard the ship would recognize it. Every time the secondary—the universe—completed a revolution on its axis, trillions of Earth years, maybe quadrillions, may have passed. The Earth's sun may have become a lightless clot in space or even have disappeared altogether. Man, who might have survived on other planets, would no longer be Homo sapiens.

Moreover, when the *Sleipnir* attained a supercosmic mass on its way out of the universe, it may have disastrously affected the other masses in the universe.

Yet none of these events may have occurred. It was possible that time inside that sphere was absolutely independent of time outside it. The notion was not so fantastic. God Almighty! Less that seventy minutes ago, Donna Wellington had been inside the ship. Now the ship was inside her.

And when the electrons and the nuclei of the atoms

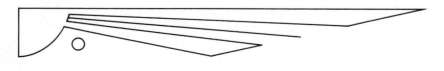

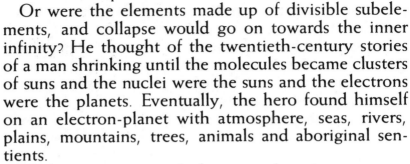

composing the ship and the crew came into contact, what then? Explosion?

Or were the elements made up of divisible subelements, and collapse would go on towards the inner infinity? He thought of the twentieth-century stories of a man shrinking until the molecules became clusters of suns and the nuclei were the suns and the electrons were the planets. Eventually, the hero found himself on an electron-planet with atmosphere, seas, rivers, plains, mountains, trees, animals and aboriginal sentients.

These stories were only fantasies. Atomic matter was composed of wavicles, stuff describable in terms of both waves and particles. The parahomunculus hero would be in a cosmos as bewildering as that encountered by the crew of the *Sleipnir* on breaking into the extra-universe space.

That fantasy galloping across the sky of his mind, swift as the original *Sleipnir*, eight-legged horse of All-Father Odin of his ancestor's religion, would have to be dismissed. Donna Wellington was not a female Ymir, the primeval giant out of whose slain corpse was formed the world, the skull the sky, the blood the sea, the flesh the Earth, the bones the mountains.

No, the heat of contraction would increase until the men cooked in their suits. What happened after that would no longer be known to the crew and hence of no consequence.

"Captain!"

MacCool's face was on the auxiliary screen, kept open to the engine room. "We'll be ready to go in a minute."

Sweat mingled with tears to blur the image of the engineer's face. "We'll make it then," Grettir said.

Four minutes later, the tumble was stopped, the ship

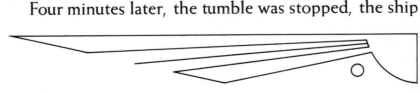

was pointed upwards and was on its way out. The temperature began dropping inside the ship at 16.7° C per thirty seconds. The blackness was relieved by a gray thread. The thread broadened into ribbon, and then the ribbon became the edges of two mountain ridges, one below and the one above hanging upside down.

"This time," Grettir said, "we'll make a hole more than large enough."

Van Voorden, much-tranquilized by a pill, entered the bridge as the *Sleipnir* passed through the break. Grettir said, "The hole repairs itself even more quickly than it did the last time. That's why the nose was cut off. We didn't know that the bigger the hole, the swifter the rate of reclosure."

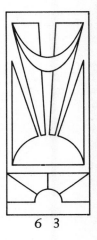

Van Voorden said, "Thirty-six hundred billion years old or even more! Why bother to go home when home no longer exists? Not that I particularly care now. Anyway, it'll all be very interesting."

"Maybe there won't be that much time gone," Grettir said. "Do you remember Minkowski's classical phrase? *From henceforth space in itself and time in itself sink to mere shadows, and only a kind of union of the two preserves an independent existence.*

"That phrase applied to the world inside the sphere, our world. Perhaps *out here* the union is somehow dissolved, the marriage of space and time is broken. Perhaps no time, or very little, has elapsed in our world."

"It's possible," Van Voorden said. "But you've overlooked one thing, Captain. If our world has not been marked by time while we've been gone, *we* have been marked. Scarred by unspace and untime. I'll never believe in cause and effect and order throughout the cosmos again. I'll always be suspicious, anxious. I'm a ruined man."

Grettir started to answer but could not make himself

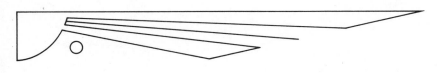

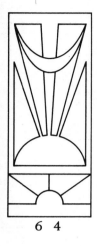

heard. The men and women on the bridge were weeping, sobbing, or laughing shrilly. Later, they would think of that *out there* as a nightmare and would try not to think of it at all. And if other nightmares faced them here, at least they would be nightmares they knew.

A BOWL BIGGER
THAN EARTH

.

Sin and punishment.

Everybody sins. Even the saints sin. But some sins are worse than others. And there's something in the species Homo sapiens that makes it strongly desire to see that others are punished for their sins. This is especially evident when somebody commits a particularly heinous sin like mutilation-murder, torture and murder of a child, brutal rape (is there any other kind?), and the blowing up of innocent bystanders, including infants, by terrorists.

If these evildoers can't be made to suffer for their sins on Earth, they must suffer in the afterlife.

People long ago noticed that sinners quite often did not get their just deserts on Earth. But people were sure that, in the economy, the check and balance of this universe, the sinners would get theirs eventually. If not here, then there. It would not be just or fair if they got off scot-free.

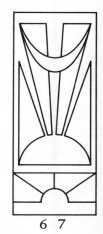

6 7

However, the idea that the more serious sins would be paid for in hell became extended to the lesser sins. Lesser, that is, from the modern viewpoint. Not attending church on Sundays, working on the Sabbaths, drinking too much or at all, taking the Lord's name in vain, disrespect for our elders, lying, cheating, usury, committing adultery, backbiting, gossiping, refusing to work hard, not belonging to a certain sect, farting in public, the sins were many and various. And, quite often, it was not only what you did but what you did not do that guaranteed burning in Hell or being cast into the outer darkness with much wailing and gnashing of teeth.

(That teeth-gnashing makes me wonder if there was a great need for dentists in hell. Are there more dentists than lawyers in hell?)

At one time, entire Christendom thought that it was right that unbaptized babies should burn in hell or suffer in purgatory or be exiled forever to a cold dark limbo. There are still many today who believe that it is right, though they will say that they don't like the idea. But they shake their heads and say that that is God's will, that's the way it is. If the infant has not had its head watered while a ritual is said over it, it's doomed. No way for it to get out of it.

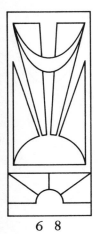

This belief in the efficacy of a ritual is a type of what the anthropologists call magical thinking. The water has ceased to be just simple H_2O because it has been magically converted. Magical thinking comes from the Old Stone Age and is still going strong. This should not surprise you; it does not surprise me. We late twentieth-centurians may make and use spacerockets and TV sets and antibiotics, but we are often as superstitious and reflex-ridden as our ancestors of 30,000 B.C. Despite all that scientists say, despite all the science and technology around us, we still believe in magic. Indeed, many scientists are not immune from this belief, though they would deny it.

The belief that following or not following a ritual behavior will ensure going to heaven or not going to heaven is a belief in magic.

There is neither scientific nor strong circumstantial evidence for an afterlife. But billions have believed in this, and billions now believe in it. Or, if some are skeptical, many of these still have hopes that perhaps, somehow, they will survive after death.

Why? Don't they know that, if they're miserable and unhappy here, they'll be so during eternity? What do they intend to do, quarrel and argue or be silently suffering, watch TV or play bridge or go to baseball games for the next billion years? Or do they expect that a magic will change their characters? Don't they know that, if such a magic could be wrought by an outside agency, it would make them different persons? That such a magic is analogous to the reprogramming of a robot and that human beings are not robots?

If you change the circuits in a robot, you make a different robot. It may look from the outside like the same robot, but its functions are different.

These people who expect to be saints in heaven, though they were not on Earth, have ignored the wisdom of the founders of the great religions. This wisdom is that the kingdom of heaven is within you and that you do not go to heaven unless you are already in it. The magic must be wrought by you and you alone. God has no fairy wand to tap the pig and turn it into the swan.

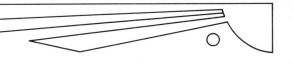

People ignore this. And those who believe in sinners burning in hell are, perhaps, not so much concerned with going to heaven as with being sure that sinners—others—roast forever in the flames.

That's an understandable attitude. It's a human one. But it's saints, the superhuman humans, who go to heaven. No mediocrities allowed. No ritual-mumbling will get you in here.

Even Mohammed, whom Christians and Jews don't think of as a nice guy, said that, eventually, the gates of hell would clang on an empty place. Having learned their lesson, having been rehabilitated through their sufferings, seen the errors of their ways—and of their thinking—the sinners would become saints.

The Buddhists don't send the dead to a supernatural place for reward or comeuppance. They insist that the soul migrates after the death of the body to a living body. Joe Smith moves, rentfree, into the body of the infant Bob Jones. Having been reincarnated, it is up to the soul to work off the evil it did in the previous life. Or, as the Buddhists put it, make the bad karma into good karma. If the reincarnated soul fails to lighten the load of the bad karma, then, when that body dies, the soul goes to another body. Joe Smith-Bob Jones now is known as Roger Brown. Roger must work off the bad karma accumulated by Smith-Jones. If he does not work off this, plus his own bad karma as Brown, then he becomes Bill Davis. Or, if his karma is too black, he may inhabit an insect named Periplaneta americana.

I don't understand how a cockroach can work off its bad karma, but I've been assured that this is possible.

Earth is hell enough for the Buddhists. They agree with George Bernard Shaw, who said, "If the other planets have a hell, it must be Earth."

Whatever the truth is, the possibility of the afterlife has always fascinated me. And it has always seemed to me that life is meaningless unless we have immortality.

Some people have been kind enough to point out to me that the universe may have no meaning.

They may be right.

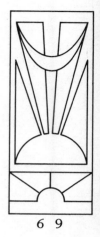

6 9

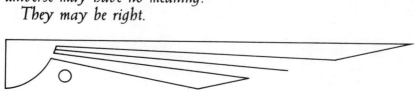

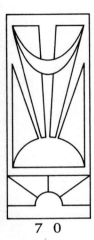

Meanwhile, with an insistence that derives from a sort of religious faith—no connection with scientific reasoning or formal logic—I believe that we will live after we die. We may not like the afterlife, but we'll be in it.

That's my irrational mind speaking. But the irrational has a wisdom which is as valid as the wisdom of the rational, though the two wisdoms spring from different premises and are constructed differently.

I've written a number of stories on the afterlife. The story at hand is one. It's mainly about our contradictory desires to be conformist and individualistic at the same time and about humanity's contrariness and stubbornness. The best of us are always trying to beat the system, and some of us are ingenious in the try.

I

No squeeze. No pain.

Death has a wide pelvis, he thought—much later, when he had time to reflect.

Now he was screaming.

He had had an impression of awakening from his deathbed, of being shot outwards over the edge of a bowl bigger than Earth seen from a space capsule. Sprawling outwards, he landed on his hands and knees on a gentle slope. So gentle it was. He did not tear his hands and knees but slid smoothly onward and downward on the great curve. The material on which he accelerated looked much like brass and felt frictionless. Though he did not think of it then—he was too panic-stricken to do anything but react—he knew later that the brassy stuff had even less resistance than oil become a solid. And the brass, or whatever it was, formed a solid seamless sheet.

The only break was in the center, where the sheet ended. There, far ahead and far below, the bowl curved briefly upward.

Gathering speed, he slipped along the gigantic chute. He tried to stay on his hands and knees, but, when he twisted his body to see behind him, he shifted his weight. Over he went onto his side. Squawling, he thrashed around, and he tried to dig his nails into the brass. No use. He met no resistance, and he began spinning around, around. He did see, during his whirlings, the rim from which he had been shoved. But he could see only the rim itself and, beyond, the blue cloudless sky.

Overhead was the sun, looking just like the Terrestrial sun.

He rolled over on his back and succeeded during

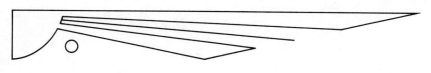

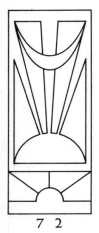

the maneuver in stopping the rotations. He also managed to see his own body. He began screaming again, the first terror driven out and replaced by—or added to as a higher harmonic—the terror of finding himself in a sexless body.

Smooth. Projectionless. Hairless. His legs hairless, too. No navel. His skin a dark brown—like an Apache's.

Morfiks screamed and screamed, and he gripped his face and the top of his head. Then he screamed higher and higher. The face was not the one he knew (the ridge of bone above the eyes and the broken nose were not there), and his head was smooth as an egg.

He fainted.

Later, although it could not have been much later, he came to his senses. Overhead was the bright sun and beneath him was the cool nonfriction.

He turned his face to one side, saw the same brass and had no sensation of sliding because he had no reference point. For a moment he thought he might be at the end of his descent. But on lifting his head he saw that the bottom of the bowl was closer, that it was rushing at him.

His heart was leaping in his chest as if trying to batter itself to a second death. But it did not fail. It just drove the blood through his ears until he could hear its roar even above the air rushing by.

He lowered his head until its back was supported by the brass, and he closed his eyes against the sun. Never in all his life (lives?) had he felt so helpless. More helpless than a newborn babe who does not know he is helpless and who cannot think and who will be taken care of if he cries.

He had screamed, but no one was running to take care of him.

Downward he slipped, brassy-yellow curving away on both sides of him, no sensation of heat against his back where the skin should have burned off a long time ago and his muscles should now be burning.

The incline began to be less downward, to straighten out. He shot across a flat space which he had no means of estimating because he was going too fast.

The flatness gave away to a curving upwards. He felt that he was slowing down; he hoped so. If he continued at the same rate of speed, he would shoot far out and over the center of the bowl.

Here it came! The rim!

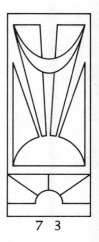

He went up with just enough velocity to rise perhaps seven feet above the edge. Then, falling, he glimpsed a city of brass beyond the people gathered on the shore of a river but lost sight of these in the green waters rushing up towards him directly below.

He bellowed in anguish, tried to straighten out, and flailed his arms and legs. In vain. The water struck him on his left side. Half-stunned, he plunged into the cool and dark waters.

By the time he had broken the surface again, he had regained his senses. There was only one thing to do. Behind him, the brassy wall reared at least thirty feet straight up. He had to swim to the shore, which was about four hundred yards away.

What if he had not been able to swim? What if he chose to drown now rather than face the unknown on the beach?

A boat was his answer. A flat-bottomed boat of brass rowed with brass oars by a brown-skinned man (man?). In the bow stood a similar creature (similar? exactly alike) extending a long pole of brass.

The manlike thing in the bow called out, "Grab hold, and I'll pull you in."

Morfiks replied with an obscenity and began swim-

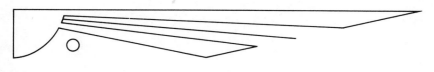

ming toward the beach. The fellow with the pole howled, "A trouble-maker, heh? We'll have no anti-social actions here, citizen!"

He brought the butt of the pole down with all his strength.

It was then that Morfiks found that he was relatively invulnerable. The pole, even if made of material as light as aluminum and hollow, should have stunned him and cut his scalp open. But it had bounced off with much less effect than the fall into the river.

"Come into the boat," said the poleman. *"Or nobody here will like you."*

II

It was this threat that cowed Morfiks. After climbing into the boat, he sat down on the bench in front of the rower and examined the two. No doubt of it. They were twins. Same height (both were sitting now) as himself. Hairless, except for long curling black eye-lashes. Same features. High foreheads. Smooth hairless brows. Straight noses. Full lips. Well developed chins. Regular, almost classical features, delicate, looking both feminine and masculine. Their eyes were the same shade of dark brown. Their skins were heavily tanned. Their bodies were slimly built and quite human except for the disconcerting lack of sex, navel and nipples on the masculine chests.

"Where am I?" said Morfiks. "In the fourth dimension?"

He had read about that in the Sunday supplements and some of the more easily digesteds.

"Or in Hell?" he added, which would have been his first question if he had been in his Terrestrial body.

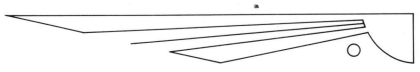

Nothing that had happened so far made him think he was in Heaven.

The pole rapped him in the mouth, and he thought that either the poleman was pulling his punches or else his new flesh was less sensitive than his Terrestrial. The last must be it. His lips felt almost as numb as when the dentist gave him novocaine before pulling a tooth. And his meager buttocks did not hurt from sitting on the hard brass.

Moreover, he had all his teeth. There were no fillings or bridges in his mouth.

"You will not use *that* word," said the poleman. "It's not nice, and it's not true. The Protectors do not like that word and will take one hundred percent effective measures to punish anybody responsible for offending the public taste with it."

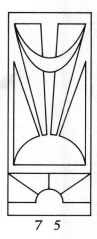

"You mean the word beginning with H?" said Morfiks cautiously.

"You're catching on fast, citizen."

"What do you call this . . . place?"

"Home. Just plain home. Allow me to introduce myself. I'm one of the official greeters. I have no name; nobody here does. Citizen is good enough for me and for you. However, being a greeter doesn't make me one whit better than you, citizen. It's just my job, that's all. We all have jobs here, all equally important. We're all on the same level, citizen. No cause for envy or strife."

"No name?" Morfiks said.

"Forget that nonsense. A name means you're trying to set yourself apart. Now, you wouldn't think it was nice if somebody thought he was better than you because he had a name that was big in We-Know-Where, would you? Of course not."

"I'm here for . . . how long?" Morfiks said.

"Who knows?"

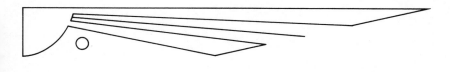

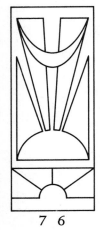

"Forever?" Morfiks said dismally.

The end of the pole butted into his lips. His head rocked back, but he did not hurt much.

"Just think of the present, citizen. Because that is all that exists. The past doesn't exist; the future can't. Only the present exists."

"There's no future?"

Again, the butt of the pole.

"Forget the word. We use it on the river when we're breaking in immigrants. But once on the shore, we're through with it. Here, we're practical. We don't indulge in fantasy."

"I get your message," Morfiks said. He damped the impulse to leap at the poleman's throat. Better to wait until he found out what the set-up was, what a man could or could not get away with.

The rower said, "Coming ashore, citizens."

Morfiks noticed that the two had voices exactly alike, and he supposed his own was the same as theirs. But he had a secret triumph. His voice would sound different to himself; he had that much edge on the bastards.

The boat nudged onto the beach, and Morfiks followed the other two onto the sand. He looked quickly behind him and now saw that there were many boats up and down the river. Here and there a body shot up over the rim of the brassy cliff and tumbled down into the waters as he had a few minutes ago.

Beyond the lip of the cliff rose the swell of the brass slide down which he had hurtled. The slide extended so far that he could not see the human figures that undoubtedly must be standing on the edge where he had stood and must just now be in the act of being pushed from behind. Five miles away, at least, five miles he had slid.

A colossal building project, he thought.

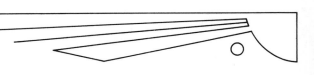

Beyond the city of brass rose another incline. He understood now that he had been mistaken in believing the city was in the middle of a bowl. As far as he could see, there was the river and the city and the cliffs and slides on both sides. And he supposed that there was another river on the other side of the city.

The city reminded him of the suburban tract in which he had lived on Earth. Rows on rows of square brass houses, exactly alike, facing each other across twenty-foot-wide streets. Each house was about twelve feet wide. Each had a flat roof and a door in front and back, a strip of windows which circled the house like a transparent belt. There were no yards. A space of two feet separated each house from its neighbor.

A person stepped out of the crowd standing on the beach. This one differed from the others only in having a band of some black metal around the biceps of its right arm.

77

"Officer of the Day," it said in a voice exactly like the two in the boat. "Your turn will come to act in this capacity. No favorites here."

It was then that Morfiks recognized the possibilities of individualism in voice, of recognizing others. Even if everybody had identical dimensions in larynxes and the resonating chambers of palate and nasal passages, they must retain their habits of intonation and choice of pitch and words. Also, despite identical bodies and legs, they must keep some of their peculiar gestures and methods of walking.

"Any complaints about treatment so far?" said the O.D.

"Yes," said Morfiks. "This jerk hit me three times with its pole."

"Only because we love it," said the poleman. "We struck it—oh, very lightly!—to correct its ways. As

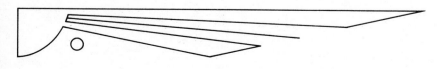

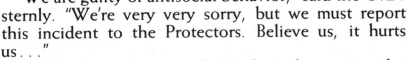

a father—pardon the word—punishes a child he loves. Or an older brother his little brother. We are all brothers. . . ."

"We are guilty of antisocial behavior," said the O.D. sternly. "We're very very sorry, but we must report this incident to the Protectors. Believe us, it hurts us . . ."

"Worse than it hurts us," said the poleman wearily. "We know."

"We'll have to add cynicism to the charge," said the O.D. "K.P. for several months if we know the Protectors. Should anybody be guilty again—"

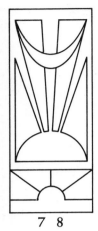

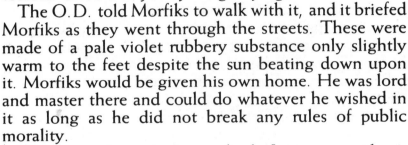

The O.D. told Morfiks to walk with it, and it briefed Morfiks as they went through the streets. These were made of a pale violet rubbery substance only slightly warm to the feet despite the sun beating down upon it. Morfiks would be given his own home. He was lord and master there and could do whatever he wished in it as long as he did not break any rules of public morality.

"You mean I can invite anybody I want to and can keep out anybody I want to?"

"Well, you can invite anybody you want. But don't throw anybody out who comes in uninvited. That is, unless the uninvited behaves antisocially. In which case, notify the O.D., and we'll notify a Protector."

"How can I be master of my house if I can't choose my guests?" Morfiks said.

"The citizen doesn't understand," said the O.D. "A citizen should not want to keep another citizen out of his house. Doing so is saying that a citizen doesn't love all citizens as brothers and sisters. It's not nice. We want to be nice, don't we?"

Morfiks replied that he had always been known as a nice guy, and he continued to listen to the O.D. But, on passing an area where a large field coated with

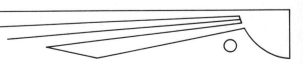

the violet rubber broke the monotonous rows of houses, he said, "Looks like a children's playground with all those swings, seesaws, games, trampolines. Where are the kids? And how—"

"Only the Protectors know what happens to the children who come from We-Know-Where," said the O.D. "It's better, much, much better, not to ask them about it. In fact, it's very good not to see or talk to a Protector.

"No, the playgrounds are for the amusement of us citizens. However, the Protectors have been thinking about taking them down. Too many citizens quarrel about who gets to use them, instead of amicably arranging precedence and turns. They actually dare to fight each other even if fighting's forbidden. And they manage, somehow, to hurt each other. We don't want anybody to get hurt, do we?"

"I guess not. What do you do for entertainment, otherwise?"

"First things first, citizen. We don't like to use any of the personal pronouns except *we*, of course, and *us* and *our* and *ours*. *I, me, they, you* all differentiate. Better to forget personal differences here, heh? After all, we're just one big happy family, heh?"

"Sure," Morfiks said. "But there must be times when a citizen has to point out somebody. How do I—we— identify someone guilty of, say, antisocial behavior?"

"It doesn't matter," said the O.D. "Point out anyone. Yourself—if you'll pardon the word—for instance. We all share in the punishment, so it makes no difference."

"You mean *I* have to be punished for someone else's crime? That isn't *fair!*"

"It may not seem so to us at first," said the O.D. "But consider. We're brothers, not only under the skin but on the skin. If a crime is committed, the guilt is

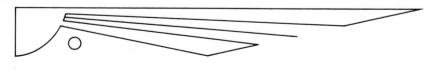

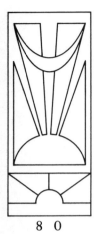

shared by all because, actually, all are responsible. And if punishment is given to all, then all will try to prevent crime. Simple, isn't it? And fair, too."

"But you—we—said that the poleman would be given K.P. Does that mean we all go on K.P.?"

"We did not commit a felony, only a misdemeanor. If we do it again, we are a felon. And we suffer. It's the only nice thing to do, to share, right?"

Morfiks did not like it. He was the one hit in the teeth, so why should he, the victim, have to take the punishment of the aggressor?

But he said nothing. He had gotten far on We-Know-Where by keeping his mouth shut. It paid off; everybody had thought he was a nice guy. And he *was* a nice guy.

There did seem to be one fallacy in the set-up. If being a stool pigeon meant you, too, suffered, why turn anybody in? Wouldn't it be smarter to keep quiet and inflict the punishment yourself on the aggressor?

"Don't do it, citizen," said the O.D.

Morfiks gasped.

The O.D. smiled and said, "No, we can't read minds. But every immigrant thinks the same thing when told about the system. Keeping quiet only results in double punishment. The Protectors—whom this citizen has never seen face to face and doesn't want to—have some means of monitoring our behavior. They know when we've been antisocial. The offender is, of course, given a certain amount of time in which to confess the injury. After that . . ."

To keep himself from bursting into outraged denunciation of the system, Morfiks asked more questions.

Yes, he would be confined to this neighborhood. If he traveled outside it, he might find himself in an area where his language was not spoken. That would result

in his feeling inferior and different because he was a foreigner. Or, worse, superior. Anyway, why travel? Any place looked like every place.

Yes, he was free to discuss any subject as long as it did not concern We-Know-Where. Talking of that place led to discussions of—forgive the term—*one's* former identity and prestige. Besides, controversial subjects might arise and so lead to antisocial behavior.

Yes, this place was not constructed, physically, like We-Know-Where. The sun might be a small body; some eggheads had estimated it to be only a mile wide. The sun orbited around the strip, which was composed of the slides, two rivers and the city between the rivers, all of which hung in space. There was some speculation that his place was in a pocket universe the dimensions of which were probably not more than fifty miles wide and twenty high. It was shaped like an intestine, closed at one end and open at the other to infinity—maybe.

At this point, O.D. cautioned Morfiks about the perils of intellectual speculation. This could be a misdemeanor or felony. In any event, eggheadedness was to be avoided. Pretending to be brainier than your neighbor, to question the unquestionable, was unegalitarian.

"There's no worry about that," Morfiks said. "If there's anything hateful and despicable, it's eggheadedness."

"Congratulations on skill in avoiding the personal," said the O.D. "We'll get along fine here."

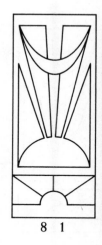

8   1

III

They entered an immense building in which citizens were sitting on brass benches and eating off brass tables running the length of the building. The O.D. told

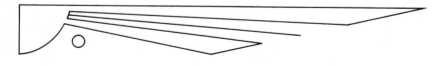

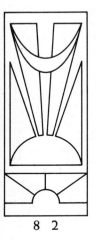

Morfiks to sit down and eat. Afterwards, Morfiks could get to his new home, No. 12634, by asking directions. The O.D. left, and a citizen on K.P. served Morfiks soup in a big brass bowl, a small steak, bread and butter, salad with garlic dressing and a pitcher of water. The utensils and cup were of brass.

He wondered where the food came from, but before he could ask, he was informed by a citizen on his right that he was not holding the spoon properly. After a few minutes of instruction and observation, Morfiks found himself able to master etiquette as practiced here.

"Having the same table manners as everybody else makes a citizen a part of the group," said the instructor. "If a citizen eats differently, then a citizen is impolite. Impoliteness is antisocial. Get it?"

"Got it," said Morfiks.

After eating, he asked the citizen where he could locate No. 12634.

"We'll show us," said the citizen. "We live near that number."

Together, they walked out of the hall and down the street. The sun was near the horizon now. Time must go faster, he thought, for it did not seem to him that he had been here for more than a few hours. Maybe the Protectors sent the sun around faster so the days would be shorter.

They came to No. 12634, and Morfiks' guide preceded him through swinging batwing doors into a large room with luminescent walls. There was a wide couchbed of the violet rubbery substance, several chairs cut out of solid blocks of the same stuff and a brass table in the center of the room. In one corner was a cubicle with a door. He investigated and found it to be the toilet. Besides the usual sanitary arrangements, the cubicle contained a shower, soap and four cups. There were no towels.

"After a shower, step outside, dry off in the sun," the guide said.

It looked at Morfiks for such a long time that Morfiks began to get nervous. Finally, the guide said, "I'll take a chance you're a pretty good Joe. What was your name on Earth?"

"John Smith," said Morfiks.

"Play it cool, then," the guide said. "But you were a man? A male?"

Morfiks nodded, and the guide said, "I was a girl. A woman, I mean. My name was Billie."

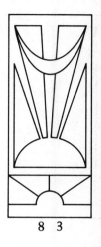

"Why tell me this?" he demanded suspiciously.

Billie came close to Morfiks and put her hands on his shoulders.

"Listen, Johnny boy," she whispered. "Those bastards think they got us behind the eight ball by putting us into these neuter bodies. But don't you believe it. There's more than one way of skinning a cat, if you know what I mean."

"I don't," Morfiks said.

Billie came even closer; her nose almost touched his. A face in a mirror.

"Inside, you're just the same," said Billie. "That's one thing They can't change without changing you so much you're no longer the same person. If They do that, They aren't punishing the same person, are They? So, you wouldn't exist any more, would you? And being here wouldn't be fair, would it?"

"I don't get it," Morfiks said. He took a step backwards; Billie took a step forwards.

"What I mean is, you and me, we're still male and female inside. When They, whoever They are, stripped off our old bodies, They had to leave us our brains and nervous systems, didn't They? Otherwise, we'd not be ourselves, right? They fitted our nervous sys-

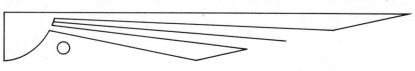

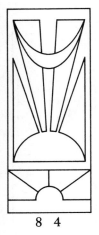

tems into these bodies, made a few adjustments here and there, like shortening or increasing nerve paths to take care of a stature different than the one you had on Earth. Or pumping something inside our skulls to take care of brains being too small for the skulls They gave us."

"Yeah, yeah," Morfiks said. He knew what Billie was going to propose, or he thought he did. He was breathing hard; a tingle was running over his skin; a warmth was spreading out from the pit of his stomach.

"Well," said Billie, "I always heard that it was all in your head. And that's true. Of course, there's only so much you can do, and maybe it isn't as good as it was on You-Know-Where. But it's better than nothing. Besides, like they say, none of it's bad. It's all good, some is just better than others."

"You mean?"

"Just close your eyes," Billie crooned, "and imagine I'm a woman. I'll tell you how I looked, how I was stacked. And you think about it. Then you tell me how you looked, don't hold anything back, no need to be bashful here, describe everything down to the last detail. And I'll imagine how you were."

"Think it'll work?" Morfiks said.

Billie, her eyes closed, softly sang, "I know it will, baby. I've been around some since I came here."

"Yeah, but what about the punishment?"

Billie half-opened her eyes and said, scornfully, "Don't believe all that jazz, Johnny boy. Besides, even if They do catch you, it's worth it. Believe me, it's worth it."

"If only I thought I could put one over on Them," Morfiks said. "It'd be worth taking any risk."

Billie's answer was to kiss him. Morfiks, though he had to repress revulsion, responded. After all, it was only the bald head that made Billie look like a half-man.

They struggled fiercely and desperately; their kisses were as deep as possible.

Suddenly Morfiks pushed Billie away from him.

"It's worse than nothing," he panted. "I think something's going to happen, but it never quite does. It's no use. Now I feel awful."

Billie came towards him again, saying, "Don't give up so easy, honey. Rome wasn't erected in a day. Believe me, you can do it. But you got to have faith."

"No, I'm licked," Morfiks said. "Maybe if you did look like a woman, instead of just a carbon copy of me. Then... no, that wouldn't be any good. I'm just not designed for the job; neither are you. They got us where it hurts."

Billie lost her half-smile; her face twisted.

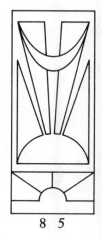

"Where it hurts!" she shrilled. "Let me tell you, Buster, if you can't get your kicks being a man here, you can by hurting somebody! That's about all that's left!"

"What do you mean?" Morfiks said.

Billie laughed loudly and long. When she mastered herself, she said, "I'll tell you one good thing about looking like everybody else. Nobody knows what you really are inside. Or what you were on Earth. Well, I'll tell you about myself.

"I was a man!"

Morfiks sputtered. His fists clenched. He walked towards Billie.

But he did not strike her... him... it.

Instead, he smiled, and he said, "Well, let me tell you something. My real name was Juanita."

Billie became pale, then red.

"You... you!"

The next few days, Morfiks spent four hours each morning on the building of new houses. It was easy work. The walls and sections of the roof were brought

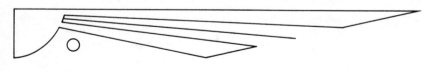

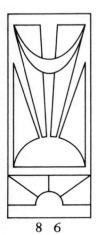

in on wagons of brass pulled by citizens. Supervised by foremen, the laborers raised the walls, secured the bottoms to the brass foundation of the city with a quick-drying glue and then fastened the walls together by gluing down strips of the violet stuff at the corners of the walls.

Morfiks took his turn being a foreman for one day after he had gotten enough experience. He asked a citizen where the material for the houses and the rubber and the glue came from.

"And where's the food grown?"

The citizen looked around to make sure no one could hear them.

"The original brass sheets and rubber are supposed to have originated from the blind end of this universe," he said. "It's spontaneously created, flows like lava from a volcano."

"How can that be?" Morfiks said.

The citizen shrugged. "How should I know? But if you remember one of the theories of creation back on You-Know-Where, matter was supposed to be continuously created out of nothing. So if hydrogen atoms can be formed from nothing, why not brass and rubber lava?"

"But brass and rubber are organized configurations of elements and compounds!"

"So what? The structure of this universe orders it."

"And the food?"

"It's brought up on dumbwaiters through shafts which lead down to the underside. The peasants live there, citizen, and grow food and raise some kind of cattle and poultry."

"Gee, I'd like that," Morfiks said. "Couldn't I get a transfer down there? I'd like to work with the soil. It'd be much more interesting than this."

"If you were supposed to be a peasant, you'd have

been transformed down there to begin with," the citizen said. "No, you're a city-dweller, brother, and you'll stay one. You predetermined that, you know, in You-Know-Where."

"I had obligations," Morfiks said. "What'd you expect me to do, shirk them?"

"I don't expect nothing except to get out of here some day."

"You mean we can get out? How? How?"

"Not so loud with that *you*," the citizen growled. "Yeah, or so we heard, anyway. We never saw a corpse but we heard about some of us dying. It isn't easy, though."

"Tell me how I can do it," Morfiks said. He grabbed the citizen's arm but the citizen tore himself loose and walked away swiftly.

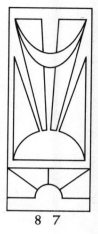

Morfiks started to follow him, then could not identify him because he had mingled with a dozen others.

In the afternoons, Morfiks spent his time playing shuffleboard, badminton, swimming or sometimes playing bridge. The brass plastic cards consisted of two thicknesses glued together. The backs were blank, and the fronts were punched with codes indicating the suits and values. Then, after the evening meals in the communal halls, there were always neighborhood committee meetings. These were to settle any disputes among the local citizens. Morfiks could see no sense in them other than devices to keep the attendants busy and tire them out so that they would be ready to go to bed. After hours of wrangling and speech-making, the disputants were always told that the fault lay equally on both sides. They were to forgive each other, shake hands and make up. Nothing was really settled, and Morfiks was sure that the disputants still burned with resentments despite their protestations that all was now well with them.

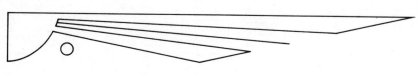

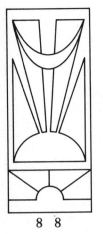

What Morfiks found particularly interesting was the public prayer—if it could be called that—said by an O.D. before each meeting. It contained hints about the origins and reasons for this place and this life but was not specific enough to satisfy his curiosity.

"Glory be to the Protectors, who give us this life. Blessed be liberty, equality and fraternity. Praise be to security, conformity and certainty. None of these did we have on We-Know-Where, O Protectors, though we desired them mightily and strove always without success to attain them. Now we have them because we strove; inevitably we came here, glory be! For this cosmos was prepared for us and when we left that vale of slippery, slidery chaos, we squeezed through the walls and were formed in the template of passage, given these bodies, sexless, sinless, suitable. O Mighty Protectors, invisible but everywhere, we know that We-Know-Where is the pristine cosmos, the basic world, dirty, many-aspected chaos under the form of seeming order, evil but necessary. The egg of creation, rotten but generative. Now, O Protectors, we are shaped forever in that which we cried for on that other unhappy universe. . . ."

There was more but most of it was a repetition in different words. Morfiks, sitting in the brass pews, his head bowed, looked up at the smooth hemisphere of the ceiling and walls and the platform on which the O.D. stood. If he understood the O.D., he was bound here forever, immortal, each day like the next, each month an almost unvarying image of the preceding, year after year, century after century, millennia after millennia.

"Stability, Unseen but Everfelt Protectors. Stability! A place for everyone and everyone in a place!"

The O.D. was saying that there were such things as souls, a configuration of energy which exactly dupli-

cated the body of the person when he had existed on We-Know-Where. It was undetectable by instruments there and so had been denied by many. But when one died there, the configuration was released from the attraction of the body, was somehow pushed from one universe into the next.

There were billions of these, all existing within the same space as the original universe but polarized and at angles to it. A "soul" went to that universe for which it had the most attraction.

Indeed, the universe to which it traveled had actually been created by men and women. The total cumulative effect of desire for just such a place had generated this place.

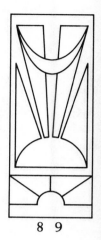

If Morfiks interpreted the vague statements of the O.D. correctly, the structure of this universe was such that when a "soul" or cohesive energy configuration came through the "walls," it naturally took the shape in which all citizens found themselves. It was like hot plastic being poured into a mold.

Morfiks dared question a citizen who claimed to have been here for a hundred years. "The O.D. said all questions have been settled, everything is explained. What's explained? I don't understand any more about the origins or reason for things here than I did on We-Know-Where."

"So what's new?" the citizen said. "How can you understand the ununderstandable? The main difference here is that you don't ask questions. There are many answers, all true, to one question, and this place is one answer. So quit bugging me. You trying to get me— uh, us—into trouble? Hey, O.D.!"

Morfiks hurried off and lost himself in a crowd before he could be identified. He burned with resentment at the implications of this world. Why should he be here?

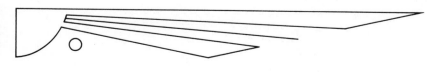

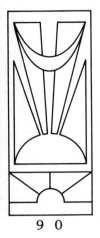

Sure, on We-Know-Where he had stayed with one company for 20 years, he had been a good family man, a pal to his kids, a faithful husband, a pillar of the best church in the neighborhood, had paid off his mortgages, joined the Lions, Elks, and Moose and the Masonic Lodge, the PTA, the Kiwanis, the Junior Chamber of Commerce and been a hard worker for the Democrats. His father before him had been a Democrat, and though he had had many misgivings about some of the policies, he had always followed the party line. Anyway, he was a right-wing Democrat, which made him practically the same thing as a left-wing Republican. He read the *Reader's Digest, Life, Time, Wall Street Journal, Saturday Evening Post,* and had always tried to keep up with the bestsellers as recommended by the local newspaper reviewer. All this, not because he really wanted it but because he felt that he owed it to his wife and kids and for the good of society. He had hoped that when he went "over yonder" he would be rewarded with a life with more freedom, with a number of unlimited avenues for the things he really wanted to do.

What were those things? He didn't remember now, but he was sure that they were not what was available here.

"There's been a mistake," he thought. "I don't belong here. Everything's all screwed up. I shouldn't be here. This is an error on somebody's part. I got to get out. But how can I get out of here any more than I could get out of We-Know-Where? There the only way out was suicide and I couldn't take that, my family would have been disgraced. Besides, I didn't feel like it.

"And here I can't kill myself. My body's too tough and there's nothing, no way for me to commit suicide. Drowning? That won't work. The river's too well guarded, and if you did slip by the guards long enough

to drown, you'd be dragged out in no time at all and resuscitated. And then punished."

IV

On the fourth night, what he had been dreading happened. His punishment. He woke up in the middle of the night with a dull toothache. As the night went on, the ache became sharper. By dawn, he wanted to scream.

Suddenly, the batwings on his doorway flew open, and one of his neighbors (he presumed) stood in the room. He/she was breathing hard and holding his/her hand to his/her jaw.

"Did you do it?" said the neighbor in a shrill voice.

"Do what?" Morfiks said, rising from the couch-bed.

"Antisocial act," the intruder said. "If the culprit confesses, the pain will cease. After a while, that is."

"Did you do it?" Morfiks said. For all he knew, he might be talking to Billie again.

"Not me. Listen, newcomers often—always—commit crimes because of a mistaken notion a crime can't be detected. But the crime is always found out."

"There are newcomers who aren't born criminals," Morfiks said. Despite his pain, he intended to keep control too.

"Then you, and I mean *you*, won't confess?"

"The pain must be breaking some people apart," said Morfiks. "Otherwise, some wouldn't be using the second person singular."

"Singular, hell!" the citizen said, breaking two tabus with two words. "Okay, so it doesn't make much difference if you or me or the poor devil down the street did it. But I got a way of beating the game."

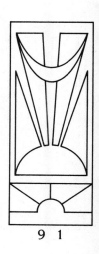

9 1

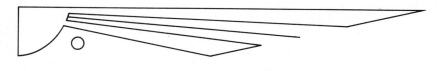

"And so bringing down more punishment on us?"

"No! Listen, I was a dental assistant on We-Know-Where. I know for a fact that you can forget one pain if you have a greater."

Morfiks laughed as much as his tooth would permit him, and he said, "So, what's the advantage there?"

The citizen smiled as much as his toothache would permit. "What I'm going to propose will hurt you. But it'll end up in a real kick. You'll enjoy your pain, get a big thrill out of it."

"How's that?" Morfiks said, thinking that the citizen talked too much like Billie.

"Our flesh is tough so we can't hurt each other too easily. But we can be hurt if we try hard enough. It takes perseverance, but then what doesn't that's worthwhile?"

The citizen shoved Morfiks onto the couch, and, before Morfiks could protest, he was chewing on his leg.

"You do the same to me," the citizen mumbled between bites. "I'm telling you, it's great! You've never had anything like it before."

Morfiks stared down at the bald head and the vigorously working jaws. He could feel a little pain, and his toothache did seem to have eased.

He said, "Never had anything like what?"

"Like blood," the citizen said. "After you've been doing this long enough, you'll get drunk on it."

"I don't know. There, uh, seems something wrong about this."

The citizen stopped gnawing.

"You're a greenhorn! Look at it this way. The Protectors tell us to love one another. So you should love me. And you can show your love by helping me get rid of this toothache. And I can do the same for you.

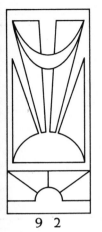

9 2

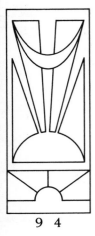

94

After a while, you'll be like all of us. You won't give a damn; you'll do anything to stop the pain."

Morfiks got into position and bit down hard. The flesh felt rubbery. Then he stopped and said, "Won't we get another toothache tomorrow because of what we're doing now?"

"We'll get an ache somewhere. But forget about tomorrow."

"Yeah," Morfiks said. He was beginning to feel more pain in his leg. "Yeah. Anyway, we can always plead we were just being social."

The citizen laughed and said, "How social can you get, huh?"

Morfiks moaned as his crushed nerves and muscles began to bleed. After a while, he was screaming between his teeth, but he kept biting. If he was being hurt, he was going to hurt the citizen even worse.

And what the hell, he was beginning to feel a reasonable facsimile to that which he had known up there on We-Know-Where.

SKETCHES AMONG
THE RUINS
OF MY MIND

.

How many times have you gone to a room and then forgotten why you went there? When have you looked for your glasses, failed to find them, then put your hand in your shirt-pocket and found them there? Or seen them on a table where you had put them at the same time that you made a strong mental note not to forget where they were?

Has someone ever asked you what your name was and, for a few hysterical seconds, you could not remember it? Have you ever read a book on how to strengthen your memory but can't recall the title?

Why is it that ten people can be present at an event, yet each recalls it as something different in detail and interpretation?

Everybody knows what memory is, but no one knows its nature. There are many theories about just how we store memory and how memories are recalled. All, so far, have remained just theories.

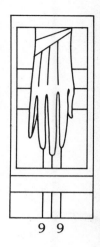

I am sixty-four years old and often vexed by my inability to recall something. I go into a room and forget why I went there. I encounter someone I have not seen for thirty years but went to grade school, high school, and college with, and I have forgotten his or her name. I could attribute this to aging and the approach of senility. But I had much the same trouble when I was twenty.

However, I do, now and then, here and there, forget something that I would not have forgotten when I was twenty. A name, a word, a definition, the title of a book or a well-known institution which I would have recalled instantly in my salad days. But if I take the trouble to think about the item, I do recall it in a few minutes or an hour or perhaps the next day. I attribute my trouble to a mind which has accumulated a tremendous amount of jewels and junk during six decades. The forgotten item is down there. All I have to do is to take some time feeling through that tangled mess, and I'll eventually find it.

I was living in a Beverly Hills apartment house in the middle 1960's (can't recall the exact year) when Gene Roddenberry asked me to write some treatments for his forthcoming Star Trek series. Before this, I had written a hundred-page manual for his show in which I detailed, among other things, what was and was not scientifically possible (that is, within the limits of our present knowledge). I had been paid for it, but I never found out what happened to it. It became evident, however, during the next three years, that no one was paying any attention to the manual. Nine-tenths of the shows were sheer fantasies, not science-fiction. Well, maybe ninety-nine-point-nine percent of the shows were fantasies.

The first treatment I submitted to Roddenberry was turned down. The reasons for that are given in the introduction to "The Shadow of Space," included in this collection.

Shortly thereafter, I got an idea for a second treatment. I don't remember the moment when I got the idea. But it must have happened when I was cursing myself for having forgotten something. And, as always, there was a click in the brain, a light went on, and I had the basic idea for a Star Trek story.

The Enterprise would land on a planet which had once been inhabited by sentients. These were gone now, for some unknown reason, but they had left behind them the ruins of their cities and various artifacts. While exploring some ruins, Captain Kirk picked up a very heavy but small idol. He took it to his quarters, even though he was supposed to turn it over to the archaeologist, and, the next morning, he awoke thinking that . . .

I can't go further into the treatment without exposing too much of the story at hand. It was a great idea, but Roddenberry rejected the treatment. His reasons for this were the same as for "The Shadow of Space." (See the introduction to that story.) At the time, I did not agree with Roddenberry's reasons for rejection, but, in retrospect, I can see that he was right. "Sketches Among the Ruins of My Mind" would make a hell of a good theater movie, and it would not go well in a forty-five-minute TV show.

However, the idea was too good to abandon. Sometime later, I changed the time of the story from the far future to the near future and the location from a distant planet to the Earth we know. Or think we know.

I'm glad now that Roddenberry (whom I referred to at that time as Rod-and-Bury) turned the treatment down. Working

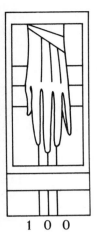

within the confines of prose fiction, which are still far beyond the confines of the visual medium, I was able to do justice to the idea.

I don't remember what the title of the treatment was. It may have been The Idol or a quotation about time from Shakespeare. In any event, the present title is based on those titles used in a certain genre of writing in the eighteenth and early nineteenth centuries.

Poets and essayists then would visit the remains of abbeys or graveyards or villas or ancient cities. There they would meditate and eventually write word-pictures of the ruins and also the philosophical thoughts evoked by the melancholy relics. "Sketches Among the Ruins of..." was a very popular title in those days.

Actually, I had used the title to this story as a subtitle for my novel, Image of the Beast. But, since the title seemed exactly right for the story herein, there was no use wasting it. So I made a major title out of a subtitle.

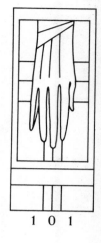

1 0 1

This is not a time-travel story except in a limited sense. We all time-travel. Every second that passes inexorably pushes us ahead in time. We also time-travel backwards via our memories, books, records, photographs, and films. Using our memories as vehicles for time-travel, however, usually takes us to bournes that never existed. Our memories reconstruct the past to fit our personal specifications for the past. This leads me to believe that memory is not, like books, records, etc., a passive, unaltered, and unaltering thing. Memory is active and creative. It makes up fictional stories and fake images.

Memory, like film and printing, is a medium. Which means that every person is a writer or painter or film director or all three and much more.

The science-fiction writer, unlike most of those in that entity we call Everyperson, has two memories. That of the past and that of the future.

I

Objective Time: June 1.

It is now 11:00 A.M., and I am afraid to go to bed. I am not alone. The whole world is afraid of sleep.

This morning I got up at 6:30 A.M., as I do every Wednesday. While I shaved and showered, I considered the case of the state of Illinois against Joseph Lankers, accused of murder. It was beginning to stink as if it were a three-day-old fish. My star witness would undoubtedly be charged with perjury.

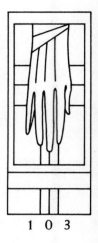

1 0 3

I dressed, went downstairs, and kissed Carole good morning. She poured me a cup of coffee and said, "The paper's late."

That put me in a bad temper. I need both coffee and the morning newspaper to get me started.

Twice during breakfast, I left the table to look outside. Neither paper nor newsboy had appeared.

At seven, Carole went upstairs to wake up Mike and Tom, aged ten and eight respectively. Saturdays and Sundays they rise early even though I'd like them to stay in bed so their horsing around won't wake me. School days they have to be dragged out.

The third time I looked out of the door, Joe Gale, the paperboy, was next door. My paper lay on the stoop.

I felt disorientated, as if I'd walked into the wrong courtroom or the judge had given my client, a shoplifter, a life sentence. I was out of phase with the world. This couldn't be Sunday. So what was the Sunday issue, bright in its covering of the colored comic section, doing there? Today was Wednesday.

I stepped out to pick it up and saw old Mrs. Douglas, my neighbor to the left. She was looking at the front page of her paper as if she could not believe it.

The world rearranged itself into the correct lines of polarization. My thin panic dwindled into nothing. I thought, the *Star* has really goofed this time. That's what comes from depending so much on a computer to put it together. One little short circuit, and Wednesday's paper comes out in Sunday's format.

The *Star's* night shift must have decided to let it go through; it was too late for them to rectify the error.

I said, "Good morning, Mrs. Douglas! Tell me, what day is it?"

"The twenty-eighth of May," she said. "I think . . ."

I walked out into the yard and shouted after Joe. Reluctantly, he wheeled his bike around.

"What is this?" I said, shaking the paper at him. "Did the *Star* screw up?"

"I don't know, Mr. Franham," he said. "None of us knows, honest to God."

By "us" he must have meant the other boys he met in the morning at the paper drop.

"We all thought it was Wednesday. That's why I'm late. We couldn't understand what was happening, so we talked a long time and then Bill Ambers called the office. Gates, he's the circulation manager, was just as bongo as we was."

"Were," I said.

"What?" he said.

"We *were*, not *was*, just as bongo, whatever that means," I said.

"For God's sake, Mr. Franham, who cares!"

"Some of us still do. All right, what did Gates say?"

"He was upset as hell. He said heads were gonna roll. The night staff had fallen asleep for a couple of hours, and some joker had diddled up the computers, or . . ."

"That's all it is?" I said. I felt relieved.

When I went inside, I got out the papers for the last

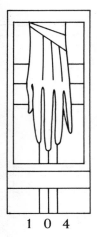

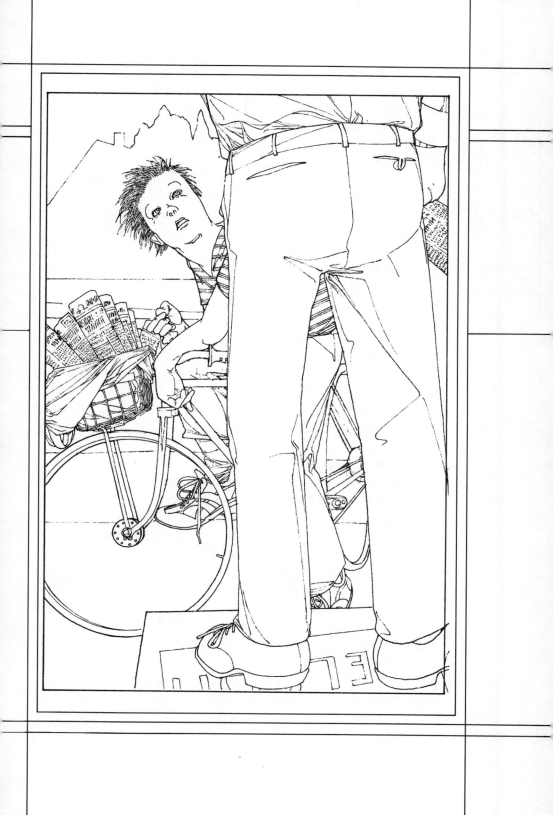

four days from the cycler. I sat down on the sofa and scanned them.

I didn't remember reading them. I didn't remember the past four days at all!

Wednesday's headline was: MYSTERIOUS OBJECT ORBITS EARTH.

I did remember Tuesday's articles, which stated that the big round object was heading for a point between the Earth and the moon. It had been detected three weeks ago when it was passing through the so-called asteroid belt. It was at that time traveling approximately 57,000 kilometers per hour, relative to the sun. Then it had slowed down, had changed course several times, and it became obvious that, unless it changed course again, it was going to come near Earth.

By the time it was eleven million miles away, the radars had defined its size and shape, though not its material composition. It was perfectly spherical and exactly half a kilometer in diameter. It did not reflect much light. Since it had altered its path so often, it had to be artificial. Strange hands, or strange some-things, had built it.

I remembered the panic and the many wild articles in the papers and magazines and the TV specials made overnight to discuss its implications.

It had failed to make any response whatever to the radio and laser signals sent from Earth. Many scientists said that it probably contained no living passengers. It had to be of interstellar origin. The sentient beings of some planet circling some star had sent it out equipped with automatic equipment of some sort. No being could live long enough to travel between the stars. It would take over four years to get from the nearest star to Earth even if the object could travel at the speed of light, and that was impossible. Even one-sixteenth the speed of light seemed incredible because

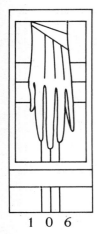

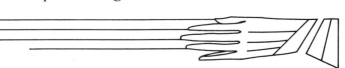

of the vast energy requirements. No, this thing had been launched with only electromechanical devices as passengers, had attained its top speed, turned off its power, and coasted until it came within the outer reaches of our solar system.

According to the experts, it must be unable to land on Earth because of its size and weight. It was probably just a surveying vessel. After it had taken some photographs and made some radar/laser sweeps, it would proceed to wherever it was supposed to go, probably back to an orbit around its home planet.

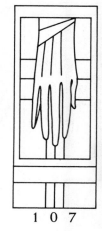

II

Last Wednesday night, the president had told us that we had nothing to fear. And he'd tried to end on an optimistic note. At least, that's what Wednesday's paper said. The beings who had sent The Ball must be more advanced than we, and they must have many good things to give us. And we might be able to make beneficial contributions to them. Like what? I thought.

Some photographs of The Ball, taken from one of the manned orbiting laboratories, were on the second page. It looked just like a giant black billiard ball. One TV comic had suggested that the other side might bear a big white 8. I may have thought that this was funny last Wednesday, but I didn't think so now. It seemed highly probable to me that The Ball was connected with the four-days' loss of memory. How, I had no idea.

I turned on the 7:30 news channels, but they weren't much help except in telling us that the same thing had happened to everybody all over the world. Even those in the deepest diamond mines or submarines had been

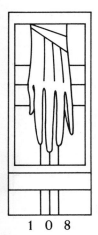

affected. The president was in conference, but he'd be making a statement over the networks sometime today. Meantime, it was known that no radiation of any sort had been detected emanating from The Ball. There was no evidence whatsoever that the object had caused the loss of memory. Or, as the jargon-crazy casters were already calling it, "memloss."

I'm a lawyer, and I like to think logically, not only about what has happened but what might happen. So I extrapolated on the basis of what little evidence, or data, there was.

On the first of June, a Sunday, we woke up with all memory of May 31 back through May 28 completely gone. We had thought that yesterday was the twenty-seventh and that this morning was that of the twenty-eighth.

If The Ball had caused this, why had it only taken four days of our memory? I didn't know. Nobody knew. But perhaps The Ball, its devices, that is, were limited in scope. Perhaps they couldn't strip off more than four days of memory at a time from everybody on Earth.

Postulate that this is the case. Then, what if the same thing happens tomorrow? We'll wake up tomorrow, June 2, with all memory of yesterday, June 1, and three more days of May, the twenty-seventh through the twenty-fifth, gone. Eight days in one solid stretch.

And if this ghastly thing should occur the following day, June 3, we'll lose another four days. All memory of June 2 will have disappeared. With it will go the memory of three more days, from May twenty-fourth through the twenty-second. Twelve days in all from June 2 backward!

And the next day? June 3 lost, too, along with May 21 through May 19. Sixteen days of a total blank. And the next day? And the next?

No, it's too hideous and too fantastic to think about.

While we were watching TV, Carole and the boys besieged me with questions. She was frantic. The boys seemed to be enjoying the mystery. They'd awakened expecting to go to school, and now they were having a holiday.

To all their questions, I said, "I don't know. Nobody knows."

I wasn't going to frighten them with my extrapolations. Besides, I didn't believe them myself.

"You'd better call up your office and tell them you can't come in today," Carole said. "Surely Judge Payne'll call off the session today."

"Carole, it's Sunday, not Wednesday, remember?" I said.

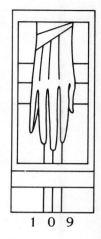

She cried for a minute. After she'd wiped away the tears, she said, "That's just it! I *don't* remember! My God, what's happening?"

The newscasters also reported that the White House was flooded with telegrams and phone calls demanding that rockets with H-bomb warheads be launched against The Ball. The specials, which came on after the news, were devoted to The Ball. These had various authorities, scientists, military men, ministers, and a few science-fiction authors. None of them radiated confidence, but they were all temperate in their approach to the problem. I suppose they had been picked for their level-headedness. The networks had screened out the hotheads and the crackpots. They didn't want to be generating any more hysteria.

But Anel Robertson, a fundamentalist faith healer with a powerful radio/TV station of his own, had already declared that The Ball was a judgment of God on a sinful planet. It was The Destroying Angel. I knew that because Mrs. Douglas, no fanatic but certainly a zealot, had phoned me and told me to dial him in.

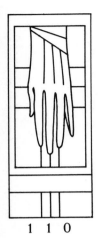

Robertson had been speaking for an hour, she said, and he was going to talk all day.

She sounded frightened, and yet, beneath the fear, was a note of joy. Obviously, she didn't think that she was going to be among the goats when the last days arrived. She'd be right in there with the whitest of the sheep. My curiosity finally overcame my repugnance for Robertson. I dialed the correct number but got nothing except a pattern. Later today, I found out his station had been shut down for some infraction of FCC regulations. At least, that was the explanation given on the news, but I suspected that the government regarded him as a hysteria monger.

At eleven, Carole reminded me that it was Sunday and that, if we didn't hurry, we'd miss church.

The Forrest Hill Presbyterian has a good attendance, but its huge parking lot has always been adequate. This morning, we had to park two blocks up the street and walk to church. Every seat was filled. We had to stand in the anteroom near the front door. The crowd stank of fear. Their faces were pale and set; their eyes, big. The air conditioning labored unsuccessfully to carry away the heat and humidity of the packed and sweating bodies. The choir was loud but quavering; their "Rock of Ages" was crumbling.

Doctor Boynton would have prepared his sermon on Saturday afternoon, as he always did. But today he spoke impromptu. Perhaps, he said, this loss of memory *had* been caused by The Ball. Perhaps there were living beings in it who had taken four days away from us, not as a hostile move but merely to demonstrate their immense powers. There was no reason to anticipate that we would suffer another loss of memory. These beings merely wanted to show us that we were hopelessly inferior in science and that we could not launch a successful attack against them.

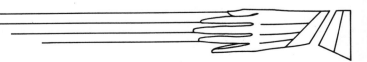

"What the hell's he doing?" I thought. "Is he trying to scare us to death?"

Boynton hastened then to say that beings with such powers, of such obvious advancement, would not, could not, be hostile. They would be on too high an ethical plane for such evil things as war, unless they were attacked, of course. They would regard us as beings who had not yet progressed to their level but had the potentiality, the God-given potentiality, to be raised to a high level. He was sure that, when they made contact with us, they would tell us that all was for the best.

They would tell us that we must, like it or not, become true Christians. At least, we must all, Buddhists, Moslems and so forth, become Christian in spirit, whatever our religion or lack thereof. They would teach us how to live as brothers and sisters, how to be happy, how to truly love. Assuredly, God had sent The Ball, since nothing happened without His knowledge and consent. He had sent these beings, whoever they were, not as Destroying Angels but as Sharers of Peace, Love and Prosperity.

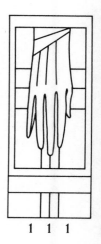

1 1 1

That last, with the big P, seemed to settle down most of the congregation. Boynton had not forgotten that most of his flock were of the big-business and professional classes. Nor had he forgotten that inscribed on the arch above the church entrance was: THEY SHALL PROSPER WHO LOVE THEE.

III

We poured out into a bright warm June afternoon. I looked up into the sky but could see no Ball, of course. The news media had said that, despite its great distance

from Earth, it was circling Earth every sixty-five minutes. It wasn't in a free fall orbit. It was applying continuous power to keep it on its path, although there were no detectable emanations of energy from it.

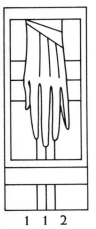

1 1 2

The memory loss had occurred all over the world between 1:00 A.M. and 2:00 A.M. Central Standard Time. Those who were not already asleep fell asleep for a minimum of an hour. This had, of course, caused hundreds of thousands of accidents in the U.S. alone. Planes not on automatic pilot had crashed, trains had collided or been derailed, ships had sunk, and more than two hundred thousand had been killed or seriously injured. At least a million vehicle drivers and passengers had been injured. The ambulance and hospital services had found it impossible to handle the situation. The fact that their personnel had been asleep for at least an hour and that it had taken them some time to recover from their confusion on awakening had aggravated the situation considerably. Many had died who might have lived if immediate service had been available.

There were many fires, too, the largest of which were still raging in Tokyo, Athens, Naples, Harlem, and Baltimore.

I thought, Would beings on a high ethical plane have put us to sleep knowing that so many people would be killed and badly hurt?

One curious item was about two rangers who had been thinning a herd of elephants in Kenya. While sleeping, they had been trampled to death. Whatever it is that's causing this, it's very specific. Only human beings are affected.

The optimism which Boynton had given us in the church melted in the sun. Many must have been thinking, as I was, that if Boynton's words were prophetic, we were helpless. Whatever the things in The Ball,

whether living or mechanical, decided to do for us or to us we were no longer masters of our own fate. Some of them must have been thinking about what the technologically superior whites had done to various aboriginal cultures. All in the name of progress and God.

But this would be, must be, different, I thought. Boynton must be right. Surely such an advanced people would not be as we were. Even we are not what we were in the bad old days. We have learned.

But then an advanced technology does not necessarily accompany an advanced ethics.

"Or whatever," I murmured.

"What did you say, dear?" Carole said.

I said, "Nothing," and shook her hand off my arm. She had clung to it tightly all through the services, as if *I* were the rock of the ages. I walked over to Judge Payne, who's sixty years old but looked this morning as if he were eighty. The many broken veins on his face were red, but underneath them was a grayishness.

I said hello and then asked him if things would be normal tomorrow. He didn't seem to know what I was getting at, so I said, "The trial will start on time tomorrow?"

"Oh, yes, the trial," he said. "Of course, Mark."

He laughed whinnyingly and said, "Provided that we all haven't forgotten today when we wake up tomorrow."

That seemed incredible, and I told him so.

"It's not law school that makes good lawyers," he said. "It's experience. And experience tells us that the same damned thing, with some trifling variations, occurs over and over, day after day. So what makes you think this evil thing won't happen again? And if it does, how're you going to learn from it when you can't remember it?"

I had no logical argument, and he didn't want to talk

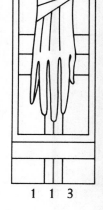

1 1 3

any more. He grabbed his wife by the arm, and they waded through the crowd as if they thought they were going to step in a sinkhole and drown in a sea of bodies.

This evening, I decided to record on tape what's happened today. Now I lay me down to sleep, I pray the Lord my memory to keep, if I forget while I sleep. . . .

Most of the rest of today, I've spent before the TV. Carole wasted hours trying to get through the lines to her friends for phone conversations. Three-fourths of the time, she got a busy signal. There were bulletins on the TV asking people not to use the phone except for emergencies, but she paid no attention to it until about eight o'clock. A TV bulletin, for the sixth time in an hour, asked that the lines be kept open. About twenty fires had broken out over the town, and the firemen couldn't be informed of them because of the tie-up. Calls to hospitals had been similarly blocked.

I told Carole to knock it off, and we quarreled. Our suppressed hysteria broke loose, and the boys retreated upstairs to their room behind a closed door. Eventually, Carole started crying and threw herself into my arms, and then I cried. We kissed and made up. The boys came down looking as if we had failed them, which we had. For them, it was no longer a fun-adventure from some science-fiction story.

Mike said, "Dad, could you help me go over my arithmetic lessons?"

I didn't feel like it, but I wanted to make it up to him for that savage scene. I said sure and then, when I saw what he had to do, I said, "But all this? What's the matter with your teacher? I never saw so much. . ."

I stopped. Of course, he had forgotten all he'd learned in the last three days of school. He had to do his lessons all over again.

This took us until eleven, though we might have

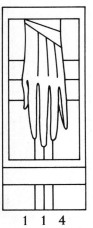

gone faster if I hadn't insisted on watching the news every half-hour for at least ten minutes. A full thirty minutes were used listening to the president, who came on at 9:30. He had nothing to add to what the newsman had said except that, within thirty days, The Ball would be completely dealt with—one way or another. If it didn't make some response to our signals within two days, then we would send up a four-man expedition, which would explore The Ball.

If it can get inside, I thought.

If, however, The Ball should commit any more hostile acts, then the United States would immediately launch, in conjunction with other nations, rockets armed with H-bombs.

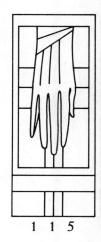

Meanwhile, would we all join the president in an interdenominational prayer?

We certainly would.

At eleven, we put the kids to bed. Tom went to sleep before we were out of the room. But about half an hour later, as I passed the door, I heard a low voice from the TV. I didn't say anything to Mike, even if he did have to go to school next day.

At twelve, I made the first part of this tape.

But here it is, one minute to one o'clock in the morning. If the same thing happens tonight as happened yesterday, then the nightside hemisphere will be affected first. People in the time zone which bisects the South and North Atlantic oceans and covers the eastern half of Greenland will fall asleep. Just in case it does happen again, all airplanes have been grounded. Right now, the TV is showing the bridge and the salon of the trans-Atlantic liner *Pax*. Its five o'clock there, but the salon is crowded. The passengers are wearing party hats and confetti, and balloons are floating everywhere. I don't know what they could be celebrating. The captain said a little while ago that the ship's on

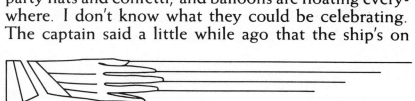

automatic, but he doesn't expect a repetition of last night. The interviewer said that the governments of the dayside nations have not been successful keeping people home. We've been getting shots from everywhere, the sirens are wailing all over the world, but, except for the totalitarian nations, the streets of the daytime world are filled with cars. The damned fools just didn't believe it would happen again.

Back to the bridge and the salon of the ship. My God! They *are* falling asleep!

The announcers are repeating warnings. Everybody lie down so they won't get hurt by falling. Make sure all home appliances, which might cause fires, are turned off. And so on and so on.

I'm sitting in a chair with a tilted back. Carole is on the sofa.

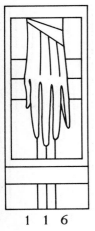

Now I'm on the sofa. Carole just said she wanted to be holding on to me when this horrible thing comes.

The announcers are getting hysterical. In a few minutes, New York will be hit. The eastern half of South America is under. The central section is going under.

IV

True Date: June 2. Subjective Date: May 25.

My God! How many times have I said, "My God!" in the last two days?

I awoke on the sofa beside Carole and Mike. The clock indicated three in the morning. Chris Turner was on the TV. I didn't know what he was talking about. All I could understand was that he was trying to reassure his viewers that everything was all right and that everything would be explained shortly.

What was I doing on the sofa? I'd gone to bed about

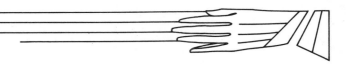

eleven the night of May 24, a Saturday. Carole and I had had a little quarrel because I'd spent all day working on the Lankers case, and she said that I'd promised to take her to see *Nova Express*. And so I had—if I finished work before eight, which I obviously had not done. So what were we doing on the sofa, where had Mike come from, and what did Turner mean by saying that today was June 2?

The tape recorder was on the table near me, but it didn't occur to me to turn it on.

I shook Carole awake, and we confusedly asked each other what had happened. Finally, Turner's insistent voice got our attention, and he explained the situation for about the fifth time so far. Later, he said that an alarm clock placed by his ear had awakened him at two-thirty.

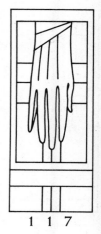

Carole made some coffee, and we drank four cups apiece. We talked wildly, with occasional breaks to listen to Turner, before we became half-convinced that we had indeed lost all memory of the last eight days. Mike slept on through it, and finally I carried him up to his bed. His TV was still on. Nate Frobisher, Mike's favorite spieler, was talking hysterically. I turned him off and went back downstairs. I figured out later that Mike had gotten scared and come downstairs to sit with us.

Dawn found us rereading the papers from May 24 through June 1. It was like getting news from Mars. Carole took a tranquilizer to quiet herself down, but I preferred Wild Turkey. After she'd seen me down six ounces, Carole said I should lay off the bourbon. I wouldn't be fit to go to work. I told her that if she thought anybody'd be working today, she was out of her mind.

At seven, I went out to pick up the paper. It wasn't there. At a quarter to eight, Joe delivered it. I tried to

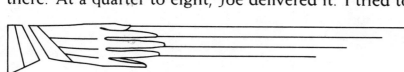

talk to him, but he wouldn't stop. All he said, as he pedaled away, was, "It ain't Saturday!"

I went back in. The entire front page was devoted to The Ball and this morning's events up to four o'clock. Part of the paper had been set up before one o'clock. According to a notice at the bottom of the page, the staff had awakened about three. It took them an hour to straighten themselves out, and then they'd gotten together the latest news and made up the front page and some of section C. They'd have never made it when they did if it wasn't for the computer, which printed justified lines from voice input.

Despite what I'd said earlier, I decided to go to work. First, I had to straighten the boys out. At ten, they went off to school. It seemed to me that it was useless for them to do so. But they were eager to talk with their classmates about this situation. To tell the truth, I wanted to get down to the office and the courthouse for the same reason. I wanted to talk this over with my colleagues. Staying home all day with Carole seemed a waste of time. We just kept saying the same thing over and over again.

Carole didn't want me to leave. She was too frightened to stay home by herself. Both our parents are dead, but she does have a sister who lives in Hannah, a small town nearby. I told her it'd do her good to get out of the house. And I just had to get to the courthouse. I couldn't find out what was happening there because the phone lines were tied up.

When I went outside to get into my car, Carole ran down after me. Her long blonde hair was straggling; she had bags under her eyes; she looked like a witch.

"Mark! Mark!" she said.

I took my finger off the starter button and said, "What is it?"

"I know you'll think I'm crazy, Mark," she said. "But I'm about to fall apart!"

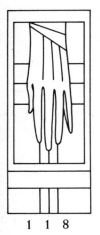

"Who isn't?" I said.

"Mark," she said, "what if I go out to my sister's and then forget how to get back? What if I forgot *you?*"

"This thing only happens at night," I said.

"So far!" she screamed. "So far!"

"Honey," I said, "I'll be home early. I promise. If you don't want to go, stay here. Go over and talk to Mrs. Knight. I see her looking out her window. She'll talk your leg off all day."

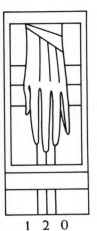

1 2 0

I didn't tell her to visit any of her close friends, because she didn't have any. Her best friend had died of cancer last year, and two others with whom she was familiar had moved away.

"If you do go to your sister's," I said, "make a note on a map reminding you where you live and stick it on top of the dashboard, where you can see it."

"You son of a bitch," she said. "It isn't funny!"

"I'm not being funny," I said. "I got a feeling . . ."

"What about?" she said.

"Well, we'll be making notes to ourselves soon. If this keeps up," I said.

I thought I was kidding then. Thinking about it later today I see that that is the only way to get orientated in the morning. Well, not the only way, but it'll have to be the way to get started when you wake up. Put a note where you can't overlook it, and it'll tell you to turn on a recording, which will, in turn, summarize the situation. Then you turn on the TV and get some more information.

I might as well have stayed home. Only half of the courthouse personnel showed up, and they were hopelessly inefficient. Judge Payne wasn't there and never will be. He'd had a fatal stroke at six that morning while listening to the TV. Walter Barbindale, my partner, said that the judge probably would have had a stroke sometime in the near future, anyway. But this

situation must certainly have hastened it.

"The stock market's about hit bottom," he said. "One more day of this, and we'll have another worldwide depression. And I can't even get through to my broker to tell him to sell everything."

"If everybody sells, then the market *will* crash," I said.

"Are you hanging onto your stocks?"

"I've been too busy to even think about it," I said. "You might say I forgot."

"That isn't funny."

"That's what my wife said. But I'm not trying to be funny, though God knows I could use a good laugh. Well, what're we going to do about Lankers?"

"I went over some of the records," he said. "We haven't got a chance. I tell you, it was a shock finding out, for the second time, mind you, though I don't remember the first, that our star witness is in jail on a perjury charge."

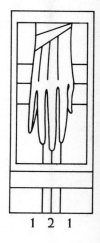

1 2 1

Since all was chaos in the courthouse, it wasn't much use trying to find out who the judge would be for the new trial for Lankers. To tell the truth, I didn't much care. There were far more important things to worry about than the fate of an undoubtedly guilty murderer.

I went to Grover's Rover Bar, which is a block from the courthouse. As an aside, for my reference or for whoever might be listening to this some day, why am I telling myself things I know perfectly well, like the location of Grover's? Maybe it's because I think I might forget them some day.

Grover's, at least, I remembered well, as I should, since I'd been going there ever since it was built, five years ago. The air was thick with tobacco and pot smoke and the odors of pot, beer and booze. And noisy. Everybody was talking fast and loud, which is to be expected in a place filled with members of the

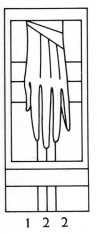

legal profession. I bellied up to the bar and bought the D.A. a shot of Wild Turkey. We talked about what we'd done that morning, and then he told me he had to release two burglars that day. They'd been caught and jailed two days before. The arresting officers had, of course, filed their reports. But that wasn't going to be enough when the trial came up. Neither the burglars nor the victims and the officers remembered a thing about the case.

"Also," the D.A. said, "at two-ten this morning, the police got a call from the Black Shadow Tavern on Washington Street. They didn't get there until three-thirty because they were too disorientated to do anything for an hour or more. When they did get to the tavern, they found a dead man. He'd been beaten badly and then stabbed in the stomach. Nobody remembered anything, of course. But from what we could piece together, the dead man must've gotten into a drunken brawl with a person or persons unknown shortly before 1:00 A.M. Thirty people must've witnessed the murder. So we have a murderer or murderers walking the streets today who don't even remember the killing or anything leading up to it."

"They might know they're guilty if they'd been planning it for a long time," I said.

He grinned and said, "But he, or they, won't be telling anybody. No one except the corpse had blood on him nor did anybody have bruised knuckles. Two were arrested for carrying saps, but so what? They'll be out soon, and nobody, but nobody, can prove they used the saps. The knife was still sticking in the deceased's belly, and his efforts to pull it out destroyed any fingerprints."

V

We talked and drank a lot, and suddenly it was 6:00 P.M. I was in no condition to drive and had sense enough to know it. I tried calling Carole to come down and get me, but I couldn't get through. At 6:30 and 7:00, I tried again without success. I decided to take a taxi. But after another drink, I tried again and this time got through.

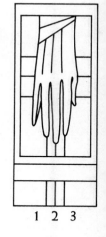

1 2 3

"Where've you been?" she said. "I called your office, but nobody answered. I was thinking about calling the police."

"As if they haven't got enough to do," I said. "When did *you* get home?"

"You're slurring," she said coldly.

I repeated the question.

"Two hours ago," she said.

"The lines were tied up. I tried."

"You knew how scared I was, and you didn't even care!"

"Can I help it if the D.A. insisted on conducting business at the Rover?" I said. "Besides, I was trying to forget."

"Forget what?" she said.

"Whatever it was I forgot," I said.

"You ass!" she screamed. "Take a taxi!"

The phone clicked off.

She didn't make a scene when I got home. She'd decided to play it cool because of the kids, I suppose. She was drinking gin and tonic when I entered, and she said, in a level voice, "*You*'ll have some coffee. And after a while you can listen to the tape you made yesterday. It's interesting but spooky."

"What tape?"

"Mike was fooling around with it," she said. "And

he found out you'd recorded what happened yesterday."

"That kid!" I said. "He's always snooping around. I told him to leave my stuff alone. Can't a man have any privacy around here?"

"Well, don't say anything to him. He's upset as it is. Anyway, it's a good thing he did turn it on. Otherwise, you'd have forgotten all about it. I think you should make a daily record."

"So you think it'll happen again?" I said.

She burst into tears. After a moment, I put my arms around her. I felt like crying, too. But she pushed me away, saying, "You stink of rotten whiskey!"

"That's because it's mostly bar whiskey," I said. "I can't afford Wild Turkey at three dollars a shot."

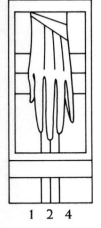

1 2 4

I drank four cups of black coffee and munched on some shrimp dip. As an aside, I can't really afford that, either, since I only make forty-five thousand dollars a year.

When we went to bed, we went to bed. Afterward, Carole said, "I'm sorry, darling, but my heart wasn't really in it."

"That wasn't all."

"You've got a dirty mind," she said. "What I meant was I couldn't stop thinking, even while we were doing it, that it wasn't any good doing it. We won't remember it tomorrow, I thought."

"How many do we really remember?" I said. "Sufficient unto the day is the, uh, good thereof."

"It's a good thing you didn't try to fulfill your childhood dream of becoming a preacher," she said. "You're a born shyster. You'd have made a lousy minister."

"Look," I said. "I remember the especially good ones. And I'll never forget our honeymoon. But we need sleep. We haven't had any to speak of for twenty-four hours. Let's hit the hay and forget everything until

tomorrow. In which case . . ."

She stared at me and then said, "Poor dear, no wonder you're so belligerently flippant! It's a defense against fear!"

I slammed my fist into my palm and shouted, "I know! I know! For God's sake, how long is this going on?"

I went into the bathroom. The face in the mirror looked as if it were trying to flirt with me. The left eye wouldn't stop winking.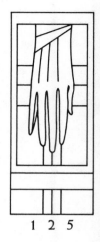

When I returned to the bedroom, Carole reminded me that I'd not made today's recording. I didn't want to do it because I was so tired. But the possibility of losing another day's memory spurred me. No, not another day, I thought. If this occurs tomorrow, I'll lose another four days. Tomorrow and the three preceding May 25. I'll wake up June 3 and think it's the morning of the twenty-second.

1 2 5

I'm making this downstairs in my study. I wouldn't want Carole to hear some of my comments.

Until tomorrow then. It's not tomorrow but yesterday that won't come. I'll make a note to myself and stick it in a corner of the case which holds my glasses.

VI

True Date: June 3.

I woke up thinking that today was my birthday, May 22. I rolled over, saw the piece of paper half-stuck from my glasses case, put on my glasses and read the note.

It didn't enlighten me. I didn't remember writing the note. And why should I go downstairs and turn on the recorder? But I did so.

As I listened to the machine, my heart thudded as

if it were a judge's gavel. My voice kept fading in and out. Was I going to faint?

And so half of today was wasted trying to regain twelve days in my mind. I didn't go to the office, and the kids went to school late. And what about the kids in school on the dayside of Earth? If they sleep during their geometry class, say, then they have to go through the class again on the same day. And that shoves the schedule forward, or is it backward, for that day. And then there's the time which workers will lose on their jobs. They have to make it up, which means they get out an hour later. Only it takes more than an hour to recover from the confusion and get orientated. What a mess it has been! What a mess it'll be if this keeps on!

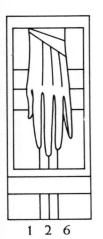

At eleven, Carole and I were straightened out enough to go to the supermarket. It was Tuesday, but Carole wanted me to be with her, so I tried to phone in and tell my secretary I'd be absent. The lines were tied up, and I doubt that she was at work. So I said to hell with it.

Our supermarket usually opens at eight. Not today. We had to stand in a long line, which kept getting longer. The doors opened at twelve. The manager, clerks and boys had had just as much trouble as we did unconfusing themselves, of course. Some didn't show at all. And some of the trucks which were to bring supplies never appeared.

By the time Carole and I got inside, those ahead of us had cleaned out half the supplies. They had the same idea we had. Load up now so there wouldn't be any standing in line so many times. The fresh milk was all gone, and the powdered milk shelf had one box left. I started for it but some teen-ager beat me to it. I felt like hitting him, but I didn't, of course.

The prices for everything were being upped by a

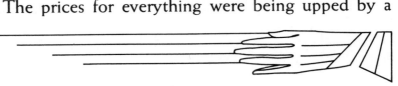

fourth even as we shopped. Some of the stuff was being marked upward once more while we stood in line at the checkout counter. From the time we entered the line until we pushed out three overflowing carts, four hours had passed.

While Carole put away the groceries, I drove to another supermarket. The line there was a block long; it would be emptied and closed up before I ever got to its doors.

The next two supermarkets and a corner grocery store were just as hopeless. And the three liquor stores I went to were no better. The fourth only had about thirty men in line, so I tried that. When I got inside, all the beer was gone, which didn't bother me any, but the only hard stuff left was a fifth of rotgut. I drank it when I went to college because I couldn't afford anything better. I put the terrible stuff and a half-gallon of cheap muscatel on the counter. Anything was better than nothing, even though the prices had been doubled.

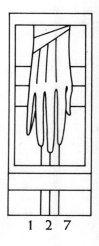

I started to make out the check, but the clerk said, "Sorry, sir. Cash only."

"What?" I said.

"Haven't you heard, sir?" he said. "The banks were closed at 2:00 P.M. today."

"The banks are closed?" I said. I sounded stupid even to myself.

"Yes, sir," he said. "By the federal government. It's only temporary, sir, at least, that's what the TV said. They'll be reopened after the stock market mess is cleared up."

"But . . ." I said.

"It's destructed," he said.

"Destroyed," I said automatically. "You mean, it's another Black Friday?"

"It's Tuesday today," he said.

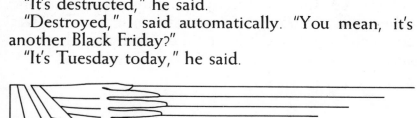

"You're too young to know the reference," I said. And too uneducated, too, I thought.

"The president is going to set up a rationing system," he said. "For The Interim. And price controls, too. Turner said so on TV an hour ago. The president is going to lay it all out at six tonight."

When I came home, I found Carole in front of the TV. She was pale and wide-eyed.

"There's going to be another depression!" she said. "Oh, Mark, what are we going to do?"

"I don't know," I said. "I'm not the president, you know." And I slumped down onto the sofa. I had lost my flippancy.

Neither of us knew what a Depression, with a big capital D, was, though we'd been through recessions, of course. We hadn't experienced it personally. But we'd heard our parents, who were kids when it happened, talk about it. Carole's parents had gotten along, though they didn't live well, but my father used to tell me about days when he had nothing but stale bread and turnips to eat and was happy to get them.

The president's TV speech was mostly about the depression, which he claimed would be temporary. At the end of half an hour of optimistic talk, he revealed why he thought the situation wouldn't last. The federal government wasn't going to wait for the sentients in The Ball—if there were any there—to communicate with us. Obviously, The Ball was hostile. So the survey expedition had been canceled. Tomorrow, the USA, the USSR, France, West Germany, Israel, India, Japan and China would send up an armada of rockets tipped with H-bombs. The orbits and the order of battle were determined this morning by computers; one after the other, the missiles would zero in until The Ball was completely destroyed. It would be overkill with a vengeance.

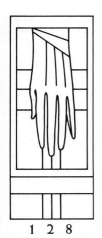

"That ought to bring up the stock market!" I said.

And so, after I've finished recording, to bed. To-morrow, we'll follow our instructions on the notes, relisten to the tapes, reread certain sections of the newspapers and await the news on the TV. To hell with going to the courthouse; nobody's going to be there anyway.

Oh, yes. With all this confusion and excitement, everybody, myself included, forgot that today was my birthday! Wait a minute! It's *not* my birthday!

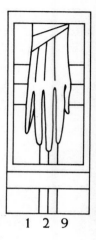

True Date: June 5. Subjective Date: May 16, same year.

I woke up mad at Carole because of our argument the previous day. Not that of June 4, of course, but our brawl of May 15. We'd been at a party given by the Burlingtons, where I met a beautiful young artist, Roberta Gardner. Carole thought I was paying too much attention to her because she looked like Myrna. Maybe I was. On the other hand, I really was interested in her paintings. It seemed to me that she had a genuine talent. When we got home, Carole tore into me, ac-cused me of still being in love with Myrna. My protests did no good whatsoever. Finally, I told her we might as well get a divorce if she couldn't forgive and forget. She ran crying out of the room and slept on the sofa downstairs.

I don't remember what reconciled us, of course, but we must have worked it out, otherwise we wouldn't still be married.

Anyway, I woke up determined to see a divorce lawyer today. I was sick about what Mike and Tom would have to go through. But it would be better for them to be spared our terrible quarrels. I can remember my reactions when I was an adolescent and overheard my parents fighting. It was a relief, though a sad one, when they separated.

Thinking this, I reached for my glasses. And I found the note. And so another voyage into confusion, disbelief and horror.

Now that the panic has eased off somewhat, May 18 is back in the saddle—somewhat. Carole and I are, in a sense, still in that day, and things are a bit cool.

It's 1:00 P.M. now. We just watched the first rockets take off. Ten of them, one after the other.

It's 1:35 P.M. Via satellite, we watched the Japanese missiles.

We just heard that the Chinese and Russian rockets are being launched. When the other nations send theirs up, there will be thirty-seven in all.

No news at 12:30 A.M., June 5. In this case, no news must be bad news. But what could have happened? The newscasters won't say; they just talk around the subject.

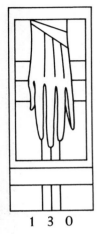

VII

True Date: June 6. Subjective Date: May 13, same year.

My records say that this morning was just like the other four. Hell.

One o'clock. The president, looking like a sad old man, though he's only forty-four, reported the catastrophe. All thirty-seven rockets were blown up by their own H-bombs about three thousand miles from The Ball. We saw some photographs of them taken from the orbiting labs. They weren't very impressive. No mushroom clouds, of course, and not even much light.

The Ball has weapons we can't hope to match. And if it can activate our H-bombs out in space, it should be able to do the same to those on Earth's surface. My God! It could wipe out all life if it wished to do so!

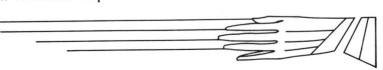

Near the end of the speech, the president did throw out a line of hope. With a weak smile—he was trying desperately to give us his big vote-winning one—he said that all was not lost by any means. A new plan, called Project Toro, was being drawn up even as he spoke.

Toro was Spanish for bull, I thought, but I didn't say so. Carole and the kids wouldn't have thought it funny, and I didn't think it was so funny myself. Anyway, I thought, maybe it's a Japanese word meaning *victory* or *destruction* or something like that.

Toro, as it turned out, was the name of a small irregularly shaped asteroid about 2.413 kilometers long and 1.609 kilometers wide. Its peculiar orbit had been calculated in 1972 by an L. Danielsson of the Swedish Royal Institute of Technology and a W. H. Ip of the University of California at San Diego. Toro, the president said, was bound into a resonant orbit with the Earth. Each time Toro came near the Earth—"near" was sometimes 12.6 million miles—it got exactly enough energy or "kick" from the Earth to push it on around so that it would come back for another near passage.

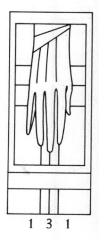

1 3 1

But the orbit was unstable, which meant that both Earth and Venus take turns controlling the asteroid. For a few centuries, Earth governs Toro; then Venus takes over. Earth has controlled Toro since A.D. 1580. Venus will take over in 2200. Earth grabs it again in 2350; Venus gets it back in 2800.

I was wondering what all this stuff about this celestial ping-pong game was about. Then the president said that it was possible to land rockets on Toro. In fact, the plan called for many shuttles to land there carrying parts of huge rocket motors, which would be assembled on Toro.

When the motors were erected on massive and deep

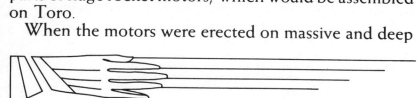

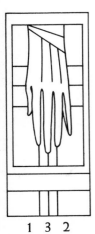

1 3 2

stands, power would be applied to nudge Toro out of its orbit. This would require many trips by many rockets with cargoes of fuel and spare parts for the motors. The motors would burn out a number of times. Eventually, though, the asteroid would be placed in an orbit that would end in a direct collision with The Ball. Toro's millions of tons of hard rock and nickel-steel would destroy The Ball utterly, would turn it into pure energy.

"Yes," I said aloud, "but what's to keep The Ball from just changing its orbit? Its sensors will detect the asteroid; it'll change course; Toro will go on by it, like a train on a track."

This was the next point of the president's speech. The failure of the attack had revealed at least one item of information, or, rather, verified it. The radiation of the H-bombs had blocked off, disrupted, all control and observation of the rockets by radar and laser. In their final approach, the rockets had gone in blind, as it were, unable to be regulated from Earth. But if the bombs did this to our sensors, they must be doing the same to The Ball's.

So, just before Toro's course is altered to send it into its final path, H-bombs will be set off all around The Ball. In effect, it will be enclosed in a sphere of radiation. It will have no sensor capabilities. Nor will The Ball *believe* that it will have to alter its orbit to dodge Toro. It will have calculated that Toro's orbit won't endanger it. After the radiation fills the space around it, it won't be able to *see* that Toro is being given a final series of nudges to push it into a collision course.

The project is going to require immense amounts of materials and manpower. The USA can't handle it alone; Toro is going to be a completely international job. What one nation can't provide, the other will.

The president ended with a few words about how Project Toro, plus the situation of memory loss, is going to bring about a radical revision of the economic setup. He's going to announce the outlines of the new structure—not just policy but structure—two days from now. It'll be designed, so he says, to restore prosperity and, not incidentally, rid society of many problems plaguing it since the industrial revolution.

"Yes, but how long will Project Toro take?" I said. "Oh, Lord, how long?"

Six years, the president said, as if he'd heard me. Perhaps longer.

Six years!

I didn't tell Carole what I could see coming. But she's no dummy. She could figure out some of the things that were bound to happen in six years, and none of them were good.

I never felt so hopeless in my life, and neither did she. But we do have each other, and so we clung tightly for a while. May 18 isn't forgotten, but it seems so unimportant. Mike and Tom cried, I suppose because they knew that this exhibition of love meant something terrible for all of us. Poor kids! They get upset by our hatreds and then become even more upset by our love.

When we realized what we were doing to them, we tried to be jolly. But we couldn't get them to smile.

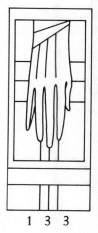

1 3 3

Subjective Date: Four years earlier than the objective date.

I'm writing this, since I couldn't get any new tapes today. The shortage is only temporary, I'm told. I could erase some of the old ones and use them, but it'd be like losing a vital part of myself. And God knows I've lost enough.

Old Mrs. Douglas next door is dead. Killed herself, according to my note on the calendar, April 2 of this year. I never would have thought she'd do it. She was

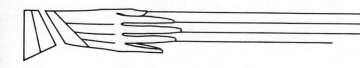

such a strong fundamentalist, and these believe as strongly as the Roman Catholics that suicide is well-nigh unforgivable. I suspect that the double shock of her husband's deaths caused her to take her own life. April 2 was the day he had died. She had had to be hospitalized because of shock and grief for two weeks after his death. Carole and I had had her over to dinner a few times after she came home, and all she could talk about was her dead husband. So I presume that, as she traveled backward to the day of his death, the grief became daily more unbearable. She couldn't face the arrival of the day he died.

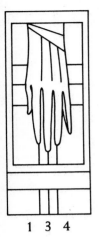

1 3 4

Hers is not the only empty house on the block. Jack Bridger killed his wife and his three kids and his mother-in-law and himself last month—according to my records. Nobody knows why, but I suspect that he couldn't stand seeing his three-year-old girl become no more than an idiot. She'd retrogressed to the day of her birth and perhaps beyond. She'd lost her language abilities and could no longer feed herself. Strangely, she could still walk, and her intelligence potential was high. She had the brain of a three-year-old, fully developed, but lacking all postbirth experience. It would have been better if she hadn't been able to walk. Confined to a cradle, she would at least not have had to be watched every minute.

Little Ann's fate is going to be Tom's. He talks like a five-year-old now. And Mike's fate...my fate ...Carole's...God! We'll end up like Ann! I can't stand thinking about it.

Poor Carole. She has the toughest job. I'm away part of the day, but she has to take care of what are, in effect, a five-year-old and an eight-year-old, getting younger every day. There is no relief for her, since they're always home. All educational institutions, except for certain research laboratories, are closed.

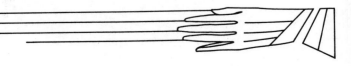

The president says we're going to convert ninety percent of all industries to cybernation. In fact, anything that can be cybernated will be. They have to be. Almost everything, from the mines to the loading equipment to the railroads and trucks and the unloading equipment and the arrangement and dispersal of the final goods at central distribution points.

Are six years enough to do this?

And who's going to pay for this? Never mind, he says. Money is on its way out. The president is a goddamned radical. He's taking advantage of this situation to put over his own ideas, which he sure as hell never revealed during his campaign for election. Sometimes I wonder *who* put The Ball up there. But that idea is sheer paranoia. At least, this gigantic WPA project is giving work to those who are able to work. The rest are on, or going to be on, a minimum guaranteed income, and I mean minimum. But the president says that, in time, everybody will have all he needs, and more, in the way of food, housing, schooling, clothing, etc. *He* says! What if Project Toro doesn't work? And what if it does work? Are we then going to return to the old economy? Of course not! It'll be impossible to abandon everything we've worked on; the new establishment will see to that.

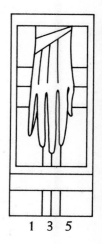

1 3 5

I tried to find out where Myrna lived. I'm making this record in my office, so Carole isn't going to get hold of it. I love her—Myrna, I mean—passionately. I hired her two weeks ago and fell headlong, burningly, in love with her. All this was in 1977, of course, but today, inside of *me*, is 1977.

Carole doesn't know about this, of course. According to the letters and notes from Myrna, which I should have destroyed but, thank God, never had the heart to do, Carole didn't find out about Myrna until two years later. At least, that's what this letter from Myrna

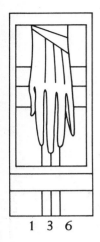

says. She was away visiting her sister then and wrote to me in answer to my letter. A good thing, too, otherwise I wouldn't know what went on then.

My reason tells me to forget about Myrna. And so I will.

I've traveled backward in our affair, from our final bitter parting, to this state, when I was most in love with her. I know this because I've just reread the records of our relationship. It began deteriorating about six months before we split up, but I don't feel those emotions now, of course. And in two weeks I won't feel anything for her. If I don't refer to the records, I won't even know she ever existed.

This thought is intolerable. I have to find her, but I've had no success at all so far. In fourteen days, no, five, since every day ahead takes three more of the past, I'll have no drive to locate her. Because I won't know what I'm missing.

I don't hate Carole. I love her, but with a cool much-married love. Myrna makes me feel like a youth again. I burn exquisitely.

But where is Myrna?

True Date: October 30, a year and four months after The Ball appeared.

I ran into Brackwell Lee, the old mystery story writer today. Like most writers who haven't gone to work for the government propaganda office, he's in a bad way financially. He's surviving on his GMI, but for him there are no more first editions of rare books, new sports cars, Western Reserve or young girls. I stood him three shots of the rotgut which is the only whiskey now served at Grover's and listened to the funny stories he told to pay me for the drinks. But I also had to listen to his tales of woe.

Nobody buys fiction or, in fact, any long works of

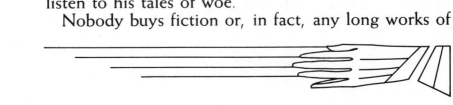

any kind anymore. Even if you're a speed reader and go through a whole novel in one day, you have to start all over again the next time you pick it up. TV writing, except for the propaganda shows, is no alternative. The same old shows are shown every day and enjoyed just as much as yesterday or last year. According to my records, I've seen the hilarious pilot movie of the "Soap Opera Blues" series fifty times.

When old Lee talked about how he had been dropped by the young girls, he got obnoxiously weepy. I told him that that didn't say much for him or the girls either. But if he didn't want to be hurt, why didn't he erase those records that noted his rejections?

He didn't want to do that, though he could give me no logical reason why he shouldn't.

"Listen," I said with a sudden drunken inspiration, "why don't you erase the old records and make some new ones? How you laid this and that beautiful young thing. Describe your conquests in detail. You'll think you're the greatest Casanova that ever lived."

"But that wouldn't be true!"

"You, a writer of lies, say that?" I said. "Anyway, you wouldn't know that they weren't the truth."

"Yeah," he said, "but if I get all charged up and come barreling down here to pick up some tail, I'll be rejected and so'll be right back where I was."

"Leave a stern note to yourself to listen to them only late at night, say, an hour before The Ball puts all to sleep. That way, you won't ever get hurt."

George Palmer wandered in then. I asked him how things were doing.

"I'm up to here handling cases for kids who can't get drivers' licenses," he said. "It's true you can teach anybody how to drive in a day, but the lessons are forgotten the next day. Anyway, it's experience that makes a good driver, and... need I explain more? The kids

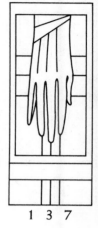

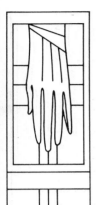

have to have cars, so they drive them regardless. Hence, as you no doubt have forgotten, the traffic accidents and violations are going up and up."

"Is that right?" I said.

"Yeah. There aren't too many in the mornings, since most people don't go to work until noon. However, the new transit system should take care of that when we get it, sometime in 1984 or 5."

"What new transit system?" I said.

"It's been in the papers," he said. "I reread some of last week's this morning. The city of Los Angeles is equipped with a model system now, and it's working so well it's going to be extended throughout Los Angeles County. Eventually, every city of any size in the country'll have it. Nobody'll have to walk more than four blocks to get to a line. It'll cut air pollution by half and the traffic load by three-fourths. Of course, it'll be compulsory; you'll have to show cause to drive a car. And I hate to think about the mess *that's* going to be, the paperwork, the pile-up in the courts and so forth. But after the way the government handled the L.A. riot, the rest of the country should get in line."

"How will the rest of the country know how the government handled it unless they're told?"

"They'll be told. Every day," he said.

"Eventually, there won't be enough time in the day for the news channels to tell us all we'll need to know," I said. "And even if there were enough time, we'd have to spend all day watching TV. So who's going to get the work done?"

"Each person will have to develop his own viewing specialty," he said. "They'll just have to watch the news that concerns them and ignore the rest."

"And how can they do that if they won't know what concerns them until they've run through everything?" I said. "Day after day."

"I'll buy a drink," he said. "Liquor's good for one thing. It makes you forget what you're afraid not to forget."

VIII

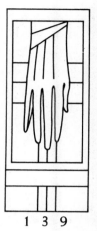

Subjective Date: Eight years before The Ball appeared.
    She came into my office, and I knew at once that she was going to be more than just another client. I'd been suffering all day from the "mirror syndrome," but the sight of her stabilized me. I forgot the thirty-seven-year-old face my twenty-nine-year-old mind had seen in the bathroom that morning. She is a beautiful woman, only twenty-seven. I had trouble at first listening to her story; all I wanted to do was to look at her. I finally understood that she wanted me to get her husband out of jail on a murder rap. It seemed he'd been in since 1976 (real time). She wanted me to get the case reopened, to use the new plea of rehabilitation by retrogression.
    I was supposed to know that, but I had to take a quick look through my resumé before I could tell her what chance she had. Under RBR was the definition of the term and a notation that a number of people had been released because of it. The main idea behind it is that criminals are not the same people they were before they became criminals, if they have lost all memory of the crime. They've traveled backward to goodness, you might say. Of course, RBR doesn't apply to hardened criminals or to someone who'd planned a crime a long time before it was actually committed.
    I asked her why she would want to help a man who had killed his mistress in a fit of rage when he'd found her cheating on him?

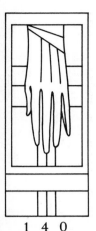

"I love him," she said.

And I love you, I thought.

She gave me some documents from the big rec bag she carried. I looked through them and said, "But you divorced him?"

"Yes, he's really my ex-husband," she said. "But I think of him now as my husband."

No need to ask her why.

"I'll study the case," I said. "You make a note to see me tomorrow. Meantime, how about a drink at the Rover so we can discuss our strategy?"

That's how it all started—again.

It wasn't until a week later, when I was going over some old recs, that I discovered it was *again*. It made no difference. I love her. I also love Carole, rather, *a* Carole. The one who married me six years ago, that is, six years ago in my memory.

But there is the other Carole, the one existing today, the poor miserable wretch who can't get out of the house until I come home. And I can't come home until late evening because I can't get started to work until about twelve noon. It's true that I could come home earlier than I do if it weren't for Myrna. I try. No use. I have to see Myrna.

I tell myself I'm a bastard, which I am, because Carole and the children need me very much. Tom is ten and acts as if he's two. Mike is a four-year-old in a twelve-year-old body. I come home from Myrna to bedlam every day, according to my records, and every day must be like today.

That I feel both guilt and shame doesn't help. I become enraged; I try to suppress my anger, which is born out of my desperation and helplessness and guilt and shame. But it comes boiling out, and then bedlam becomes hell.

I tell myself that Carole and the kids need a tower

of strength now. One who can be calm and reassuring and above all, loving. One who can handle the thousand tedious and aggravating problems that infest every household in this world of diminishing memory. In short, a hero. Because the real heroes, and heroines, are those who deal heroically with the everyday cares of life, though God knows they've been multiplied enormously. It's not the guy who kills a dragon once in his lifetime and then retires that's a hero. It's the guy who kills cockroaches and rats every day, day after day, and doesn't rest on his laurels until he's an old man, if then.

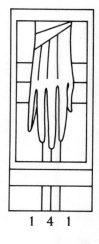

1 4 1

What am I talking about? Maybe I could handle the problems if it weren't for this memory loss. I can't adjust because I can't ever get used to it. My whole being, body and mind, must get the same high-voltage jolt every morning.

The insurance companies have canceled all policies for anybody under twelve. The government's contemplated taking over these policies but has decided against it. It will, however, pay for the burials, since this service is necessary. I don't really think that that many children are being "accidentally" killed because of the insurance money. Most fatalities are obviously just results of neglect or parents going berserk.

I'm getting away from Myrna, trying to, anyway, because I wish to forget my guilt. I love her, but if I didn't see her tomorrow, I'd forget her. But I *will* see her tomorrow. My notes will make sure of that. And each day is, for me, love at first sight. It's a wonderful feeling, and I wish it could go on forever.

If I just had the guts to destroy all reference to her tonight. But I won't. The thought of losing her makes me panic.

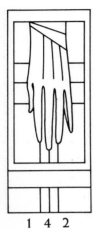

1 4 2

Subjective Date: Sixteen years before The Ball appeared.

I was surprised that I woke up so early.

Yesterday, Carole and I had been married at noon. We'd driven up to this classy motel near Lake Geneva. We'd spent most of our time in bed after we got there, naturally, though we did get up for dinner and champagne. We finally fell asleep about four in the morning. That was why I hadn't expected to wake up at dawn. I reached over to touch Carole, wondering if she would be too sleepy. But she wasn't there.

She's gone to the bathroom, I thought. I'll catch her on the way back.

Then I sat up, my heart beating as if it had suddenly discovered it was alive. The edges of the room got fuzzy, and then the fuzziness raced in toward me.

The dawn light was filtered by the blinds, but I had seen that the furniture was not familiar. I'd never been in this place before.

I sprang out of bed and did not, of course, notice the note sticking out of my glass case. Why should I? I didn't wear glasses then.

Bellowing, "Carole!" I ran down a long and utterly strange hall and past the bathroom door, which was open, and into the room at the other end of the hall. Inside it, I stopped. This was a kids' bedroom: bunks, pennants, slogans, photographs of two young boys, posters and blowups of faces I'd never seen, except one of Laurel and Hardy, some science fiction and Tolkien and Tarzan books, some school texts, and a large flat piece of equipment hanging on the wall. I would not have known that it was a TV set if its controls had not made its purpose obvious.

The bunks had not been slept in. The first rays of

the sun fell on thick dust on a table.

I ran back down the hall, looked into the bathroom again, though I knew no one was there, saw dirty towels, underwear and socks heaped in a corner, and ran back to my bedroom. The blinds did not let enough light in, so I looked for a light switch on the wall. There wasn't any, though there was a small round plate of brass where the switch should have been. I touched it, and the ceiling lights came on.

Carole's side of the bed had not been slept in.

The mirror over the bureau caught me, drew me and held me. Who was this haggard old man staring out from my twenty-three-year-old self? I had gray hair, big bags under my eyes, thickening and sagging features, and a long scar on my right cheek.

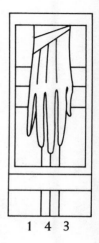

1 4 3

After a while, still dazed and trembling, I picked up a book from the bureau and looked at it. At this close distance, I could just barely make out the title, and, when I opened it, the print was a blur.

I put the book down, *Be Your Own Handyman Around Your House,* and proceeded to go through the house from attic to basement. Several times, I whimpered, "Carole! Carole!" Finding no one, I left the house and walked to the house next door and beat on its door. No one answered; no lights came on inside.

I ran to the next house and tried to wake up the people in it. But there weren't any.

A woman in a house across the street shouted at me. I ran at her, babbling. She was about fifty years old and also hysterical. A moment later, a man her age appeared behind her. Neither listened to me; they kept asking me questions, the same questions I was asking them. Then I saw a black and white police car of a model unknown to me come around the corner half a block away. I ran toward it, then stopped. The car was so silent that I knew even in my panic that it was

electrically powered. The two cops wore strange uniforms, charcoal gray with white helmets topped by red panaches. Their aluminum badges were in the shape of a spread eagle.

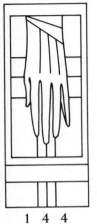

I found out later that the police throughout the country had been federalized. These two were on the night shift and so had had enough time to get reorientated. Even so, one had such a case of the shakes that the other told him to get back into the car and take it easy for a while.

After he got us calmed down, he asked us why we hadn't listened to our tapes.

"What tapes?" we said.

"Where's your bedroom?" he said to the couple.

They led him to it, and he turned on a machine on the bedside table.

"Good morning," a voice said. I recognized it as the husband's. "Don't panic. Stay in bed and listen to me. Listen to everything I say."

The rest was a resumé, by no means short, of the main events since the first day of memory loss. It ended by directing the two to a notebook that would tell them personal things they needed to know, such as where their jobs were, how they could get to them, where their area central distributing stores were, how to use their I.D. cards and so on.

The policeman said, "You have the rec set to turn on at 6:30, but you woke up before then. Happens a lot."

I went back, reluctantly, to the house I'd fled. It was mine, but I felt as if I were a stranger. I ran off my own recs twice. Then I put my glasses on and started to put together my life. The daily rerun of "Narrative of an Old-Young Man Shipwrecked on the Shoals of Time."

I didn't go anyplace today. Why should I? I had no

job. Who needs a lawyer who isn't through law school yet? I did have, I found out, an application in for a position on the police force. The police force was getting bigger and bigger but at the same time was having a large turnover. My recs said that I was to appear at the City Hall for an interview tomorrow.

If I feel tomorrow as I do today, and I will, I probably won't be able to make myself go to the interview. I'm too grief-stricken to do anything but sit and stare or, now and then, get up and pace back and forth, like a sick leopard in a cage made by Time. Even the tranquilizers haven't helped me much.

I have lost my bride the day after we were married. And I love Carole deeply. We were going to live a long happy life and have two children. We would raise them in a house filled with love.

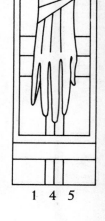

1 4 5

But the recs say that the oldest boy escaped from the house and was killed by a car and Carole, in a fit of anguish and despair, killed the youngest boy and then herself.

They're buried in Springdale Cemetery.

I can't feel a retroactive grief for those strangers called Mike and Tom.

But Carole, lovely laughing Carole, lives in my mind.

Oh, God, why don't I just erase all my recs? Then I'd not have to suffer remorse for all I've done or failed to do. I wouldn't know what a bastard I'd been.

Why don't I do it? Take the past and shed its heartbreaks and its guilts as a snake sheds its skin. Or as the legislature cancels old laws. Press a button, fill the wastebasket, and you're clean and easy again, innocent again. That's the logical thing to do, and I'm a lawyer, dedicated to logic.

Why not? Why not?

But I can't. Maybe I like to suffer. I've liked to inflict suffering, and according to what I understand, those who like to inflict, unconsciously hope to be inflicted upon.

No, that can't be it. At least, not all of it. My main reason for hanging on to the recs is that I don't want to lose my identity. A major part of me, a unique person, is not in the neurons of my mind, where it belongs, but in an electro-mechanical device or in tracings of lead or ink on paper. The protein, the flesh for which I owe, can't hang on to *me*.

I'm becoming less and less, dwindling away, like the wicked witch on whom Dorothy poured water. I'll become a puddle, a wailing voice of hopeless despair, and then . . . nothing.

God, haven't I suffered enough! I said I owe for the flesh and I'm down in Your books. Why do I have to struggle each day against becoming a dumb brute, a thing without memory? Why not rid myself of the struggle? Press the button, fill the wastebasket, discharge my grief in a chaos of magnetic lines and pulped paper?

Sufficient unto the day is the evil thereof.

I didn't realize, Lord, what that really meant.

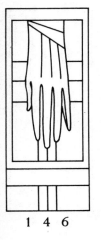

146

X

I will marry Carole in three days. No, I would have. No, I did.

I remember reading a collection of Krazy Kat comic strips when I was twenty-one. One was captioned: COMA REIGNS. Coconino County was in the doldrums, comatose. Nobody, Krazy Kat, Ignatz Mouse, Officer Pupp, nobody had the energy to do anything. Mouse was too lazy even to think about hurling his brickbat. Strange how that sticks in my mind. Strange

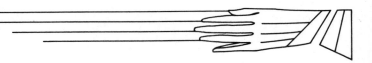

to think that it won't be long before it becomes forever unstuck.

Coma reigns today over the world.

Except for Project Toro, the TV says. And that is behind schedule. But the Earth, Ignatz Mouse, will not allow itself to forget that it must hurl the brickbat, the asteroid. But where Ignatz expressed his love, in a queer perverted fashion, by banging Kat in the back of the head with his brick, the world is expressing its hatred, and its desperation, by throwing Toro at The Ball.

I did manage today to go downtown to my appointment. I did it only to keep from going mad with grief. I was late, but Chief Moberly seemed to expect that I would be. Almost everybody is, he said. One reason for my tardiness was that I got lost. This residential area was nothing in 1968 but a forest out past the edge of town. I don't have a car, and the house is in the middle of the area, which has many winding streets. I do have a map of the area, which I forgot about. I kept going eastward and finally came to a main thoroughfare. This was Route 98, over which I've traveled many times since I was a child. But the road itself, and the houses along it, were strange. The private airport which should have been across the road was gone, replaced by a number of large industrial buildings.

A big sign near a roofed bench told me to wait there for the RTS bus. One would be along every ten minutes, the sign stated.

I waited an hour. The bus, when it came, was not the fully automated vehicle promised by the sign. It held a sleepy-looking driver and ten nervous passengers. The driver didn't ask me for money, so I didn't offer any. I sat down and watched him with an occasional look out of the window. He didn't have a

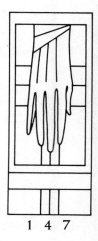

1 4 7

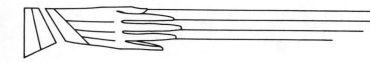

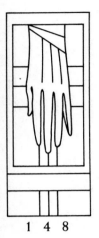

steering wheel. When he wanted the bus to slow down or stop he pushed a lever forward. To speed it up, he pulled back on the lever. The bus was apparently following a single aluminum rail in the middle of the right-hand lane. My recs told me that the automatic pilot and door-opening equipment had never been delivered and probably wouldn't be for some years—if ever. The grand plan of cybernating everything possible had failed. There aren't enough people who can provide the know-how or the man-hours. In fact, everything is going to hell.

The police chief, Adam Moberly, is fifty years old and looks as if he's sixty-five. He talked to me for about fifteen minutes and then had me take a short physical and intelligence test. Three hours after I had walked into the station, I was sworn in. He suggested that I room with two other officers, one of whom was a sixty-year-old veteran, in the hotel across the street from the station. If I had company, I'd get over the morning disorientation more quickly. Besides, the policemen who lived in the central area of the city got preferential treatment in many things, including the rationed supplies.

I refused to move. I couldn't claim that my house was a home to me, but I feel that it's a link to the past, I mean the future, no, I mean the past. Leaving it would be cutting out one more part of me.

Subjective Date: Seventeen years before The Ball appeared.

My mother died today. That is, as far as I'm concerned, she did. The days ahead of me are going to be full of anxiety and grief. She took a long time to die. She found out she had cancer two weeks after my father died. So I'll be voyaging backward in sorrow through my mother and then through my father, who was also sick for a long time.

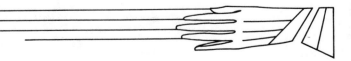

Thank God I won't have to go through every day of that, though. Only a third of them. And these are the last words I'm going to record about their illnesses.

But how can I record them unless I make a recording reminding me not to do so?

I found out from my recs how I'd gotten this big scar on my face. Myrna's ex-husband slashed me before I laid him out with a big ashtray. He was shipped off this time to a hospital for the criminally insane where he died a few months later in the fire that burned every prisoner in his building. I haven't the faintest idea what happened to Myrna after that. Apparently I decided not to record it.

I feel dead tired tonight, and, according to my recs, every night. It's no wonder, if every day is like today. Fires, murders, suicides, accidents and insane people. Babies up to fourteen years old abandoned. And a police department which is ninety percent composed, in effect, of raw rookies. The victims are taken to hospitals where the nurses are only half-trained, if that, and the doctors are mostly old geezers hauled out of retirement.

I'm going to bed soon even if it's only nine o'clock. I'm so exhausted that even Jayne Mansfield couldn't keep me awake. And I dread tomorrow. Besides the usual reasons for loathing it, I have one which I can hardly stand thinking about.

Tomorrow my memory will have slid past the day I met Carole. I won't remember her at all.

Why do I cry because I'll be relieved of a great sorrow?

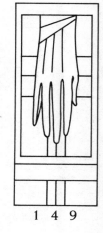

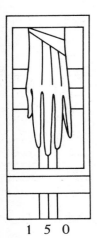

Subjective Date: Twenty-four years before The Ball appeared.

I'm nuts about Jean, and I'm way down because I can't find her. According to my recs, she went to Canada three years after this subjective date. Why? We surely didn't fall in and then out of love? Our love would never die. Her parents must've moved to Canada. And so here we both are in this subjective date. Halfway in it, anyway. Amphibians of time. Is she thinking about me now? Is she unable to think about me, about anything, because she's dead or crazy? Tomorrow I'll start the official wheels grinding. The Canadian government should be able to find her through the International Information Computer Network, according to the recs. Meanwhile, I burn, though with a low flame. I'm so goddamn tired.

Even Marilyn Monroe couldn't get a rise out of me tonight. But Jean. Yeah, Jean. I see her as seventeen years old, tall, slim but full-busted, with creamy white skin and a high forehead and huge blue eyes and glossy black hair and the most kissable lips ever. And broadcasting sex waves so thick you can see them, like heat waves. Wow!

And so tired old Wow goes to bed.

Objective Time: February 6, almost seven years after The Ball appeared.

While I was watching TV to get orientated this morning, a news flash interrupted the program. The president of the United States had died of a heart attack a few minutes before.

"My God!" I said. "Old Eisenhower is dead!"

But the picture of the president certainly wasn't that of Eisenhower. And the name was one I never heard, of course.

I can't feel bad for a guy I never knew.

I got to thinking about him, though. Was he as confused every morning as I was? Imagine a guy waking up, thinking he's a senator in Washington and then he finds he's the president? At least, he knows something about running the country. But it's no wonder the old pump conked out. The TV says we've had five prexies, mostly real old guys, in the last seven years. One was shot; one dived out of the White House window onto his head; two had heart attacks; one went crazy and almost caused a war, as if we didn't have grief enough, for crying out loud.

Even after the orientation, I really didn't get it. I guess I'm too dumb for anything to percolate through my dome.

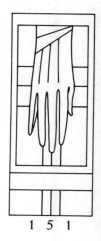

A policeman called and told me I'd better get my ass down to work. I said I didn't feel up to it, besides, why would I want to be a cop? He said that if I didn't show, I might go to jail. So I showed.

True Date: Eight and one-half years post-Ball. Subjective Date: Twenty-four years pre-Ball.

Here I am, eleven years old, going on ten.

In one way, that is. The other way, here I am forty-three and going on about sixty. At least, that's what my face looks like to me. Sixty.

This place is just like a prison except some of us get treated like trusties. According to the work chart, I leave through the big iron gates every day at twelve noon with a demolition crew. We tore down five partly burned houses today. The gang chief, old Rogers, says it's just WPA work, whatever that is. Anyway, one of the guys I work with kept looking more and more familiar. Suddenly, I felt like I was going to pass out. I put down my sledgehammer and walked over to him, and I said, "Aren't you Stinky Davis?"

He looked funny and then he said, "Jesus! You're Gabby! Gabby Franham!"

I didn't like his using the Lord's name in vain, but I guess he can be excused.

Nothing would've tasted good the way I felt, but the sandwiches we got for breakfast, lunch and supper tasted like they had a dash of oil in them. Engine oil, I mean. The head honcho, he's eighty if he's a day, says his recs told him they're derived from petroleum. The oil is converted into a kind of protein and then flavoring and stuff is added. Oilburgers, they call them.

Tonight, before lights-out, we watched the prez give a speech. He said that, within a month, Project Toro will be finished. One way or the other. And all this memory loss should stop. I can't quite get it even if I was briefed this morning. Men on the moon, un-manned ships on Venus and Mars, all since I was eleven years old. And The Black Ball, the thing from outer space. And now we're pushing asteroids around. Talk about your science fiction!

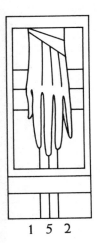

1 5 2

XII

Objective Time: September 4, eight years post-Ball.

Today's the day.

Actually, the big collision'll be tomorrow, ten min-utes before 1:00 A.M. . . . but I think of it as today. Toro, going 150,000 miles an hour, will run head-on into The Ball. Maybe.

Here I am again, Mark Franham, recording just in case The Ball does dodge out of the way and I have to depend on my recs. It's 7:00 P.M. and after that raunchy supper of oilburgers, potato soup and canned carrots, fifty of us gathered around set No. 8. There's

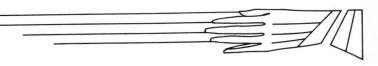

a couple of scientists talking now, discussing theories about just what The Ball is and why it's been taking our memories away from us. Old Doctor Charles Presley—any relation to Elvis?—thinks The Ball is some sort of unmanned survey ship. When it finds a planet inhabited by sentient life, sentient means intelligent, it takes specimens. Specimens of the mind, that is. It unpeels people's minds four day's worth at a time, because that's all it's capable of. But it can do it to billions of specimens. It's like it was reading our minds but destroying the mind at the same time. Presley said it was like some sort of Heisenberg principle of the mind. The Ball can't observe our memories closely without disturbing them.

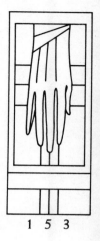

This Ball, Presley says, takes our memories and stores them. And when it's through with us, sucked us dry, it'll take off for another planet circling some far-off star. Someday, it'll return to its home planet, and the scientists there will study the recordings of our minds.

The other scientist, Dr. Marbles—he's still got his, ha! ha!—asked why any species advanced enough to be able to do this could be so callous? Surely, the extees must know what great damage they're doing to us. Wouldn't they be too ethical for this?

Doc Presley says maybe they think of us as animals, they are so far above us. Doc Marbles says that could be. But it could also be that whoever built The Ball have different brains than we do. Their mind-reading ray, or whatever it is, when used on themselves doesn't disturb the memory patterns. But we're different. The extees don't know this, of course. Not now, anyway. When The Ball comes home, and the extees read our minds, they'll be shocked at what they've done to us. But it'll be too late then.

Presley and Marbles got into an argument about how the extees would be able to interpret their recordings.

How could they translate our languages when they have no references—I mean, referents? How're they going to translate *chair* and *recs* and *rock and roll* and *yucky* and so on when they don't have anybody to tell them their meanings. Marbles said they wouldn't have just words; they'd have mental images to associate with the words. And so on. Some of the stuff they spouted I didn't understand at all.

I do know one thing, though, and I'm sure those bigdomes do, too. But they wouldn't be allowed to say it over TV because we'd be even more gloomy and hopeless-feeling. That is, what if right now the computers in The Ball are translating our languages, reading our minds, as they're recorded? Then they know all about Project Toro. They'll be ready for the asteroid, destroy it if they have the weapons to do it, or, if they haven't, they'll just move The Ball into a different orbit.

I'm not going to say anything to the other guys about this. Why make them feel worse?

It's ten o'clock now. According to regulations posted up all over the place, it's time to go to bed. But nobody is. Not tonight. You don't sleep when the End of the World may be coming up.

I wish my Mom and Dad were here. I cried this morning when I found they weren't in this dump, and I asked the chief where they were. He said they were working in a city nearby, but they'd be visiting me soon. I think he lied.

Stinky saw me crying, but he didn't say anything. Why should he? I'll bet he's shed a few when he thought nobody was looking, too.

Twelve o'clock. Midnight. Less than an hour to go. Then, the big smash! Or, I hate to think about it, the big flop. We won't be able to see it directly because the skies are cloudy over most of North America. But we've got a system worked out so we can see it on

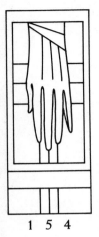

TV. If there's a gigantic flash when the Toro and The Ball collide, that is.

What if there isn't? Then we'll soon be just like those grown-up kids, some of them twenty years old, that they keep locked up in the big building in the northwest corner of this place. Saying nothing but Da Da or Ma Ma, drooling, filling their diapers. If they got diapers, because old Rogers says he heard, today, of course, they don't wear nothing. The nurses come in once a day and hose them and the place down. The nurses don't have time to change and wash diapers and give personal baths. They got enough to do just spoon-feeding them.

Three and a half more hours to go, and I'll be just like them. Unless, before then, I flip, and they put me in that building old Rogers calls the puzzle factory. They're all completely out of their skulls, he says, and even if memloss stops tonight, they won't change any.

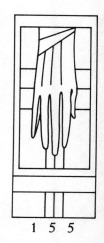

1 5 5

Old Rogers says there's fifty million less people in the United States than there were in 1980, according to the recs. And a good thing, too, he says, because it's all we can do to feed what we got!

Come on, Toro! You're our last chance!

If Toro doesn't make it, I'll kill myself! I will! I'm not going to let myself become an idiot. Anyway, by the time I do become one, there won't be enough food to go around for those that do have their minds. I'll be starving to death. I'd rather get it over with now than go through that.

God'll forgive me.

God, You know I want to be a minister of the gospel when I grow up and that I want to help people. I'll marry a good woman, and we'll have children that'll be brought up right. And we'll thank You every day for the good things of life and battle the bad things.

Love, that's what I got, Lord. Love for You and love

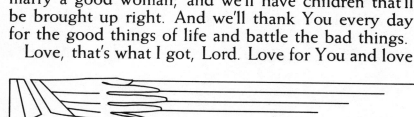

for Your people. So don't make me hate You. Guide Toro right into The Ball, and get us started on the right path again.

I wish Mom and Dad were here.

Twelve-thirty. In twenty minutes, we'll know.

The TV says the H-bombs are still going off all around The Ball.

The TV says the people on the East Coast are falling asleep. The rays, or whatever The Ball uses, aren't being affected by the H-bomb radiation. But that doesn't mean that its sensors aren't. I pray to God that they are cut off.

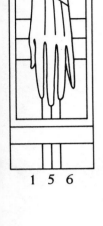

156

Ten minutes to go. Toro's got twenty-five thousand miles to go. Our sensors can't tell whether or not The Ball's still on its original orbit. I hope it is; I hope it is! If it's changed its path, then we're through! Done! Finished! Wiped out!

Five minutes to go; twelve thousand five hundred miles to go.

I can see in my mind's eyes The Ball, almost half a mile in diameter, hurtling on its orbit, blind as a bat, I hope and pray, the bombs, the last of the five thousand bombs, flashing, and Toro, a mile and a half long, a mile wide, millions of tons of rock and nickel-steel, charging toward its destined spot.

If it *is* destined.

But space *is* big, and even the Ball and Toro are small compared to all that emptiness out there. What if the mathematics of the scientists is just a little off, or the rocket motors on Toro aren't working just like they're supposed to, and Toro just tears on by The Ball? It's got to meet The Ball at the exact time and place, it's just *got* to!

I wish the radars and lasers could see what's going on.

Maybe it's better they can't. If we knew that The

Ball had changed course... but this way we still got hope.

If Toro misses, I'll kill myself, I swear it.

Two minutes to go. One hundred and twenty seconds. The big room is silent except for kids like me praying or talking quietly into our recs or praying and talking and sobbing.

The TV says the bombs have quit exploding. No more flashes until Toro hits The Ball—if it does. Oh, God, let it hit, let it hit!

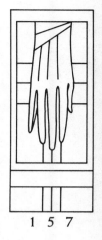

The unmanned satellites are going to open their camera lenses at the exact second of impact and take a quick shot. The cameras are encased in lead, the shutters are lead, and the equipment is special, mostly mechanical, not electrical, almost like a human eyeball. If the cameras see the big flash, they'll send an electrical impulse through circuits, also encased in lead, to a mechanism that'll shoot a big thin-shelled ball out. This is crammed with flashpowder, the same stuff photographers use, and mixed with oxygen pellets so the powder will ignite. There's to be three of the biggest flashes you ever saw. Three. Three for Victory.

If Toro misses, then only one flashball'll be set off.

Oh, Lord, don't let it happen!

Planes with automatic pilots'll be cruising above the clouds, and their equipment will see the flashes and transmit them to the ground TV equipment.

One minute to go.

Come on, God!

Don't let it happen, please don't let it happen, that some place way out there, some thousands of years from now, some weird-looking character reads this and finds out to his horror what his people have done to us. Will he feel bad about it? Lot of good that'll do. You, out there, I hate you! God, how I hate you!

Our Father which art in Heaven, fifteen seconds,

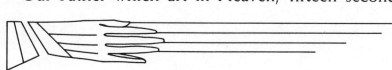

Hallowed be Thy name, ten seconds, Thy will be done, five seconds, Thy will be done, but if it's thumbs down, God, why? Why? What did I ever do to You?

The screen's blank! Oh, my God, the screen's blank! What happened? Transmission trouble? Or they're afraid to tell us the truth?

It's on! It's on!

YAAAAAAY!

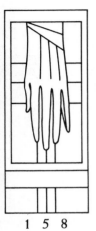

XIII

July 4, Twenty-two years post-Ball.

I may erase this. If I have any sense, I will. If I had any sense, I wouldn't make it in the first place.

Independence Day, and we're still under an iron rule. But old Dick the Dictator insists that when there's no longer a need for strict control, the Constitution will be restored, and we'll be a democracy again. He's ninety-five years old and can't last much longer. The vice-president is only eighty, but he's as tough an octogenarian as ever lived. And he's even more of a totalitarian than Dick. And when have men ever voluntarily relinquished power?

I'm one of the elite, so I don't have it so bad. Just being fifty-seven years old makes me a candidate for that class. In addition, I have my Ph.D. in education and I'm a part-time minister. I don't know why I say part-time, since there aren't any full-time ministers outside of the executives of the North American Council of Churches. The People can't afford full-time divines. Everybody has to work at least ten hours a day. But I'm better off than many. I've been eating fresh beef and pork for three years now. I have a nice house I don't have to share with another family. The house

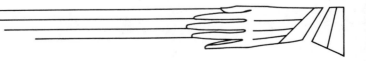

isn't the one my recs say I once owned. The People took it over to pay for back taxes. It did me no good to protest that property taxes had been canceled during The Interim. That, say The People, ended when The Ball was destroyed.

But how could I pay taxes on it when I was only eleven years old, in effect?

I went out this afternoon, it being a holiday, with Leona to Springdale. We put flowers on her parents' and sisters' graves, none of whom she remembers, and on my parents' and Carole's and the children's graves, whom I know only through the recs. I prayed for the forgiveness of Carole and the boys.

Near Carole's grave was Stinky Davis's. Poor fellow, he went berserk the night The Ball was destroyed and had to be put in a padded cell. Still mad, he died five years later.

I sometimes wonder why I didn't go mad, too. The daily shocks and jars of memloss should have made everyone fall apart. But a certain number of us were very tough, tougher than we deserved. Even so, the day-to-day attack by alarm syndromes did its damage. I'm sure that years of life were cut off the hardiest of us. We're the shattered generation. And this is bad for the younger ones, who'll have no older people to lead them in the next ten years or so.

Or is it such a bad thing?

At least, those who were in their early twenties or younger when The Ball was smashed are coming along fine. Leona herself was twenty then. She became one of my students in high school. She's thirty-five physically but only fifteen in what the kids call "intage" or internal age. But since education goes faster for adults, and all those humanities courses have been eliminated, she graduated from high school last June. She still wants to be a doctor of medicine, and God knows we

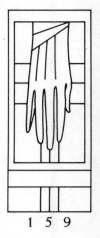

1 5 9

need M.D.'s. She'll be forty-two before she gets her degree. We're planning on having two children, the maximum allowed, and it's going to be tough raising them while she's in school. But God will see us through.

As we were leaving the cemetery, Margie Oleander, a very pretty girl of twenty-five, approached us. She asked me if she could speak privately to me. Leona didn't like that, but I told her that Margie probably wanted to talk to me about her grades in my geometry class.

Margie did talk somewhat about her troubles with her lessons. But then she began to ask some questions about the political system. Yes, I'd better erase this, and if it weren't for old habits, I'd not be doing this now.

After a few minutes, I became uneasy. She sounded as if she were trying to get me to show some resentment about the current situation.

Is she an agent provocateur or was she testing me for potential membership in the underground?

Whatever she was doing, she was in dangerous waters. So was I. I told her to ask her political philosophy teacher for answers. She said she'd read the textbook, which is provided by the government. I muttered something about, "Render unto Caesar's what is Caesar's," and walked away.

But she came after me and asked if I could talk to her in my office tomorrow. I hesitated and then said I would.

I wonder if I would have agreed if she weren't so beautiful?

When we got home, Leona made a scene. She accused me of chasing after the younger girls because she was too old to stimulate me. I told her that I was no senile King David, which she should be well aware of, and she said she's listened to my recs and she knew

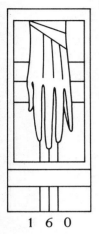

what kind of man I was. I told her I'd learned from my mistakes. I've gone over the recs of the missing years many times.

"Yes," she said, "you know about them intellectually. But you don't *feel* them!"

Which is true.

I'm outside now and looking up into the night. Up there, out there, loose atoms and molecules float around, cold and alone, debris of the memory records of The Ball, atoms and molecules of what were once incredibly complex patterns, the memories of thirty-two years of the lives of four and a half billion human beings. Forever lost, except in the mind of One.

Oh, Lord, I started all over again as an eleven-year-old. Don't let me make the same mistakes again.

You've given us tomorrow again, but we've very little past to guide us.

Tomorrow I'll be very cool and very professional with Margie. Not too much, of course, since there should be a certain warmth between teacher and pupil.

If only she did not remind me of . . . whom?

But that's impossible. I can remember nothing from The Interim. Absolutely nothing.

But what if there are different kinds of memory?

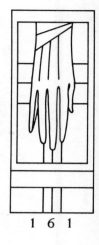

THE SLICED-
CROSSWISE ONLY-
ON-TUESDAY
WORLD

.

The dream, like so many of my dreams, was edged in gray fog. Before me on the perfectly flat gray plain were a dozen or so circular dwellings with conical roofs. These were about eight feet tall and made of some gray material which I knew was the dried gelatinous stuff spat out by some giant insect, probably a Brobdingnagian termite. A rectangular opening was in the front of each bullet-shaped or rocket-shaped or penis-shaped hut, and tall, thin, melancholy white people, as pale as if they had never known sunlight, went silently in and out of the openings.

Then the dream faded. Or perhaps, I do not remember the rest of it.

This dream was the genesis of the story you are about to read.

I wish I could explain how the dream metamorphosed from something meaningless to me into something meaningful. I have dived into myself and swum through heavy wetness, through dark deep-sea pressures and twisting tunnels and murky caverns to find the key to this dream. But I still do not know how the brief bizarre scene became a story which describes, among other things, how to solve overpopulation and the problems attendant thereto. There seems to be no connection between the night-flickerings in my mind and what is produced by conscious story-building.

My unconscious was trying to tell me something, to flash some kind of illumination, but it spoke in a foreign tongue or flashed a movie without subtitles.

I have had dreams with subtitles, but this was not one of them.

In any event, waking that morning, I at once saw how, if certain scientific discoveries could be made, then Homo sapiens would have the solution for cutting down food, energy, and materials comsumption and living space use to one-seventh of what they are now. Or to one-seventh of what they will be when Earth's human swarm becomes even more numerous.

The concept of "freezing" inanimate objects or living beings by quickly stopping atomic motion in them is not new. As far as I know, the concept originated in a science-fiction magazine in the early 1930's. I wish I could remember the title and the author. I can't; I read too many stories when I was young—hundreds of them.

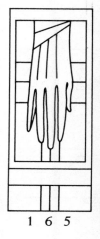

1 6 5

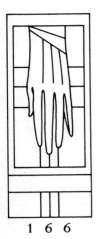

However, the writer probably got the idea from the Biblical story of Lot's wife. Poor wretch, she was too curious and looked back at the destruction of Sodom and Gomorrah even though God and her husband had warned her not to do so. So God turned her into a pillar of salt for her disobedience and monkey curiosity. Just why is not explained. I would think that witnessing the horrible destruction of the cities of the plain would have been required. The spectacle would have been a valuable lesson in morality, branded in Mrs. Lot's mind. It would also not have hurt Mr. Lot.

We can surmise, however, that the earthquake which actually shook down these two ancient San Franciscos also toppled the salt pillar. And that, when the rains came, they dissolved the unmortal remains.

Did Lot covertly chip off a chunk of his wife as a souvenir before leaving her? We'll never know. The Old Testament is admirably lacking in such details, preferring to stick to just plain, mainly unadorned story-telling except when it deviates tiresomely into genealogies and Jeremiads.

If he did chip off a hunk of sodium chloride, what part of her body did he take? Such things naggle at me, and that question might be the basis for a story. The choice of the part would show to the reader just what sort of man Lot was. However, we do know that he was a lush and that he impregnated his daughters later on. Perhaps he wanted to get rid of his wife so that he could drink without her nagging at him and also so that he could lay his daughters. (It's only fair to point out that this was their idea, not his. But then the Bible was written by men, and we may not be getting the true story.) I suspect that the story about the conversion of Mrs. Lot to salt was a coverup for murder.

Whatever really happened, I have this idea for a tale which might be titled: "A Piece of Lot's Wife." The story could go to Playboy.

I hope that the reader will forgive me for wandering off the highway of this essay. The ramble is not irrelevant; it shows how a writer's mind—mine, anyway—works.

Before writing the story at hand, I sketched out the background of the society based on the means for stopping (and starting up again) atomic motion. I figured out by the calendar just how long the seasons would be for a person who lived only one day of the week or four days out of every twenty-eight days. I also tackled other problems, and, I thought, solved them all. I did, too, as far the short story was concerned.

Some years later, I decided that the exposition of this once-a-week Earthwide society should not be the last. I'd write a novel in which it could be much more detailed. The gears, sprockets, and electrical circuitry would be shown en passant while my protagonist was hunting and being hunted through the flickering labyrinth of days and nights.

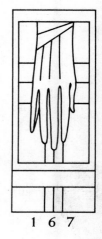

The outline of the novel became very long and complex. I had to make the society work realistically, and I had to consider every weak part in it and every objection to it. I had to make a coherent whole of it, make it as logical and functional as I could. Also, show the illogic and dysfunctions in the society.

It would not be perfect. No human society has been, is, or will be perfect. Human societies are not ant hills. They function at what I would estimate is fifty percent efficiency. Nevertheless, the once-a-week society had to function well enough to keep from breaking down. It can change, of course. All societies change. And what people think of as "breaking down" is often only change for better or worse. Better for some people; worse, for others.

This novel will be titled Dayworld and will probably be written in 1984. This seems to be an appropriate date for the writing, though the society of Dayworld will be far more desirable and optimistic than Orwell's.

The locale will be Manhattan in about a thousand years after the story at hand takes place.

The protagonist is, at this time, named Lewis Clark Cortez. He'll be descended from Daniel Boone and also from, among others, a twentieth-century Puerto Rican, Hernando Cortez. He won't be "ethnic." The Spanish-speaking citizens of the area now known as the United States of America will have been assimilated.

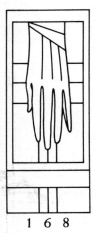

But the process of assimilation will have resulted somewhat in changing the assimilators, too. The becomers become part of the becomees and vice versa. What goes in comes out changed and changing.

I pause to point out to the reader that what is mislabeled as WASP is also "ethnic." Think about this, and then start rejecting all categories. It probably won't do much good, since you'll at once make new categories to fill in the holes left by rejecting the old. But the process might make your mind more flexible. You might slough off, snakelike, old prejudices, old habits, and old mental and emotional reflexes. Not that the new is always necessarily better than the old. It's always best to dive for the ground if you hear bullets whistling nearby or a voice crying hate. Of course, you might fall on a land mine while you're seeking cover.

One of the land mines in science-fiction is scientific credibility. Is such a device as an atom-stopper possible? I'd say yes, it's possible. But neither the theory of atomic-motion-halting nor the power needed if we did have the means exists now, as far as I know. This story assumes that the means and power are available. I will have to supply a scientific or at least quasi-scientific means and power for making the "stoners" in this tale credible when I write the novel.

You'll have to wait until 1985 before the novel comes out. Meanwhile, read about the man who unknowingly prepared a land mine and became its victim.

Getting into Wednesday was almost impossible. Tom Pym had thought about living on other days of the week. Almost everybody with any imagination did. There were even TV shows speculating on this. Tom Pym had even acted in two of these. But he had no genuine desire to move out of his own world. Then his house burned down.

This was on the last day of the eight days of spring. He awoke to look out the door at the ashes and the firemen. A man in a white asbestos suit motioned for him to stay inside. After fifteen minutes, another man in a suit gestured that it was safe. He pressed the button by the door, and it swung open. He sank down in the ashes to his ankles; they were a trifle warm under the inch-thick coat of water-soaked crust.

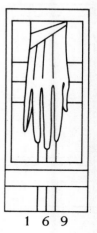

169

There was no need to ask what had happened, but he did anyway.

The fireman said, "A short-circuit, I suppose. Actually, we don't know. It started shortly after midnight, between the time that Monday quit and we took over."

Tom Pym thought that it must be strange to be a fireman or a policeman. Their hours were so different, even though they were still limited by the walls of midnight.

By then the others were stepping out of their stoners or "coffins" as they were often called. That left sixty still occupied.

They were due for work at 08:00. The problem of getting new clothes and a place to live would have to be put off until off-hours, because the TV studio where they worked was behind in the big special it was due to put on in 144 days.

They ate breakfast at an emergency center. Tom Pym asked a grip if he knew of any place he could stay. Though the government would find one for him, it might not look very hard for a convenient place.

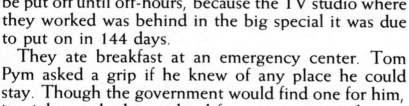

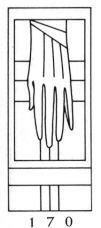

The grip told him about a house only six blocks from his former house. A makeup man had died, and as far as he knew the vacancy had not been filled. Tom got onto the phone at once, since he wasn't needed at that moment, but the office wouldn't be open until ten, as the recording informed him. The recording was a very pretty girl with red hair, tourmaline eyes, and a very sexy voice. Tom would have been more impressed if he had not known her. She had played in some small parts in two of his shows, and the maddening voice was not hers. Neither was the color of her eyes.

At noon he called again, got through after a ten-minute wait, and asked Mrs. Bellefield if she would put through a request for him. Mrs. Bellefield reprimanded him for not having phoned sooner; she was not sure that anything could be done today. He tried to tell her his circumstances and then gave up. Bureaucrats! That evening he went to a public emergency place, slept for the required four hours while the inductive fields speeded up his dreaming, woke up, and got into the upright cylinder of eternium. He stood for ten seconds, gazing out through the transparent door at other cylinders with their still figures, and then he pressed the button. Approximately fifteen seconds later he became unconscious.

He had to spend three more nights in the public stoner. Three days of fall were gone; only five left. Not that that mattered in California so much. When he had lived in Chicago, winter was like a white blanket being shaken by a madwoman. Spring was a green explosion. Summer was a bright roar and a hot breath. Fall was the topple of a drunken jester in garish motley.

The fourth day, he received notice that he could move into the very house he had picked. This surprised and pleased him. He knew of a dozen who had spent a whole year—forty-eight days or so—in a public

station while waiting. He moved in the fifth day, with three days of spring to enjoy. But he would have to use up his two days off to shop for clothes, bring in groceries and other goods, and get acquainted with his housemates. Sometimes he wished he had not been born with the compulsion to act. TV'ers worked five days at a stretch, sometimes six, while a plumber, for instance, only put in three days out of seven.

The house was as large as the other, and the six extra blocks to walk would be good for him. It held eight people per day, counting himself. He moved in that evening, introduced himself, and got Mabel Curta, who worked as a secretary for a producer, to fill him in on the household routine. After he made sure that his stoner had been moved into the stoner room, he could relax somewhat.

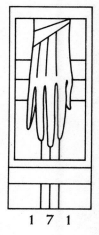

Mabel Curta had accompanied him into the stoner room, since she had appointed herself his guide. She was a short, overly curved woman of about thirty-five (Tuesday time). She had been divorced three times, and marriage was no more for her unless, of course, Mr. Right came along. Tom was between marriages himself, but he did not tell her so.

"We'll take a look at your bedroom," Mabel said. "It's small but it's soundproofed, thank God."

He started after her, but stopped. She looked back through the doorway and said, "What is it?"

"This girl . . ."

There were sixty-three of the tall gray enternium cylinders. He was looking through the door of the nearest at the girl within.

"Wow! Really beautiful!"

If Mabel felt any jealousy, she suppressed it.

"Yes, isn't she!"

The girl had long, black, slightly curly hair, a face that could have launched him a thousand times a thousand times, a figure that had enough but not too much, and long legs. Her eyes were open; in the dim light they looked a purplish-blue. She wore a thin silvery dress.

The plate by the top of the door gave her vital data. Jennie Marlowe. Born 2031 A.D., San Marino, California. She would be twenty-four years old. Actress. Unmarried. Wednesday's child.

"What's the matter?" Mabel said.

"Nothing."

How could he tell her that he felt sick in his stomach from a desire that could never be satisfied? Sick from beauty?

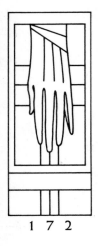

> For will in us is over-ruled by fate.
> Who ever loved, that loved not at first sight?

"What?" Mabel said, and then, after laughing, "You must be kidding."

She wasn't angry. She realized that Jennie Marlowe was no more competition than if she were dead. She was right. Better for him to busy himself with the living of this world. Mabel wasn't too bad; cuddly, really, and, after a few drinks, rather stimulating.

They went downstairs afterward after 18:00 to the TV room. Most of the others were there, too. Some had their ear plugs in; some were looking at the screen but talking. The newscast was on, of course. Everybody was filling up on what had happened last Tuesday and today. The Speaker of the House was retiring after his term was up. His days of usefulness were over, and his recent ill health showed no signs of disappearing. There was a shot of the family graveyard in Mississippi with the pedestal reserved for him. When science someday learned how to rejuvenate, he would come out of stonerment.

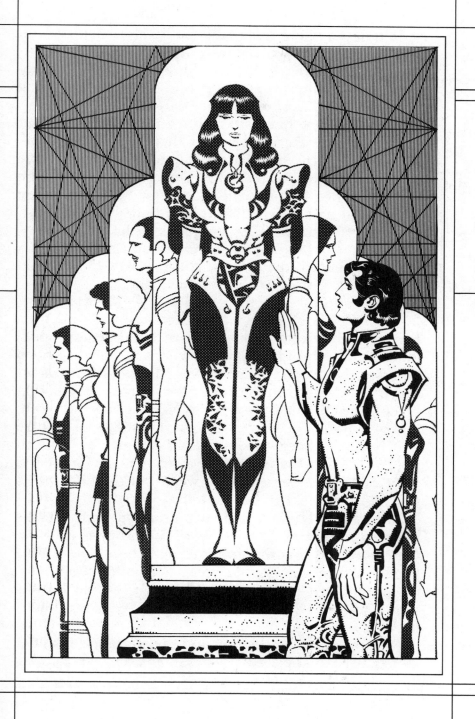

"That'll be the day!" Mabel said. She squirmed on his lap.

"Oh, I think they'll crack it," he said. "They're already on the track; they've succeeded in stopping the aging of rabbits."

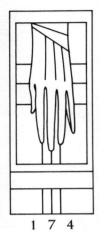

"I don't mean that," she said. "Sure, they'll find out how to rejuvenate people. But then what? You think they're going to bring them all back? With all the people they got now, and then they'll double, maybe triple, maybe quadruple the population? You think they won't just leave them standing out there?" She giggled, and said, "What would the pigeons do without them?"

He squeezed her waist. At the same time, he had a vision of himself squeezing *that* girl's waist. Hers would be soft enough but with no hint of fat.

Forget about her. Think of now. Watch the news.

A Mrs. Wilder had stabbed her husband and then herself with a kitchen knife. Both had been stonered immediately after the police arrived, and they had been taken to the hospital. An investigation of a work slow-down in the county government offices was taking place. The complaints were that Monday's people were not setting up the computers for Tuesday's. The case was being referred to the proper authorities of both days. The Ganymede base reported that the Great Red Spot of Jupiter was emitting weak but definite pulses that did not seem to be random.

The last five minutes of the program was a precis devoted to outstanding events of the other days. Mrs. Cuthmar, the housemother, turned the channel to a situation comedy with no protests from anybody.

Tom left the room, after telling Mabel that he was going to bed early—alone, and to sleep. He had a hard day tomorrow.

He tiptoed down the hall and the stairs and into the stoner room. The lights were soft, there were many

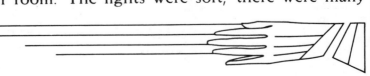

shadows, and it was quiet. The sixty-three cylinders were like ancient granite columns of an underground chamber of a buried city. Fifty-five faces were white blurs behind the clear metal. Some had their eyes open; most had closed them while waiting for the field radiated from the machine in the base. He looked through Jennie Marlowe's door. He felt sick again. Out of his reach: never for him. Wednesday was only a day away. No, it was only a little less than four and a half hours away.

He touched the door. It was slick and only a little cold. She stared at him. Her right forearm was bent to hold the strap of a large purse. When the door opened, she would step out, ready to go. Some people took their showers and fixed their faces as soon as they got up from their sleep and then went directly into the stoner. When the field was automatically radiated at 05:00, they stepped out a minute later, ready for the day.

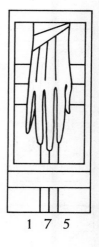

He would like to step out of his "coffin," too, at the same time.

But he was barred by Wednesday.

He turned away. He was acting like a sixteen-year-old kid. He had been sixteen about one hundred and six years ago, not that that made any difference. Physiologically, he was thirty.

As he started up to the second floor, he almost turned around and went back for another look. But he took himself by his neck-collar and pulled himself up to his room. There he decided he would get to sleep at once. Perhaps he would dream about her. If dreams were wish-fulfillments, they would bring her to him. It still had not been "proved" that dreams always expressed wishes, but it had been proved that man deprived of dreaming did go mad. And so the somniums radiated a field that put man into a state in which he got all

the sleep, and all the dreams, that he needed within a four-hour period. Then he was awakened and a little later went into the stoner where the field suspended all atomic and subatomic activity. He would remain in that state forever unless the activating field came on.

He slept, and Jennie Marlowe did not come to him. Or, if she did, he did not remember. He awoke, washed his face, went down eagerly to the stoner, where he found the entire household standing around, getting in one last smoke, talking, laughing. Then they would step into their cylinders, and a silence like that at the heart of a mountain would fall.

He had often wondered what would happen if he did not go into the stoner. How would he feel? Would he be panicked? All his life, he had known only Tuesdays. Would Wednesday rush at him, roaring, like a tidal wave? Pick him up and hurl him against the reefs of a strange time?

What if he made some excuse and went back upstairs and did not go back down until the field had come on? By then, he could not enter. The door to his cylinder would not open again until the proper time. He could still run down to the public emergency stoners only three blocks away. But if he stayed in his room, waiting for Wednesday?

Such things happened. If the breaker of the law did not have a reasonable excuse, he was put on trial. It was a felony second only to murder to "break time," and the unexcused were stoned. All felons, sane or insane, were stoned. Or *mañanaed*, as some said. The *mañanaed* criminal waited in immobility and unconsciousness, preserved unharmed until science had techniques to cure the insane, the neurotic, the criminal, the sick. *Mañana*.

"What was it like in Wednesday?" Tom had asked a man who had been unavoidably left behind because of an accident.

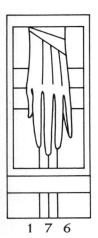

"How would I know? I was knocked out except for about fifteen minutes. I was in the same city, and I had never seen the faces of the ambulance men, of course, but then I've never seen them here. They stonered me and left me in the hospital for Tuesday to take care of."

He must have it bad, he thought. Bad. Even to think of such a thing was crazy. Getting into Wednesday was almost impossible. Almost. But it could be done. It would take time and patience, but it could be done.

He stood in front of his stoner for a moment. The others said, "See you! So long! Next Tuesday!" Mabel called, "Good night, lover!"

"Good night," he muttered.

"What?" she shouted.

"Good night!"

He glanced at the beautiful face behind the door. Then he smiled. He had been afraid that she might hear him say good night to a woman who called him lover.

He had ten minutes left. The intercom alarms were whooping. Get going, everybody! Time to take the six-day trip! Run! Remember the penalties!

He remembered, but he wanted to leave a message. The recorder was on a table. He activated it and said, "Dear Miss Jennie Marlowe. My name is Tom Pym, and my stoner is next to yours. I am an actor, too; in fact, I work at the same studio as you. I know this is presumptuous of me, but I have never seen anybody so beautiful. Do you have a talent to match your beauty? I would like to see some run-offs of your shows. Would you please leave some in room five? I'm sure the occupant won't mind. Yours, Tom Pym."

He ran it back. It was certainly bald enough, and that might be just what was needed. Too flowery or too pressing would have made her leary. He had commented on her beauty twice but not overstressed it.

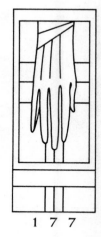

177

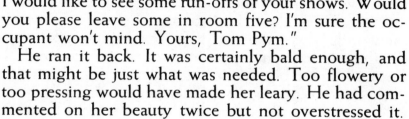

And the appeal to her pride in her acting would be difficult to resist. Nobody knew better than he about that.

He whistled a little on his way to the cylinder. Inside, he pressed the button and looked at his watch. Five minutes to midnight. The light on the huge screen above the computer in the police station would not be flashing for him. Ten minutes from now, Wednesday's police would step out of their stoners in the precinct station, and they would take over their duties.

There was a ten-minute hiatus between the two days in the police station. All hell could break loose in these few minutes and it sometimes did. But a price had to be paid to maintain the walls of time.

He opened his eyes. His knees sagged a little and his head bent. The activation was a million microseconds fast—from eternium to flesh and blood almost instantaneously, and the heart never knew that it had been stopped for such a long time. Even so, there was a little delay in the muscles' response to a standing position.

He pressed the button, opened the door, and it was as if his button had launched the day. Mabel had made herself up last night so that she looked dawn-fresh. He complimented her and she smiled happily. But he told her he would meet her for breakfast. Halfway up the staircase he stopped, and he waited until the hall was empty. Then he sneaked back down and into the stoner room. He turned on the recorder.

A voice, husky but also melodious, said, "Dear Mr. Pym. I've had a few messages from other days. It was fun to talk back and forth across the abyss between the worlds, if you don't mind my exaggerating a little. But there is really no sense in it, once the novelty has worn off. If you become interested in the other person, you're frustrating yourself. That person can only be a voice in a recorder and a cold waxy face in a metal

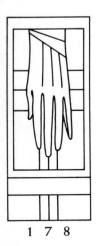

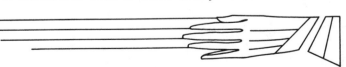

coffin. I wax poetic. Pardon me. If the person doesn't interest you, why continue to communicate? There is no sense in either case. And I *may* be beautiful. Anyway, I thank you for the compliment, but I am also sensible.

"I should have just not bothered to reply. But I want to be nice; I didn't want to hurt your feelings. So please don't leave any more messages."

He waited while silence was played. Maybe she was pausing for effect. Now would come a chuckle or a low honey-throated laugh, and she would say, "However, I don't like to disappoint my public. The run-offs are in your room."

The silence stretched out. He turned off the machine and went to the dining room for breakfast.

Siesta time at work was from 14:40 to 14:45. He lay down on the bunk and pressed the button. Within a minute he was asleep. He did dream of Jennie this time; she was a white shimmering face solidifying out of the darkness and floating toward him. She was even more beautiful than she had been in her stoner.

The shooting ran overtime that afternoon, so that he got home just in time for supper. Even the studio would not dare to keep a man past his supper hour, especially since the studio was authorized to serve food only at noon.

He had time to look at Jennie for a minute before Mrs. Cuthmar's voice screeched over the intercom. As he walked down the hall, he thought, "I'm going bananas over her. It's ridiculous. I'm a grown man. Maybe . . . maybe I should see a psycher."

Sure, make your petition, and wait until a psycher has time for you. Say about three hundred days from now, if you are lucky. And if the psycher doesn't work out for you, then petition for another, and wait six hundred days.

Petition. He slowed down. Petition. What about a

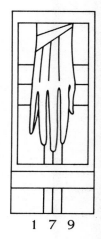

1 7 9

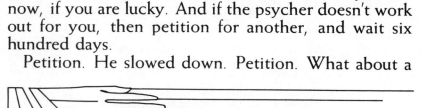

request, not to see a psycher, but to move? Why not? What did he have to lose? It would probably be turned down, but he could at least try.

Even obtaining a form for the request was not easy. He spent two nonwork days standing in line at the Center City Bureau before he got the proper forms. The first time, he was handed the wrong form and had to start all over again. There was no line set aside for those who wanted to change their days. There were not enough who wished to do this to justify such a line. So he had had to queue up before the Miscellaneous Office counter of the Mobility Section of the Vital Exchange Department of the Interchange and Cross Transfer Bureau. None of these titles had anything to do with emigration to another day.

When he got his form the second time, he refused to move from the office window until he had checked the number of the form and asked the clerk to double-check it. He ignored the cries and the mutterings behind him. Then he went to one side of the vast room and stood in line before the punch machines. After two hours, he got to sit down at a small rolltop desk-shaped machine, above which was a large screen. He inserted the form into the slot, looked at the projection of the form, and punched buttons to mark the proper spaces opposite the proper questions. After that, all he had to do was to drop the form into a slot and hope it did not get lost. Or hope he would not have to go through the same procedure because he had improperly punched the form.

That evening, he put his head against the hard metal and murmured to the rigid face behind the door, "I must really love you to go through all this. And you don't even know it. And worse, if you did, you might not care one bit."

To prove to himself that he had kept his gray stuff,

he went out with Mabel that evening to a party given by Sol Voremwolf, a producer. Voremwolf had just passed a civil service examination giving him an A-13 rating. This meant that, in time, with some luck and the proper pull, he would become an executive vice-president of the studio.

The party was a qualified success. Tom and Mabel returned about half an hour before stoner time. Tom had managed to refrain from too many blowminds and liquor, so he was not tempted by Mabel. Even so, he knew that when he became unstonered he would be half-loaded and he'd have to take some dreadful counter-actives. He would look and feel like hell at work, since he had missed his sleep.

He put Mabel off with an excuse and went down to the stoner room ahead of the others. Not that that would do him any good if he wanted to get stonered early. The stoners only activated within narrow time limits.

He leaned against the cylinder and patted the door. "I tried not to think about you all evening. I wanted to be fair to Mabel; it's not fair to go out with her and think about you all the time."

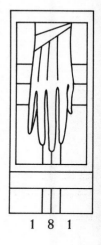

1 8 1

All's fair in love . . .

He left another message for her, then wiped it out. What was the use? Besides, he knew that his speech was a little thick. He wanted to appear at his best for her.

Why should he? What did she care for him?

The answer was, he cared, and there was no reason or logic connected with it. He loved this forbidden, untouchable, far-away-in-time, yet-so-near woman.

Mabel had come in silently. She said, "You're sick!"

Tom jumped away. Now why had he done that? He

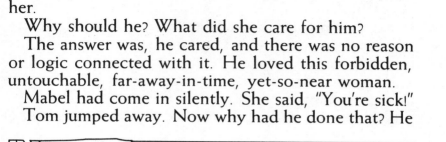

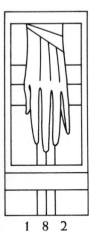

had nothing to be ashamed of. Then why was he so angry with her? His embarrassment was understandable but his anger was not.

Mabel laughed at him, and he was glad. Now he could snarl at her. He did so, and she turned away and walked out. But she was back in a few minutes with the others. It would soon be midnight.

By then he was standing inside the cylinder. A few seconds later he left it, pushed Jennie's backward on its wheels, and pushed his around so that it faced hers. He went back in, pressed the button, and stood there. The double doors only slightly distorted his view. But she seemed even more removed in distance, in time, and in unattainability.

Three days later, well into winter, he received a letter. The box inside the entrance hall buzzed just as he entered the front door. He went back and waited until the letter was printed and had dropped out from the slot. It was the reply to his request to move to Wednesday.

Denied. Reason: He had no reasonable reason to move.

That was true. But he could not give his real motive. It would have been even less impressive than the one he had given. He had punched the box opposite No. 12. REASON: TO GET INTO AN ENVIRONMENT WHERE MY TALENTS WILL BE MORE LIKELY TO BE ENCOURAGED.

He cursed and he raged. It was his human, his civil right to move into any day he pleased. That is, should be his right. What if a move did cause much effort? What if it required a transfer of his I.D. and all the records connected with him from the moment of his birth? What if . . . ?

He could rage all he wanted to, but it would not change a thing. He was stuck in the world of Tuesday.

Not yet, he muttered. Not yet. Fortunately, there

is no limit to the number of requests I can make in my own day. I'll send out another. They think they can wear me out, huh? Well, I'll wear them out. Man against the machine. Man against the system. Man against the bureaucracy and the hard cold rules.

Winter's twenty days had sped by. Spring's eight days rocketed by. It was summer again. On the second day of the twelve days of summer, he received a reply to his second request.

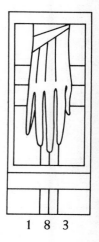

It was neither a denial nor an acceptance. It stated that if he thought he would be better off psychologically in Wednesday because his astrologer said so, then he would have to get a psycher's critique of the astrologer's analysis. Tom Pym jumped into the air and clicked his sandaled heels together. Thank God that he lived in an age that did not classify astrologers as charlatans! The people—the masses—had protested that astrology was a necessity and that it should be legalized and honored. So laws were passed, and because of that, Tom Pym had a chance.

He went down to the stoner room and kissed the door of the cylinder and told Jennie Marlowe the good news. She did not respond, though he thought he saw her eyes brighten just a little. That was, of course, only his imagination, but he liked his imagination.

Getting a psycher for a consultation and getting through the three sessions took another year, another forty-eight days. Doctor Sigmund Traurig was a friend of Doctor Stelhela, the astrologer, and so that made things easier for Tom.

"I've studied Doctor Stelhela's chart carefully and analyzed carefully your obsession for this woman," he said. "I agree with Doctor Stelhela that you will always be unhappy in Tuesday, but I don't quite agree with him that you will be happier in Wednesday. However, you have this thing going for this Miss Marlowe, so I

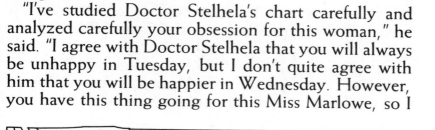

think you should go to Wednesday. But only if you sign papers agreeing to see a psycher there for extended therapy."

Only later did Tom Pym realize that Doctor Traurig might have wanted to get rid of him because he had too many patients. But that was an uncharitable thought.

He had to wait while the proper papers were transmitted to Wednesday's authorities. His battle was only half-won. The other officials could turn him down. And if he did get to his goal, then what? She could reject him without giving him a second chance.

It was unthinkable, but she could.

He caressed the door and then pressed his lips against it.

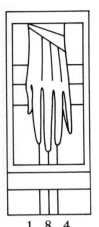

"Pygmalion could at least touch Galatea," he said. "Surely, the gods—the big dumb bureaucrats—will take pity on me, who can't even touch you. Surely."

The psycher had said that he was incapable of a true and lasting bond with a woman, as so many men were in this world of easy-come-easy-go liaisons. He had fallen in love with Jennie Marlowe for several reasons. She may have resembled somebody he had loved when he was very young. His mother, perhaps? No? Well, never mind. He would find out in Wednesday—perhaps. The deep, the important, truth was that he loved Miss Marlowe because she could never reject him, kick him out, or become tiresome, complain, weep, yell, insult, and so forth. He loved her because she was unattainable and silent.

"I love her as Achilles must have loved Helen when he saw her on top of the walls of Troy," Tom said.

"I wasn't aware that Achilles was ever in love with Helen of Troy," Doctor Traurig said drily.

"Homer never said so, but I *know* that he must have been! Who could see her and *not* love her?"

"How the hell would I know? I never saw her! If I had suspected these delusions would intensify..."

"I am a poet!" Tom said.

"Overimaginative, you mean! Hmmm. She must be a douser! I don't have anything particular to do this evening. I'll tell you what.... My curiosity is aroused. ...I'll come down to your place tonight and take a look at this fabulous beauty, your Helen of Troy."

Doctor Traurig appeared immediately after supper, and Tom Pym ushered him down the hall and into the stoner room at the rear of the big house as if he were a guide conducting a famous critic to a just-discovered Rembrandt.

The doctor stood for a long time in front of the cylinder. He hmmmed several times and checked her vital-data plate several times. Then he turned and said, "I see what you mean, Mr. Pym. Very well. I'll give the go-ahead."

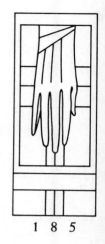

"Ain't she something?" Tom said on the porch. "She's out of this world, literally and figuratively, of course."

"Very beautiful. But I believe that you are facing a great disappointment, perhaps heartbreak, perhaps, who knows, even madness, much as I hate to use that unscientific term."

"I'll take the chance," Tom said. "I know I sound nuts, but where would we be if it weren't for nuts? Look at the man who invented the wheel, at Columbus, at James Watt, at the Wright brothers, at Pasteur, you name them."

"You can scarcely compare those pioneers of science with their passion for truth with you and your desire to marry a woman. But, as I have observed, she is strikingly beautiful. Still, that makes me exceedingly cautious. Why isn't she married? What's wrong with her?"

"For all I know, she may have been married a dozen

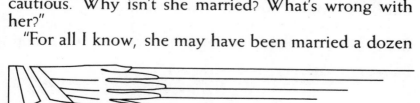

times!" Tom said. "The point is, she isn't now! Maybe she's disappointed and she's sworn to wait until the right man comes along. Maybe..."

"There's no maybe about it; you're neurotic," Traurig said. "But I actually believe that it would be more dangerous for you *not* to go to Wednesday than it would be *to* go."

"Then you'll say yes!" Tom said, grabbing the doctor's hand and shaking it.

"Perhaps. I have some doubts."

The doctor had a faraway look. Tom laughed and released the hand and slapped the doctor on the shoulder. "Admit it! You were really struck by her! You'd have to be dead not to!"

"She's all right," the doctor said. "But you must think this over. If you do go there and she turns you down, you might go off the deep end, much as I hate to use such a poetical term."

"No, I won't. I wouldn't be a bit the worse off. Better off, in fact. I'll at least get to see her in the flesh."

Spring and summer zipped by. Then, a morning he would never forget, the letter of acceptance. With it, instructions on how to get to Wednesday. These were simple enough. He was to make sure that the technicians came to his stoner sometime during the day and readjusted the timer within the base. He could not figure out why he could not just stay out of the stoner and let Wednesday catch up to him, but by now he was past trying to fathom the bureaucratic mind.

He did not intend to tell anyone at the house, mainly because of Mabel. But Mabel found out from someone at the studio. She wept when she saw him at supper time, and she ran upstairs to her room. He felt badly, but he did not follow to console her.

That evening, his heart beating hard, he opened the door to his stoner. The others had found out by then;

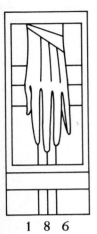

1 8 6

he had been unable to keep the business to himself. Actually, he was glad that he had told them. They seemed happy for him, and they brought in drinks and had many rounds of toasts. Finally Mabel came downstairs, wiping her eyes, and she said she wished him luck, too. She had known that he was not really in love with her. But she did wish someone would fall in love with her just by looking inside her stoner.

When she found out that he had gone to see Doctor Traurig, she said, "He's a very influential man. Sol Voremwolf had him for his analyst. He says he's even got influence on other days. He edits the *Psyche Cross-currents*, you know, one of the few periodicals read by other people."

Other, of course, meant those who lived in Wednesdays through Mondays.

Tom said he was glad he had gotten Traurig. Perhaps he had used his influence to get the Wednesday authorities to push through his request so swiftly. The walls between the worlds were seldom broken, but it was suspected that the very influential did it when they pleased.

Now, quivering, he stood before Jennie's cylinder again. The last time, he thought, that I'll see her stonered. Next time, she'll be warm, colorful, touchable flesh.

"*Ave atque vale!*" he said aloud. The others cheered. Mabel said, "How corny!" They thought he was addressing them, and perhaps he had included them.

He stepped inside the cylinder, closed the door, and pressed the button. He would keep his eyes open, so that . . .

And today was Wednesday. Though the view was exactly the same, it was like being on Mars.

He pushed open the door and stepped out. The seven people had faces he knew and names he had

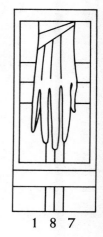

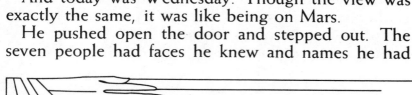

187

read on their plates. But he did not know them.

He started to say hello, and then he stopped.

Jennie Marlowe's cylinder was gone.

He seized the nearest man by the arm.

"Where's Jennie Marlowe?"

"Let go. You're hurting me. She's gone. To Tuesday."

"Tuesday! Tuesday?"

"Sure. She's been trying to get out of here for a long time. She had something about this day being unlucky for her. She was unhappy, that's for sure. Just two days ago, she said her application had finally been accepted. Apparently, some Tuesday psycher had used his influence. He came down and saw her in her stoner and that was it, brother."

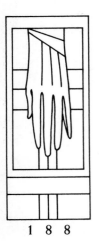

The walls and the people and the stoners seemed to be distorted. Time was bending itself this way and that. He wasn't in Wednesday; he wasn't in Tuesday. He wasn't in *any* day. He was stuck inside himself at some crazy date that should never have existed.

"She can't do that!"

"Oh, no? She just did that!"

"But . . . you can't transfer more than once!"

"That's her problem."

It was his, too.

"I should never have brought him down to look at her!" Tom said. "The swine! The unethical swine!"

Tom Pym stood there for a long time, and then he went into the kitchen. It was the same environment, if you discounted the people. Later, he went to the studio and got a part in a situation play which was, really, just like all those in Tuesday. He watched the newscaster that night. The president of the USA had a different name and face, but the words of his speech could have been those of Tuesday's president. He was introduced to a secretary of a producer; her name wasn't Mabel, but it might as well have been.

The difference here was that Jennie was gone, and oh, what a world of difference it made to him.

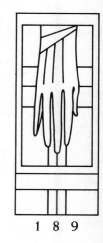

AFTER
KING KONG
FELL

.

This is one of my favorite stories. While rereading it for preparation for this collection, I felt cold run over my skin when I was near the end.

Unlike so many of my stories, the idea for this one was not born from a dream. Just like the grandfather in the story, I was sitting before the TV set with my granddaughter, Kimberly Dana Ladd, watching a rerun of the original *King Kong* film. The year was 1970, she was five years old, I was fifty-two, and we were in the big Moorish-style house on Burnside Avenue in Los Angeles. This was a few blocks south of the Miracle Mile section of Wilshire Boulevard and a few more blocks from the La Brea Tar Pits. Within a few minutes you could pass through the late twentieth-century to the one hundred-twentieth-century B.C.

Just as the granddaughter does in the story, Kim asked me some questions about King Kong. Her five-year-old mind thought that the film was based on reality, and I thought, Why not? This led to the idea for this tale based on the modern mythology of the forlorn ogre, the Giant Ape.

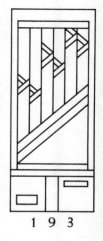

I did not write the story, however, until I had returned to my home town, Peoria. When I was invited to be a guest of honor at the first science-fiction convention to be held in Kansas City, Missouri, I wrote this story and read it instead of giving a speech. It was well-received, and I later sent it to my agent to sell. "Kong" has been in a number of anthologies since, here and abroad, and was included in a Nebula Awards issue.

Both my daughter and granddaughter saw the movie when they were very young; both were powerfully affected by it. It still holds up very well, though it should be seen for best effect on the big screen of a movie theater and without interruptions from commercials. Nowadays, though, the many imitations of it have somewhat diminished its power for the young viewer. The Di Laurentis remake was not very good and did not at all evoke the awe and sympathy we felt for the doomed god-human-beast when we saw the original in 1933, 1950, or 1970.

The first King Kong was a classic that vibrated the deep unconscious chords in us, the feelings still surviving from the Old

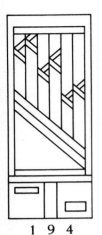

Stone Age. At the same time that it stirred up clouds of awe and horror, it evoked sympathy, even empathy, for this hairy colossus questing after a love he could never have in a land that he could never understand, a quest destined for rejection and death. Kong was both pathetic and tragic, dramatic states which a human actor cannot simultaneously portray on the stage, but, which, apparently, apes can. Or a monster made by Doctor Frankenstein.

When I read the story at Kansas City, the audience understood the references to the giant, bronze-skinned, and yellow-eyed man and to the tall, pale, and hawk-nosed man who appear briefly during the crowd scene around Kong's body. Unfortunately, there will be many readers of this collection who won't know who these two are. I had considered removing them because of this, but I decided to leave them in. This story is, after all, a lesser myth based on a greater, and the two strangers about whom young Howller wondered are also of lesser myths.

The former is Doc Savage, a hero of the pulp-magazine series in the 30's and the 40's, reborn in paperback reprints in the middle 60's, still being reprinted, and popular with later generations. He was one of my heroes when I was young, and Howller would have been a fan of Doc Savage.

The latter stranger is the Shadow, a mysterious superman crimefighter of a pulp-magazine series of the 30's and 40's and rejuvenated in several paperback series since. He originated in a radio show, titled The Shadow, and then became a very popular hero of the magazines. The Shadow is perhaps better known than Doc Savage because he has become a sort of American folk legend. Many writers refer to him en passant in their fiction. "Who knows what evil lurks in the hearts of men? The Shadow knows!"

Surely, many of you have heard this quotation, even if you were born in 1960 or later.

"Who knows what evil lurks in the hearts of men?"

Not to mention in the hearts of women.

It might be said that not only the Shadow, but King Kong and young Howller also knew.

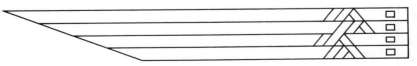

The first half of the movie was grim and gray and somewhat tedious. Mr. Howller did not mind. That was, after all, realism. Those times had been grim and gray. Morever, behind the tediousness was the promise of something vast and horrifying. The creeping pace and the measured ritualistic movements of the actors gave intimations of the workings of the gods. Unhurriedly, but with utmost confidence, the gods were directing events toward the climax.

Mr. Howller had felt that at the age of fifteen, and he felt it now while watching the show on TV at the age of fifty-five. Of course, when he first saw it in 1933, he had known what was coming. Hadn't he lived through some of the events only two years before that?

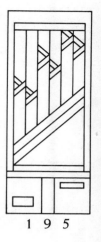

The old freighter, the *Wanderer*, was nosing blindly through the fog toward the surflike roar of the natives' drums. And then: the commercial. Mr. Howller rose and stepped into the hall and called down the steps loudly enough for Jill to hear him on the front porch. He thought, Commercials can be a blessing. They give us time to get into the bathroom or the kitchen or time to light up a cigarette and decide about continuing to watch this show or go on to that show.

And why couldn't real life have its commercials?

Wouldn't it be something to be grateful for if reality stopped in mid-course while the Big Salesman made His pitch! The car about to smash into you, the bullet on its way to your brain, the first cancer cell about to break loose, the boss reaching for the phone to call you in so he can fire you, the spermatozoon about to be launched toward the ovum, the final insult about to be hurled at the once, and perhaps still, beloved, the final drink of alcohol which would rupture the abused blood vessel, the decision which would lead to the light that would surely fail?

If only you could step out while the commercial

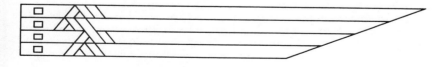

interrupted these, think about it, talk about it, and then, returning to the set, switch it to another channel.

But that one is having technical difficulties, and the one after that is a talk show whose guest is the archangel Gabriel himself and after some urging by the host he agrees to blow his trumpet, and...

Jill entered, sat down, and began to munch the cookies and drink the lemonade he had prepared for her. Jill was six and a half years old and beautiful, but then what granddaughter wasn't beautiful? Jill was also unhappy because she had just quarreled with her best friend, Amy, who had stalked off with threats never to see Jill again. Mr. Howller reminded her that this had happened before and that Amy always came back the next day, if not sooner. To take her mind off of Amy, Mr. Howller gave her a brief outline of what had happened in the movie. Jill listened without enthusiasm, but she became excited enough once the movie had resumed. And when Kong was feeling over the edge of the abyss for John Driscoll, played by Bruce Cabot, she got into her grandfather's lap. She gave a little scream and put her hands over her eyes when Kong carried Ann Redman into the jungle (Ann played by Fay Wray).

But by the time Kong lay dead on Fifth Avenue, she was rooting for him, as millions had before her. Mr. Howller squeezed her and kissed her and said, "When your mother was about your age, I took her to see this. And when it was over, she was crying, too."

Jill sniffled and let him dry the tears with his handkerchief. When the Roadrunner cartoon came on, she got off his lap and went back to her cookie-munching. After a while she said, "Grandpa, the coyote falls off the cliff so far you can't even see him. When he hits, the whole earth shakes. But he always comes back, good as new. Why can he fall so far and not get hurt?

Why couldn't King Kong fall and be just like new?"

Her grandparents and her mother had explained many times the distinction between a "live" and a "taped" show. It did not seem to make any difference how many times they explained. Somehow, in the years of watching TV, she had gotten the fixed idea that people in "live" shows actually suffered pain, sorrow, and death. The only shows she could endure seeing were those that her elders labeled as "taped." This worried Mr. Howller more than he admitted to his wife and daughter. Jill was a very bright child, but what if too many TV shows at too early an age had done her some irreparable harm? What if, a few years from now, she could see, and even define, the distinction between reality and unreality on the screen but deep down in her there was a child that still could not distinguish?

"You know that the Roadrunner is a series of pictures that move. People draw pictures, and people can do anything with pictures. So the Roadrunner is drawn again and again, and he's back in the next show with his wounds all healed and he's ready to make a jackass of himself again."

"A jackass? But he's a coyote."

"Now . . ."

Mr. Howller stopped. Jill was grinning.

"O.K., now you're pulling my leg."

"But is King Kong alive or is he taped?"

"Taped. Like the Disney I took you to see last week. *Bedknobs and Broomsticks.*"

"Then *King Kong* didn't happen?"

"Oh, yes, it really happened. But this is a movie they made about King Kong after what really happened was all over. So it's not exactly like it really was, and actors took the parts of Ann Redman and Carl Denham and all the others. Except King Kong himself. He was a toy model."

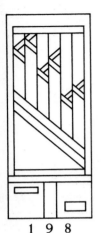

Jill was silent for a minute and then she said, "You mean, there really *was* a King Kong? How do you know, Grandpa?"

"Because I was there in New York when Kong went on his rampage. I was in the theater when he broke loose, and I was in the crowd that gathered around Kong's body after he fell off the Empire State Building. I was thirteen then, just seven years older than you are now. I was with my parents, and they were visiting my Aunt Thea. She was beautiful, and she had golden hair just like Fay Wray's—I mean, Ann Redman's. She'd married a very rich man, and they had a big apartment high up in the clouds. In the Empire State Building itself."

"High up in the clouds! That must've been fun, Grandpa!"

It would have been, he thought, if there had not been so much tension in that apartment. Uncle Nate and Aunt Thea should have been happy because they were so rich and lived in such a swell place. But they weren't. No one said anything to young Tim Howller, but he felt the suppressed anger, heard the bite of tone, and saw the tightening lips. His aunt and uncle were having trouble of some sort, and his parents were upset by it. But they all tried to pretend everything was as sweet as honey when he was around.

Young Howller had been eager to accept the pretense. He didn't like to think that anybody could be mad at his tall, blonde, and beautiful aunt. He was passionately in love with her; he ached for her in the daytime; at nights he had fantasies about her of which he was ashamed when he awoke. But not for long. She was a thousand times more desirable than Fay Wray or Claudette Colbert or Elissa Landi.

But that night, when they were all going to see the première of *The Eighth Wonder of the World*, King Kong

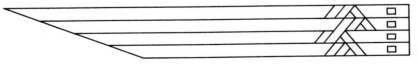

himself, young Howller had managed to ignore whatever it was that was bugging his elders. And even they
seemed to be having a good time. Uncle Nate, over
his parents' weak protests, had purchased orchestra
seats for him. These were twenty dollars apiece, big
money in Depression days, enough to feed a family
for a month. Everybody got all dressed up, and Aunt
Thea looked too beautiful to be real. Young Howller
was so excited that he thought his heart was going to
climb up and out through his throat. For days the
newspapers had been full of stories about King Kong—
speculations, rather, since Carl Denham wasn't telling
them much. And he, Tim Howller, would be one of
the lucky few to see the monster first.

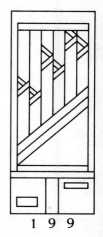

Boy, wait until he got back to the kids in seventh
grade at Peoria, Illinois! Would their eyes ever pop
when he told them all about it!

But his happiness was too good to last. Aunt Thea
suddenly said she had a headache and couldn't possibly
go. Then she and Uncle Nate went into their bedroom,
and even in the front room, three rooms and a hallway
distant, young Tim could hear their voices. After a
while Uncle Nate, slamming doors behind him, came
out. He was red-faced and scowling, but he wasn't
going to call the party off. All four of them, very
uncomfortable and silent, rode in a taxi to the theater
on Times Square. But when they got inside, even Uncle
Nate forgot the quarrel or at least he seemed to. There
was the big stage with its towering silvery curtains and
through the curtains came a vibration of excitement
and of delicious danger. And even through the curtains
the hot hairy ape-stink filled the theater.

"Did King Kong get loose just like in the movie?"
Jill said.

Mr. Howller started. "What? Oh, yes, he sure did.
Just like in the movie."

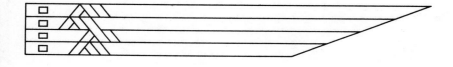

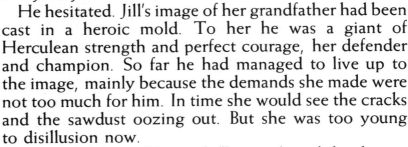

"Were you scared, Grandpa? Did you run away like everybody else?"

He hesitated. Jill's image of her grandfather had been cast in a heroic mold. To her he was a giant of Herculean strength and perfect courage, her defender and champion. So far he had managed to live up to the image, mainly because the demands she made were not too much for him. In time she would see the cracks and the sawdust oozing out. But she was too young to disillusion now.

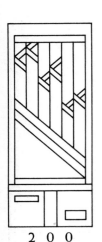

"No, I didn't run," he said. "I waited until the theater was cleared of the crowd."

This was true. The big man who'd been sitting in the seat before him had leaped up yelling as Kong began tearing the bars out of his cage, had whirled and jumped over the back of his seat, and his knee had hit young Howller on the jaw. And so young Howller had been stretched out senseless on the floor under the seats while the mob screamed and tore at each other and trampled the fallen.

Later he was glad that he had been knocked out. It gave him a good excuse for not keeping cool, for not acting heroically in the situation. He knew that if he had not been unconscious, he would have been as frenzied as the others, and he would have abandoned his parents, thinking only in his terror of his own salvation. Of course, his parents had deserted him, though they claimed that they had been swept away from him by the mob. This *could* be true; maybe his folks *had* actually tried to get to him. But he had not really thought they had, and for years he had looked down on them because of their flight. When he got older, he realized that he would have done the same thing, and he knew that his contempt for them was really a disguised contempt for himself.

He had awakened with a sore jaw and a headache.

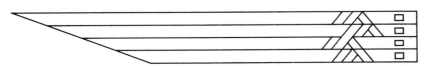

The police and the ambulance men were there and starting to take care of the hurt and to haul away the dead. He staggered past them out into the lobby and, not seeing his parents there, went outside. The sidewalks and the streets were plugged with thousands of men, women, and children, on foot and in cars, fleeing northward.

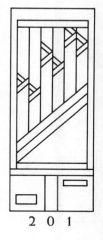

He had not known where Kong was. He should have been able to figure it out, since the frantic mob was leaving the midtown part of Manhattan. But he could think of only two things. Where were his parents? And was Aunt Thea safe? And then he had a third thing to consider. He discovered that, when he had seen the great ape burst loose, he had wet his pants.

Under the circumstances, he should have paid no attention to this. Certainly no one else did. But he was a very sensitive and shy boy of thirteen, and, for some reason, the need for getting dry underwear and trousers seemed even more important than finding his parents. In retrospect he would tell himself that he would have gone south anyway. But he knew deep down that if his pants had not been wet he might not have dared return to the Empire State Building.

It was impossible to buck the flow of the thousands moving like lava up Broadway. He went east on 43rd Street until he came to Fifth Avenue, where he started southward. There was a crowd to fight against here, too, but it was much smaller than that on Broadway. He was able to thread his way through it, though he often had to go out into the street and dodge the cars. These, fortunately, were not able to move faster than about three miles an hour.

"Many people got impatient because the cars wouldn't go faster," he told Jill, "and they just abandoned them and struck out on foot."

"Wasn't it noisy, Grandpa?"

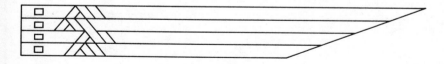

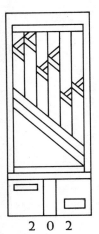

"Noisy? I've never heard such noise. I think that everyone in Manhattan, except those hiding under their beds, was yelling or talking. And every driver in Manhattan was blowing his car's horn. And then there were the sirens of the fire trucks and police cars and ambulances. Yes, it was noisy."

Several times he tried to stop a fugitive so he could find out what was going on. But even when he did succeed in halting someone for a few seconds, he couldn't make himself heard. By then, as he found out later, the radio had broadcast the news. Kong had chased John Driscoll and Ann Redman out of the theater and across the street to their hotel. They had gone up to Driscoll's room, where they thought they were safe. But Kong had climbed up, using windows as ladder steps, reached into the room, knocked Driscoll out, grabbed Ann, and had then leaped away with her. He had headed, as Carl Denham figured he would, toward the tallest structure on the island. On King Kong's own island, he lived on the highest point, Skull Mountain, where he was truly monarch of all he surveyed. Here he would climb to the top of the Empire State Building, Manhattan's Skull Mountain.

Tim Howller had not known this, but he was able to infer that Kong had traveled down Fifth Avenue from 38th Street on. He passed a dozen cars with their tops flattened down by the ape's fist or turned over on their sides or tops. He saw three sheet-covered bodies on the sidewalks, and he overheard a policeman telling a reporter that Kong had climbed up several buildings on his way south and reached into windows and pulled people out and thrown them down onto the pavement.

"But you said King Kong was carrying Ann Redman in the crook of his arm, Grandpa," Jill said. "He only had one arm to climb with, Grandpa, so . . . so wouldn't he fall off the building when he reached in to grab those poor people?"

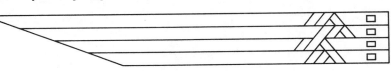

"A very shrewd observation, my little chickadee," Mr. Howller said, using the W C. Fields voice that usually sent her into giggles. "But his arms were long enough for him to drape Ann Redman over the arm he used to hang on with while he reached in with the other. And to forestall your next question, even if you had not thought of it, he could turn over an automobile with only one hand."

"But . . . but why'd he take time out to do that if he wanted to get to the top of the Empire State Building?"

"I don't know why *people* often do the things they do," Mr. Howller said. "So how would I know why an *ape* does the things he does?"

When Kong was a block away from the Empire State, a plane crashed onto the middle of the avenue two blocks behind him and burned furiously. Tim Howller watched it for a few minutes, then he looked upward and saw the red and green lights of the five planes and their silvery bodies slipping in and out of the searchlights.

"Five airplanes, Grandpa? But the movie . . ."

"Yes, I know. The movie showed about fourteen or fifteen. But the book says that there were six to begin with, and the book is much more accurate. The movie also shows King Kong's last stand taking place in the daylight. But it didn't; it was still nighttime."

The Army Air Force plane must have been going at least 250 mph as it dived down toward the giant ape standing on the top of the observation tower. Kong had put Ann Redman by his feet so he could hang on to the tower with one hand and grab out with the other at the planes. One had come too close, and he had seized the left biplane structure and ripped it off. Given the energy of the plane, his hand should have been torn off, too, or at least he should have been pulled loose from his hold on the tower and gone down with the plane. But he hadn't let loose, and that told

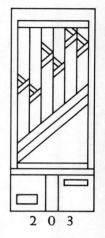

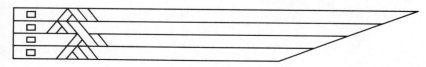

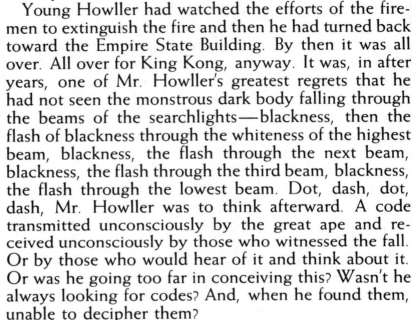

something of the enormous strength of that towering body. It also told something of the relative fragility of the biplane.

Young Howller had watched the efforts of the firemen to extinguish the fire and then he had turned back toward the Empire State Building. By then it was all over. All over for King Kong, anyway. It was, in after years, one of Mr. Howller's greatest regrets that he had not seen the monstrous dark body falling through the beams of the searchlights—blackness, then the flash of blackness through the whiteness of the highest beam, blackness, the flash through the next beam, blackness, the flash through the third beam, blackness, the flash through the lowest beam. Dot, dash, dot, dash, Mr. Howller was to think afterward. A code transmitted unconsciously by the great ape and received unconsciously by those who witnessed the fall. Or by those who would hear of it and think about it. Or was he going too far in conceiving this? Wasn't he always looking for codes? And, when he found them, unable to decipher them?

Since he had been thirteen, he had been trying to equate the great falls in man's myths and legends and to find some sort of intelligence in them. The fall of the tower of Babel, of Lucifer, of Vulcan, of Icarus, and, finally, of King Kong. But he wasn't equal to the task; he didn't have the genius to perceive what the falls meant, he couldn't screen out the—to use an electronic term—the "noise." All he could come up with were folk adages. What goes up must come down. The bigger they are, the harder they fall.

"What'd you say, Grandpa?"

"I was thinking out loud, if you can call that thinking," Mr. Howller said.

Young Howller had been one of the first on the scene, and so he got a place in the front of the crowd.

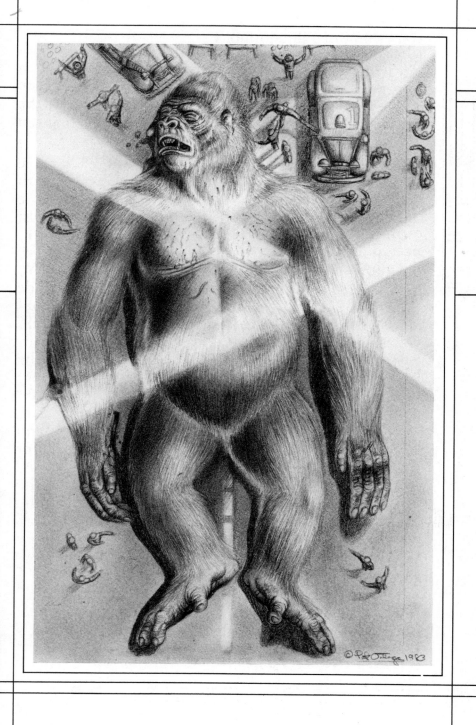

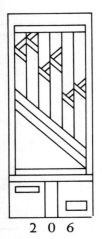

He had not completely forgotten his parents or Aunt Thea, but the danger was over, and he could not make himself leave to search for them. And he had even forgotten about his soaked pants. The body was only about thirty feet from him. It lay on its back on the sidewalk, just as in the movie. But the dead Kong did not look as big or as dignified as in the movie. He was spread out more like an apeskin rug than a body; and blood and bowels and their contents had splashed out around him.

After a while Carl Denham, the man responsible for capturing Kong and bringing him to New York, appeared. As in the movie, Denham spoke his classical lines by the body: "It was Beauty. As always, Beauty killed the Beast."

This was the most appropriately dramatic place for the lines to be spoken, of course, and the proper place to end the movie.

But the book had Denham speaking these lines as he leaned over the parapet of the observation tower to look down at Kong on the sidewalk. His only audience was a police sergeant.

Both the book and the movie were true. Or half true. Denham did speak those lines way up on the 102nd floor of the tower. But, showman that he was, he also spoke them when he got down to the sidewalk, where the newsmen could hear them.

Young Howller didn't hear Denham's remarks. He was too far away. Besides, at that moment he felt a tap on his shoulder and heard a man say, "Hey, kid, there's somebody trying to get your attention!"

Young Howller went into his mother's arms and wept for at least a minute. His father reached past his mother and touched him briefly on the forehead, as if blessing him, and then gave his shoulders a squeeze. When he was able to talk, Tim Howller asked his mother what

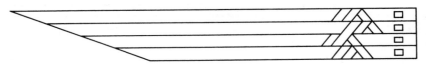

had happened to them. They, as near as they could remember, had been pushed out by the crowd, though they had fought to get to him, and had run up Broadway after they found themselves in the street because King Kong had appeared. They had managed to get back to the theater, had not been able to locate Tim, and had walked back to the Empire State Building.

"What happened to Uncle Nate?" Tim said.

Uncle Nate, his mother said, had caught up with them on Fifth Avenue and just now was trying to get past the police cordon into the building so he could check on Aunt Thea.

"She must be all right!" young Howller said. "The ape climbed up her side of the building, but she could easily get away from him, her apartment's so big!"

"Well, yes," his father had said. "But if she went to bed with her headache, she would've been right next to the window. But don't worry. If she'd been hurt, we'd know it. And maybe she wasn't even home."

Young Tim had asked him what he meant by that, but his father had only shrugged.

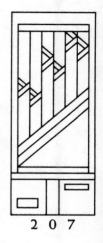

2 0 7

The three of them stood in the front line of the crowd, waiting for Uncle Nate to bring news of Aunt Thea, even though they weren't really worried about her, and waiting to see what happened to Kong. Mayor Jimmy Walker showed up and conferred with the officials. Then the governor himself, Franklin Delano Roosevelt, arrived with much noise of siren and motorcycle. A minute later a big black limousine with flashing red lights and a siren pulled up. Standing on the runningboard was a giant with bronze hair and strange-looking gold-flecked eyes. He jumped off the runningboard and strode up to the mayor, governor, and police commissioner and talked briefly with them. Tim Howller asked the man next to him what the giant's name was, but the man replied that he didn't

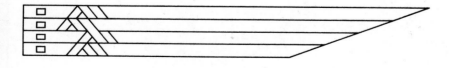

know because he was from out of town also. The giant finished talking and strode up to the crowd, which opened for him as if it were the Red Sea and he were Moses, and he had no trouble at all getting through the police cordon. Tim then asked the man on the right of his parents if he knew the yellow-eyed giant's name. This man, tall and thin, was with a beautiful woman dressed up in an evening gown and a mink coat. He turned his head when Tim called to him and presented a hawklike face and eyes that burned so brightly that Tim wondered if he took dope. Those eyes also told him that here was a man who asked questions, not one who gave answers. Tim didn't repeat his question, and a moment later the man said, in a whispering voice that still carried a long distance, "Come on, Margo. I've work to do." And the two melted into the crowd.

Mr. Howller told Jill about the two men, and she said, "What about them, Grandpa?"

"I don't really know," he said. "Often I've wondered . . . well, never mind. Whoever they were, they're irrelevant to what happened to King Kong. But I'll say one thing about New York—you sure see a lot of strange characters there."

Young Howller had expected that the mess would quickly be cleaned up. And it was true that the sanitation department had sent a big truck with a big crane and a number of men with hoses, scoop shovels, and brooms. But a dozen people at least stopped the cleanup almost before it began. Carl Denham wanted no one to touch the body except the taxidermists he had called in. If he couldn't exhibit a live Kong, he would exhibit a dead one. A colonel from Roosevelt Field claimed the body and, when asked why the Air Force wanted it, could not give an explanation. Rather, he refused to give one, and it was not until an hour later that a

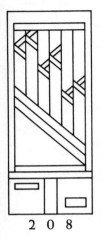

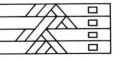

phone call from the White House forced him to reveal the real reason. A general wanted the skin for a trophy because Kong was the only ape ever shot down in aerial combat.

A lawyer for the owners of the Empire State Building appeared with a claim for possession of the body. His clients wanted reimbursement for the damage done to the building.

A representative of the transit system wanted Kong's body so it could be sold to help pay for the damage the ape had done to the Sixth Avenue Elevated.

The owner of the theater from which Kong had escaped arrived with his lawyer and announced he intended to sue Denham for an amount which would cover the sums he would have to pay to those who were inevitably going to sue him.

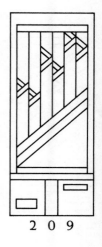

The police ordered the body seized as evidence in the trial for involuntary manslaughter and criminal negligence in which Denham and the theater owner would be defendants in due process.

The manslaughter charges were later dropped, but Denham did serve a year before being paroled. On being released, he was killed by a religious fanatic, a native brought back by the second expedition to Kong's island. He was, in fact, the witch doctor. He had murdered Denham because Denham had abducted and slain his god, Kong.

His Majesty's New York consul showed up with papers which proved that Kong's island was in British waters. Therefore, Denham had no right to anything removed from the island without permission of His Majesty's government.

Denham was in a lot of trouble. But the worst blow of all was to come next day. He would be handed notification that he was being sued by Ann Redman. She wanted compensation to the tune of ten million

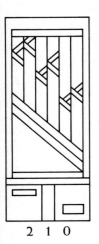

dollars for various physical indignities and injuries suffered during her two abductions by the ape, plus the
mental anguish these had caused her. Unfortunately
for her, Denham went to prison without a penny in
his pocket, and she dropped the suit. Thus, the public
never found out exactly what the "physical indignities
and injuries" were, but this did not keep it from making
many speculations. Ann Redman also sued John
Driscoll, though for a different reason. She claimed
breach of promise. Driscoll, interviewed by newsmen,
made his famous remark that she should have been
suing Kong, not him. This convinced most of the
public that what it had suspected had indeed happened. Just how it could have been done was difficult
to explain, but the public had never lacked wiseacres
who would not only attempt the difficult but would
not draw back even at the impossible.

Actually, Mr. Howller thought, the deed was not
beyond possibility. Take an adult male gorilla who
stood six feet high and weighed three hundred and
fifty pounds. According to Swiss zoo director Ernst
Lang, he would have a full erection only two inches
long. How did Professor Lang know this? Did he enter
the cage during a mating and measure the phallus? Not
very likely. Even the timid and amiable gorilla would
scarcely submit to this type of handling in that kind
of situation. Never mind. Professor Lang said it was
so, and so it must be. Perhaps he used a telescope with
gradations across the lens like those on a submarine's
periscope. In any event, until someone entered the
cage and slapped down a ruler during the action,
Professor Lang's word would have to be taken as the
last word.

By mathematical extrapolation, using the square-cube
law, a gorilla twenty feet tall would have an erect penis
about twenty-one inches long. What the diameter
would be was another guess and perhaps a vital one,

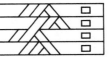

for Ann Redman anyway. Whatever anyone else thought about the possibility, Kong must have decided that he would never know unless he tried. Just how well he succeeded, only he and his victim knew, since the attempt would have taken place before Driscoll and Denham got to the observation tower and before the searchlight beams centered on their target.

But Ann Redman must have told her lover, John Driscoll, the truth, and he turned out not to be such an understanding man after all.

"What're you thinking about, Grandpa?"

Mr. Howller looked at the screen. The Roadrunner had been succeeded by the Pink Panther, who was enduring as much pain and violence as the poor old coyote.

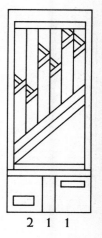

2 1 1

"Nothing," he said. "I'm just watching the Pink Panther with you."

"But you didn't say what happened to King Kong," she said.

"Oh," he said, "we stood around until dawn, and then the big shots finally came to some sort of agreement. The body just couldn't be left there much longer, if for no other reason than that it was blocking traffic. Blocking traffic meant that business would be held up. And lots of people would lose lots of money. And so Kong's body was taken away by the Police Department, though it used the Sanitation Department's crane, and it was kept in an icehouse until its ownership could be thrashed out."

"Poor Kong."

"No," he said, "not poor Kong. He was dead and out of it."

"He went to heaven?"

"As much as anybody," Mr. Howller said.

"But he killed a lot of people, and he carried off that nice girl. Wasn't he bad?"

"No, he wasn't bad. He was an animal, and he didn't

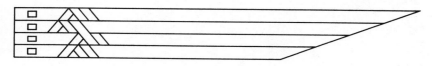

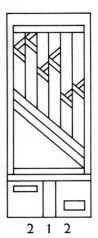

2 1 2

know the difference between good and evil. Anyway, even if he'd been human, he would've been doing what any human would have done."

"What do you mean, Grandpa?"

"Well, if you were captured by people only a foot tall and carried off to a far place and put in a cage, wouldn't you try to escape? And if these people tried to put you back in or got so scared that they tried to kill you right now, wouldn't you step on them?"

"Sure, I'd step on them, Grandpa."

"You'd be justified, too. And King Kong was justified. He was only acting according to the dictates of his instincts."

"What?"

"He was an animal, and so he can't be blamed, no matter what he did. He wasn't evil. It was what happened around Kong that was evil."

"What do you mean?" Jill said.

"He brought out the bad and the good in the people."

But mostly bad, he thought, and he encouraged Jill to forget about Kong and concentrate on the Pink Panther. And as he looked at the screen, he saw it through tears. Even after forty-two years, he thought, tears. This was what the fall of Kong had meant to him.

The crane had hooked the corpse and lifted it up. And there were two flattened-out bodies under Kong; he must have dropped them onto the sidewalk on his way up and then fallen on them from the tower. But how explain the nakedness of the corpses of the man and the woman?

The hair of the woman was long and, in a small area not covered by blood, yellow. And part of her face was recognizable.

Young Tim had not known until then that Uncle Nate had returned from looking for Aunt Thea. Uncle

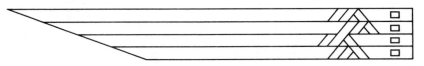

Nate gave a long wailing cry that sounded as if he, too, were falling from the top of the Empire State Building.

A second later young Tim Howller was wailing. But where Uncle Nate's was the cry of betrayal, and perhaps of revenge satisfied, Tim's was both of betrayal and of grief for the death of one he had passionately loved with a thirteen-year-old's love, for one whom the thirteen-year-old in him still loved.

"Grandpa, are there any more King Kongs?"

"No," Mr. Howller said. To say yes would force him to try to explain something that she could not understand. When she got older, she would know that every dawn saw the death of the old Kong and the birth of the new.

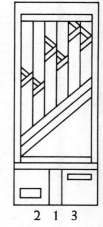

2 1 3

TOTEM AND TABOO

Not very far in the future, the lion, tiger, wolf, jackal, vulture, elephant, gorilla, whale, and many other creatures will be extinct. They may survive in zoos, but they will no longer roam wild and free. And still people will be complimenting or insulting each other by references to the beasts, birds, reptiles, and fishes. Brave as a lion, fierce as a tiger, cross as a bear, dumb as a cow, bird-brain, cowardly as a jackal, fat as a hippo, and so on. Probably, those who use these terms will only be vaguely aware of the referents themselves. Some may never have even seen photographs of the animals whose names they will so glibly use.

Such references must have been made in the Old Stone Age and perhaps before then. Humans had much more and closer contact with the other members of the animal kingdom than we do now. Many even claimed descent from certain animals. Early civilizations worshipped some. Even today, many people worship Hollywood actors and actresses and rock stars though these may be, in many respects, weasels or pigs, wolves or hyenas, crows or vultures.

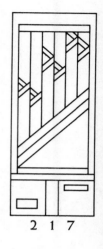

2 1 7

Many years ago, I made some notes about a novel or a play in which the characters would all have the heads of birds or beasts. Thus, one would be jackal-headed like the Egyptian god Anubis, another ibis-headed like Thoth, another cow-headed like Hathor, and so on. The heads would indicate the drives, motives, and temperaments of the characters. At the same time, their human bodies would indicate the conflicts between their beastlike nature and human nature.

I never did anything beyond the notes with the idea because it was too much like a simple morality play. Also, it was rather demeaning of the animals. Jackals and hyenas are not, in reality, cowardly. Pigs are seldom fat in the wilds and are no more voracious than other animals. Vultures perform services analogous to those of human garbage collectors. Stallions and bulls and rams are responding to hormonal effects over which they have no control.

Animals do not have morals. Why should they? And, if they did, how could we humans breed them for certain desirable (to

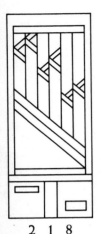

us) features? What would you do with a bull if he refused on moral grounds to impregnate hundreds of cows? What if cattle destined to be slaughtered for their meat sued us in court because we were violating their civil rights? Nor should a housecat be rebuked because it slays songbirds or toys with mice before killing them. It is just obeying its instinct-drives.

Another reason for not doing anything with my projected play about beast-headed humans was that I finally realized that we are beastlike in many respects. It is almost impossible to discriminate, to segregate or classify, what is beastlike in us and what is humanlike. Humans are part beasts, and the two threads of beastishness and humanity are so intertwined that you can't unravel one without making the whole fall apart.

Yet, to this day, sometimes when I look at certain persons, I see, quite vividly, not the human face but that of a bird, beast, reptile, fish, or insect. Their personalities suggest these, and my imagination supplants the human head with that of one of the "lower" animals. Curiously enough, this only happens in a pejorative sense. That is, if I admire a person's courage, I never see the head of a lion or tiger on him or her. The features of Homo sapiens remain unblurred. But if I regard a person as an inanely chattering magpie, then I see the bird's head. Or, if I regard a person as not too bright, I see a cow's or kangaroo's head, or a pig's if the person is selfish or self-centered, self-indulgent, or overly fat.

Despite knowing that animals cannot help their behavior and that humans isolate certain fancied characteristics of animals to use as insults or compliments, I still react sometimes on a purely conditioned-reflex level.

Which makes me more animal than I want to be.

But then humans are animals, and they quite often react to stimuli in what seems to be an instinct-fixed manner. I am talking of psychological stimuli, not physical. The reactions to these psychological stimuli vary widely among people; they are not rigid uniform reactions such as we find in animals reacting to physical stimuli. Thus, some groups, the fundamentalists, for

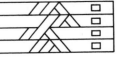

instance, persist in believing, despite all evidence to the contrary, in a literal interpretation of the Bible. Other groups persist in believing that all Negroes are inferior to all Caucasians, despite the evidence to the contrary. There is even a group, though a small one, that insists, despite overwhelming evidence to the contrary, that the Earth is flat.

I suggest that these people are subject to instinct and that it is instinct which makes them deny their rational powers. Various types of such rationality-denying instincts exist in people. But whereas animals have a common and uniform type of instinct, varying according to the species, humans have individual instincts. They inherit certain complexes of genes which determine their rationality-denying behavior.

In other words, human beings are like beasts in that they do have instincts, reactions punched-in by their genetic inheritance. But the instincts vary among human beings. Every person is his or her own species—in a sense.

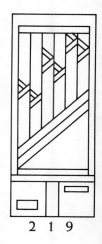

What beast sometimes stares back at me when I look into a mirror? After all, I should see in myself what I see in other people. What is sauce for the goose is sauce for the gander. We're all birds of a feather. So, I see now and then, not the theriomorphic head I put on others, but the visage of an Arcturan or Rigelian. The exotic features of a creature from outer space, the face of a sentient nonhuman yet near-human being born on a planet revolving around the star Arcturus or the star Rigel. I used to see a Martian's face, but, since we now know that Mars has no animal life, I've abandoned that vision.

Yet, I'm not entirely sure that Mars does not have life. We have not eliminated the possibility that things do creep, walk, and fly under the red rock on the surface. Deep beneath the crust may be all sorts of creatures, imaginable and unimaginable.

When and where did the idea for this short story, "Totem and Taboo," originate? I was in Peoria then, it was 1954, and I was working as a laborer and bottle-and-vat washer on the second shift at Roszell's Sealtest Dairy. Mornings and weekends, I was either reading or writing—when, of course, I was not cutting

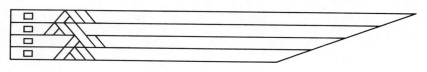

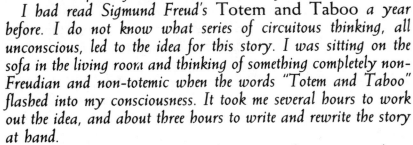

grass or grocery-shopping or doing one of the hundred tasks and chores inescapable for a married man and father.

I had read Sigmund Freud's Totem and Taboo a year before. I do not know what series of circuitous thinking, all unconscious, led to the idea for this story. I was sitting on the sofa in the living room and thinking of something completely non-Freudian and non-totemic when the words "Totem and Taboo" flashed into my consciousness. It took me several hours to work out the idea, and about three hours to write and rewrite the story at hand.

Freud's book tries to explain the origins of totemism and exogamy in ancient preliterate societies. Totemism is the belief in totems and totemic relationships. A totem is an animal or natural object considered by preliterates to be related by blood to a certain family or clan and taken as its symbol. Exogamy is the custom among certain tribes, clans, etc., which prohibits a man from marrying a woman of his own tribe, clan, etc.

Freud's explanations are not generally accepted by psychoanalysts or anthropologists, but the book is interesting. Those who have read his work and will read my story will see that the story has nothing to do with Freud's thesis. Or does it? There is a psycholanalyst in it, and he has a practice based upon a theory which is as invalid and nonsensical as some of Freud's conclusions. Or are they really so nonsensical? Whatever works in psychotherapy with the patient is valid; never mind the theory.

No psychologist or psychoanalyst, as far as I know, has thought to combine zoology with his or her particular school of theory and technique. Maybe they should look into this.

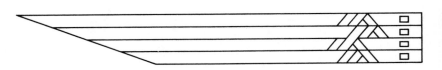

Kathy Phelan told her fiancé, "Jay, you can take your choice. Give up drinking or give up me."

Jay Martin was convinced she meant it. Her triangular face was set in tense lines, and her slanting green eyes burned.

He made one more protest. "But, kitten, I'm not an alcoholic. Just a light-heavy drinker, almost a middleweight, you might say."

She bared little sharp teeth with extraordinarily long canines.

"Flyweight, shmyweight, what's the difference? You're no champ. You never go more than six rounds before you're flat on your back."

Pretty as a prize Siamese—and her bite was as sharp. Sadly, Jay Martin said he would, of course, not hesitate a moment about his choice. She smiled and purred and ran her little red-pink tongue out to moisten her lips for his goodby kiss.

Like a wounded crow dragging his broken wing behind him, Jay Martin limped into the Green Lizard Lounge. It was the best place he could think of in which to brood over his decision not to drink anymore. A dry martini was just the thing in which to mingle sorrow and anger.

Ivan Tursiops entered a moment later, almost literally dived into a huge schooner of beer, rolled and reveled in it, then, after blowing and snorting relief and rhapsody, condescended to listen to Jay's story. He was properly sympathetic.

"You can't help your urge towards the bottle, you know," he said. "What you need is a good psychiatrist."

"The only one I know is an alcoholic."

"Oh, now, he's not the only one in the world. The trouble with you, my boy, is you don't hobnob with enough neurotics. Now I've dozens for friends, and every one swears by a different witch doctor. But I've

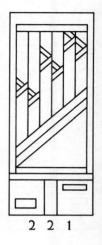

2 2 1

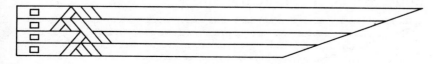

heard recently of one fellow who's so good I'm afraid to see him. I might lose my neurosis, you know, and I couldn't afford that."

"You mean your total inability to hear your mother-in-law?"

"Exactly. Look, here's his address. The new Medical Arts Building."

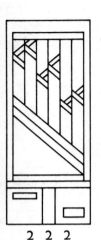

Doctor Capra pulled on his chin-whiskers and said, "Yes, I'm of a new school of thought. We take the anthropological approach. Have you read the recent authoritative article on our theories in the August *Commuter's Digest?*"

Jay nodded. Dr. Capra looked pleased and glanced at his watch. His waiting room was full.

"Then you know the essentials. Why waste time repeating them? You must be an intelligent man; you graduated from college. Business administration, I believe?"

"Yes, Doctor. Look, Kathy loves me, but she dominates me. She wants to run every minute of my life. And . . ."

"Never mind that, Mr. Martin. Or may I call you Jay? Pay no attention to what your fiancée is doing. I assure you the Freudians and their mother-complexes were way off. It's not at all necessary that I know your personal difficulties. We—"

"But she's made me give up almost everything I like. Now, I don't mind . . ."

"All that's of no consequence at all, Jay. Ha! *Hmm!*"

The doctor was holding up four photographs of Jay, each made from a different angle. He stroked his chin-whiskers. "Excellent. No border case here. You're definitely the avian type."

Ignoring Jay's torrential story of his conflicts with Kathy, he said, "Look at the tall thin and gangling body. Stork. Look at the shock of hair. Kingfisher.

Big round eyes. Owl. Hooked nose. Falcon. Big and friendly but slightly mocking grin. Laughing jackass."

"Say!" said Jay. "I resent—"

"No doubt of it, young man. You're a classical type. There'll be no trouble at all, at all."

Doctor Capra rubbed his hands in professional glee and then handed Jay Martin a pillbox. "One every two hours, my boy, until your tutelary totem appears."

"What?"

"You read the article, didn't you? You know that primitive societies were quite correct in dividing their people into clans, each of which had a guiding and protecting spirit or totem modeled after a particular animal, don't you? We psychiatrists of the anthropological school have found that the primitives unconsciously stumbled over a great truth. Every man is, in his subconscious, a bear or fox or weasel or magpie or pig, or what have you. Watch your friends. Observe their types of bodies, their faces, their actions, their characters. All modeled upon some zoological prototype.

"This pill is the result of our collaborations with the neurologists and biochemists. It organizes your subconscious so that your subjective totem seems to be projected objectively. In fact, it may be, for all we know, for we've never succeeded in catching one. However..."

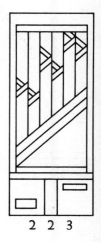

2 2 3

"But, Doctor, don't you want to hear what my trouble is? Kathy says..."

Capra glanced at his wrist watch, stood up, smiling, and gently butted Jay out of the office with his hands.

"Come back at this time next week. I can give you five minutes."

"But, Doc, Kathy says I drink too much!"

Capra stopped, frowned, and pulled on his yellow-brown goatee.

"I knew there was something. Ah, yes, don't drink

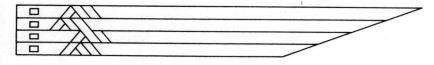

any liquor while you're taking these pills, my boy. Might disorganize the subconscious, you know."

"But, but...!"

"Not now, Mr. Martin."

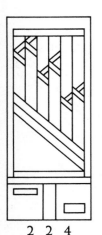

Ivan Tursiops looked up from the depths of his beer. "How'd it go?"

"I just told Kathy. Her fur really bristled; I was lucky to get away with only a verbal mauling. She says I should ignore Capra's corn. All I need is a strong will power. If I loved her enough, I'd..."

Ivan beckoned to the waitress.

"Dry martini."

"No, thanks," said Jay. "Doctor's orders. And Kathy threatened to scratch my eyes out if I ever came around with liquor on my breath again. Everybody's against me...."

The waitress set down the martini. Absently, broodingly, Jay sipped. Ivan said, "Pay no attention to either, my boy. I was just talking to Bob White, and he said he knows a hell of a good psychiatrist who uses the overdo-it approach. Just what you need. If your neurosis is alcohol, you don't try to quit hitting the bottle. You try to drink *too* much."

Jay downed his martini. His eyes were bright. "Yeah? Tell me more."

"Waitress!"

Jay Martin awoke at noon the following day. Because it was Saturday and he didn't have to work, he didn't care that it was so late. But he did mind that he had to wake up at all. Seven martinis before he lost count. That meant a head the size of the *Hindenburg* and one just as ready to burst into flames. He'd be riding a seismograph of nausea and...

But he wasn't. His head was clear as a freshly wiped

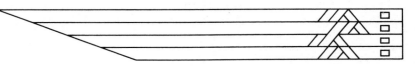

cocktail glass, and his nerves firm as a bartender's hand scooping up a tip.

It was then that he saw, perched on the foot of his bed, the bird.

The jagbird.

It was big as a bald eagle. It *was* bald, and the bags under its squinting bloodshot eyes were packed with dissipation. Its long bulbous red beak hung open to expose a swollen tongue with purple hair. Its frizzled black plumage reeked of stale beer; its breath was the morning-after's.

If Jay had not felt so healthy, he would have sworn that this was the first hallucination of an attack of D.T.'s.

"Go away!" he said.

"Nevermore!" croaked the jagbird.

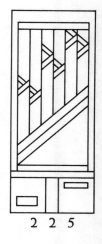

It was some time before Jay understood that the phrase was not a reply to his request that it leave. It was, literally, Jay's usual vow on awakening after a hard night.

Jay got up and made some coffee. While he was drinking it, the bird flew in and perched on the chair across the table.

"Nevermore!"

If it hadn't been for the creature, Jay would have been able to eat a hearty breakfast, something he hadn't done for several years.

He got up and walked out. The bird flew through the door just as he opened it. And it insisted on perching upon his shoulder and croaking every sixty seconds, regular and monotonous as a metronome, "Nevermore!"

When he brushed it away, it flapped heavily above him so its shadow always fell on Jay's head.

Jay was afraid to visit Kathy, so he went to a movie. The bird flew in with him, nor was it asked for a ticket.

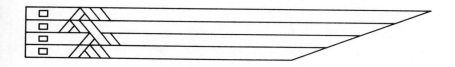

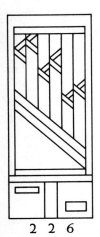

When Jay sat down, it perched upon his shoulder. The woman behind Jay did not seem to be bothered by it, so he decided that it must be an hallucination. It was a visual, auditory, tactile, and olfactory triumph for Doctor Capra's little pills. Jay wanted to read the riot act to the psychiatrist, but he was afraid that he would be asked if he'd been drinking liquor while taking the pills. Not only had he done so, he had swallowed all of them at once during a fit of bravado when Ivan Tursiops had said that they were probably nothing but sugar.

At exactly five o'clock, the jagbird disappeared. Puzzled but elated, Jay left the movie a few minutes later. It was not until he was just about to step into the Green Lizard that he remembered his hangovers always left him at that time.

He raised his eyebrows and went on in. His eyebrows soared even higher when he saw the bird sitting on the bar, waiting for him. Jay ignored it and ordered a martini. He lifted it to his lips.

"Hic!" belched the bird.

At the same time it breathed in his face.

"Aagh!"

"What's the matter?" said the bartender. "You chokin' or somepin?"

"Can't you smell it?" wheezed Jay.

"Smell what?"

"Nothing."

The jagbird had put one heavy foot on the edge of the glass. Its talon, like a waiter's dirty thumb, dipped into the drink. Its red eyes, purple in the lounge's dim light, squinted reproachfully.

"Hic!" it said.

"Haec!" sneered Jay.

"Hoc!" trumped the bird.

"Heck!" groaned Jay.

He left the martini untouched. He couldn't argue with a bird who could decline Latin.

Kathy was so pleased to see Jay sober and with not even the hint of liquor on his breath that she almost purred. Her suspicion-slanted eyes widened into a soft golden-green.

"Oh, Jay, you've really sworn off. You love me!"

Her kiss was more than warm. He didn't enjoy it as much as he should, and she felt it. She stiffened, narrowed her eyes, and put her sharp nails on his arm.

"What's the matter? Aren't you happy? Do you regret doing this for me?"

"Bring me a drink."

"What? I will not!"

"Oh, I won't touch it . . . I think."

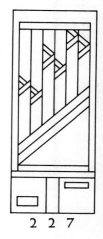

Kathy sensed urgency. She went to the liquor cabinet and poured a scotch. He watched her and wondered again why he had to give up drinking when she wouldn't. She had explained that she did not *have* to drink, but he did. Would he be a dog-in-the-manger and ask her to give up her harmless enjoyment because it was for him a vicious habit? Feeling like a selfish brute, he had said no. But he couldn't help a little bitterness.

She handed him the scotch. Instantly, the jagbird stuck its big bulbous beak between cup and lip.

"Hic!"

Jay handed the glass back to Kathy.

"See?"

She didn't. He explained. Instead of relaxing, her eyes slitted even more, and her nails scratched his arm.

"Do you mean this bird will *always* be with us? Even after we're married? We'll *never* be alone?"

There was no soft plaintive note in her voice. Only a hiss of anger and determination.

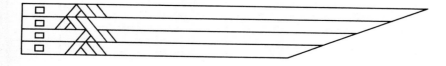

He patted her arm. "It's not a real bird, kitten. *You* can't see it."

"No, but I'll know it's there! I won't be able to forget it. It'll make me nervous as a cat! Not only that, but I don't like your giving up liquor because of some crazy bird. I want you to do it on your own will power, to stand on your own two feet."

"If it weren't for my totem," he said, "I'd not be standing on my feet now. I'd be under the table at the Green Lizard."

"That's what I thought!" she spat. "Where is the jag-bird now?"

He jerked his thumb at the end table, where it perched, sleepy-eyed, upon the ceramic bust of a Silenus. She stared vainly, burst into tears, and said, "Oh, if only I could see it! If only . . ."

She stopped and dried her eyes. She became soft and furry-voiced.

"What is the address of this Doctor Capra, honey?"

It was a moment before he could see what she intended doing. She looked unconcernedly at him and even yawned, as if the whole matter had all at once become of no importance.

He blinked rapidly, like a startled owl. The outlines of her body had wavered and then congealed. They had remained fixed for only the space of a wink, but long enough. There was no mistaking the long bristling whiskers, the fangs revealed by the yawn, and the narrow-pupiled eyes. Nor the I'm-about-to-swallow-the-canary expression.

He strode past her, scooped up the jagbird, and lunged through the door.

Kathy screamed, "Jay, come back!"

"Nevermore!" croaked the bird, its head sticking out from under its owner's arm.

•

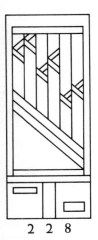

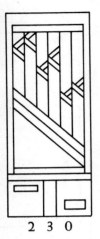

Jay Martin is now married to a little woman with a spaniel's big brown eyes. Her devotion to him has been described by their friends as dog-like. They act like two lovebirds. He no longer drinks like a fish, and he has become a whale of a success in the business world. He seems to be gifted with some uncanny instinct which enables him to judge a person's character at a glance. Last year he joined the bulls, cornered the bears, and made a big killing among the wolves of Wall Street.

THE ADVENTURE
OF THE
THREE MADMEN

.

This story was, in a different version, a very short novel titled The Adventure of the Peerless Peer. *The version at hand, now a novella in this collection, has been retitled and extensively rewritten and revised. The reason for this is a tale in itself.*

At the time I wrote the original, 1973, I was living in a small house in the Knollcrest area of Peoria, Illinois. Only two years before, my wife and I sold our big Moorish house on Burnside Street in Los Angeles and returned to Peoria after an absence of thirteen years. As I have said elsewhere, the smog and dense population of Los Angeles were factors in this decision. Also, I had started freelancing full-time in the middle of 1969, and by 1970 I was convinced that a writer could live more cheaply and peacefully in Peoria (though he'd have to lose certain things), and so weather the bad times, the ups and downs, of a self-employer. The major factor, though, was that my daughter, Kristen, and granddaughter, Kimberly Dana, had moved back to Peoria. We wanted to be near them.

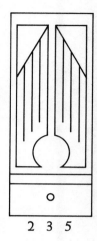

2 3 5

At this time, I was happy and in a good mood. So, when a devout Sherlockian, a small-house publisher, asked me to write a Holmes-Watson-feral man parody, I eagerly accepted. I had been thinking for some time about such a story, but I might not have written it at this time—or perhaps ever—if it had not been for the request.

So I sat down and wrote a 24,000-word pastiche which was also somewhat of a parody. I had a lot of fun doing it and am still amused when I reread it. The Adventure of the Peerless Peer *was first published as a hardcover by Aspen Press. The limited edition of two thousand was almost sold out before it was printed.*

Dell brought it out in paperback in 1974. The cover illustration by Gadino was magnificent. The original hangs on the wall in front of my desk now beside an oil reconstruction of an original for a Shadow *magazine. The Gadino shows an African veldt on which are zebras and giraffes and water birds in the background along with a Zeppelin and two Allied World War I fighter biplanes. To the left in the foreground is a chimpanzee reading*

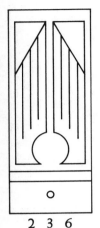

The Casebook of Sherlock Holmes. *To the right is Ron Ely, holding a big hunting knife, clad only in a brown deerskin. He does look much like the Ape-Man, Lord of the Jungle, whom he portrayed in films. Behind him are Basil Rathbone and Nigel Bruce as Holmes and Watson.*

Fabulous!

Due to objections from the Burroughs estate, the original version of Peer could not be reprinted until 1999, when the Tarzan copyright runs out. I at once purchased all copies I could and have been looking for others since. Once the news gets out, the two editions of Peer will become even more valuable collector's items. I want as many as possible for investments against my retirement or poverty, whichever comes first.

(Oh, how I wish I'd managed to keep all my Doc Savage, Shadow, and Weird Tales magazines, all my Burroughs, Doyle, Lovecraft, and Oz first editions, my early Mad magazines and Superman and Pogo comic books! I could retire right now if I had them. But they were all destroyed in a flash flood when I was living on South Holt Street, just off Burton Way, in Los Angeles.)

The refusal by the Burroughs estate left Preiss and me in a predicament. Should I write an entirely new 24,000-word story, or should I write Lord Greystoke out and write in a new character? Time available determined what I did. I had a contract to write a long novel and hand it in by January, 1983. To write a new novella would cut into the time needed for the novel. As it was, rewriting this version took much more time than I had estimated. But I am always underestimating.

So I decided to rewrite the tale, and the result is at hand.

I retitled it "The Adventure of the Three Madmen" because there is no longer a peer—a nobleman—in the story. The replacement is, however, a baronet, a rank between that of a knight and a baron. A baronet is a sort of titled knight. Some baronetcies are hereditary; some, for a lifetime only.

The new title is appropriate because Holmes does encounter three madmen, and Holmes has figured in "The Adventure of the

Three Gables," "The Adventure of the Three Students," and "The Adventure of the Three Garridebs." And I hope to write three Holmes adventures, of which this is the first, even though it has two versions. The second will take place in Mecca, the Muslim holy city, when Holmes was in the midst of the Great Hiatus. The third will be in Ireland in 1919, when Holmes and Watson are vacationing there.

The original Peer was supposed to have been written by Doctor Watson, and I appeared only as the editor. I have abandoned this pretense and now admit that I am the true author. I don't think I fooled anybody, anyway.

The reader, however, should understand that the manuscript was in first draft and that Watson would never have permitted certain passages to be printed. Hence, certain parenthetical phrases and certain footnotes.

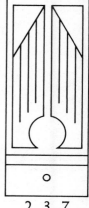

I

It is with a light heart that I take up my pen to write these the last words in which I shall ever record the singular genius which distinguished my friend Sherlock Holmes. I realise that I once wrote something to that effect, though at that time my heart was as heavy as it could possibly be. This time I am certain that Holmes has retired for the last time. At least, he has sworn that he will no more go a-detectiving. The adventure of the three madmen has made him financially secure, and he foresees no more grave perils menacing our country now that our great enemy has been laid low. Moreover, he has sworn that never again will he set foot on any soil but that of his native land. Nor will he ever again get near an aircraft. The mere sight or sound of one freezes his blood.

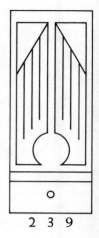

The peculiar narrative which occupies these pages began on the second day of February, 1916. At this time I was, despite my advanced age, serving on the staff of a military hospital in London. Zeppelins had made bombing raids over England for two nights previously, mainly in the Midlands. Though these were comparatively ineffective, seventy people had been killed, one hundred and thirteen injured, and a monetary damage of fifty-three thousand eight hundred and thirty-two pounds had been inflicted. These raids were the latest in a series starting the nineteenth of January. There was no panic, of course, but even stout British hearts were experiencing some uneasiness. There were rumours, no doubt originated by German agents, that the Kaiser intended to send across the channel a fleet of a thousand airships. I was discussing this rumour with my young friend, Doctor Fell, over a brandy in my quarters when a knock sounded on the door. I opened it to admit a messenger. He handed me a telegram which I wasted no time in reading.

"Great Scott!" I cried.

"What is it, my dear fellow?" Fell said, heaving himself from the chair. Even then, on war rations, he was putting on overly much weight.

"A summons to the F.O.," I said. "From Holmes. And I am on special leave."

"Sherlock?" said Fell.

"No, Mycroft," I replied. Minutes later, having packed my few belongings, I was being driven in a limousine toward the Foreign Office. An hour later, I entered the small austere room in which the massive Mycroft Holmes sat like a great spider spinning the web that ran throughout the British Empire and many alien lands. There were two others present, both of whom I knew. One was young Merrivale, a baronet's son, the brilliant aide to the head of the British Military Intelligence Department and soon to assume the chieftainship. He was also a qualified physician and had been one of my students when I was lecturing at Bart's. Mycroft claimed that Merrivale was capable of rivalling Holmes himself in the art of detection and would not be far behind Mycroft himself. Holmes' reply to this "needling" was that only practise revealed true promise.

I wondered what Merrivale was doing away from the War Office but had no opportunity to voice my question. The sight of the second person there startled me at the same time it delighted me. It had been over a year since I had seen that tall, gaunt figure with the greying hair and the unforgettable hawklike profile.

"My dear Holmes," I said. "I had thought that after the Von Bork affair..."

"The east wind has become appallingly cold, Watson," he said. "Duty recognises no age limits, and so I am called from my bees to serve our nation once more."

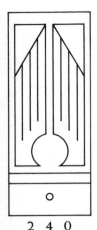

Looking even more grim, he added, "The Von Bork business is not over. I fear that we underestimated the fellow because we so easily captured him. He is not always taken with such facility. Our government erred grievously in permitting him to return to Germany with Von Herling. He should have faced a firing squad. A motor-car crash in Germany after his return almost did for us what we had failed to do, according to reports that have recently reached me. But, except for a permanent injury to his left eye, he has recovered.

"Mycroft tells me that Von Bork has done us and is doing us inestimable damage. Our intelligence tells us that he is operating in Cairo, Egypt. But just where in Cairo and what disguise he has assumed is not known."

"The man is indeed dangerous," Mycroft said, reaching with a hand as ponderous as a grizzly's paw for his snuff-box. "It is no exaggeration to say that he is the most dangerous man in the world, as far as the Allies are concerned, anyway."

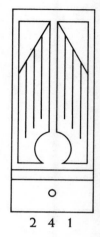

2   4   1

"Greater than Moriarty was?" Holmes said, his eyes lighting up.

"Much greater," replied Mycroft. He breathed in the snuff, sneezed, and wiped his jacket with a large red handkerchief. His watery grey eyes had lost their inward-turning look and burned as if they were searchlights probing the murkiness around a distant target.

"Von Bork has stolen the formula of a Hungarian refugee scientist employed by our government in Cairo. The scientist recently reported to his superiors the results of certain experiments he had been making on a certain type of bacillus peculiar to the land of the Pharaohs. He had discovered that this bacillus could be modified by chemical means to eat only sauerkraut. When a single bacillus was placed upon sauerkraut, it multiplied at a fantastic rate. It would become within sixty minutes a colony which would consume a pound of sauerkraut to its last molecule.

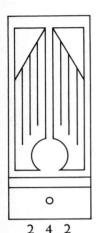

2 4 2

"You see the implications. The bacillus is what the scientists call a mutated type. After treatment with a certain chemical both its form and function are changed. Should we drop vials containing this mutation in Germany, or our agents directly introduce the germs, the entire nation would shortly become sauerkrautless. Both their food supply and their morale would be devastated.

"But Von Bork somehow got wind of this, stole the formula, destroyed the records and the chemicals with fire, and murdered the only man who knew how to mutate the bacillus.

"However, his foul deed was no sooner committed than detected. A tight cordon was thrown around Cairo, and we have reason to believe that Von Bork is hiding in the native quarter somewhere. We can't keep that net tight for long, my dear Sherlock, and that is why you must be gotten there quickly to track him down. England expects much from you, brother, and much, I am sure, will be given."

I turned to Holmes, who looked as shaken as I felt. "Surely, my dear fellow, we are not going to Cairo?"

"Surely, indeed, Watson," he replied. "Who else could sniff out the Teutonic fox, who else could trap him? We are not so old that we cannot settle Von Bork's hash once and for all."

Holmes, I observed, was still in the habit of using Americanisms, I suppose because he had thrown himself so thoroughly into the role of an Irish-American while tracking down Von Bork in that adventure which I have titled "His Last Bow."

"Unless," he said, "you really feel that the old warhorse should not leave his comfortable pasture?"

"I am as good a man as I was a year and a half ago," I protested. "Have you ever known me to call it quits?"

He chuckled and patted my shoulder, a gesture so rare that my heart warmed.

"Good old Watson."

Mycroft called for cigars, and while we were lighting up, he said, "You two will leave tonight from a Royal Naval Air Service strip outside London. You will be flown by two stages to Cairo, by two different pilots, I should say. The fliers have been carefully selected because their cargo will be precious. The Huns may already know your destination. If they do, they will make desperate efforts to intercept you, but our fliers are the pick of the lot. They are fighter pilots, but they will be flying bombers. The first pilot, the man who'll take you under his wing tonight, is a young fellow. You may know of him, at least you knew his great-uncle."

He paused and said, "You remember, of course, the late Duke of Greyminster?"*

"I will never forget the size of the fee I collected from him," Holmes said, and he chuckled.

"Your pilot, Leftenant John Drummond, is the adopted son of the present Lord Greyminster," Mycroft continued.

"But wait!" I said. "Haven't I heard some rather strange things about Lord Greyminster? Doesn't he live in Africa?"

"Oh, yes, in darkest Africa," Mycroft said. "In a tree house, I believe."

"Lord Greyminster lives in a tree house?" I said.

"Ah, yes," Mycroft said. "Greyminster is living in a tree house with an ape."

"Lord Greyminster is living with an ape?" I said. "A female ape, I trust."

"Oh, yes," Mycroft said. "There's nothing queer about Lord Greyminster, you know."

"I have heard," Merrivale said, "that there is another

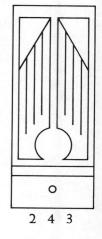

2 4 3

---

*Referring to "The Adventure of the Priory School."

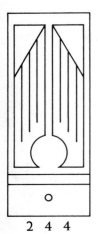

feral man, that is, a human being raised by animals from infancy, in Africa at this time. I refer to the Indian baronet, Sir Mowgli of the Seeonee. He, as I understand it, was raised by wolves, not apes."

"What is he doing in Africa?" Holmes said. "India is his native land, and its central area his domain."

"You haven't read the recent accounts of him in the *Times?*"

"No. I read only accounts of crimes and the agony column."

I do not know why Holmes lied about this. It had long been evident to me and the readers of my accounts of his adventures that he reads almost everything in many London and some foreign journals.

"He is in central Africa with an American film company which is making a movie based on his life. He is playing himself as a boy of eighteen, though he is forty-three years old or thereabouts. His leading lady is the British actress, Countess Mary Anne Liza Murdstone-Malcon, better known under her stage name of Liza Borden."

"Making a movie? During wartime?" I said. "Isn't the baronet a major in the Army?"

"There are neither British nor German forces in that area," Merrivale said. "Major Sir Mowgli is on leave to make this film, which I understand contains much anti-German propaganda."

Mycroft slammed his palm against the top of the table, startling all of us and making me wonder what had caused this unheard-of violence from the usually phlegmatic Mycroft.

"Enough of this time-wasting chitchat!" he said. "The Empire is crumbling around our ears and we're talking as if we're in a pub and all's well with the world!"

He was right, of course, and all of us, including Holmes, I'm sure, felt abashed. But that conversation was not as irrelevant as we thought at the time.

An hour later, after receiving verbal instructions from Mycroft and Merrivale, we left in the limousine for the secret airstrip outside London.

II

Our chauffeur drove off the highway onto a narrow dirt road which wound through a dense woods of oaks. After a half-mile, during which we passed many signs warning trespassers that this was military property, we were halted by a barbed wire gate across the road. Armed R.N.A.S. guards checked our documents and then waved us on. Ten minutes later, we emerged from the woods onto a very large meadow. At its northern end was a tall hill, the lower part of which gaped as if it had a mouth which was open with surprise. The surprise was that the opening was not to a cavern but to a hangar which had been hollowed out of the living rock of the hill. As we got out of the car men pushed from the hangar a huge aeroplane, the wings of which were folded against the fuselage.

After that, events proceeded swiftly—too swiftly for me, I admit, and perhaps a trifle too swiftly for Holmes. After all, we had been born about a half century before the first aeroplane had flown. We were not sure that the motor-car, a recent invention from our viewpoint, was altogether a beneficial device. And here we were being conducted by a commodore toward the monstrously large aircraft. Within a few minutes, according to him, we would be within its fuselage and leaving the good earth behind and beneath us.

Even as we walked toward it, its biplanes were unfolded and locked into place. By the time we reached

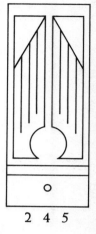

it, its propellors had been spun by mechanics and the two motors had caught fire. Thunder rolled from its rotaries, and flames spat from its exhausts.

Whatever Holmes' true feelings, and his skin was rather grey, he could not suppress his driving curiosity, his need to know all that was relevant. However, he had to shout at the commodore to be heard above the roar of the warming-up motors.

"The Admiralty ordered it to be outfitted for your use," the commodore said. His expression told us that he thought that we must be very special people indeed if this aeroplane was equipped just for us.

"It's the prototype model of the Handley Page 0/100," he shouted. "The first of the 'bloody paralyser of an aeroplane' the Admiralty ordered for the bombing of Germany. It has two two hundred-fifty-horsepower Rolls-Royce Eagle II motors, as you see. It has an enclosed crew cabin. The engine nacelles and the front part of the fuselage were armour-plated, but the armour has been removed to give the craft more speed."

"What?" Holmes yelled. "Removed?"

"Yes," the commodore said. "It shouldn't make any difference to you. You'll be in the cabin, and it was never armour-plated."

Holmes and I exchanged glances. The commodore continued, "Extra petrol tanks have been installed to give the craft extended range. These will be just forward of the cabin..."

"And if we crash?" Holmes said.

"Poof!" the commodore said, smiling. "No pain, my dear sir. If the smash doesn't kill you, the flaming petrol sears the lungs and causes instantaneous death. The only difficulty is in identifying the corpse. Charred, you know."

We climbed up a short flight of wooden mobile steps and stepped into the cabin. The commodore closed

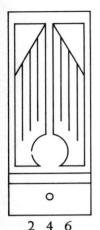

2 4 6

the door, thus somewhat muting the roar. He pointed out the bunks that had been installed for our convenience and the W. C. This contained a small washbowl with a gravity-feed water tank and several thundermugs bolted to the deck.

"The prototype can carry a four-man crew," the commodore said. "There is, as you have observed, a cockpit for the nose gunner, with the pilot in a cockpit directly behind him. There is a cockpit near the rear for another machine gunner, and there is a trap-door through which a machine gun may be pointed to cover the rear area under the plane. You are standing on the trap-door."

Holmes and I moved away, though not, I trust, with unseemly haste.

"We estimate that with its present load the craft can fly at approximately eighty-five miles per hour. Under ideal conditions, of course. We have decided to eliminate the normal armament of machine guns in order to lighten the load. In fact, to this end, all of the crew except the pilot and co-pilot are eliminated. The pilot, I believe, is bringing his personal arms: a dagger, several pistols, a carbine, and his specially mounted Spandau machine gun, a trophy, by the way, taken from a Fokker E-1 which Captain Wentworth downed when he dropped an ash-tray on the pilot's head. Wentworth has also brought in several cases of hand grenades and a case of Scotch whisky."

The door, or port, or whatever they call a door in the Royal Naval Air Service, opened, and a young man of medium height but with very broad shoulders and a narrow waist, entered. He wore the uniform of the R. N. A. S. He was a handsome young man with eyes as steely grey and as magnetic as Holmes'. There was also something strange about them. If I had known *how* strange, I would have stepped off that plane at that very second. Holmes would have preceded me.

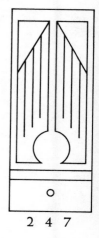

He shook hands with us and spoke a few words. I was astonished to hear a flat midwestern American accent. When Wentworth had disappeared on some errand toward the stern, Holmes asked the commodore, "Why wasn't a British pilot assigned to us? No doubt this Yank volunteer is quite capable, but really . . ."

"There is only one pilot who can match Wentworth's aerial genius. He is an American in the service of the Tsar. The Russians know him as Kentov, though that is not his real name. They refer to him with the honorific of *Chorniy Oryol*, the French call him *l'Aigle Noir* and the Germans are offering a hundred thousand marks for *Der Schwarz Adler*, dead or alive. The English translation is *The Black Eagle*."

"Is he a Negro?" I said.

"No, the adjective refers to his sinister reputation," replied the commodore. "Kentov will take you on from Marseilles. Your mission is so important that we borrowed him from the Russians. Wentworth is being used only for the comparatively short haul since he is scheduled to carry out another mission soon. If you should crash, and survive, he would be able to guide you through enemy territory better than anyone we know of, excluding Kentov. Wentworth is an unparalleled master of disguise. . . ."

"Really?" Holmes said, drawing himself up and frostily regarding the officer.

Aware that he had made a gaffe, the commodore changed the subject. He showed us how to don the bulky parachutes, which were to be kept stored under a bunk.

"What happened to young Drummond?" I asked him. "Lord Greyminster's adopted son? Wasn't he supposed to be our pilot?"

"Oh, he's in hospital," he said, smiling. "Nothing

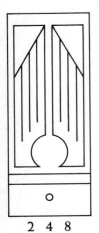

serious. Several broken ribs and clavicle, a liver that may be ruptured, a concussion and possible fracture of the skull. The landing gear of his craft collapsed as he was making a deadstick landing, and he slid into a brick wall. He sends his regards."

Captain Wentworth suddenly reappeared. Muttering to himself, he looked under our blankets and sheets and then under the bunks. Holmes said, "What is it, captain?"

Wentworth straightened up and looked at us with those strange grey eyes. "Thought I heard bats," he said. "Wings fluttering. Giant bats. But no sign of them."

He left the cabin then, heading down a narrow tunnel which had been specially installed so that the pilot could get into the cockpit without having to go outside the craft. His co-pilot, a Lieutenant Nelson, had been warming the motors. The commodore left a minute later after wishing us luck. He looked as if he thought we'd need it.

Presently, Wentworth phoned in to us and told us to lie down in the bunks or grab hold of something solid. We were getting ready to take off. We got into the bunks, and I stared at the ceiling while the plane slowly taxied to the starting point, the motors were "revved" up, and then it began to bump along the meadow. Within a short time its tail had lifted and we were suddenly aloft. Neither Holmes nor I could endure just lying there any more. We had to get up and look through the window in the door. The sight of the earth dropping away in the dusk, of houses, cows, horses and wagons, and brooks and then the Thames itself dwindling caused us to be both uneasy and exhilarated.

Holmes was still grey, but I am certain that it was not fear of altitude that affected him. It was being

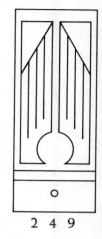

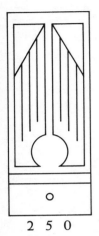

completely dependent upon someone else, being *not* in control of the situation. On the ground Holmes was his own master. Here his life and limb were in the hands of two strangers, one of whom had already impressed us as being very strange. It also became obvious only too soon that Holmes, no matter how steely his nerves and how calm his digestion on earth, was subject to airsickness.

The plane flew on and on, crossing the channel in the dark, crossing the westerly and then the southwestern part of France. We landed on a strip lighted with flames. Holmes wanted to get out and stretch his legs but Wentworth forbade that.

"Who knows what's prowling around here, waiting to identify you and then to crouch and leap, destroying utterly?" he said.

After he had gone back to the cockpit, I said, "Holmes, don't you think he puts the possibility of spies in somewhat strange language? And didn't you smell Scotch on his breath? Should a pilot drink while flying?"

"Frankly," Holmes said, "I'm too sick to care," and he lay down outside the door to the W.C.

Midnight came with the great plane boring through the dark moonless atmosphere. Lieutenant Nelson crawled into his bunk with the cheery comment that we would be landing at a drome outside Marseilles by dawn. Holmes groaned. I bade the fellow, who seemed quite a decent sort, good-night. Presently I fell asleep, but I awoke some time later with a start. As an old veteran of Holmes' campaigns, however, I knew better than to reveal my awakened state. While I rolled over to one side as if I were doing it in my sleep, I watched through narrowed eyes.

A sound, or a vibration, or perhaps it was an old veteran's sixth sense, had awakened me. Across the aisle, illumined by the single bulb overhead, stood Lieutenant Nelson. His handsome youthful face bore an expression which the circumstances certainly did not seem to call for. He looked so malignant that my heart began thumping and perspiration poured out from me despite the cold outside the blankets. In his hand was a revolver, and when he lifted it my heart almost stopped. But he did not turn toward us. Instead he started toward the front end, toward the narrow tunnel leading to the pilot's cockpit.

Since his back was to me, I leaned over the edge of the bunk and reached down to get hold of Holmes. I had no need to warn him. Whatever his physical condition, he was still the same alert fox—an old fox, it is true, but still a fox. His hand reached up and touched mine, and within a few seconds he was out of the bunk and on his feet. In his one hand he held his trusty Webley, which he raised to point at Nelson's back, crying out to halt at the same time.

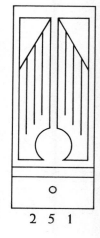

I do not know if he heard Holmes above the roar of the motors. If he did, he did not have time to consider it. There was a report, almost inaudible in the din, and Nelson fell back and slid a few feet along the floor backward. Blood gushed from his shattered forehead.

The dim light fell on the face of Captain Wentworth, whose eyes seemed to blaze, though I am certain that was an optical illusion. The face was momentarily twisted, and then it smoothed out, and he stepped out into the light. I got down from the bunk and with Holmes approached him. I could smell the heavy, though fragrant, odour of excellent Scotch on his breath.

Wentworth looked at the revolver in Holmes' hand, smiled, and said, "So—you are not overrated, Mr. Holmes! But I was waiting for him, I expected him to

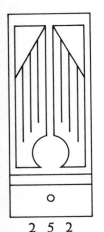

252

sneak in upon me while I should be concentrating on the instrument board. He thought he'd blow my a*s off!"

"He is, of course, a German spy," Holmes said. "But how did you determine that he was?"

"I suspect everybody," Wentworth replied. "I kept my eye on him, and when I saw him talking over the wireless, I listened in. It was too noisy to hear clearly, but he was talking in German. I caught several words, *schwanz* and *schweinhund*. Undoubtedly, he was informing the Imperial German Military Aviation Service of our location. If he didn't kill me, then we would be shot down. The Huns must be on their way to intercept us now."

This was alarming enough, but both Holmes and I were struck at the same time with a far more disturbing thought. Holmes, as usual, was more quick in his reactions. He screamed, "Who's flying the plane?"

Wentworth smiled lazily and said, "Nobody. Don't worry. The controls are connected to a little device I invented last month. As long as the air is smooth, the plane will fly on an even keel all by itself."

He stiffened suddenly, cocked his head to one side, and said, "Do you hear it?"

"Great Scott, man!" I cried. "How could we hear anything above the infernal racket of those motors?"

"Cockroaches!" Wentworth bellowed. "Giant flying cockroaches! That evil scientist has released another horror upon the world!"

He whirled, and he was gone into the blackness of the tunnel.

Holmes and I stared at each other. Then Holmes said, "We are at the mercy of a madman, Watson. And there is nothing we can do until we have landed."

"We could parachute out," I said.

"I would prefer not to," Holmes said stiffly. "Besides,

it somehow doesn't seem cricket. The pilots have no parachutes, you know. These two were provided only because we are civilians."

"I wasn't planning on asking Wentworth to ride down with me," I mumbled, somewhat ashamed of myself for saying this.

Holmes didn't hear me; once again his stomach was trying to reject contents that did not exist.

III

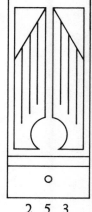

Shortly after dawn, the German planes struck. These, as I was told later, were Fokker E-III's, single-seater monoplanes equipped with two Spandau machine guns. These were synchronized with the propellors to shoot bullets through the empty spaces between the whirling of the propellor blades.

Holmes was sitting on the floor, holding his head and groaning, and I was commiserating with him, though getting weary of his complaints, when the telephone bell rang. I removed the receiver from the box attached to the wall, or bulkhead, or whatever they call it. Wentworth's voice bellowed, "Put on the parachutes and hang on to something tight! Twelve ****ing Fokkers, a whole *staffel*, coming in at eleven o'clock!"

I misunderstood him. I said, "Yes, but what type of plane are they?"

"Fokkers!" he cried, adding, "No, no! My eyes played tricks on me. They're giant flying cockroaches! Each one is being ridden by a Prussian officer, helmeted and goggled and armed with a boarding cutlass!"

"What did you say?" I screamed into the phone, but it had been disconnected.

I told Holmes what Wentworth had said, and he

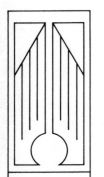

forgot about being airsick, though he looked no better than before. We staggered out to the door and looked through its window.

The night was now brighter than day, the result of flares thrown out from the attacking aeroplanes. Their pilots intended to use the light to line up the sights of their machine guns on our helpless craft. Then, as if that were not bad enough, shells began exploding, some so near that our aeroplane shuddered and rocked under the impact of the blasts. Giant searchlights began playing about, some of them illuminating monoplanes with black crosses on their fuselages.

"Archy!" I exclaimed. "The French anti-aircraft guns are firing at the Huns! The fools! They could hit us just as well!"

Something flashed by. We lost sight of it, but a moment later we saw a fighter diving down toward us through the glare of the flares and the searchlights, ignoring the bursting shells around it. Two tiny red eyes flickered behind the propellor, but it was not until holes were suddenly punched in the fabric only a few feet from us that we realised that those were the muzzles of the machine guns. We dropped to the floor while the great plane rolled and dipped and rose and dropped and we were shot this way and that across the floor and against the bulkheads.

"We're doomed!" I cried to Holmes. "Get the parachutes on! He can't shoot back at the planes, and our plane is too slow and clumsy to get away!"

How wrong I was. And what a demon that madman was. He did things with that big lumbering aeroplane that I wouldn't have believed possible. Several times we were upside down and we only kept from being smashed, like mice shaken in a tin, by hanging on desperately to the bunkposts.

Once, Holmes, whose sense of hearing was somewhat keener than mine, said, "Watson, isn't that a******e shooting a machine gun? How can he fly this plane, put it through such manoeuvres, and still operate a weapon which he must hold in both hands to use effectively?"

"I don't know," I confessed. At that moment both of us were dangling from the post, failing to fall only because of our tight grip. The plane was on its left side. Through the window beneath my feet I saw a German plane, smoke trailing from it, fall away. And then another followed it, becoming a ball of flame about a thousand feet or so from the ground.

The Handley Page righted itself, and I heard faint thumping noises overhead, followed by the chatter of a machine gun. Something exploded very near us and wreckage drifted by the window.

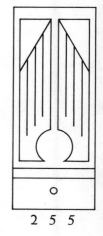

This shocked me, but even more shocking was the rapping on the window. This, to my astonishment, originated from a fist hammering on the door. I crawled over to it and stood up and looked through it. Upside down, staring at me through the isinglass, was Wentworth's face. His lips formed the words, "Open the door! Let me in!"

Numbly, I obeyed. A moment later, with an acrobatic skill that I still find incredible, he swung through the door. In one hand he held a Spandau with a rifle stock. A moment later, while I held on to his waist, he had closed the door and shut out the cold shrilling blast of wind.

"There they are!" he yelled, and he pointed the machine gun at a point just past Holmes, lying on the floor, and sent three short bursts past Holmes' ear.

Holmes said, "Really, old fellow..." Wentworth, raving, ran past him and a moment later we heard the chatter of the Spandau again.

"At least, he's back in the cockpit," Holmes said

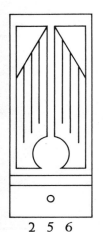

weakly. However, this was one of the times when Holmes was wrong. A moment later the captain was back. He opened the trap-door, poked the barrel of his weapon through, let loose a single burst, said, "Got you, you ****ing son of a *****!" closed the trap-door, and ran back toward the front.

Forty minutes later, the plane landed on a French military aerodrome outside of Marseilles. Its fuselage and wings were perforated with bullet holes in a hundred places, though fortunately no missiles had struck the petrol tanks. The French commander who inspected the plane pointed out that more of the holes were made by a gun firing from the inside than from guns firing from the outside.

"Damn right!" Wentworth said. "The cockroaches and their allies, the flying leopards, were crawling all over inside the plane! They almost got these two old men!"

A few minutes later a British medical officer arrived. Wentworth, after fiercely fighting six men, was subdued and put into a straitjacket and carried off in an ambulance.

Wentworth was not the only one raving. Holmes, his pale face twisted, his fists clenched, was cursing his brother Mycroft, young Merrivale, and everyone else who could possibly be responsible, excepting, of course, His Majesty.

We were taken to an office occupied by several French and British officers of very high rank. The highest, General Chatson-Dawes-Overleigh, said, "Yes, my dear Mr. Holmes, we realise that he sometimes has these hallucinatory fits. Becomes quite mad, to be frank. But he is the best pilot and also the best espionage agent we have, even if he is a Colonial, and he has done heroic work for us. He never hallucinates negatively, that is, he never harms his fellows—though

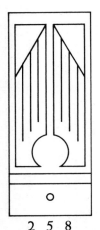

he did shoot an Italian once, but the fellow *was* only a private and he *was* an Italian and it *was* an accident—and so we feel that we must permit him to work for us. We can't permit a word of his condition to get back to the civilian populace, of course, so I must require you to swear silence about the whole affair. Which you would have to do as a matter of course, and, of course, of patriotism. He'll be given a little rest cure, a drying-out, too, and then returned to duty. Britain sorely needs him."*

Holmes raved some more, but he always was one to face realities and to govern himself accordingly. Even so, he could not resist making some sarcastic remarks about his life, which was also extremely valuable, being put into the care of a homicidal maniac. At last, cooling down, he said, "And the pilot who will fly us to Egypt? Is he also an irresponsible madman? Will we be in more danger from him than from the enemy?"

"He is said to be every bit as good a pilot as Wentworth," the general said. "He is an American..."

"Great Scott!" Holmes said. He groaned, and he added, "Why can't we have a pilot of good British stock, tried and true?"

"Both Wentworth and Kentov are of the best British stock," Overleigh said stiffly. "They're descended from some of the oldest and noblest stock of England. They have royal blood in them, as a matter of fact. But they happen to be Colonials. The man who will fly you from here has been working for His Majesty's cousin, the Tsar of all the Russias, as an espionage agent. The Tsar was kind enough to loan both him and one of the great Sikorski *Ilya Mourometz* Type V aeroplanes to us. Kentov flew here in it with a full crew, and it is ready to take off."

Holmes' face became even paler, and I felt every minute of my sixty-four years of age. We were not to get a moment's rest, and yet we had gone through an experience which would have sent many a youth to bed for several days.

IV

General Overleigh himself conducted us to the colossal Russian aeroplane. As we approached it, he described certain features in answer to Holmes' questions.

"So far, the only four-engined heavier-than-air craft in the world has been built by the Russians," he said. "Much to the shame of the British. The first one was built, and flown, in 1913. This, as you can see, is a biplane, fitted with wheels and a ski undercarriage. It has four 150-horsepower Sunbeam water-cooled Vee-type engines. The Sunbeam, unfortunately, leaves much to be desired."

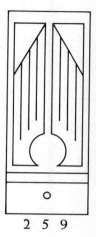

"I would rather not have known that," I murmured. The sudden ashen hue of Holmes' face indicated that his reactions were similar to mine.

"Its wing span is ninety-seven feet, nine and a half inches; the craft's length is fifty-six feet, one inch; its height is fifteen feet, five and seven-eighths inches. Its maximum speed is seventy-five miles per hour; its operational ceiling is 9,843 feet. And its endurance is five hours—under ideal conditions. It carries a crew of five, though it can carry more. The rear fuselage is

*This mad, but usually functioning, American must surely be the great aviator and espionage agent who, after transferring to the U.S. forces in 1917, was known under the code name of G-8. While in the British service, he apparently went under the name of Wentworth, his half-brother's surname. For the true names of G-8, the Spider, and the Shadow, see my *Doc Savage: His Apocalyptic Life.*

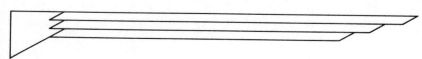

fitted with compartments for sleeping and eating."

Overleigh shook hands with us after he had handed us over to a Lieutenant Obrenov. The young officer led us to the steps into the fuselage and to the rear, where he showed us our compartment. Holmes chatted away with him in Russian, of which he had gained a certain mastery during his experience in Odessa with the Trepoff case. Holmes' insistence on speaking Russian seemed to annoy the officer somewhat, since, like all upper-class people of his country, he preferred to use French. But he was courteous, and after making sure we were comfortable, he bowed himself out. Certainly, we had little to complain about except possibly the size of the cabin. It had been prepared especially for us, had two swing-down beds, a thick rug which Holmes said was a genuine Persian, oil paintings on the walls which Holmes said were genuine Maleviches (I thought they were artistic nonsense), two comfortable chairs bolted to the deck, and a sideboard also bolted to the deck and holding alcoholic beverages. In one corner was a tiny cubicle containing all the furniture and necessities that one finds in a W.C.

Holmes and I lit up the fine Cuban cigars we found in a humidor and poured out some Scotch whisky, Duggan's Dew of Kirkintilloch, I believe. Suddenly, both of us leaped into the air, spilling our drinks over our cuffs. Seemingly from nowhere, a tall figure had silently appeared. How he had done it, I do not know, since the door had been closed and under observation at all times by one or both of us.

Holmes groaned and said, under his breath, "Not another madman?"

The fellow certainly looked eccentric. He wore the uniform of a colonel of the Imperial Russian Air Service, but he also wore a long black opera cloak and a big black slouch hat. From under its floppy brim burned

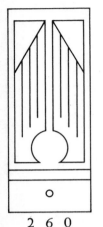

two of the most magnetic and fear-inspiring eyes I have ever seen. My attention, however, was somewhat diverted from these by the size and the aquilinity of the nose beneath them. It could have belonged to Cyrano de Bergerac.*

I found that I had to sit down to catch my breath. The fellow introduced himself, in an Oxford accent, as Colonel Kentov. He had a surprisingly pleasant voice, deep, rich, and shot with authority. It was also heavily laced with bourbon.

"Are you all right?" he said.

"I think so," I said. "You gave me quite a start. A cloud seemed to pass over my mind. But I'm fine now, thank you."

"I must go forward now," he said, "but I've assigned a crew member, a tail gunner now but once a butler, to serve you. Just ring that bell beside you if you need him."

And he was gone, though this time he opened the door. At least, I think he did.

"I fear, my dear fellow, that we are in for another trying time," Holmes said.

Actually, the voyage seemed quite pleasant once one got used to the roar of the four motors and the nerve-shaking jack-out-of-the-box appearances of Kentov. The trip was to take approximately twenty-eight hours if all went well. About every four and a half hours, we put down at a hastily constructed landing strip to which petrol and supplies had been rushed by ship, air, or camel some days before. With the Mediterranean Sea on our left and the shores of North Africa below us,

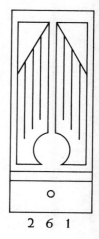

*The description of this man certainly fits that of a notable crime fighter operating out of Manhattan in the '30's through the '40's. If he is who I think he is, then one of his many aliases was Lamont Cranston.

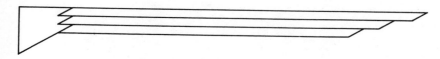

we sped toward Cairo at an amazing average speed of seventy-point-three miles per hour, according to our commander. While we sipped various liquors or liqueurs and smoked Havanas, we read to pass the time. Holmes commented several times that he could use a little cocaine to relieve the tedium, but I believe that he said that just to needle me. Holmes had brought along a work of his own authorship, the privately printed *Practical Handbook of Bee Culture, with Some Observations Upon the Segregation of the Queen.* He had often urged me to read the results of his experience with his Sussex bees and so I now acceded to his urgings, mainly because all the other books available were in Russian.

I found it more interesting than I had expected, and I told Holmes so. This seemed to please him, though he had affected an air of indifference to my reaction before then.

"The techniques and tricks of apiculture are intriguing and complex enough," he said. "But I was called away from a project which goes far beyond anything any apiculturist—scientist or not—has attempted. It is my theory that bees have a language and that they communicate such important information as the location of new clover, the approach of enemies, and so forth, by means of symbolic dancing. I was investigating this with a view to turning theory into fact when I got Mycroft's wire."

I sat up so suddenly that the ash dropped off my cigar into my lap, and I was busy for a moment brushing off the coals before they burned a hole in my trousers. "Really, Holmes," I said, "you are surely pulling my leg! Bees have a language? Next you'll be telling me they compose sonnets in honour of their queen's inauguration! Or perhaps epitases when she gets married!"

"Epitases?" he said, regarding me scornfully. "You

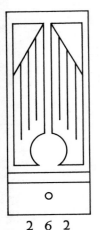

mean epithalamiums, you blockhead! I suggest you use moderation while drinking the national beverage of Russia. Yes, Watson, bees do communicate, though not in the manner which *Homo sapiens* uses."*

"I understand that Lord Mowgli of the Seeonee claims that he can talk to beasts and reptiles..." I said, but I was interrupted by that sudden vagueness of mind which signalled the appearance of our commander. I always jumped and my heart beat hard when the cloud dissolved and I realized that Kentov was standing before me. My only consolation was that Holmes was just as startled.

"Confound it, man!" Holmes said, his face red. "Couldn't you behave like a civilised being for once and knock before entering? Or don't Americans have such customs?"

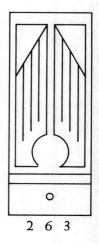

This, of course, was sheer sarcasm, since Holmes had been to the States several times.

"We are only two hours from Cairo," Kentov said, ignoring Holmes' remarks. "But I have just learned from the wireless station in Cairo that a storm of severe proportions is approaching us from the north. We may be blown somewhat off our course. Also, our spies at Cos, in Turkey, report that a Zeppelin left there yesterday. They believe that it intends to pick up Von Bork. Somehow, he's slipped out past the cordon and is waiting in the desert for the airship."

Holmes, gasping and sputtering, said, "If this execrable voyage turns out to be for nothing... if I was forced to endure that madman's dangerous antics only to have...!"

Suddenly, the colonel was gone. Holmes regained

---

*For the first time we learn that Holmes anticipated the discovery of the Austrian scientist, von Frisch, by many decades.

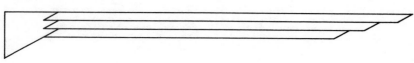

his normal colour and composure, and he said, "Do you know, Watson, I believe I know that man! Or, at least, his parents. I've been studying him at every opportunity, and though he is doubtless a master at dissimulation, that nose is false, he has a certain bone structure and a certain trait of walking, of turning his head, which leads me to believe..."

At that moment the telephone rang. Since I was closest to the instrument, I answered it. Our commander's voice said, "Batten down all loose objects and tie yourself in to your beds. We are in for a hell of a storm, the worst of this century, if the weather reports are accurate."

For once, the meteorologists had not exaggerated. The next three hours were terrible. The giant aeroplane was tossed about as if it were a sheet of writing paper. The electric lamps on the walls flickered again and again and finally went out, leaving us in darkness. Holmes groaned and moaned and finally tried to crawl to the W.C. Unfortunately, the craft was bucking up and down like a wild horse and rolling and yawing like a rowboat caught in a rapids. Holmes managed to get back to his bed without breaking any bones but, I regret to say, proceeded to get rid of all the vodka and brandy (a combination itself not conducive to good digestion, I believe), beef stroganoff, cabbage soup, and black bread on which we had dined earlier. Even more regrettably, he leaned over the edge of the bed to perform this undeniable function, and though I did not get all of it, I did get too much. I did not have the heart to reprimand him. Besides, he would have killed me, or at least attempted to do so, if I had made any reproaches. His mood was not of the best.

Finally, I heard his voice, weak though it was, saying, "Watson, promise me one thing."

"What is that, Holmes?"

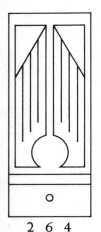

2 6 4

"Swear to me that once we've set foot on land you'll shoot me through the head if ever I show the slightest inclination to board a flying vehicle again. I don't think there's much danger of that, but even if His Majesty himself should plead with me to get into an aeroplane, or anything that flies, dirigible, balloon, anything, you will mercifully tender euthanasia of some sort. Promise me."

I thought I was safe in promising. For one thing, I felt almost as strongly as he did about it.

At that moment, the door to our cabin opened, and our attendant, Ivan, appeared with a small electric lamp in his hand. He exchanged some excited words in Russian with Holmes and then left, leaving the lamp behind. Holmes crawled down from the bunk, saying, "We've orders to abandon ship, Watson. We've been blown far south of Cairo and will be out of petrol in half an hour. We'll have to jump then, like it or not. Ivan says that the colonel has looked for a safe landing place, but he can't even see the ground. The air's filled with sand; visibility is nil; the sand is getting into the bearings of the engines and pitting the windshields. So, my dear old friend, we must don the parachutes."

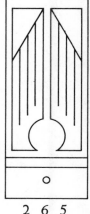

My heart warmed at being addressed so fondly, though my emotion was somewhat tempered in the next few minutes while we were assisting each other in strapping on the equipment. Holmes said, "You have an abominable effluvia about you, Watson," and I replied, testily, I must admit, "You stink like the W.C. in an East End pub yourself, my dear Holmes. Besides, any odour emanating from me has originated from, or in, you. Surely you are aware of that."

Holmes muttered something about the direction upwards, and I was about to ask him to clarify his comment when Ivan appeared again. This time he carried weapons which he distributed among the three of us.

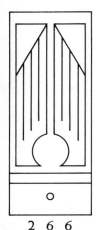

I was handed a cavalry sabre, a stiletto, a knout (which I discarded), and a revolver of some unknown make but of .50 calibre. Holmes was given a cutlass, a carbine, a belt full of ammunition, and a coil of rope at one end of which were grappling hooks. Ivan kept for himself another cutlass, two hand grenades dangling by their pins from his belt, and a dagger in his teeth.

We walked (rolled, rather) to the door, where three others stood, also fully, perhaps even over-, armed. There was a window further forward, and so Holmes and I went to it after a while to observe the storm. We could see little except clouds of dust for a few minutes and then the dust was suddenly gone. A heavy rain succeeded it, though the wind buffeted us as strongly as before. There was also much lightning, some of it exploding loudly close by.

A moment later Ivan joined us, pulling at Holmes' arm and shouting something in Russian. Holmes answered him and turning to me said, "Kentov has sighted a Zeppelin!"

"Great Scott!" I cried. "Surely it must be the one sent to pick up Von Bork! It, too, has been caught by the storm!"

"An elementary deduction," Holmes said. But he seemed pleased about something. I surmised that he was happy because Von Bork had either missed the airship or, if he was in it, was in as perilous a plight as we. I failed to see any humour in the situation.

Holmes lost his grin several minutes later when we were informed that we were going to attack the Zeppelin.

"In this storm?" I said. "Why, the colonel can't even keep us at the same altitude or attitude from one second to the next."

"The man's a maniac!" Holmes shouted.

Just how mad, we were shortly to discover. Presently

the great airship hove into view, painted silver above and black below to conceal it from search lights, the large designation on its side painted out, the control car in front, its pusher propellor spinning, the propellors on the front and rear of the two midships and one aft engine-gondolas spinning, the whole looking quite monstrous and sinister and yet beautiful.

The airship was bobbing and rolling and yawing like a toy boat afloat on a Scottish salmon stream. Its crew had to be airsick and they had to have their hands full just to keep from being pitched out of their vessel. This was heartening to some degree, since none of us on the aeroplane, except possibly Kentov, were in any state remotely resembling good health or aggression.

Ivan mumbled something, and Holmes said, "He says that if the storm keeps up the airship will soon break up. Let us hope it does and so spares us aerial combat."

But the Zeppelin, though it did seem to be somewhat out of line, its frame slightly twisted, held together. Meanwhile, our four-engined colossus, so small compared to the airship, swept around to the vessel's stern. It was a ragged approach what with the constantly buffeting blasts, but the wonder was that it was accomplished at all.

"What's the fool doing?" Holmes said, and he spoke again to Ivan. Lightning rolled up the heavens then, and I saw that his face was a ghastly blue-grey.

"This Yank is madder than the other!" he said. "He's going to try to land on top of the Zeppelin!"

"How could he do that?" I gasped.

"How would I know what techniques he'll use, you dunce!" he shouted. "Who cares? Whatever he does, the plane will fall off the ship, probably break its wings, and we'll fall to our deaths!"

"We can jump *now!*" I shouted.

"What? Desert?" he cried. "Watson, we are British!"

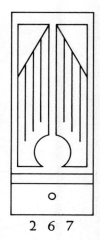

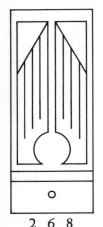

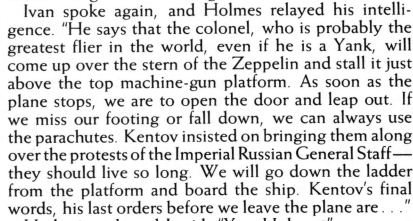

"It was only a suggestion," I said. "Forgive me. Of course, we will stick it out. No Slav is going to say that we English lack courage."

Ivan spoke again, and Holmes relayed his intelligence. "He says that the colonel, who is probably the greatest flier in the world, even if he is a Yank, will come up over the stern of the Zeppelin and stall it just above the top machine-gun platform. As soon as the plane stops, we are to open the door and leap out. If we miss our footing or fall down, we can always use the parachutes. Kentov insisted on bringing them along over the protests of the Imperial Russian General Staff—they should live so long. We will go down the ladder from the platform and board the ship. Kentov's final words, his last orders before we leave the plane are . . ."

He hesitated, and I said, "Yes, Holmes?"

"Kill! Kill! Kill!"

"Good heavens!" I said. "How barbaric!"

"Yes," he answered. "But one has to excuse him. He is obviously not sane."

V

Following orders communicated through Obrenov, we lay down on the deck and grabbed whatever was solid and anchored in a world soon to become all too fluid and foundationless. The plane dived and we slid forward and then it rose sharply upward and we slid backward and then its nose suddenly lifted up, the roaring of the four engines becoming much more highly pitched, and suddenly we were pressed against the floor. And then the pressure was gone.

Slowly, but far too swiftly for me, the deck tilted to the left. This was in accordance with Kentov's plans.

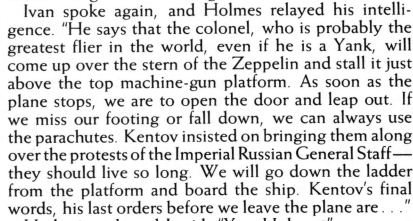

He had stalled the craft with its longitudinal axis, or centre-line, a little to the left of the airship's centre-line. Its weight would thus cause the airship on whose back it rode to roll to the left.

For a second, I did not realize what was happening. To be quite frank, I was scared out of my wits, numb with terror. I would never allow Holmes to see this, and so I overcame my frozen state, though not the stiffness and slowness due to my age and recent hardships. I got up and stumbled out through the door, the parachute banging the upper parts of the back of my thighs and feeling as if it were made of lead, and sprawled out onto the small part of the platform left to me. I grabbed for the lowest end of an upright pipe forming the enclosure about the platform. The hatch had already been opened and Kentov was inside the airship. I could hear the booming of several guns. It was comparatively silent now, since Kentov had cut the engines just before the stalling. Nevertheless, one could hear the creaking of the girders of the ship's structure as it bent under the varying pressures. My ears hurt abominably because the airship was dropping swiftly under the weight of the giant aeroplane. The aeroplane was also making its own unmistakable noises, groaning, as its structure bent, tearing the fabric of the ship's covering as it slipped more and more to the left, then there was a loud ripping, and the ship beneath me rolled swiftly back, relieved of the enormous weight of the aeroplane. At the same time the Zeppelin soared aloft, and the two motions, the rolling and the levitation, almost tore me loose from my hold.

When the dirigible had ceased its major oscillations, the Russians rose and one by one disappeared into the well. Holmes and I worked our way across, passed the pedestals of the two quilt-swathed eight-millimetre Maxim machine guns, and descended the ladder. Just

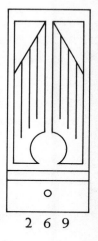

269

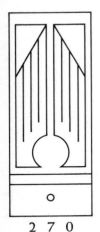

before I was all the way into the hatch, I looked across the back of the great beast that we were invading. I would have been shocked if I had not been so numb. The wheels and the ski undercarriage of the plane had ripped open a great wound along the thin skin of the vessel. Encountering the duralumin girders and rings of the framework, it had torn some apart and then its landing gear had itself been ripped off. The propellors, though no longer turning, had also done extensive damage. I wondered if the framework of the ship, the skeleton of the beast, as it were, might not have suffered so great a blow it would collapse and carry all of us down to our death.

I also had a second's admiration for the skill, no, the genius, of the pilot who had landed us.

And then I descended into the vast complex spiderweb of the ship's hull with its rings and girders and bulging hydrogen-filled gas cells and ballast sacks of water. I emerged at the keel of the ship, on the foot-wide catwalk that ran the length of the ship between triangular girders. It had been a nightmare before then; after that it became a nightmare having a nightmare. I remember dodging along, clinging to girders, swinging out and climbing around to avoid the fire of the German sailors in the bow. I remember Lieutenant Obrenov falling with fatal bullet wounds after sticking two Germans with his sabre (there was no room to swing it and so use the edge as regulations required).

I remember others falling, some managing to retain their grip and so avoiding the fall through the fabric of the cover and into the abyss below. I remember Holmes hiding behind a gas cell and firing away at the Germans who were afraid of firing back and perhaps setting the hydrogen aflame.*

Most of all I remember the slouch-hatted cloaked form of Kentov leaping about, swinging from girders and brace wires, bouncing from a beam onto a great gas cell and back again, flitting like a phantom of the opera through the maze, firing two huge .45 automatic pistols (not at the same time, of course, otherwise he would have lost his grip). German after German cried out or fled while the maniac cackled with a blood-chilling laugh between the booming of the huge guns. But though he was worth a squadron in himself, his men died one by one. And so the inevitable happened.

Perhaps it was a ricocheting bullet or perhaps he slipped. I do not know. All of a sudden he was falling off a girder, through a web of wires, miraculously missing them, falling backward, now in each hand a thundering flame-spitting .45, killing two sailors as he fell, laughing loudly even as he broke through the thin fabric and disappeared into the dark rain over Africa.

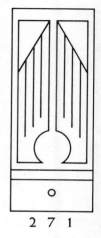

Since he was wearing a parachute, he may have survived. I never heard of him again, though.

Presently the Germans approached cautiously, having heard Holmes and me call out that we surrendered. (We were out of ammunition and too nerveless even to lift a sabre.) We stood on the catwalk with our hands up, two tired beaten old men. Yet it was our finest hour. Nothing could ever rob us of the pleasure of seeing Von Bork's face when he recognised us. If the shock had been slightly more intense, he would have dropped dead from a heart attack.

*There was actually no danger of fire since phosphorous-coated bullets were not being used. Apparently, the grenades, which might have set off the hydrogen, were not used.

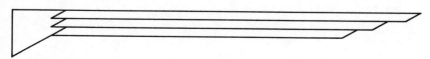

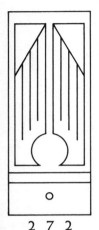

A few minutes later, we had climbed down the ladder from the hull to the control gondola under the fore part of the airship. Behind us, raving, restrained by a petty officer and the executive officer, Oberleutnant zur *See* Heinrich Tring, came Von Bork. He had ordered us thrown overboard then and there, but Tring, a decent fellow, had refused to obey his orders. We were introduced to the commander, Kapitänleutnant Victor Reich. He was also a decent fellow, openly admiring our feat of landing and boarding his ship even though it and his crew had suffered terribly. He rejected Von Bork's suggestion that we should be shot as spies since we were in civilian clothes and on a Russian warcraft. He knew of us, of course, and he would have nothing to do with a summary execution of the great Holmes and his colleague. After hearing our story, he made sure of our comfort. However, he refused to let Holmes smoke, cast his tobacco overboard then and there, in fact, and this made Holmes suffer. He had gone through so much that he desperately needed a pipeful of shag.

"It is fortunate that the storm is breaking up," Reich said in excellent English. "Otherwise, the ship would soon break up. Three of our motors are not operating. The clutch to the port motor has overheated, the water in the radiator of a motor in the starboard mid-car has boiled out, and something struck the propellor of the control car and shattered it. We are so far south that even if we could operate at one hundred percent efficiency, we would be out of petrol somewhere over Egypt on the return trip. Moreover, the controls to the elevators have been damaged. All we can do at

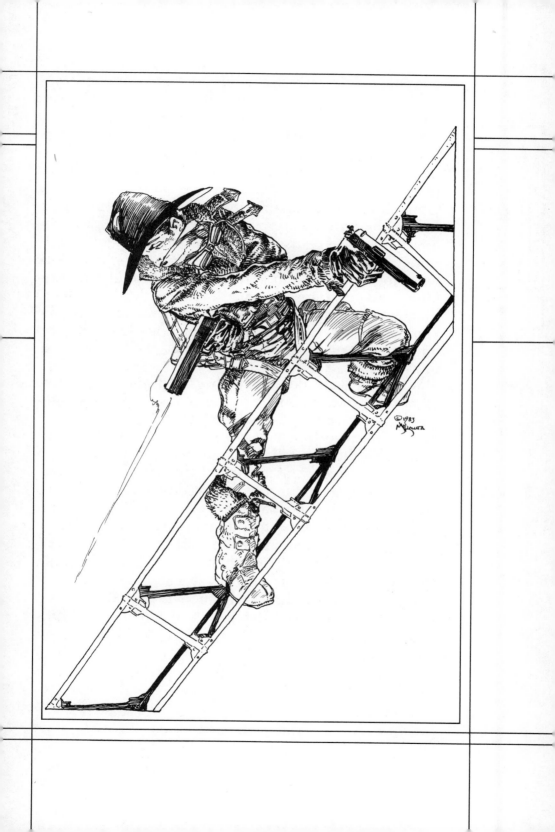

present is drift with the wind and hope for the best."

The days and nights that followed were full of suffering and anxiety. Seven of the crew had been killed during the fight, leaving only six to man the vessel. This alone was enough to make a voyage back to Turkey or Palestine impossible. Reich told us that he had received a radio message ordering him to get to the German forces in East Africa under Von Lettow-Vorbeck. There he was to burn the Zeppelin and join the forces. This, of course, was not all the message. Surely something must have been said about getting Von Bork back to Germany, since he had the formula for mutating and culturing the "sauerkraut bacilli." I wondered then why the formula was not sent via radio to the German-Turkish base, but I found out later that no one aboard understood the formula well enough to transmit it.

When we were alone in the port mid-gondola, where we were kept during part of the voyage, Holmes commented on what he called the "SB."

"We must get possession of the formula, Watson," he said. "I did not tell you, but before you arrived at Mycroft's office I was informed that the SB is a two-edged weapon. It can be mutated to eat other foods. Imagine what would happen to our food supply, not to mention the blow to our morale, if the SB were changed to eat boiled meat? Or cabbage? Or potatoes?"

"Great Scott!" I said, and then, in a whisper, "It could be worse, Holmes, far worse. What if the Germans dropped an SB over England which devoured stout and ale? Or think of how the spirits of our valiant Scots would sink if their whisky supply vanished before their eyes?"

Von Bork had been impressed into airship service but, being as untrained as we, was not of much use. Also, his injured left eye handicapped him as much as

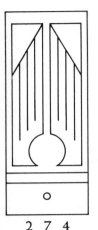

our age did us. It was very bloodshot and failed to coordinate with its partner. My professional opinion was that it was totally without sight. The other eye was healthy enough. It glared every time it lighted upon us. Its fires reflected the raging hatred in his heart, the lust to murder us.

However, the airship was in such straits that no one had much time or inclination to think about anything except survival. Some of the motors were still operating, thus enabling some kind of control. As long as we went south, with the wind behind us, we made headway. But due to the jammed elevators, the nose of the ship was downward and the tail was up. It flew at roughly five degrees to the horizontal for some time. Reich put everybody to work, including us, since we had volunteered, at carrying indispensable equipment to the rear to help weigh it down. Anything that was dispensable, and there was not much, went overboard. In addition, much water ballast in the front was discharged.

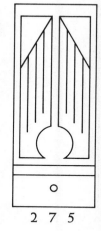

2 7 5

Below us the sands of Sudan reeled by while the sun flamed in a cloudless blue. Its fiery breath heated the hydrogen in the cells, and great amounts hissed out from the automatic valves. The hot wind blew into the hull through the great hole made by the aeroplane when it had stalled into a landing on its top. The heat, of course, made the hydrogen expand, thus causing the ship to rise despite the loss of gas from the valves. At night, the air cooled very swiftly, and the ship dropped swiftly, too swiftly for the peace of mind of its passengers. During the day the updrafts of heat from the sands made the vessel buck and kick. All of us aboard got sick during these times.

By working like Herculeses despite all handicaps, the crew managed to get all the motors going again. On the fifth day, the elevator controls were fixed. Her

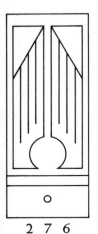

hull was still twisted, and this, with the huge gap in the surface covering, made her aerodynamically unstable. At least, that was how Reich explained it to us. He, by the way, was not at all reticent in telling us about the vessel itself though he would not tell us our exact location. Perhaps this was because he wanted to make sure that we would not somehow get to the radio and send a message to the British in East Africa.

The flat desert gave way to rugged mountains. More ballast was dropped, and the vessel just barely avoided scraping some of the peaks. Night came with its cooling effects, and the ship dropped. The mountains were lower at this point, fortunately for us.

Two days later, as we lay sweltering on the catwalk that ran along the keel, Holmes said, "I estimate that we are now somewhere over British East Africa, somewhere in the vicinity of Lake Victoria. It is evident that we will never get to Mahenge or indeed anywhere in German East Africa. The ship has lost too much hydrogen. I have overheard some guarded comments to this effect by Reich and Tring. They think we'll crash sometime tonight. Instead of seeking out the nearest British authorities and surrendering, as anyone with good sense would, they are determined to cross our territory to German territory. Do you know how many miles of veldt and jungle and swamp swarming with lions, rhinoceri, vipers, savages, malaria, dengue, and God knows what else we will have to walk? Attempt to walk, rather?"

"Perhaps we can slip away some night?"

"And then what will we do?" he said bitterly. "Watson, you and I know the jungles of London well and are quite fitted to conduct our safaris through them. But here... no, Watson, any black child of eight is more competent, far more so, to survive in these wilds."

"You don't paint a very good picture," I said grimly.

"Though I am descended from the Vernets, the great French artists," he said, "I myself have little ability at painting pretty pictures."

He chuckled then, and I was heartened by this example of pawky humour, feeble though it was. Holmes would never quit; his indomitable English spirit might be defeated, but it would go down fighting. And I would be at his side. And was it not after all better to die with one's boots on while one still had some vigour than when one was old and crippled and sick and perhaps an idiot drooling and doing all sorts of pitiful, sickening things?

That evening preparations were made to abandon the ship. Ballast water was put in every portable container, the food supply was stored in sacks made from the cotton fabric ripped off the hull, and we waited. Sometime after midnight, the end came. It was fortunately a cloudless night with a moon bright enough for us to see, if not too sharply, the terrain beneath. This was a jungle up in the mountains, which were not at a great elevation. The ship was steered down a winding valley through which a stream ran silvery. Then, abruptly, we had to rise, and we could not do it.

We were in the control car when the hillside loomed before us. Reich gave the order and we threw our supplies out, thus lightening the load and giving us a few more seconds of grace. We two prisoners were allowed to drop out first. Reich did this because the ship would rise as the crew members left, and he wanted us to be closest to the ground. We were old and not so agile, and he thought that we needed all the advantages we could get.

He was right. Even though Holmes and I fell into some bushes which eased our descent, we were still bruised and shaken up. We scrambled out, however,

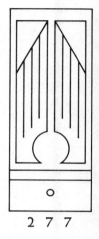

and made our way through the growth toward the supplies. The ship passed over us, sliding its great shadow like a cloak, and then it struck something. The whirring propellors were snapped off, the cars crumpled and came loose with a nerve-scraping sound, the ship lifted again with the weight of the cars gone, and it drifted out of sight. But its career was about over. A few minutes later, it exploded. Reich had left several time-bombs next to some gas cells.

The flames were very bright and very hot, outlining the dark skeleton of its framework. Birds flew up and around it. No doubt they and the beasts of the jungle were making a loud racket, but the roar of the flames drowned them out.

By their light we could see back down the hill, though not very far. We struggled through the heavy vegetation, hoping to get to the supplies before the others. We had agreed to take as much food and water as we could carry and set off by ourselves, if we got the chance. Surely, we reasoned, there must be some native village nearby, and once there we would ask for guidance to the nearest British post.

By pure luck, we came across a pile of food and some bottles of water. Holmes said, "Dame Fortune is with us, Watson!" but his chuckle died the next moment when Von Bork stepped out of the bushes. In his hand was a Luger automatic and in his one eye was the determination to use that before the others arrived. He could claim, of course, that we were fleeing or had attacked him and that he was forced to shoot us.

"Die, you pig-dogs!" he snarled, and he raised the gun. "Before you do, though, know that I have the formula on me and that I will get it to the Fatherland and it will doom you English swine and the French swine and the Italian swine. The bacilli can be adapted to eat Yorkshire pudding and snails and spaghetti, any-

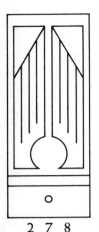

thing that is edible! The beauty of it is that it's specific, and unless it's mutated to eat sauerkraut, it will starve rather than do so!"

We drew ourselves up, prepared to die as British men should. Holmes muttered out of the corner of his mouth, "Jump to one side, Watson, and then we'll rush him! You take his blind side! Perhaps one of us can get to him!"

This was a noble plan, though I didn't know what I could do even if I got hold of Von Bork. After all, he was a young man and had a splendid physique.

At that moment there was a crashing in the bushes, Reich's loud voice commanding Von Bork not to shoot, and the commander, tears streaming from his face, stumbled into the little clearing. Behind him came others. Von Bork said, "I was merely holding them until you got here."

Reich, I must add, was not weeping because of any danger to us. The fate of his airship had dealt him a terrible blow; he loved his vessel and to see it die was to him comparable to seeing his wife die. Perhaps it had even more impact, since, as I later found out, he was on the verge of a divorce.

Though he had saved us, he knew that we were ready to skip out at the first chance. He kept a close eye on us, though it was not as close as Von Bork's. Nevertheless, he allowed us to retreat behind bushes to attend to our comforts. And so, three days later, we strolled on away.

"Well, Watson," Holmes said, as we sat panting under a tree several hours later, "we have given them the slip. But we have no water and no food except these pieces of mouldy biscuit in our pockets. At this moment I would trade them for a handful of shag."

We went to sleep finally and slept like the two old and exhausted men we were. I awoke several times, I

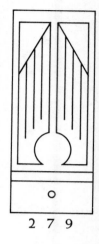

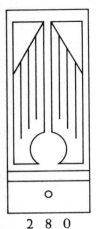

think because of insects crawling over my face, but I always went back to sleep quickly. About eight in the morning, the light and the uproar of jungle life awoke us. I was the first to see the cobra slipping through the tall growths toward us. I got quickly, though unsteadily and painfully, to my feet. Holmes saw the reptile then and started to get up. The snake raised its upper part, its hood swelled, and it swayed as it turned its head this way and that.

"Steady, Watson!" Holmes said, though the advice would better have been given to himself. He was much closer to the cobra, within striking range, in fact, and he was shaking more violently than I. He could not be blamed for this, of course. He was in a more shakeable situation.

"I knew we should have brought along that flask of brandy," I said. "We have absolutely nothing for snakebite."

"No time for reproaches, you imbecile!" Holmes said. "Besides, what kind of medical man are you? It's sheer superstitious nonsense that alcohol helps prevent the effects of venom."

"Really, Holmes," I said. He had been getting so irascible lately, so insulting. Part of this could be excused, since he became very nervous without the solace of tobacco. Even so, I thought...

The thought was never finished. The cobra struck, and Holmes and I jumped, yelling.

VII

For a moment both Holmes and I thought that he had been bitten. The blunt nose of the cobra, however, had only touched Holmes' leg. But he was in as perilous a situation as before, having jumped straight up instead of away and having come down in the same place, in his footprints in the mud, in fact. The cobra, meanwhile, had moved closer and now could not miss.

"Don't move, Holmes!" I cried. "It may not strike again!"

"The cobra is like lightning; it always strikes the same place twice!" he said. "For heaven's sake, Watson, divert it!"

I started to move around Holmes toward the creature, though not too closely, when I saw a bush ahead of me shake. Great Scott, I thought, is another venomous killer, perhaps its mate, coming to join it?

The bush ceased shaking, and from behind it stepped out a man such as I had never seen before. At least, I've never seen a totally naked man in a public place before, if the African jungle may be classed as such.*
I have viewed few with such a heavy bone structure and superb muscles, more like Apollo's than Hercules' though, more leopardish than lionish.

He stood perhaps six feet two inches and was very dark, definitely not an Englishman but not as dark as a Negro. His shoulder-length hair was straight and blue-black. Below the bulging atavistic supraorbital ridges were large long-lashed deep brown eyes. His face was indeed handsome, and he had the biggest [word blotted out by ink] I've ever seen, and as a medical man I've seen some startlers.†

He was a magnificent specimen, unflawed except for an angry-red spot between and on the big toe and next toe of his left foot. This, I assumed, was caused by a

---

*Watson forgot "The Case of the Mortlake Flasher."
†The last phrase is crossed over with the notation "delete" in the margin.

birthmark or one of the fungi so rife in the jungle.

My statement that he was altogether unclothed is not quite accurate. He did wear a broad belt of crocodile hide, secured at the front by thongs tied in a knot, and the belt supported a crocodile-hide scabbard in which was a huge hunting knife.

The man advanced toward us, saying in English with an Oxford accent, "Don't move a muscle, gentlemen."

He looked at Holmes.

"Try to keep your teeth from chattering."

He walked up quite close to the cobra and spoke to it in a language totally unfamiliar to me. Holmes, an accomplished linguist, later confessed to me that the language was also unknown to him.

The cobra twisted its body towards him and hissed a few times, its forked tongue shooting out. Then its hood collapsed, and it crawled off into the bush.

"White Hood is my brother," the dark man said, "and I explained to her that you were no danger to her and that she was under no obligation to the Law of the Jungle to attack you."

Holmes surprised me by his reply, which I thought under the circumstances was remarkably ungrateful.

"Really?" he said, sneering. "Just how could she hear you, since cobras are totally deaf? And why do you call it brother, since it's a female?"

The man's dark eyes seemed to flame, and his hand went to the handle of the knife.

"Are you calling me a liar, sir?"

"My friend has been under a series of strains and stresses of high degree," I hastily said. "He is not quite himself. I assure you, sir, whoever you may be, that we are both very grateful to you for having rescued us from a possibly fatal situation. Nor do we doubt for a moment that you and the snake were carrying on a dialogue.

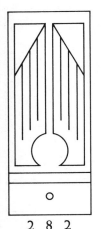

"Allow me to introduce us. That gentleman is Mr. Sherlock Holmes, of whom you may have heard, and I am his colleague, Doctor John H. Watson."

"Another madman!" Holmes said, though softly. The ears of the stranger must have been singularly keen because he frowned and looked strangely at Holmes. However, he then grinned, but this did not ease my apprehension. His facial expression reminded me of Chaucer's line about "the smiler with the knife."

Holmes had by then somewhat regained his composure and was no doubt regretting his hasty and ill-considered words. He said, "Yes, we owe you a great debt of gratitude."

Then, his keen grey eyes narrowed, a slight smile— of triumph?—playing about his lips, he said, "Sir Mowgli of the Seeonee, I presume?"

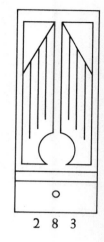

VIII

Our savior was visibly startled. He said, "We have met before? I don't remember your odor!"

"There is no reason to get personal," Holmes said. "No, Sir Mowgli, we have not met elsewhere. But it is obvious to me that you must be that man who claims to have been reared from infancy by wolves, the man of whom Rudyard Kipling wrote so strikingly and beautifully. You are Mowgli—that is, translated from the universal jungle language, Frog. You are obviously of that branch of the dark Caucasian race which principally inhabits the chief jewel on the diadem of the British Empire, India. You are not of the light-skinned Caucasian branch to which several feral human beings of the African area belong. That is, to name a few, Tarzan the Ape-Man, Kaspa the Lion-Man, Kungai

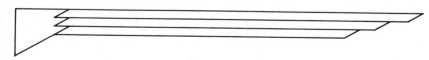

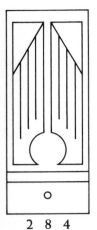

the Leopard-Man, Miota the Jackal-Girl, Ka-Zar the Lion-Man, Kalu the Baboon-Boy, Azan the Ape-Man, and several others whose names and titles I do not recall. * All are said to be roaming the jungles and veldts of the Dark Continent, consorting with their various hairy companions, and breaking the necks or gashing the throats of evil men.

"You claim . . . I mean . . . you speak with a cobra and call it your brother, White Hood. So did Mowgli, according to your biographer, Kipling. You go naked, whereas the others I named, though not clad as if they were walking through Trafalgar Square, still are modest enough to wear loincloths of animal origin. Also, I happen to know that Sir Mowgli is in Africa, though I was informed that he was in Central, not East, Africa."

"Yes, it is obvious, now that you explain it," the baronet said.

Holmes' face twisted with anger as it does sometimes when I make the same remark.

The baronet said, "I have heard of both of you, and I have read some of the chronicles of your adventures. I am as surprised at finding you here in this jungle, far away from the great but dingy and misery-ridden metropolis of London, as you are at encountering me here. How did you happen to come here?"

Holmes told our story. When my companion had finished it, the baronet said, "You are indeed fortunate to have survived such harrowing experiences."

He turned and gestured at the bush behind which he had hidden and which again was shaking. He seemed to be indicating to someone to come out from hiding. Presently, that turned out to be so. The head of a white woman came from behind the bush and was followed after some hesitation by the body. She was, it was embarrassingly clear, clad only in a ragged and exceedingly dirty slip. I could not help observing that she had a magnificent figure—much like Irene Adler's, if I may reminisce—but the effect was spoiled by the mud, scratches, and rashes which seemed to cover most of the skin that was exposed, which was considerable.

Her long and curly auburn hair was a tangle of dirt and burrs. One big blue eye was quite beautiful, but the other was swollen shut by an insect bite. Or so I thought at the time.

Despite the scanty and torn attire, the lack of coiffure, and the various disfigurements, I recognized Liza Borden, the actress, whose true name was Mary Anne Liza Murdstone-Malcon, daughter of the Viscount of Utter Bickring, widow of the Earl of Murdstone-Malcon. Who would not recognize the face and body of this beauty who had played the lead female role in such movies as *The Divine Aspasia, Socrates' Wife, The Motor Maid, She Stooped to Holly, The Scarlet Mark,* and *The Witch of Endor?*

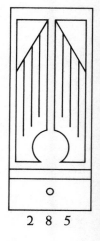

But the voice that accompanied that goddess-like beauty made me glad that the movies were silent. Its effect was that of a screech owl's shriek issuing from a nightingale's throat. It was high and whining and nasal and strident, what one might expect from a fishwife or a Siamese cat.

"Oh, gentlemen!" she cried as she ran toward us, purple and red furrowed arms outstretched. "Save me! Save me!"

She fell sobbing into my arms, and her body shook with uncontrolled grief.

"There, there, you're all right. You are saved," I said, patting her back.

---

*This era and locale seems to have been peculiarly productive of feral humans.

"Save you from what, Madame?" Holmes said.

She tore herself from my embrace, whirled, and thrust an accusing finger at Sir Mowgli.

"From him the beast! He's an absolute savage, he doesn't know what decency or honor or kindness or consideration or civilization means! He has wronged me, wronged me, violated me many times over, night and day, day and night, despite all my pleas, my tearful protestations . . . !"

There was much more, but I would have felt more strongly abut her accusations if I had not recognized that her words were exactly the same as those she had delivered in the film *Mrs. Milton's Revenge*. I will never forget those words, burning white in the subtitles.

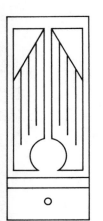

"Now, now, my dear," I said, "just what do you mean, wronged you? When you say *violated* do you mean by that that . . . ?"

"Yes, I do!" she cried, her rasping voice not only scraping my nerves but driving birds for some distance around to soar screaming from the trees. "He ravished me, took me against my will! It tears my heart out to utter such words, but I must!"

These words were not from *Mrs. Milton's Revenge* but from *The Divine Aspasia*.

"Sir, is this true?" I sputtered at the wild man. "And have you no decency, standing naked before a white woman, a noble lady?"

"She's no lady," he said, grinning, "except in the titular sense. As for being ravished, it is the ravisher who accuses me, the ravishee-to-be, of being the ravisher. Though, actually, there was no foul deed, no carnal knowledge except for some brief unavoidable contact while I was fighting her off. I even had to blacken her eye and knock her down a few times before she understood that I am faithful to my marriage vows. The wolves take only one mate during their lifetime, and I am brother to the wolf."

"You lie, you utter cad!" she screamed. She turned to me, and she said, "Oh, sir, you look like a gentleman! Please defend me!"

"But... but..." I said, "he's not attacking you!"

"Then please don't let him! Keep the beast away from me!"

"He will not touch you, I assure you, while I am alive to protect you," I said.

"Don't worry," Sir Mowgli said. "The panther does not mate with the crocodile. Nor the eagle with the skunk. That is the Law of the Jungle, but she knows only the Law of Hollywood, the Law of the British Nobility, and both are decadent."

"Sir!" I cried, "a gentleman does not say anything about a lady's honor even if he is wronged!"

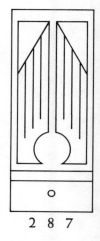

"*Ngaayah!*" he said. I supposed that it was an exclamation of disgust in the jungle language, and his spitting on the ground with vigor and his grimace confirmed my surmise.

"If you want to fill your bellies, follow me," he said, and he walked around the bush out of our sight.

"Aren't you going to do anything?" the countess said.

I harrumphed several times and said, "Under the, uh, circumstances, there seems little that I can do."

"Or should," Holmes said. "We are not policemen to arrest Sir Mowgli or judges to sentence him. I suggest, Your Ladyship, that you can bring suit against him when we return to civilisation. If we ever do."

Holmes had winced every time she spoke. To him she was only a rather unpleasant creature who might or might not have just cause for her complaints. He never attended movies, and he had little regard for those who did and for those involved in their making.

He said, "Your Ladyship, perhaps you would be kind enough to tell me how you came here?"

The countess, suddenly looking nervous, said, "We'd best follow him. We might get lost."

"From what you said," I spoke, "I'd suppose that you'd like to get rid of him."

"I don't want to starve to death, you decrepit old simp!" she said. "Or get eaten by a leopard."

"Really?" I said coolly.

"Come, Watson," Holmes said. "Let's go after the baronet. He may be insane, but he seems to be adjusted to the jungle. He is at present our only hope for survival."

We walked swiftly after the wild-man baronet, Lady Liza in the lead, and soon we saw his broad brown back, dappled by sunlight and the shadows of leaves. The countess told us her story while we continued to follow the baronet.

The movie, *Mowgli's Revenge,* was being filmed near a village about three hundred miles west of the place where we were. Only a few days had remained before its completion when a messenger had arrived. Though he had carried the letter on a forked stick, he was a British soldier, and the message was an order for Major Sir Mowgli to report to the East African Headquarters as soon as his part in the film was done. The baronet had received orders to that effect when the filming started, but the letter was a reminder. On the final day of shooting, however, trouble with the local natives had erupted. The tribe, led by its chief, had tried to abduct the countess.

"He wanted my fair white body," she said.

"More likely, she had insulted him, and he wanted revenge," Holmes muttered in my ear.

The baronet had played in his final scene and had set out on foot for the east an hour before the tribe made its raid.

"If it was a raid," Holmes said softly.

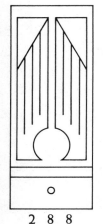

The countess had eluded the lustful chief and his henchmen and had fled eastward. Eventually, she had caught up with Sir Mowgli. To her indignation, he had refused to return and punish the chief and the other troublemakers.

"Probably with good reason," Holmes said to me. "He knew who was at fault."

To her, he said, "Your Ladyship, you claim that the chief was willing to incur the wrath of the white authorities, perhaps suffer execution, imprisonment certainly, because of his overriding lechery? What tribe, may I ask, did he belong to?"

"The Mbandwana," she replied. "What difference does that make?"

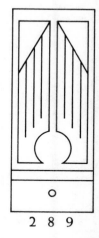

"Ah, the Mbandwana," he said, his eyebrows shooting up. "I am no anthropologist, My Lady, except among the denizens of London, but I happen to know something about that tribe."

"Really?" she said coolly, if loudly. After a pause, she said, "What of them?"

He said in a low voice to me, "The Mbandwana have as their female ideal very fat women, the closer to a tub of lard, the better. They would regard the countess' body with indifference and even contempt."

To her, he said, "My Lady, were some of the tribesmen carrying a circular device of iron, a narrow band with a large square piece attached to the front?"

"Why, yes," she screeched. "So they were. I have no idea what they were for, but I supposed they were some form of torture instrument."

"They were," Holmes said. Aside, he said, "Actually, they were instruments designed to prevent torture. The Mbandwana put them on the mouths of loud and nagging shrews to shut off their offending voices. Doubtless, the tribesmen intended to silence her. They must have been desperate indeed to attempt muzzling a

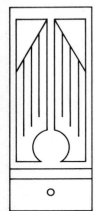

wealthy, white, and well-known woman, but I can well understand and sympathize with them."

"What are you saying?" the countess shrilled.

"Nothing of any importance, Your Ladyship," Holmes said.

She glared at him but did not press her curiosity. A few minutes later, we came into a glade where the baronet was waiting for us. Near him, hanging head down, its hind legs tied by a grass rope to a tree-branch, was a freshly killed forest pig. The baronet had gutted it, and, despite the flies swarming over his face, was devouring a raw and bloody hunk of haunch.

"Lunch!" he said cheerfully, and he handed each of us a slice.

"Good God, are we supposed to eat this uncooked?" Holmes said.

"He's an utter filthy disgusting troglodytish cannibalistic Calibanian boorish savage lycanthropic freak," the countess said. "Utterly beyond the pale of humanity."

"Thank you, Your Ladyship," the baronet said gravely. "You are too kind. However, though I'll eat just about anything if circumstances dictate it for survival, I would never eat you, My Lady. And, despite the fact that we have been eating raw flesh, I really prefer my meat well-cooked. A fire, however, attracts certain creatures whom I would prefer did not suspect our presence.

"For instance, just now I hear sounds in the jungle which indicate that a group of men are moving toward us. They may be Germans and their native askaris. Thus, no fire to draw their attention. Also, I request, and it's a strong request, that you lower your voice. In fact, why don't you just shut up?"

I tried to eat the piece of stinking pork, but I could not manage it despite my hunger. Holmes, however, munched on his as if it were a delicacy offered by one of the finer restaurants in London.

He caught my glance, and he said, "It's superior to most examples of English cooking."

I went to the edge of the glade where the loud noises of the countess devouring her pork would not interfere with my hearing. Though I strained my ears, I could detect only the usual sounds one heard in the jungle. After a while, driven by my conscienceless stomach, I returned to the flesh that I had cast down on the ground, wiped it off on my sleeve, and began chewing on it. Holmes was right; it was not so bad.

The wild man wiped some of the blood from his hands with leaves, licked the rest off, and said, "Those men are getting closer. I'll go see who they are and what they're up to. You all stay here. And keep quiet. That means you, too, Your Ladyship, even if it kills you to do so. Which I hope it does."

The countess had been squatting like one of those troglodytes she had referred to. Now she rose up and threw her piece of meat at the baronet, but he was disappearing into the green tangle surrounding us. The missile missed him.

Minutes passed. We sat silently until the countess said, "I'm going into the bushes."

"Sir Mowgli said to wait here," Holmes said sharply.

"To hell with that nigger baronet, that crazy sex-obsessed beast-man!" she said loudly, causing more birds to fly screaming from the trees. "Anyway, I really have to go!"

"Go?" Holmes said, his eyebrows rising. "Go where? And why?"

"Yes, go, you dunderhead!" she said. "I have to take a [word blotted out and a marginal note by Watson to rephrase this scene]! Don't you know that even we aristocracy have to [word blotted out]!"

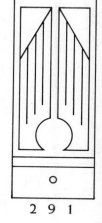

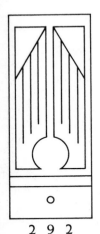

Holmes blushed, but he said, "I am well aware that they do; they are no better than Hollywood film actresses or washerwomen and not as good as some."

"[Word blotted out] you!" the countess cried, and she strode down the trail for about twenty feet and went around a bush.

"I hope a leopard gets her," said Holmes. "Or ants crawl up her [word blotted out]."

"Really, Holmes!" I gasped.

"The jungle brings out the worst in us," he said. "But it also demands the best—if we are to survive."

"Your comment was uncharitable," I said, "but understandable."

More silence ensued. Then Holmes burst out, "How I miss my pipe, Watson! Nicotine is more than an aid to thought, it is a necessity! It's a wonder that anything was done in the sciences and the arts before the discovery of America!"

Absently, he reached out and picked up a stick off the ground. He put it in his mouth, no doubt intending to suck on it as a substitute, however unsatisfactory, for the desiderated pipe. The next moment he leaped up with a yell that startled me. I cried, "What have you found, Holmes? What is it?"

"That, curse it!" he shouted and pointed at the stick. It was travelling at a fast rate on a number of thin legs toward a refuge under a log.

"Great Scott!" I said. "It's an insect, a mimetic!"

"How observant of you," he said, snarling. But the next moment he was down on his knees and groping after the creature.

"What on earth are you doing?" I said.

"It does taste like tobacco," he said. "Expediency is the mark of a . . ."

I never heard the rest. An uproar broke out in the jungle nearby, the shouts of men mortally wounded.

"What is it?" I said. "Could Mowgli have found the Germans?"

Then I fell silent and clutched him, as he clutched me, while a yell pierced the forest, a yell that froze our blood and hushed the jungle. It sounded to me like the victory cry of a wolf. There are no wild wolves in Africa, so I knew who had uttered that terrifying ululation.

IX

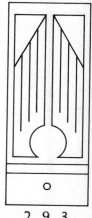

Holmes unfroze and started in the direction of the sound. I said, "Wait, Holmes! Mowgli ordered us not to leave this place! He must have his reasons for that!"

"He isn't going to order me around! Not now!" Holmes said. Nevertheless, he halted. It was not a change of mind about the command; it was the crashing of men thrusting through the jungle toward us. We turned and plunged into the bush in the opposite direction while a cry behind us told us that we had been seen. A moment later, heavy hands fell upon us and dragged us down. Someone gave an order in a language unknown to me, and we were jerked roughly to our feet.

Our captors were four tall men of a dark Caucasian race with features somewhat like those of the ancient Persians. They wore thick quilted helmets of some cloth, thin sleeveless shirts, short kilts, and knee-high leather boots. They were armed with small round steel shields, short heavy two-edged swords, heavy two-headed steel axes with long wooden shafts, and bows and arrows.

They said something to us. We looked blank. Then they turned as a weak cry came from the other side of the clearing. One of their own staggered out from the

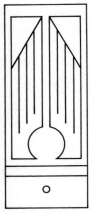

bush only to fall flat on his face and lie there unmoving. His own sword projected from his back.

Seeing this, the men became alarmed, though I suppose they had been alarmed all along. One ran out, examined the man, shook his head, and raced back. We were half-lifted, half-dragged along with them in a mad dash through vegetation that tore and ripped our clothes and us. Evidently they had run up against Mowgli, which was not a thing to be recommended at any time. I didn't know why they burdened themselves with two exhausted old men, but I surmised that it was for no beneficent purpose.

I will not recount in detail that terrible journey. Suffice it to say that we were four days and nights in the jungle, walking all day, trying to sleep at night. We were scratched, bitten, and torn, tormented with itches that wouldn't stop and sometimes sick from insect bites. We went through almost impenetrable jungle and waded waist-deep in swamps which held hordes of blood-sucking leeches. Half of the time, however, we progressed fairly swiftly along paths whose ease of access convinced me that they must be kept open by regular work parties.

The third day we started up a small mountain. The fourth day we went down it by being let down in a bamboo cage suspended by ropes from a bamboo boom. Below us lay the end of a lake that wound out of sight among the precipices that surrounded it. We were moved along at a fast pace toward a canyon into which the arm of the lake ran. Our captors pulled two dugouts out of concealment and we were paddled into the fjord. After rounding a corner, we saw before us a shore that sloped gently upward to a precipice several miles beyond it. A village of bamboo huts with thatched roofs spread along the shore and some distance inland.

The villagers came running when they saw us. A

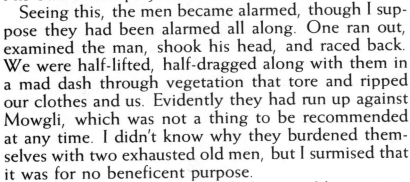

drum began beating some place, and to its beat we were marched up a narrow street and to a hut near the biggest hut. We were thrust into this, a gate of bamboo bars was lashed to the entrance, and we sat against its back wall while the villagers took turns looking in at us. As a whole, they were a good-looking people, the average of beauty being much higher than that seen in the East End of London, for instance. The women wore only long cloth skirts, though necklaces of shells hung around their necks and their long hair was decorated with flowers. The prepubescent children were stark naked.

Presently, food was brought to us. This consisted of delicious baked fish, roasted pygmy antelope, unleavened bread, and a brew that would under other circumstances have been too sweet for my taste. I am not ashamed to admit that Holmes and I gorged ourselves, devouring everything set before us.

I went to sleep shortly afterward, waking after dusk with a start. A torch flared in a stanchion just outside the entrance, at which two guards stood. Holmes was sitting near it, reading his *Practical Handbook of Bee Culture, With Some Observations Upon the Segregation of the Queen.* "Holmes," I began, but he held up his hand for silence. His keen ears had detected a sound a few seconds before mine did. This swelled to a hubbub with the villagers swarming out while the drum beat again. A moment later we saw the cause of the uproar. Six warriors, with Reich and Von Bork among them, were marching toward us. And while we watched curiously the two Germans were shoved into our hut.

Though both were much younger than Holmes and I, they were in equally bad condition—probably, I suppose, because they had not practiced the good old British custom of walking whenever possible. Von Bork refused to talk to us, but Reich, always a gentleman,

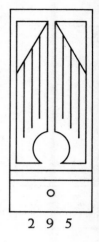

told us what had happened to his party.

"We too heard the noises and that horrible cry," he said, referring to the baronet's attack on our captors. "We made our way cautiously toward it until we saw the carnage in a clearing. There were five dead men sprawled there, and six running in one direction and four in another. Standing with his foot on the chest of the largest corpse was a dark white man, utterly naked, a bloody knife in his hand. He was the one giving that awful cry, which I would swear no human throat could make.

"Three of the men had been pierced with arrows. The other two had obviously had their necks broken. The arrows were just like the dead men's, so I suppose that the killer stole a bow and arrows from them. Or perhaps he is a renegade seeking vengeance on his fellow tribesmen for some reason or other. I whispered to my men to fire at him. Before we could do so, he had leaped up and pulled himself by a branch into a tree, and he was gone. We searched for him for some time without success. Then we started out to the east, but at dusk one of my men fell with an arrow through his neck. The angle of the arrow showed that it had come from above. We looked upward but could see nothing. Then a voice, speaking in excellent German, but with an Oxford accent yet, ordered us to turn back. We were to march to the southwest. If we did not, one of us would die at dusk each day until no one was left. I asked him why we should do this, but there was no reply. Obviously, he had us entirely at his mercy — which, I suspected, from the looks of him, he utterly lacked."

"He is Major Sir Mowgli of the Seeonee, a British officer and baronet of Indian origin," Holmes said. "He is the same Mowgli — or at least claims to be — the same Mowgli of whom Rudyard Kipling wrote in his *Jungle Book.*"

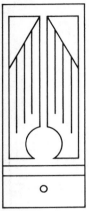

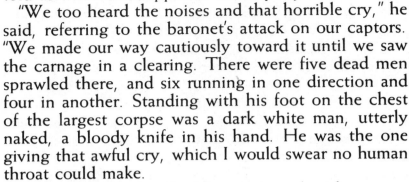

"*Ach, der Wolfmensch!*" Von Bork said. "But I had thought that he was a myth, a creation of Herr Kipling's imagination!"

"Surely you must have read that the real Mowgli, or a man claiming to be the real one, appeared some time after Kipling's book was published. You must know that he was accepted as the genuine article and eventually inherited a vast fortune and was made a baronet by the queen. For what reason, I forget, though I'm sure that his monetary contributions to certain causes had something to do with it."

"I read about him, yes," Von Bork said. "But . . . ?"

Holmes smiled and shrugged and also said, "But . . . ?"

Reich continued his story:

"My first concern was the safety and well-being of my men. To have ignored the savage would have been to be brave but stupid. So I ordered the march to the southwest. After two days it became evident that the stalker intended for us to starve to death. All our food was stolen that night, and we dared not leave the line of march to hunt, even though I doubt that we would have been able to shoot anything. The evening of the second day, I called out, begging that he let us at least hunt for food. He must have had some pangs of conscience, some mercy in him after all. That morning we woke to find a freshly killed wild pig, one of those orange-bristled swine, in the center of the camp. From somewhere in the branches overhead his voice came mockingly. 'Pigs should eat pigs!'

"And so we struggled southwestward until today. We were attacked by these people. The stalker had not ordered us to lay down our arms, so we gave a good account of ourselves. But only Von Bork and I survived, and we were knocked unconscious by the flats of their axes. And marched here, the Lord only knows for what end."

"I suspect that the Lord of the Jungle, one of Mow-

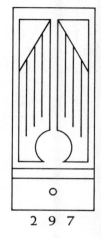

gli's unofficial titles, knows," Holmes said. "No doubt, he is lurking out there in the jungle somewhere. Oh, by the way, did you happen to see a white woman, an Englishwoman, while you were out there?"

"No, we did not," Reich said.

"That's good," Holmes said.

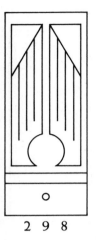

X

If the wild man did know, he did not appear to tell us what to expect. Several days passed while we slept and ate and talked to Reich. Von Bork continued to ignore us, even though Holmes several times addressed him. Holmes asked him about his health, which I thought a strange concern for a man who had not killed us only because he lacked the opportunity.

Holmes seemed especially interested in his left eye, once coming up to within a few inches of it and staring at it. Von Bork became enraged at this close scrutiny.

"Get away from me, British swine!" he yelled. "Or I will ruin both of your eyes!"

"Permit Dr. Watson to examine it," Holmes said. "He might be able to save it."

"I want no incompetent English physician poking around it," Von Bork said.

I became so indigant that I lectured him on the very high standards of British medicine, but he only turned his back on me. Holmes chuckled at this and winked at me.

At the end of the week, we were allowed to leave the hut during the day, unaccompanied by guards. Holmes and I were not restrained in any way, though the Germans were hobbled with shackles so that they could not walk very fast. Apparently, our captors decided that Holmes and I were too old to give them much of a run for their money.

We took advantage of our comparative freedom to stroll around the village, inspecting everything and also attempting to learn the language.

"I don't know what family it belongs to," Holmes said. "But it is related neither to Cornish nor Chaldean, of that I'm sure."

Holmes was also interested in the white china of these people, which represented their highest art form. The black figures and designs they painted upon it reminded me somewhat of early Greek vase paintings. The vases and dishes were formed from kaolin deposits which existed to the north near the precipices. I mention this only because the white clay was to play an important part in our salvation in the near future.

At the end of the second week, Holmes, a superb linguist, had attained some fluency in the speech of our captors. "It belongs to a completely unknown language family," he said. "But there are certain words which, degenerated though they are, obviously come from ancient Persian. I would say that at one time these people had contact with a wandering party of descendants of Darius. The party settled down here, and these people borrowed some words from their idiom."

The village consisted of a hundred huts arranged in concentric circles. Each held a family ranging from two to eight members. Their fields lay north of the village on the slopes leading up to the precipices. The stock consisted of goats, pigs, and dwarf antelopes. Their alcoholic drink was a sort of mead made from the honey of wild bees. A few specimens of these ventured near the village, and Holmes secured some for study. They were about an inch long, striped black and white, and were armed with a long venom-ejecting

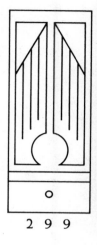

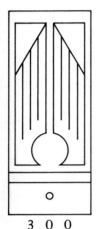

3 0 0

barb. Holmes declared that they were of a new species, and he saw no reason not to classify them as *Apis holmesi*.

Once a week a party set out to the hills to collect honey. Its members were always clad in leather clothing and gloves and wore veils over their hats. Holmes asked permission to accompany them, explaining that he was wise in the ways of bees. To his disappointment, they refused him. A further inquiry by him resulted in the information that there was a negotiable, though difficult, pass through the precipices. It was used only for emergency purposes because of the vast number of bees that filled the narrow pass. Holmes obtained his data by questioning a child. Apparently, the adults had not thought to tell their young to keep silent about this means of exit.

"The bee-warding equipment is kept locked up in their temple," Holmes said. "And that makes it impossible to obtain it for an escape attempt."

The temple was the great hut in the village's centre. We were not allowed to enter it or even to approach it within fifty feet. Through some discreet inquiries, and unashamed eavesdropping, Holmes discovered that the high priestess-and-queen lived within the temple. We had never seen her nor were we likely to do so. She had been born in the temple and was to reside there until she died. Just why she was so restricted Holmes could not determine. His theory was that she was a sort of hostage to the gods.

"Perhaps, Watson, she is confined because of a superstition that arose after the catastrophe which their myths say deluged this land and the great civilisation it harboured. The fishermen tell me that they often see on the bottom of this lake the sunken ruins of the stone houses in which their ancestors lived. A curse was laid upon the land, they say, and they hint that only by keeping the high priestess-cum-queen inviolate, unseen by profane eyes, untouched by anyone after pubescence, can the wrath of the gods be averted. They are cagey in what they say, so I have had to surmise certain aspects of their religion."

"That's terrible!" I said.

"The deluge?"

"No, that a woman should be denied freedom and love."

"She has a name, but I have never overheard it. They refer to her as The Beautiful One."

"Is there nothing we can do for her?" I said.

"I do not know that she wants to be helped. You must not allow your well-known gallantry to endanger us. But to satisfy a legitimate scientific interest, if anthropology is a science, we could perhaps attempt a look inside the temple. Its roof has a large circular hole in its center. If we could get near the top of the high tree about twenty yards from it, we could look down into the building."

"With the whole village watching us?" I said. "No, Holmes, it is impossible to get up the tree unobserved during the day. And if we did so during the night, we could see nothing because of the darkness. In any event, it would probably mean instantaneous death even to make the attempt."

"There are torches lit in the building at night," he said. "Come, Watson, if you have no taste for this arboreal adventure, I shall go it alone."

And that was why, despite my deep misgivings, we climbed that towering tree on a cloudy night. After Von Bork and Reich had fallen asleep and our guards had dozed off and the village was silent except for a chanting in the temple, we crept out of our hut. Holmes had hidden a rope the day before, but even with this it was no easy task. We were not youths of twenty, agile as monkeys and as fearless aloft. Holmes threw

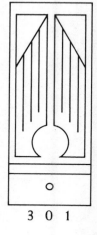

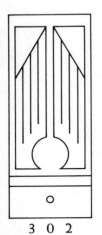

the weighted end of the rope over the lowest branch,
which was twenty feet up, and tied the two ends together. Then, grasping the rope with both hands, and
bracing his feet against the trunk, he half-walked almost perpendicular to the trunk, up the tree. On reaching the branch, he rested for a long time while he
gasped for breath so loudly that I feared he would
wake up the nearest villagers. When he was quite recovered, he called down to me to make the ascent.
Since I was heavier and several years older, and lacked
his feline muscles, having more the physique of a bear,
I experienced great difficulty in getting up. I wrapped
my legs around the rope—no walking at a ninety-
degree angle to the tree for me—and painfully and
gaspingly hauled myself up. But I persisted—after all,
I am British—and Holmes pulled me up at the final
stage of what I was beginning to fear was my final
journey.

After resting, we made a somewhat easier ascent via
the branches to a position about ten feet below the
top of the tree. From there we could look almost directly down through the hole in the middle of the
roof. The torches within enabled us to see its interior
quite clearly.

Both of us gasped when we saw the woman standing
in the center of the building by a stone altar. She was
a beautiful woman, surely one of the daintiest things
that ever graced this planet. She had long golden hair
and eyes that looked dark from where we sat but which,
we later found out, were a deep grey. She was wearing
nothing except a necklace of some stones that sparkled
as she moved. Though I was fascinated, I also felt
something of shame, as if I were a peeping tom. I had
to remind myself that the women wore nothing above
the waist in their everyday attire and that when they
swam in the lake they wore nothing at all. So we were

doing nothing immoral by this spying. Despite this reasoning, my face (and other things) felt inflamed. *

She stood there, doing nothing for a long time, which I expected would make Holmes impatient. He did not stir or make any comment, so I suppose that this time he did not mind a lack of action. The priestesses chanted and the priests walked around in a circle making signs with their hands and their fingers. Then a bound he-goat was brought in and placed on the altar, and, after some more mumbo-jumbo, the woman cut its throat. The blood was caught in a golden bowl and passed around in a sort of communion, the woman drinking first.

"A most unsanitary arrangement," I murmured to Holmes.

"These people are, nevertheless, somewhat cleaner than your average Londoner," Holmes replied. "And much more cleanly than your Scots peasant."

I was about to take umbrage at this, since I am of Scots descent on my mother's side. Holmes knew this and my sensitivity about it. He had been making too many remarks of this nature recently, and though I attributed them to irritability arising from nicotine withdrawal, I was, to use an American phrase, getting fed up with them. I was about to remonstrate when my heart leaped into my throat and choked me.

A hand had come from above and clamped down upon my shoulder. I knew that it wasn't Holmes' because I could see both of his hands.

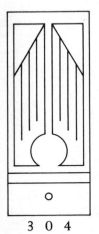

3 0 4

XI

Holmes almost fell off the branch but was saved by another hand, which grasped him by the collar of his shirt. A familiar voice said, "Silence!"

"Mowgli!" I gasped. And then, remembering that, after all, he was a baronet, I said, "Your pardon. I mean, Sir Mowgli."

"What are you doing up here, you baboon!" Holmes said.

I was shocked at this, though I knew that Holmes spoke thus only because he must have been thoroughly frightened. To address a baronet in this manner was not his custom.

"Tut, tut, Holmes," I said.

"Tut, tut yourself," he replied. "He's not paying me a fee! He's no client of mine. Besides, I doubt that he is entitled to his title!"

A growl that lifted the hairs on the back of my neck came from above. It was followed by the descent of the baronet's heavy body upon our branch, which bent alarmingly. But he squatted upon it, his hands free, with all the sense of balance of the baboon he had been accused of being.

"What does that last remark mean?" the baronet said.

At that moment the moon broke through the clouds. A ray fell upon Holmes' face, which had become as pale as when he was pretending to be sick in that case which I have titled "The Adventure of the Dying Detective."

Holmes said, "This is neither the time nor the place for an investigation of your credentials. We are in a desperate plight, and..."

"You don't realize how desperate," the baronet interrupted. "I usually abide by human laws when I am in civilisation. But this is the jungle, and here I obey

*The parentheses are the editor's. Watson had crossed out this phrase, though not enough to make it illegible.

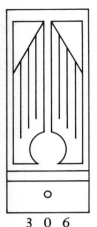

the Law of the Jungle as I learned it from Baloo, the Blind Brown Bear, the Law of the Seeonee Wolf-Pack, of Chil the Kite, Bagheera the Black Panther, and Kaa the Rock Python. And here, even though this is not my native land, India, in the central part of which I am king, not a mere baronet, I revert to my primal and happiest state, that of Mowgli, the Frog, brother to the Wolf and to Hathi, the Silent One, the Elephant..."

Good Lord! I thought. How this man does run on! I had supposed that feral men were reticent and laconic types who spoke seldom and then only in short declarative sentences. This man talked as if he were one of James Fenimore Cooper's noble savages.

". . . then I obey my own laws, not those of humanity, for which I have the greatest contempt, barring a few specimens of such . . ."

(There was much more in this single statement, the length of which would have made any German philosopher proud. The gist of it was that if Holmes did not explain his remark now, he would have no chance to do so later. Nor was the baronet backward in stating that I would not be taking any news of Holmes' fate to the outside world.)

"He means it, Holmes!" I said.

"I am well aware of that, Watson. He is covered only with a thin veneer of civilisation. Very well, Your Highness. It is not my custom to set forth a theory until I have enough evidence to make it a fact. But under the circumstances . . ."

I looked for Sir Mowgli to show some resentment at Holmes' sarcastic use of a title appropriate only to a monarch. He, however, only smiled. This, I believe, was a reaction of pleasure, of ignorance of Holmes' intent to cut him. He was sure that he deserved the title, and now that I have had time to reflect on it, I agree with him. He ruled a kingdom many times larger than our tight little isle. And he paid no taxes in it.

"The very fact that you threaten me," Holmes said, "tells me that I have some basis of validity in my reasoning."

I thought that he spoke bravely but indiscreetly and it was discretion that was called for now. But I kept silent.

"I believe that the real Mowgli, if he exists or ever did exist, would be incapable of such a threat. Kipling's accounts of the Wolf-Boy's exploits lead me to believe that Mowgli would be of a high moral character. The genuine Mowgli, if he existed, would only have laughed at my hints of fraud."

The baronet shifted his weight so that the branch under him creaked. The moon glittered on the sharp blade. He was scowling fiercely.

"What do you know of the true nature of the Wolf's Brother, Two-Legs?" he said harshly.

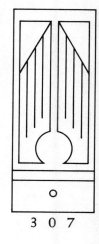

307

Holmes, seemingly unperturbed, replied, "As I said, I know only what I've read about him. However, I have arrived at my conclusions through observation of you combined with my trifling powers of deduction. Which some, however, have been kind enough to state are those of a genius. Disregarding this, I still have some gifts worthy of consideration..."

Holmes, I thought, you are as wordy as the wild man.

"One of my dictums is that, when you have eliminated the impossible, whatever is left, however improbable, is the truth."

"I have read that statement in Doctor Watson's narratives," the baronet said. "It's full of [word blotted out]. What if you haven't included everything that could happen? What if you've overlooked something or are incapable of enough deductive powers to see all the patterns of certain clues? You may be a genius, Mr. Detective, but I have read some cases in which you made some serious, even stupid, errors."

Even in the moonlight, I could see Holmes flush. But he did not reply sharply, perhaps because of the sharp edge so close to his jugular vein.

"Nevertheless," he said determinedly, "it is impossible for animals to talk. They may communicate by a rather limited system of signals. But they cannot use language. They are not sentient creatures like *Homo sapiens.*

"It is improbable, though barely possible, that a human infant could be raised by wolves. But it is impossible that wolves could have true speech. Therefore, Kipling's account is obviously fictitious. His *Jungle Book* is merely an extension of ancient myths, primitive folktales, and medieval fairy tales wherein animals do have speech.

"Thus, there was no Mowgli who talked to animals. It is highly improbable that there was a Mowgli of any kind.

"But, in 1899, a man claiming to be the genuine Wolf-Boy appeared in Bombay, having travelled all the way from the Seeonee Hills on foot. Or so he said. His claim was widely publicized, and he was the subject of much speculation, pro and con, by various notable personages and authorities. Not to mention some rather lunatic people.

"Investigation showed, or seemed to show, that the alleged Mowgli was indeed the son of a woodchopper and his wife and that they had been killed by a tiger and that the infant had disappeared.

"Further investigation revealed that the woodchopper was not a Hindu but a Parsee. Parsees are, as you know, the descendants of Persian fire-worshippers, Zoroastrians, who fled their native land when the Arab Moslems conquered it. They settled in India so that

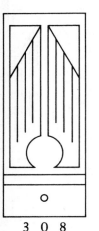

they could have freedom of worship.

"The woodchopper was a poor relative of Sir Jametsee Jejeebhoy, the Parsee baronet of Bombay. The woodchopper had at one time visited his wealthy second cousin to show him his son. The infant was flawless except for a red birthmark between the big toe and the next toe on the left foot. The man claiming to be Mowgli had such a birthmark."

"As you see," the baronet said, sticking out a singularly muscular leg and spreading his toes.

"That could be a fortunate coincidence and, in fact, the basis for action in a fraudulent claim," Holmes said.

"*Ngaayah!*" the baronet snarled. "You disgust me."

"Sir Jametsse, son of the late baronet and himself childless, adopted Mowgli. When Sir Jametsee died, Mowgli inherited his vast fortune and, a few years later, was given a baronetcy by our queen."

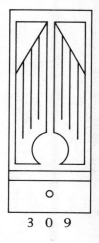

"I was investigated by Scotland Yard," Sir Mowgli said. "They found nothing wrong."

"But they did not prove your claim," Holmes said. "They did not apply my deductive and investigative techniques. Their methods were, I regret to say, much like those of the inept and late Inspector Lestrade."

Sir Mowgli shrugged his heavy shoulders.

"What do I care what you believe?"

"What I plan to do," Holmes said, "is to go to India when the war is over and investigate your claim. I will be a bloodhound, relentless, sniffing out every clue, true or false. I will pursue the trail to its end."

"Why should you do that?" the baronet said.

"The truth is not only a means but the end. It is its own reward."

I was trying to puzzle that out when the baronet said, "I could kill you now and prevent all that trouble and publicity. I am heartily tired of such, I assure you. However..."

After a long pause, Holmes said, "Yes?"

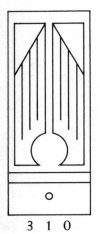

"It would be worth it to avoid such an investigation. Not because I am afraid of the truth, I'm not, but because I am weary of publicity."

"Is that why you played yourself in a movie which will be shown everywhere on Earth?" Holmes said.

"Don't try me!" the baronet said huskily, and his knife flashed.

"Yes, my dear Holmes," I said in, I fear, a trembling voice. "There is no need to antagonize our only ally, our only hope for escape."

"You are a sensible man, Doctor Watson," the baronet said. "Would that your colleague were. Very well. I have a proposition to make, Mr. Holmes. What if I hired you to investigate my claim, to ferret out the truth of my story?"

"What?" I said. His offer was so unexpected.

Holmes, however, was not startled. He seemed to have anticipated the suggestion.

"Such a project would require great expenses," he said calmly.

"I believe it would. Tell me, what is the largest fee you ever received?"

"The highest was in the case of the Priory School. Twelve thousand pounds."

Quickly, he added, "Of course, that sum was only *my* fee. Watson, as my colleague in the case, received the same amount."

"Really, Holmes," I murmured.

"Twenty-four thousand pounds," the baronet said, frowning.

"That fee was paid in 1901," Holmes said. "Inflation has sent prices sky-high since then, and the income tax rate is ascending as if it were a rocket."

"For Heaven's sake, Holmes!" I cried. "I do not see the necessity for this fishmarket bargaining! Surely..."

Holmes coldly interrupted. "You will please leave

the financial arrangements to me, the senior partner and the true professional in this matter."

"You'll antagonize Sir Mowgli and..."

"Would sixty thousand pounds be adequate?" the baronet said.

"Well," Holmes said, hesitating, "God knows how wartime conditions will continue to cheapen the price of money in the next few years."

The baronet turned the knife over as if he were considering using it.

"You are most generous," Holmes said quickly. "Sixty thousand pounds... quite satisfactory."

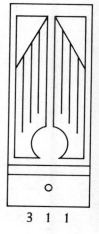

I could not understand why the baronet would hire anyone to look into his claim unless he truly believed that it was valid. But Holmes, I was certain from his expression, did not have the same faith. I was wondering how I could find out just what Holmes was thinking when the baronet changed the subject.

"I travelled in this area before I agreed to make the movie. I went alone, unencumbered by a safari, and I discovered, rediscovered, I should say, this hidden land. I said nothing about it when I returned to civilization because I did not want these people invaded by hordes of Europeans bearing their usual gifts of gin, disease, and their thousand means of exploitation."

He paused, then said, "I also discovered that this is the land of Zu-Vendis."

"What?" I said. "You mean that the unknown civilization described by H. Rider Haggard in his novel, *Allan Quatermain*, is not fiction?"

"Exactly," the baronet said. "Haggard presented the true adventures of the hunter and explorer, Allan Quatermain, as fiction because he, like me, did not want this country devastated."

"Then we are the prisoners of the people of Zu-Vendis?" I said.

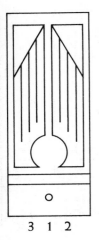

3 1 2

"Not for long, if I can help it," said the baronet. "However, either Quatermain or his agent and editor, Haggard, exaggerated the size of Zu-Vendis. It was supposed to be about the size of France but actually covered an area equal to that of Liechtenstein. In the main, however, except for the size and location of Zu-Vendis, Quatermain's account is true. He was accompanied on his expedition by two Englishmen, a baronet, Sir Henry Curtis, and a naval captain, John Good. And that great Zulu warrior, Umslopogaas, a man whom I would have liked to have known. After the Zulu and Quatermain died, Curtis sent Quatermain's manuscript of the adventure to Haggard. Haggard apparently added some things of his own to give more verisimilitude to the chronicle. For one thing, he said that several British commissions were investigating Zu-Vendis with the intent of finding a more accessible means of travel to it. This was not so. Zu-Vendis was never found, except by me, and that is why most people concluded that the account was pure fiction. Shortly after the manuscript was sent out by one of the natives who had accompanied the Quatermain party, the entire valley except for this high end was flooded."

"Then poor Curtis and Good and their lovely Zu-Vendis wives were drowned?" I said.

"No," the baronet said. "They were among the dozen or so who reached safety. Apparently, they either could not get out of the valley then or decided to stay here. After all, Nylepthah, Curtis' wife, was the queen, and she would not want to abandon her people, few though they were. The two Englishmen settled down, taught the people the use of the bow, among other things, and died here. They were buried up in the hills."

"What a sad story!" I said.

"All people must die," Sir Mowgli replied, as if that told the whole story of the world. And perhaps it did.

He looked out at the temple, saying, "That woman at whom you have been staring with a non-quite-scientific detachment..."

"Yes?" I said.

"Her name is also Nylepthah. She is the granddaughter of both Good and Curtis."

"Will wonders never cease!" I said.

The baronet cleared his throat and said, "Oh, yes, before I forget it..."

Holmes smiled as if he had been expecting that the baronet would recall something.

"I will pay you your fee as soon as possible. But you must not begin your investigation until I tell you that the time is ripe for it. I am a very busy man, I have much business to conduct, and it might be inconvenient for me to have to attend to you until I have certain matters cleared up. This might take a long time. Meanwhile, you will have the fee in your hands, and there will be no question asked about how you two handle the sums.

"Do you understand?"

"Perfectly," Holmes said, smiling even more broadly. "We will await your consent to begin the investigation. No matter how much time passes."

"Ah, then you do understand," the baronet said quietly.

"Yes. The fee will enable me to live quite well in my retirement. I had enough when I first retired, but many of my investments went bad, and..."

"Can't you think about anything but money, Holmes!" I said. "We must do something about that poor British woman parading around naked before those savages and held in close captivity!"

The baronet shrugged and said, "It's their custom."

"We must rescue her and get her back to the home of her ancestors!" I cried.

"Be quiet, Watson, or you'll have the whole pack

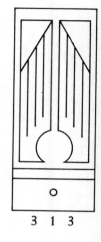

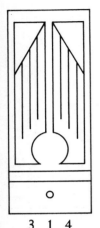

3   1   4

howling for our blood," Holmes growled. "She seems quite contented with her lot. Or could it be," he added, looking hard at me, "that you have once again fallen into love?"

He made it sound as if the grand passion were an open privy. Blushing, I said, "I must admit that there is a certain feeling..."

"Well, the fair sex is your department," he said. "But really, Watson, at your age!"

("The Americans have a proverb," I said. "The older the buck, the stiffer the horn.")*

"Be quiet, both of you," the baronet said. "I permitted the Zu-Vendis to capture you because I knew you'd be safe for a while. I drove the Germans this way because I expected that they would, like you, be picked up by the Zu-Vendis. Tomorrow night, all four of you prisoners are scheduled to be sacrificed on the temple altar. I got back an hour ago to get you two out."

"That was cutting it close, wasn't it?" Holmes said.

"You mean to leave Von Bork and Reich here?" I said. "To be slaughtered like sheep? And what about the woman, Nylepthah? What kind of life is that, being confined from birth to death in that house, being denied the love and companionship of a husband, forced to murder poor devils of captives?"

"Yes," said Holmes. "Reich is a very decent fellow and should be treated like a prisoner of war. I wouldn't mind at all if Von Bork were to die, but only he knows the location of the SB papers. The fate of Britain, of her allies, hangs on those papers. As for the woman, well, she is of good British stock and it seems a shame to leave her here in this squalidness."

"So she can go to London and perhaps live in squalour there?" the baronet said.

"I'll see to it that that does not happen," I said. "You can have back my fee if you take that woman along."

The baronet laughed softly and said, "I couldn't refuse a man who loves love more than he loves money.
And you can keep the fee."

XII

At some time before dawn, the baronet entered our
hut. The Germans were also waiting for him, since we
had told them what to expect if they did not leave
with us. He gestured for silence, unnecessarily, I
thought, and we followed him outside. The two guards,
gagged and trussed-up, lay by the door. Near them
stood Nylepthah, also gagged, her hands bound before
her and a rope hobbling her. Her glorious body was
concealed in a cloak. The baronet removed the hobble,
gestured at us, took the woman by the arm, and we
walked silently through the village. Our immediate
goal was the beach, where we intended to steal two
boats. We would paddle to the foot of the cliff on top
of which was the bamboo boom and ascend the ropes.
Then we would cut the ropes so that we could not be
followed. Sir Mowgli had come down on the rope after
disposing of the guards at the boom. He would climb
back up the rope and then pull us up.

Our plans died in the bud. As we approached the
beach, we saw torches flaring on the water. Presently,
as we watched from behind a hut, we saw fishermen
paddling in with their catch of night-caught fish.
Someone stirred in the hut beside which we crouched,
and before we could get away, a woman, yawning and

*The parentheses are the editor's, indicating another passage crossed
out by Watson.

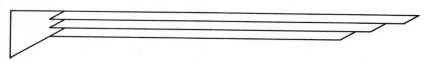

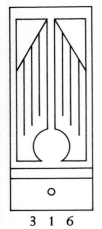

stretching came out. She must have been waiting for her fisherman husband. Whatever the case, she surprised us.

The baronet moved swiftly, but too late, toward her. She screamed loudly, and though she quit almost immediately, she had aroused the village.

There is no need to go into detail about the long and exhausting run we made through the village, while the people poured out, and up the slopes toward the faraway pass in the precipices. The baronet smote right and left and before him, and men and women went down like the Philistines before Samson. We were armed with the short swords he had stolen from the armory and so were of some aid to him. But by the time we had left the village and reached the fields, Holmes and I were breathing very hard.

"You two help the woman along between you," Sir Mowgli commanded the Germans. Before we could protest, though what good it would have done if we had I don't know, we were picked up, one under each arm, and carried off. Burdened though he was, the baronet ran faster than the three behind him. The ground, only about a foot away from my face since I was dangling like a rag doll in his arm, reeled by. After about a mile, Sir Mowgli stopped and released us. He did this by simply dropping us. My face hit the dirt at the same time my knees did. I was somewhat pained, but I thought it indiscreet to complain. Holmes, however, displayed a knowledge of swear words which would have delighted a dock worker. The baronet ignored him, urging us to push on. Far behind us we could see the torches of our pursuers and hear their clamour.

By dawn the Zu-Vendis had gotten closer. All of us, except for the indefatigable Wolf-Man, were tiring swiftly. The pass was only half a mile away, and once

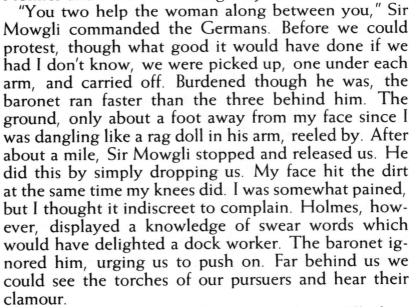

we were through that, he said, we would be safe. The savages behind us, though, were beginning to shoot their arrows at us.

"We can't get through the pass anyway!" I said between gasps to Holmes. "We have no equipment to keep the bees off us! If the arrows don't kill us, the bee-stings will!"

Ahead of us, where the hills suddenly moved in and formed the entrance to the path, a vast buzzing filled the air. Fifty thousand tiny, but deadly, insects swirled in a thick cloud as they prepared to voyage to the sea of flowers which held the precious nectar.

We stopped to catch our breath and consider the situation.

"We can't go back and we can't go ahead!" I said. "What shall we do?"

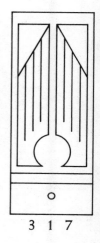

The baronet pointed at the nearby hill, at the base of which was the white clay used by the Zu-Vendis to make their fine pots and dishes.

"Coat yourselves with that!" he said. "It should be somewhat of a shield!" And he hastened to take his own advice.

I hesitated. The baronet had stripped off his loincloth and had jumped into the stream which ran nearby. Then he had scooped out with his hands a quantity of clay, had mixed it with water, and was smearing it over him everywhere. Holmes was removing his clothing before going into the stream. The Germans were getting ready to do likewise, while the beautiful Nylepthah stood abandoned. I did the only thing a gentleman could do. I went to her and removed her cloak, under which she wore nothing. I told her in my halting Zu-Vendis that I was ready to sacrifice myself for her. Though the bees, alarmed, were now moving in a great cloud toward us, I would make sure that I smeared the clay all over her before I took care of myself.

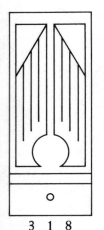

Nylepthah said, "I know an easier way to escape the bees. Let me run back to the village."

"Poor deluded girl!" I said. "You do not know what is best for you! Trust me, and I will see you safely to England, the home of your ancestors. And then . . ."

I did not get a chance to promise to marry her. Holmes and the Germans cried out, causing me to look up just in time to see Sir Mowgli falling unconscious to the ground. An arrow had hit him in the head, and though it had struck a glancing blow, it had knocked him out and made a large nasty wound.

I thought we were indeed lost. Behind us was the howling horde of savages, their arrows and spears and axes flying through the air at us. Ahead was a swarm of giant bees, a cloud so dense that I could barely see the hills behind them. The buzzing was deafening. The one man who was strong enough and jungle-wise enough to pull us through was out of action for the time being. And if the bees attacked soon, which they would do, he would be in that state permanently. So would all of us.

Holmes shouted at me, "Never mind taking advantage of that woman, Watson! Come here, quickly, and help me!"

"This is no time to indulge in jealousy, Holmes," I muttered, but nevertheless I obeyed him. "No, Watson," Holmes said. "I'll put on the clay! You daub on me that excellent black dirt there along the banks of the stream! Put it on in stripes, thus, white and black alternating!"

"Have you gone mad, Holmes?"

"There's no time to talk," said Holmes. "The bees are almost upon us! Oh, they are deadly, deadly, Watson! Quick, the mud!"

Within a minute, striped like a zebra, Holmes stood before me. He ran to the pile of clothes and took from the pocket of his jacket the large magnifying glass that had been his faithful companion all these years. And then he did something that caused me to cry out in utter despair. He ran directly toward the deadly buzzing cloud.

I shouted after him as I ran to drag him away from his futile and senseless act. It was too late to get him away from the swiftly advancing insects. I knew that, just as I knew that I would die horribly with him. Nevertheless, I would be with him. We had been comrades too many years for me to even contemplate for a second abandoning him.

He turned when he heard my voice and shouted, "Go back, Watson! Go back! Get the others to one side! Drag the baronet out of their path! I know what I'm doing! Get away! I command you, Watson!"

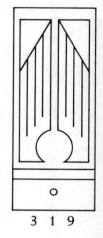

The conditioning of our many years of association turned me and sent me back to the group. I'd obeyed his orders too long to refuse them now. But I was weeping, convinced that he was out of his mind, or, if he did have a plan, it would fail. I got Reich to help me drag the senseless and heavily bleeding baronet half into the stream, and I ordered Von Bork and Nylepthah to lie down in the stream. The clay coating, I was convinced, was not an adequate protection. We could submerge ourselves when the bees passed over us. The stream was only inches deep, but perhaps the water flowing over our bodies would discourage the insects.

Lying in the stream, holding Sir Mowgli's head up to keep him from drowning, I watched Holmes.

He had indeed gone crazy. He was dancing around and around, stopping now and then to bend over and wiggle his buttocks in a most undignified manner. Then he would hold up the magnifying glass so that the sunlight flashed through it at the Zu-Vendis. These, by the way, had halted to stare open-mouthed at Holmes.

"Whatever are you doing?" I shouted.

He shook his head angrily at me to indicate that I should keep quiet. At that moment I became aware that he was himself making a loud buzzing sound. It was almost submerged in the louder noise of the swarm, but I was near enough to hear it faintly.

Again and again Holmes whirled, danced, stopped, pointing his wriggling buttocks at the Zu-Vendis savages and letting the sun pass through the magnifying glass at a certain angle. His actions seemed to puzzle not only the humans but the bees. The swarm had stopped its forward movement and it was hanging in the air, seemingly pointed at Holmes.

Suddenly, as Holmes completed his obscene dance for the seventh time, the swarm flew forward. I cried out, expecting to see him covered with the huge black-and-white-striped horrors. But the mass split in two, leaving him an island in their midst. And then they were all gone, and the Zu-Vendis were running away screaming, their bodies black and fuzzy with a covering of bees. Some of them dropped in their flight, rolling back and forth, screaming, batting at the insects, and then becoming still and silent.

I ran to Holmes, crying, "How did you do it?"

"Do you remember your scepticism when I told you that I had made an astounding discovery? One that will enshrine my name among the greats in the hall of science?"

"You don't mean . . . ?"

He nodded. "Yes, bees do have a language, even African bees. It is actually a system of signals, not a true language. Bees who have discovered a new source of honey return to the hive and there perform a dance which indicates clearly the direction of and the dis-

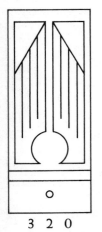

tance at which the honey lies. I have also discovered that the bee communicates the advent of an enemy to the swarm. It was this dance which I performed, and the swarm attacked the indicated enemy, the Zu-Ven-dis. The dance movements are intricate, and certain polarisations of light play a necessary part in the message. These I simulated with my magnifying glass. But come, Watson, let us get our clothes on and be off before the swarm returns! I do not think I can pull that trick again. We do not want to be the game afoot."

We got the baronet to his feet and half-carried him to the pass. Though he recovered consciousness, he seemed to have reverted to a totally savage state. He did not attack us but he regarded us suspiciously and made threatening growls if we got too close. We were at a loss to explain this frightening change in him. The frightening part came not so much from any danger he represented as from the dangers he was supposed to save us from. We had depended upon him to guide us and to feed and protect us on the way back. Without him even the incomparable Holmes was lost.

Fortunately, the baronet recovered the next day and provided the explanation himself.

"For some reason I seem to be prone to receiving blows on the head," he said. "I have a thick skull, but every once in a while I get such a blow that even its walls cannot withstand the force. Sometimes, say about one out of three times, a complete amnesia results. I then revert to the state in which I was before I encountered white people. I am once again the uncivilised Wolf-Man; I have no memory of anything that occurred before I was fourteen years old. This state may last for only a day, as you have seen, or it may persist for months."

"I would venture to say," Holmes said, "that this readiness to forget your contact with civilised peoples

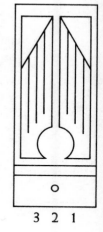

3 2 1

indicates an unconscious desire to avoid them. You are happiest when in the jungle and with no obligations. Hence your unconscious seizes upon every opportunity, such as a blow on the head, to go back to the happy primal time."

"Perhaps you are right," the baronet said. "I would like to forget civilisation even exists."

Later, when Holmes and I were alone, Holmes said, "The man is a fraud but a magnificent fraud, I'm convinced of that. However, he is in a sense not a liar. He truly believes that he is Mowgli, brother to the Wolves, the Black Panther, and the Brown Bear. In the beginning, he was a hoaxer, for profit, I'm certain. But he cast himself so thoroughly into the role that he became insane, descended into a madness reflecting Kipling's world of *The Jungle Book*. It is, however, a rather harmless insanity and one profitable for us."

"Holmes," I said, "I've been meaning to speak to you about this. Don't you think that there's extortion involved in this, a form of blackmail..."

He drew himself up and cut me off sharply.

"Not at all! I am ready to begin the investigation, a sincere one to which I shall apply a lifetime of experience, the moment he gives the word."

"Which he is not going to do," I said.

"We don't know that," he said. "Besides, that's his business."

It took more than a month for us to get to Nairobi. During the journey, I had ample time to teach Nylepthah the English language and to get well-acquainted with her. Before we reached the Lake Victoria railhead, I had proposed to her and been accepted. I will never forget that night. The moon was bright, and a hyena was laughing nearby.

The day before we reached the railhead, the baronet went up a tree to check out the territory. A branch

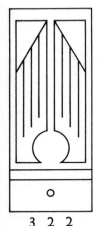

322

broke under his feet, and he landed on his head. When he regained consciousness, he was again the Wolf-Man. We could not come near him without his baring his teeth and growling menacingly. And that night he disappeared.

Holmes was very downcast by this. "What if he never gets over his amnesia, Watson? Then we will be cheated out of our fees."

"My dear Holmes," I said, somewhat coolly, "we never earned the fee in the first place. Actually, we were allowing ourselves to be bribed by the baronet to keep silent."

"You never did understand the subtle interplay of economics and ethics," Holmes replied.

"These goes Von Bork," I said, glad to change the subject. I pointed to the fellow, who was sprinting across the veldt as if a lion were after him.

"He is mad if he thinks he can make his way alone to German East Africa," Holmes said. "But we must go after him! He has on him the formula for the SB."

"Where?" I asked for the hundredth time. "We have stripped him a dozen times and gone over every inch of his clothes and his skin. We have looked into his mouth and up . . ."

At that moment I observed Von Bork turn his head to the right to look at a rhinoceros which had come around a tall termite hill. The next moment, he had run the left side of his head and body into an acacia tree with such force that he bounced back several feet. He did not get up, which was just as well. The rhinoceros was looking for him and would have detected any movement by Von Bork. After prancing around and sniffing the air in several directions, the weak-eyed beast trotted off. Holmes and I hastened to Von Bork before he got his senses back and ran off once more.

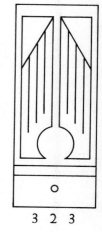

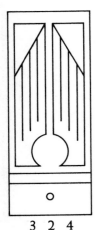

3 2 4

"I believe I know where the formula is," Holmes said.

"And how could you know that?" I said, for the thousandth time since I had first met him.

"I will bet my fee against yours that I can show you the formula within the next two minutes," he said, but I did not reply.

He kneeled down beside the German, who was lying on his back, his mouth and his eyes open. His pulse, however, beat strongly.

Holmes placed the tips of his thumbs under Von Bork's left eye. I stared aghast as the eye popped out.

"It's glass, Watson," Holmes said. "I had suspected that for some time, but I saw no reason to verify my suspicions until he was in a British prison. I was certain that his vision was limited to his right side when I saw him run into that tree. Even with his head turned away he would have seen it if his left eye had been effective."

He rotated the glass eye between thumb and finger while examining it through the magnifying glass. "Aha!" he exclaimed and then, handing the eye and glass to me, said, "See for yourself, Watson."

"Why," I said, "what I had thought were massive haemorrhages due to eye injury are tiny red lines of chemical formulae on the surface of the glass—if it *is* glass, and not some special material prepared to receive inscriptions."

"Very good, Watson," Holmes said. "Undoubtedly, Von Bork did not merely receive an injury to the eye in that motor-car crash of which I heard rumours. He lost it, but the wily fellow had it replaced with an artificial eye which had more uses than—ahem—met the eye.

"After stealing the SB formula, he inscribed the surface of this false organ with the symbols. These, except through a magnifier, look like the results of dissipation or of an accident. He must have been laughing at us when we examined him so thoroughly, but he will laugh no more."

He took the eye back and pocketed it. "Well, Watson, let us rouse him from whatever dreams he is indulging in and get him into the proper hands. This time he shall pay the penalty for espionage."

Two months later we were back in England. We travelled by water, despite the danger of U-boats, since Holmes had sworn never again to get into an aircraft of any type. He was in a bad humour throughout the voyage. He was certain that the baronet, even if he recovered his memory, would not send the promised cheques.

He turned the glass eye over to Mycroft, who sent it on to his superiors. That was the last we ever heard of it, and since the SB was never used, I surmise that the War Office decided that it would be too horrible a weapon. I was happy about this, since it just did not seem British to wage germ warfare. I have often wondered, though, what would have happened if Von Bork's mission had been successful. Would the Kaiser have countenanced SB as a weapon against his English cousins?

There were still two years of war to get through. I found lodgings for my wife and myself, and, despite the terrible conditions, the air raids, the food and material shortages, the dismaying reports from the front, we managed to be happy. In 1917 Nylepthah did what none of my previous wives had ever done. She presented me with a son. I was delirious with joy, even though I had to endure much joshing from my colleagues about fatherhood at my age. I did not inform Holmes of the baby. I dreaded his sarcastic remarks.

On November 11, 1919, however, a year after the news that turned the entire Allied world into a carnival of happiness, though a brief one, I received a wire.

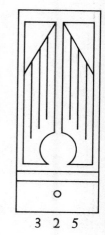

"Bringing a bottle and cigars to celebrate the good tidings. Holmes."

I naturally assumed that he referred to the anniversary of the Armistice. My surprise was indeed great when he showed up not only with the bottle of Scotch and a box of Havanas but a bundle of new clothes and toys for the baby and a box of chocolates for Nylepthah. The latter was a rarity at this time and must have cost Holmes some time and money to obtain.

"Tut, tut, my dear fellow," he said when I tried to express my thanks. "I've known for some time that you were the proud father. I have always intended to show up and tender my respects to the aged, but still energetic, father and to the beautiful Mrs. Watson. Never mind waking the infant up to show him to me, Watson. All babies look alike, and I will take your word for it that he is beautiful."

"You are certainly jovial," I said. "I do not ever remember seeing you more so."

"With good reason, Watson, with good reason!"

He dipped his hand into his pocket and brought out a cheque.

I looked at it and almost staggered. It was made out to me for the sum of thirty thousand pounds.

"I had given up on Sir Mowgli," he said. "I heard that he was missing, lost somewhere in deepest Africa, probably dead. Then I heard that that utter bitch, Countess Murdstone-Malcon, had managed to get to safety and civilisation. It seemed to me to be one of the ironies of fate, or of the vast indifference of Nature, that she should survive and he die. But, Watson, he did surface eventually, he was in good health, and, most fortunate for us, he had recovered his memory!

"And so, my dear fellow, one of the first things he did on getting to Nairobi was to send the cheques! Both in my care, of course!"

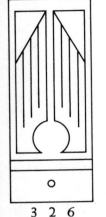

"I can certainly use it," I said. "This will enable me to retire instead of working until I am eighty."

I poured two drinks for us and we toasted our good fortune. Holmes sat back in the chair, puffing upon the excellent Havana and watching Mrs. Watson bustle about her housework.

"She won't allow me to hire a maid," I said. "She insists on doing all the work, including the cooking, herself. Except for the baby and myself, she does not like to touch anyone or be touched by anyone. Sometimes I think. . . ."

"Then she has shut herself off from all but you and the baby," he said.

"You might say that," I replied. "She is happy, though, and that is what matters."

Holmes took out a small notebook and began making notes in it. He would look up at Nylepthah, watch her for a minute, and record something.

"What are you doing, Holmes?" I said.

His answer showed me that he, too, could indulge in a pawky humour when his spirits were high.

"I am making some observations upon the segregation of the queen."

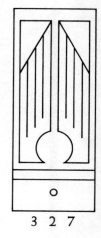

More Adventure

What would happen if you were Captain of the spaceship Sleipnir in THE SHADOW OF SPACE?

. . . Or if you were in charge of Operation Toro in SKETCHES AMONG THE RUINS OF MY MIND?

. . . Or if you were alive only one day of each week as in SLICED-CROSSWISE ONLY-ON-TUESDAY WORLD?

THE GRAND ADVENTURE computer adventure software game puts you in the middle of Philip José Farmer's outrageous fantasies and lets you make the decisions. You may enter the pavilions at the Fair, and wander around New Atlantis, but Arcturan spies are everywhere—even in the adventures!

The adventure game is produced for personal computers by Byron Preiss Video Productions, Inc. It will be released by Trillium Corporation, 1 Kendall Square, Cambridge, MA 02139. Interested computer owners may write them for more information.